Praise for Pulled

"It's one of the best books I've read so far this year."
–Grace, Feeding My Book Addiction

"This one is going to be one that I will recommended again and again."
–Teresa, Teresa's Reading Corner

"What an emotional roller coaster of a book. I honestly haven't spent so much time crying and smiling while reading in a long time. I loved it!"
–Chrystal, Snowdrop Dreams of Books

"This is one amazing book…a MUST READ novel for anyone wanting to read a true love story of two people trying to overcome and beat all odds."
–Nattie, Books from the Purple Jelly Bean Chair

"This story was exactly what I've been dying to read in a romance…Beautiful, captivating, achingly romantic and heartbreaking."
–Author Courtney Lyn Batten

Pulled

A. L. Jackson

A.L. Jackson
www.aljacksonauthor.com
First A.L. Jackson trade paperback edition, April 2012

The characters and events in this book are fictitious. Names, characters, places, and plots are a product of the author's imagination. Any similarity to real persons, living or dead, is coincidental and not intended by the author.

ISBN-13: 978-1-938404-83-2

Cover Image by Regina Wamba

Dedication

To Chad. Always.

Acknowledgments

To Katie who was there from the moment the first word was set in place. For the countless hours you gave, your ideas, and your unending support. To Ginger for your time, encouragement, and invaluable honesty. I love you both.

To Gail for seeing this story as it was meant to be, your insight and guidance, and above all, your belief in me. Thank you, and I love you.

And to Chad for putting up with it all. I love you more than you could know.

Chapter One

I glanced at the clock.

Shit—nearly six o'clock. I needed to hurry. I'd lost track of time and Nicholas would be home soon. I wiped the tears from my face before carefully gathering the pictures from the bedroom floor. My chest weighed heavy as I collected each one, cherishing the memories a moment longer as I tucked them away in the envelope.

The memories were all I had and I clung to them as if they were my last breath, knowing that once they faded, there would truly be no reason to go on. I hid the envelope at the bottom of the large jewelry box in the back of the closet, mindful to spread the necklaces out over the hidden compartment. Nicholas had never found them, but I was certain he would destroy them if he ever did.

Drawing in a deep breath, I ran my hands through my hair and dragged myself from the past I had immersed myself in for the last two hours and forced myself downstairs.

My footsteps echoed against the marble floor, each an accent of emptiness. I entered the kitchen, the only sanctuary I had. Every room of this house was gaudy and overdone, designed by the pompous for the pompous, except for this haven. It was no less extravagant, but held a warmth missing from all of the others.

As I worked, my thoughts inevitably wandered back to those beloved pictures hidden away in the back of my closet, but even they weren't enough to ward off the anxiety steadily building within me as the passing minutes warned of Nicholas's arrival. At six thirty-one, I heard the garage door open. Bile rose in my throat.

"Melanie?" Nicholas called from the entryway.

"In the kitchen," I called weakly. Maybe he would go upstairs and spare me a few more minutes, but of course, I never had that kind of luck. I heard his footsteps approaching and prepared myself.

"Dinner ready?" He yanked at his tie as he came through the door.

"Um, not quite, just a couple more minutes," I said, not meeting his face.

I felt him pause, though I refused to look up. I'd learned a long time ago how to survive in hell. The less I interacted with him the better.

He snorted through his nose, muttering, "Worthless whore," under his breath.

I gritted my teeth, holding in the anger his accusation triggered.

He set his briefcase on the island next to me and tossed his tie over the top of it. "What time do I get home from work, Melanie?" Nicholas dipped his head, forcing me to look at him.

"Six-thirty."

"Is it too much to ask that dinner is ready when I get home?" he said, "or do you have something better to do with your useless life?"

I cringed but said nothing. He was the one who didn't want me to work.

"I didn't think so." He leaned in closer, his words a low warning. "When I tell you dinner needs to be ready at six-thirty, it means dinner is to be ready at six-thirty. Do you understand?"

I saw the threat in his eyes. He had never hurt me physically, but he made sure I knew who was in charge. I'd given up any control nine years ago when I'd followed him here to Chicago, looking for an escape from the pain.

I knew then what this life would be like. I'd met him at the airport when I'd fled Colorado that final time, the trip that severed the last thread holding my heart together.

Nicholas hadn't seen the broken girl who sat numb with nothing but pain swimming in her eyes. He saw the young, beautiful girl, the one who said nothing at all but seemed to be willing to do whatever he said.

I wasn't stupid. I had known exactly what he wanted, but I could never go back to Colorado Springs to face what I could no longer have, and I refused to stay with my mother in Dallas.

So I left all of it behind, moving with Nicholas to Chicago just days after I returned from Colorado.

I knew then Nicholas would never bring me happiness. That had never been the point. My heart belonged to another and would never be his. All I wanted was a way out, while Nicholas got the trophy wife he thought he deserved. The only thing I hadn't anticipated was how the numbness I felt for him would evolve over nine years into bitterness and loathing.

"I'm going upstairs to change, and I expect dinner to be on the table when I get back down here." He had been this way since the first day I arrived; I had a role to play, and he expected me to play it well.

When he left the room, I gathered our plates and took them into the dining room. I wasn't really afraid of Nicholas, but I didn't want to fight. It was exhausting and got me nowhere, and even if it did, I still wouldn't be happy, so it really didn't matter anyway. It was just easier to do what he said.

Ten minutes later, I heard him returning. Just the sound of his heavy steps made my stomach turn. It still shocked me that I could feel so much hatred for one person. I watched him bound down the stairs, his tall body well muscled and agile for his forty-four years. His black hair hadn't thinned and it was usually meticulously styled, though he obviously had run his hands through it. His eyes were nearly as dark as his hair and filled with unmerited pride. He may have been attractive, though that was something I could never see. His mere presence warned my instincts to escape, always smarter than my head.

"About fucking time," he spat, letting me know just how disappointing I was.

Asshole.

Taking a seat across from me, he lifted his fork and began to eat. I picked at my chicken, pushing it around my plate. I could rarely stomach anything when he was around.

As he ate, I lost myself in the silence, my mind drawn back to Colorado.

"We have a dinner Thursday," he abruptly broke through the quiet, pulling me from my daydream. I had to run his words through my mind again before I realized what he had said.

I closed my eyes, suppressing a sigh. Great. Another business dinner. It was the perfect time for me to play my part—the perfect wife with her perfect smile plastered across her perfect face, nodding mindlessly while her husband gave his proposal as if her presence would somehow change the outcome. The whole thing was ridiculous. It was part of my job though, so I nodded that I'd heard him and looked back to my plate.

"This is a huge account, Melanie." He sat back, eyeing me critically as if I didn't already understand my role in this little charade. "It's a medical complex that'll bring in a couple million in profit, so I don't want you fucking this up for me."

I almost laughed. Did he really think that my presence would sway the decision?

Nicholas went on about details I really didn't care to know, about how much money he would make and how much recognition his company would gain if they built this complex.

The only comfort I found was in knowing Shane would be at the dinner. Shane Preston was Nicholas's business partner and the nicest guy I knew. While Nicholas was cocky and arrogant and felt the world owed him, Shane was modest and thankful for all he had. He continually cleaned up the messes Nicholas caused, soothing clients' nerves and regaining their trust after Nicholas had done something unethical.

The dinner also meant that Katie, Shane's wife, would be there. She was the one friend I had in this world. She knew the real me and was the only one I had ever taken into my confidence since I'd married Nicholas. Shane and Katie's presence there would at least make the evening bearable.

Nicholas finished his food, while I cleared the table and took the dishes into the kitchen. I was exhausted. I wondered how much more of this I could take. Surely, I would never survive this life sentence I'd imposed on myself. I loaded the dishwasher and went upstairs to take a bath.

Turning the hot water valve full blast, I let it run, anxious to feel the heat relax my muscles. I unbuttoned my pants and slid them down, shrugging them off my feet. As I pulled my shirt over my head, my gaze reflexively dropped to my stomach as I caught my reflection in the mirror, my first instinct to seek out the marred skin that bore her wounds.

I caressed along the puckered, angry scar that slanted in a long, jagged line across my lower abdomen, wishing she could somehow find comfort in my touch. Chills shook my body as I ran my fingers over the still sensitive skin and, just like every night, the bitterness and anger I found myself feeling faded away into sadness as I lost myself in this tangible reminder of my child. I loved her so much.

Steam filled the room, and I eased myself into the water and allowed myself to drift back to Daniel. I missed him, almost more than I could bear. This was never supposed to have happened to us. We were supposed to make it—we *should* have made it.

"Melanie, hurry up and get in here!" I cringed as Nicholas yelled from the bedroom.

Shit. I'd hoped he'd be asleep by now.

Reluctantly, I rose and pushed the memories aside. I wrapped myself in my robe, slow to finish my normal routine. I shouldn't have been stalling; he'd wait. Still, I took my time as I brushed my teeth and ran a brush through my long brown curls. I inhaled deeply and took one last look at myself before going into the bedroom.

"Don't keep me waiting like that," Nicholas rebuked from his place under the covers.

This was by far the worst part of our arrangement. I couldn't help but feel like a prostitute, cheating on my own heart, when I lay beneath this man. I crawled into bed next to him, praying he would at least have the decency to turn off the light.

He untied the belt on my robe and groped my breast with his callused hand. My body roiled with disgust that he mistook as anticipation. "You like that, don't you," he growled as his foulness spread across my face. I fought against my instinct to flee and, instead, reached over to the bedside table and flicked off the lamp.

The blackness enveloped the room, allowing me to remove myself mentally from the sick situation. I closed my eyes to find an image of Daniel—*a flash of messy blond hair.*

"You're mine." Nicholas's voice jerked me back into reality, making me acutely aware of his sweaty panting body hovering above me. I closed my eyes tighter, willing my mind away.

"Melanie, my love. You're so beautiful," he said as he held my body against his, tender caresses igniting a fire deep within me.

"Daniel," was all I could manage as he made love to me, each touch a whisper across my skin. He gently kissed my neck as he moved against me, and I felt the pressure build with each stroke of his body.

"Melanie, you feel so good," he ground out, his voice rough with emotion.

I couldn't help the little moan that escaped my lips, the flash of desire that washed over my body as it remembered the way only Daniel could make me feel.

"That's right. I feel good, don't I?" Nicholas grunted as he finished and collapsed with all of his weight on me.

The nausea swept through me, and I pushed Nicholas away. "I need to clean up," I choked over my standard excuse as I rushed to the bathroom. I fell to my knees at the toilet, desperate to purge away the hate I had for myself. The act only left me feeling more empty and alone.

Holding onto the vanity for support, I pulled myself up to stand. I rinsed my mouth and splashed water on my face—anything to make me feel clean again—but there was nothing that could wash away the shame.

I stared at myself in the mirror, the reflection no longer one I recognized. The girl I remembered was seventeen—full of life and love. The one staring back at me may as well have been dead. The only life left flickered in the periphery of my consciousness where a familiar comfort waited in the darkness. As I climbed into bed, I grasped for it, desperate to feel *him* for one moment more.

Chapter Two

"Work, Daniel. Come on, get your shit together," I mumbled to myself under my breath, raking my hands through my hair for the hundredth time today. Thoughts of *her* kept creeping in, and I found it impossible to focus on the contracts in front of me. After nine years, I should've been able to forget, but I knew I never would.

Melanie.

Part of me hated her, and that part still wanted to track her down to tell her how she had torn my heart out. How could I hold it against her, though? I knew what I'd done. Even then, I'd still believed we'd get through it together.

Sighing, I ran my palm over my face in an attempt to wake myself up and read the submission in front of me one more time. I was completely exhausted, having substituted coffee for sleep for the last week.

Since arriving in Chicago five months ago, I'd sifted through countless contractor proposals for our new medical complex, weeding out the under-qualified and over-priced. I'd begun to think there wasn't a single competent contractor in all of Chicago before I finally received, what looked to be, a promising bid. I'd spoken with their project manager just this morning and was now awaiting a call from their CEO.

After Melanie had left me, I'd buried myself in school, lost myself in the years of undergrad, medical school, and ultimately, my residency. As it turned out, I was a damn good doctor, even if there had been a point in my life when I thought I'd never make it through.

Dad had been insistent I come back to Colorado Springs to join his practice once I finished my rotation in New York City. He didn't have to ask twice.

My dad, Patrick Montgomery, was a brilliant surgeon and researcher, devoting his life to breast cancer research and treatment. When I moved back home to Colorado, I'd known it was only temporary. A new practice in Chicago, headed by my father, was already in the works. I honestly didn't care where we settled; *she* wouldn't be there, so it made no difference to me.

I wouldn't begin seeing patients until I got the new building well under way, and if I was going to meet my deadline, I needed to decide on the contractor by the end of the week.

"Hey, Daniel?" Dad appeared at my office door, his brown hair peppered with gray. It was the only part of him that hinted at his age. Even at fifty-six years, he still had his lean, muscled body, his build the one trait I seemed to have inherited from him. I took more after my mother, Julia, with her hazel eyes and dark blond curls.

"Yeah, Dad, what's up?" I took another sip of my coffee as I looked at him.

"Erin is coming into town this weekend, and we're having dinner at the house on Friday. Can you make it?"

"Erin? Yeah, I'll be there. How long will she be in town?" My little sister had been living in Los Angeles for the last three years after accepting a position with a marketing firm. It felt wrong for her to be so far away while the rest of the family lived here in Chicago.

I'd always been close with my family. They'd stood by me during my hardest years, unwavering in their love and support. I owed them everything.

"She'll be here for the week. Your mom can hardly contain herself." His brown eyes lit up. You'd think after being with someone for thirty years, a person would get bored, but not Dad. It was obvious he and Mom loved each other just as much today as they did the day they married.

I once believed Melanie and I shared a love like that.

He gestured to my desk with his head. "So, how's the search coming?"

We'd both felt the pressure of the approaching deadline, but neither of us was willing to settle on anything less than the best.

I held up the small pile of papers. "I think this may be the one." I grinned—finally some good news.

A satisfied smile spread over his face. "You don't know how glad I am to hear that." That satisfaction shifted, looking a lot more like sympathy. "I'm proud of you, son."

I suppressed a groan, shaking my head in frustration. "Dad...don't."

I knew exactly where this was heading. What could he say that hadn't been said before?

"Daniel," he said, stepping forward and letting the door shut behind him, "It's been *nine* years. I'm tired of seeing you this way. It's time to live your life."

"I'm fine," I snapped.

As much as I loved my family and respected my father, I was growing tired of their constant interference.

He shook his head as he retreated to the door. He paused to look over his shoulder, his eyes full of concern as they searched my face for understanding. "We just worry about you."

With a sigh, I rocked back in my chair, feeling guilty for lashing out at him. "Yeah, I know."

⁂

Flopping into my chair, I thumbed through the messages Lisa had taken while I'd stepped out for coffee. I stopped when I came to the one from Nicholas Borelli, happy to see he'd called me back.

I dialed the number. He answered on the third ring, "Nicholas Borelli."

"Hello, Mr. Borelli. This is Dr. Daniel Montgomery calling you back about the medical building off Chicago Avenue. I spoke with Shane Preston this morning, and I wanted to see when the three of us could get together to go over your proposal in more detail."

"Yes, I've been expecting your call." His voice was strong, confident, and held a distinct tone of arrogance. It caught me off guard, especially after speaking with his partner this morning.

"Well, uh, I was hoping we could get together in the next couple of days to go over specifics so you could give me a final cost."

"I was under the impression that there's a senior Dr. Montgomery? I assumed I'd be working with him," Borelli said, his voice condescending.

I found myself gritting my teeth, fighting to rein in my temper. Anger was an issue I dealt with constantly. It always simmered just below the surface. I didn't know if I was angrier with Melanie or myself, but from wherever it came, it was always there ready to unleash its fury on the first person who rubbed me the wrong way.

But losing it now would get me nowhere, so I swallowed my irritation.

"No…" I drew out, "I'm in charge of all building decisions."

"I see." Borelli's dissatisfaction traveled through the phone. "Well, I can meet you for dinner on Friday."

There was no way I was giving up dinner with my sister, and beyond that, nights were not good for me. It was hard enough to concentrate during the day and not think about Melanie. By the time evening rolled around, she'd be all I could think about. "I have plans Friday night. How about Thursday around lunchtime?"

Borelli paused. "I'm completely booked up Thursday during the day. Are you free for dinner?"

Inwardly, I groaned. I was up against the wire on this. I ran my free hand over my face, forcing myself to agree.

"Thursday night will work. Where were you thinking?" I asked.

"How about Cushing Grill on Michigan at seven?"

"Okay, I have you down for seven at Cushing Grill."

"Shane and I'll see you then, Daniel. I'm sure our wives will be very pleased to meet you as well."

This time I couldn't suppress the exasperated sigh. I wasn't surprised that they'd try to woo me with an expensive dinner, but what I didn't get was why they thought they needed to bring their wives along. This wasn't the first time this sort of thing had happened, and it seemed really inappropriate to me. Did they think that once I met their family and knew a little of their personal life it would somehow sway me? All I cared about was the cost, the quality, and how fast they could get it done. I considered telling him to forget it, but then I'd be right back to square one.

"Fine, I'll see you Thursday."

Frustrated, I slammed my phone down. Now I'd have to find somebody to go with me, and I had no idea where to start. I thought about asking Lisa, but knew her husband wouldn't be the only one who thought it was weird.

And I didn't date.

ಌ

I left my office at five-thirty completely spent. Evenings were always the worst. I walked to the parking lot, clicked off the car alarm, and slid into the leather seat of my black 650i.

I drove the short distance to the luxury condo Mom and Erin had found for me. It was nice, but to me it was nothing more than a place to sleep. My head was spinning by the time I pulled into the underground garage. It had been a long day, and I just wanted to get upstairs and take a shower. I gathered the papers from the passenger seat, shoved them into my bag, and got out. I should have stopped to get something to eat, but I didn't have the energy. I nodded absently to the elderly couple exiting the elevator as I entered it and pushed the button for the top floor.

I never felt more alone than when I walked into the emptiness of my apartment at the end of the day. I flicked on the light switch, set my things down, and closed the door. The all-too-familiar sadness washed over me, and again, I wished I were coming home to my girls instead.

I took a quick shower and went into the kitchen, hoping to find something to eat. I was starving, but all I could find was some stale pizza. I threw it into the microwave, grabbed a beer, and swallowed half of it as I sank into one of the four chairs set around the small dining table.

It was how I spent every night—utterly fucking alone.

Tonight that loneliness felt unbearable.

I slammed the empty bottle on the table, strode to my room where I threw on a T-shirt and jeans, and then grabbed my keys. Ten minutes later, I stood outside a downtown club, showing my ID to the bouncer.

Stepping inside, I allowed my eyes to adjust to the dim room and flashing lights. The bar was crowded, crawling with college students, some trying to converse over the deafening level of music, others with their bodies pressed together on the dance floor.

I found an empty booth in the back, ordered a whiskey, and waited.

It was obvious why I was here. No other twenty-eight year old man would be alone in a place like this if he wasn't after one thing.

I sat back, sipping my whiskey while my eyes roamed the hazy room, finally stopping on the blonde watching me from where she sat across the room at the bar. She tipped her beer to her mouth and drained it, before she stood and crossed the room.

~

It was nearing two in the morning when I turned the lock to my condo.

I went straight for the shower, desperate to wash the night from my body. I lingered under the stream, knowing the second I lay down the memories would take over. When the water grew cold, I gave in to the inevitable. I crawled into the king-size bed Erin had insisted upon—why, I'll never know—and wrapped myself around a pillow. I felt the energy surge and she was there.

I whispered, "I miss you, Melanie," into the darkness, and I felt a faint tug of the force that bound her to me. I relished in the remnant of her presence before I closed my eyes and gave up the fight for the night.

Chapter Three

Heaven. So safe, laying in his arms; never was there a place I'd rather be. His presence all around me, soothing me with each breath. I curled closer to him, sinking my body into his as if we could become one.

I breathed deeper, struck with panic as he began to fade. Frantic, I struggled, desperate to lock his body to mine, but it was no use. He drifted away as fast as my mind rushed to consciousness.

A sense of dread washed over me as my eyes flickered open. I looked at the bedside table. The red light displayed five forty-three.

"Shit."

It wasn't the dreams of him that bothered me; it was waking to the reality that he was no longer mine that nearly destroyed me each day. I woke every morning with my heart laid bare, wounds torn open, fresh pain oozing from every pore in my body.

I pushed it aside, put back up the walls to shut it all out. I couldn't allow myself to feel in front of those who just didn't understand.

I pulled the covers back, rubbing my stiff neck. Nicholas still slept, snoring with his back turned toward me. Sighing, I stood and padded to the bathroom, preparing myself for another day of nothing.

Showered, I went downstairs to start breakfast. Nicholas would be up soon and he demanded a hot breakfast before he left. I went to the cupboard, pulled out the coffee, and started a pot, breathing it in as it began to brew.

I made a quick breakfast, finishing the eggs and placing them on plates just as Nicholas came downstairs.

I handed him his food when he walked into the kitchen and received nothing more than a grunt of recognition when he took it from my hands.

"You're welcome," I muttered under my breath.

We ate in silence with me lost in thought and Nicholas buried in the pages of the newspaper.

He finished eating, and I took his plate over to the sink to rinse it and put it in the dishwasher. He put on his jacket, grabbed his briefcase, and strode to the door. He paused and turned to look at me. "I'll be home by six-thirty, so don't be late with dinner again tonight. And don't forget about dinner Thursday."

"Yeah, I remember."

If only I *could* forget.

There was nothing worse than having your husband parade you around while you feigned some type of affection for him. The disdain I held for him had to be apparent. This act was getting harder and harder to pull off.

I finished loading the dishwasher and looked around, searching for a job to keep my hands busy while I lost myself in my thoughts. Nicholas didn't trust housekeepers in his house, so the upkeep was relegated to me. I didn't mind. If I sat idle, I was certain I would lose my mind.

I worked, scrubbing down the entire kitchen and enjoying the silence of the house when my phone vibrated in my pocket. I looked up, realizing two hours had passed. I pulled out the phone and smiled when I saw the name displayed on the screen.

"Hey, Katie, what's up?"

We talked several times a week and got together at least once a week, so her early morning calls were not unexpected.

"Hey, hon. You up for coffee?"

"You have no idea how good that sounds." I flipped on the faucet, squeezing the sponge under the stream. "Just give me a few minutes to get cleaned up...say...half an hour?"

"Sounds good."

"All right. See you soon," I said before I ended the call and rushed upstairs to change my clothes.

A half hour later, I pulled my black four-door sedan into the lot of our favorite coffee house and slid into the first open parking space. Katie stood across the lot waving. She was a natural blonde with striking blue eyes, but she had to tip the scales. With hair dyed the deepest black and vibrant tattoos on her back and arms, most found her captivating and a little bit intimidating.

I'd been surprised by the instant connection we'd made when we first met. She was straightforward and strong, and I'd been afraid she would judge me, tell me to grow up and forget about my past, but she never did.

She was just there for me.

"Hey, babe." She grinned as I approached.

"Hey, how are you?" I asked, not hesitating to reach out and hug my closest friend. She was about an inch shorter than I was, though I had to look up at her with the extra height her boots gave her.

"I'm great." Her blue eyes danced as she stepped back and took my hand, pulling me behind her into the shop.

We ordered and found a quiet spot in the back where I sank down into the cushions. I moaned in pleasure as I took the first sip of my mocha latte, allowing its warmth to soothe me.

Katie lounged deep in a plush maroon chair. "So, can you believe the bid the guys put in? If they land it, it'll bring in enough money that Shane will finally be able to start his own company."

Shane was almost as miserable with Nicholas as I was. He couldn't wait to tell his partner goodbye, and I'd been praying for the day when he could finally escape Nicholas's influence.

It also broke my heart. I knew once Shane split with Nicholas, I'd no longer be allowed to have Katie and Shane in my life and, once again, I'd lose the only people who meant anything to me.

"Listen," she said, her voice softening, "I need to talk to you." I braced myself for what was coming. "Shane and I were talking. When he makes his break, we think you should make one too." She looked up at me hesitantly, gauging my reaction. She had been trying to get me to leave Nicholas from the moment we'd met.

"Katie," I choked out. Did I want to be with Nicholas? No. But I had no other place to go. After I'd left Dallas, my mom and I had never been the same, and there was no way I was going back to Colorado Springs. I hadn't talked to my dad since I'd first left, and the last I'd heard, the Montgomerys were still there. "You know I can't do that."

"There's no reason for you to stay with Nicholas. Look," she said, shifting to the edge of the chair and inclining her head toward me, "Shane and I want you to come and stay with us...for as long as you need." She had fire behind her eyes. "You have to get away from that asshole. I'm not going to stand by and watch him tear you down any further."

"You know I appreciate it, but I chose this life a long time ago," I said. *What's done is done.*

"It doesn't have to be that way. Just let me take care of you, please?" I knew she just wanted me to be happy, but what she didn't understand was that I would be unhappy wherever I was, with or without Nicholas, and it was just easier to stay. My heart was already dead, so no more damage could be done.

Sighing, I finished my last sip of coffee and hurried to the door, hoping for a way to escape the conversation.

Katie was right behind me. She grabbed my arm, spinning me around. "I'm serious, Melanie. We're going to talk about this."

"Can we just go? Please? We've talked about this before, and you need to just drop it, okay?"

Pleading, she took my hand, squeezing it, "Shane and I love you. You don't have to spend your life like this."

"I know you do, Katie. I love you too." I bit my lip where it trembled, refusing to shed the tears gathering in my eyes. "But it doesn't change anything."

Sadness clouded her face. "Melanie—"

I cut her off. "Listen, I'm going to head home." The memories were starting to creep in after our talk, and I knew I'd hit my breaking point soon.

"Okay." She stepped to me, wrapping me in her arms. She hugged me closer and whispered against my ear. "But I won't give up on you."

* * *

Wearing old jeans and a thin white T-shirt, I headed out the back door. The weather was still warm and it drew me outside. I moved across the vast lawn to the hedge lining the back of the yard and the flowerbed running along it. Resting on my knees, I began to pull the weeds that had sprouted up between the flowering plants. My hands worked while my mind went back to him, to his beautiful face, to hazel eyes I could never forget. It was as if they watched me across the distance separating us. They both haunted me and comforted me at the same time.

"Daniel, I miss you."

I prayed he could somehow feel me. I wondered if he knew how often I thought of him. I could only imagine that he had another family by now.

Family.

I grasped the weed in my hand as if it were an anchor. If I held on tight enough, maybe I could feel that joy for a moment, the anticipation we'd had for our little family. I took in measured breaths, willing the hurt away, only allowing myself to feel the love I had for her. I'd never even held her, but I *knew* her. I could see the amazing little girl she'd be right now, her brown hair flying around her face, hazel eyes blazing as she played in the back yard.

My thoughts swirled around her for the longest time before they drifted to Patrick and Julia. They had been like parents to me, and I'd loved them like they were. I would never forget all that they had done, the support they'd given. I knew they had felt the same way about me.

And Erin. Tears streamed down my face as I thought of the one person who had been both my best friend and the sister I'd never had. She'd always been there for me, standing by me during the most uncertain times of my young life. I'd known why Daniel no longer wanted me. What I couldn't understand was why she'd abandoned me too.

The phone ringing inside brought me back. I didn't know how long I'd been out here, but my hands were covered in mud and I'd nearly cleared out the flowerbed. Wiping my hands on my pants, I jogged inside and grabbed the phone on the fourth ring. "Hello?" I said, panting.

"Melanie? Honey, are you okay?"

"Mom?" It took me a second to wrap my head around the fact she was on the line. "Yeah, I'm fine. I was just outside and ran in."

I couldn't believe she was calling. We hadn't talked since I'd made a quick, obligatory happy birthday call to her five months before.

"How are you and Mark?" I asked.

After I'd left for Chicago, things had never been the same between Mom and me. I still loved her, of course, but I harbored a lot of resentment toward her. I was angry with her for putting so much blame on Daniel, but in the end, she'd been right. He'd left me for someone else when things got rough. Beyond that, I guess I felt even more betrayed by how taken she seemed to be with Nicholas. But how was that her fault? I was the one who'd chosen this life.

I wasn't the only one, though. She'd been holding back, too. Maybe she'd just been too disappointed in me and couldn't look at me the same. I didn't have all the answers, but what I did know was my relationship with my mom never recovered after that summer.

"I'm pretty good." She sounded off. "How have you been?"

"Um, well, you know, same old Melanie." I couldn't bring myself to lie to her about being happy. It was just too obvious I wasn't.

She didn't say anything.

"Mom, what's going on?" As distant as we were, the thought of something being wrong with her sent a wave of terror through me.

"Nothing's wrong, Melanie. I just miss you. I mean, I miss *you*, the girl I used to know." I could hear the sadness in her voice and was certain she was crying. We hadn't talked like this once in the last nine years, and I wasn't quite sure how to handle it.

"Mom...that girl doesn't exist anymore."

An audible sob came through the line. I sagged against the wall for support. This was not where I'd expected this conversation to go.

"Melanie, sweetheart, I need to come and see you. Will you let me?"

It was clear how far we'd allowed ourselves to drift from each other when it was obvious neither of us wanted it that way. It was as much my fault as it was hers. She was just taking the first step to make it right.

She'd dropped by overnight a couple of times when she and Mark were passing through over the years, but I'd never gone to visit her once. I knew this trip would be different.

"Yeah, Mom. I think I'd like that. When?" The emotion was thick in my words, and I hoped she knew just how much I wanted to see her. I missed her so much, but I'd allowed all of the other hurt I had to cloud that.

"I was thinking I could come out the week of Thanksgiving and stay during the holiday? Only if it's not too much trouble. I don't want to impose on you and Nicholas."

I was a little disappointed it would still be eight weeks before I could see her, another confirmation of just how much I needed her.

"No, Mom, I really do want you here. Please...come." It was more than an invitation for a simple visit.

She sniffled, though I could sense her relief. "Okay...I'll be there."

It was time to make right this one thing that had been wronged so long ago.

Chapter Four

"Daniel, it's too late."

I wouldn't listen, refused to accept his words. Instead, I pled, "No. Please. Save her. You have to save her."

Hands restrained me, but my body pushed forward, desperate.

"No!" If I said it enough, I could make it true.

She couldn't be gone. I just saw her.

"God, no. Please!"

Why weren't they fighting for her? Why were they all standing here, doing nothing?

I had to get past him, to go to her, to protect her.

"It's too late," he said the words again, his arms tightening around me as he abandoned his efforts to restrain me in an attempt to comfort me.

His words crushed me as reality brought me to my knees, images of the perfect face I barely knew flashing through my mind, cutting my soul in two.

Panic burned through my body and sweat broke out across my flesh.

The alarm blared, shocking my mind back into the present, bringing me to a consciousness I didn't want to face. I squeezed my eyes, willing them shut a moment longer, unable to tell what was worse—reliving the nightmare every night or waking to the life I didn't want to live.

My stomach rolled, recoiling with the acids burning in my throat. I barely made it to the bathroom before my body rid itself of the ache the only way it knew how, as if the act would somehow give my body peace.

If only it were that simple.

The heaves finally subsided, and I sank the rest of the way to the floor, trying to catch my breath and slow my breathing.

"Fuck."

Pulling myself off the floor, I held onto the sink for support. I turned on the water, splashed it on my face, and washed the strain away.

Every morning, just the same. Tuesday would prove to be no different.

I showered and dressed, dreading this dinner thing. Feeling desperate, I even considered asking Mom, but figured it would not be cute to bring my mother. I was sure it ran more along the lines of pathetic.

I walked to the front door, bent over to pick up my bag, and reached for my keys on the entryway table. I paused, looking at the photo atop it, the one of me with my arms wrapped around Melanie. We were both smiling, just moments after I'd walked across the stage for my high school diploma, back when we believed nothing could tear us apart.

God, I missed her.

I arrived at the office just before eight, trying to ignore the steady increase of pressure in my head. I had so much to do. I couldn't believe the amount of stress one building could cause.

"Good morning, Lisa."

"Good morning, Dr. Montgomery." Her smile was warm.

"Any messages for me this morning?"

"Um...there are a couple here from the answering service." She searched through the stacks of papers on her desk, digging out the small pile of notes and handing them to me. I tipped her a small nod in thanks and walked into my office.

Sinking into my desk, I checked my appointments for the day before thumbing through the messages. The first two were from the bank.

The last was from Vanessa.

"Shit," I mumbled under my breath.

That girl had been hounding me for months. I really screwed that one up. I should have known better, but she'd completely caught me off guard.

She was a drug rep from one of the larger pharmaceutical companies, and it was clear she wanted to get her foot in the door. I met her the first week we'd arrived in Chicago. A mixer had been set up to get the word out about the new practice, generating interest and referrals right away.

I knew it the first time I saw her. She was just the same as the rest, looking for an easy way to get ahead and using whatever means she thought would get her what she wanted. She'd sought me out, knowing exactly who I was and what I could do for her. My first instinct was to run. But she was relentless, and I'd had too much to drink.

Nine years before, I'd learned it best to stay away, but there were times when I became weak, tired—tired of being alone—and I'd relent to the small voice in my head that insisted it was okay. Just like last night. Never once had I not regretted it.

The first time had been the worst. Stephanie had been my study partner in college. I'd really believed she was my friend. I'd been naive and allowed her to use my pain as a means to get close to me.

It only happened once, and it was the last time I ever saw Stephanie. I'd been so angry that she'd taken advantage of my vulnerability, angry with myself for being so weak. Later I realized that I'd wanted to believe somebody else could make me feel the same way Melanie had, the complete ecstasy we felt when we were one. But that feeling could not be replicated. Melanie's body fit mine as if we'd been carved from the same stone, each made for the other.

She could not be replaced.

Knowing that, you'd think I'd be stronger, that I'd run from the regret I'd have after waking up next to a girl I knew I could never love or even care for.

But sometimes experiencing that regret was better than falling asleep alone.

With Vanessa, though, it was different. It hadn't been about two people giving into their bodies, succumbing to the physical. It was about someone exploiting another's weakness.

She was a predator, and now the bitch thought I owed her something.

"Shit." I threw her message down, knowing I couldn't avoid her any longer.

To top it all off, I had to find a date for dinner Thursday.

I picked up the phone and dialed her number. I knew all she wanted from me was free reign to push her product in my office, as if fucking me somehow had earned her that right, and it pissed me off. But I accepted it as my fault; I knew better than to sleep with a rep.

I prayed it'd go to voicemail, but she picked up on the second ring. "Good morning, this is Vanessa." Always the professional; it reminded me of the sex, all just part of the job.

"Yeah, Vanessa, it's Daniel Montgomery...returning your call." I didn't even know what to say. The whole situation made me uncomfortable.

"Daniel...I've been trying to get in touch with you." Her voice was low and laced with irritation.

What the hell was I supposed to tell her, that I didn't want to talk to her and had been avoiding her?

"Uh, well, sorry. I've been busy," I said as if I couldn't have spared five minutes sometime in the last three months to return her call.

"I really need to meet with you."

Was I seriously agreeing to this?

"Uh, sure, Vanessa. I have some free time during lunch on Thursday. Can we get together then?" She started to say something, so I cut her off before I lost the nerve. "Listen, I need a favor." I couldn't believe I was about to do this. I raked my hand through my hair, hoping the gesture would give me some kind of courage to see this through. "I have a meeting Thursday night and I need to take somebody. Are you free that night?"

I felt like I was selling my soul.

"Are you asking me out after avoiding my phone calls for the last three months?" I couldn't tell if she was mad or surprised, but it really didn't matter. It wasn't as if I actually wanted to go out with her.

I paused before answering. "I guess I am." Now I did owe her. I'd just given her what she'd set her sights on five months ago.

She paused as if she were struggling to find my intent and then released an audible breath into the phone. "Okay...I can go with you Thursday night, as long as we can meet Thursday for lunch."

"Fine."

There was nothing fine about the whole situation, but what was I going to do?

"Can you meet me at Tavalindo's at noon?" she asked.

"Yeah...I'll be there." I hung up the phone and rocked back in my chair, wondering how I got myself into this shit.

ණ

I glanced at the clock. Noon. I had no appetite, but I had to get out of my small office. I felt caged, irritable.

I passed through the lobby, throwing Lisa a halfhearted wave as I walked out the front door. I shoved my hands in the pockets of my slacks and walked the half-block to my favorite coffee shop just up the street from our temporary office.

I ordered my regular, a large latte with a double shot of espresso, careful not to make eye contact with the brown-haired barista taking my order. She handed me my coffee, and I took a sip of it as I stuffed a couple of bucks in the tip jar and mumbled, "Thanks," before I hurried outside.

I plopped into a metal chair at a small bistro table sitting on the sidewalk, needing to escape reality for a couple of minutes. Closing my eyes, I raised my face to the sky and allowed my mind to drift in the cool Chicago breeze.

September 1997

"Good morning, sweetheart," Mom said as I walked into the kitchen. I smiled in her direction where she sat at the small breakfast bar with Dad and Erin.

"Morning." I yawned and rubbed my face, trying to wake myself up. I filled a bowl with cereal and milk and took my place next to Erin. Dad and Erin were talking about the upcoming school year. Erin was nervous about the two sophomore AP classes she had signed up for, and Mom and Dad were trying to give her encouragement.

I nudged my sister's shoulder, her blond wavy hair swaying across her back.

"Hey, don't worry about it. I had both of those classes last year. I'll help you study if you need me to."

Erin's face brightened and she nodded. "Thanks, Daniel."

"No problem." I grinned at her. Of course I'd help her. I adored her, even if she drove me crazy sometimes.

Dad glanced at his watch and reluctantly stood, draining the last bit of coffee from his mug. "I have to get to the hospital."

He patted my shoulder, kissed Erin's head, and stopped to pull Mom up to him. He wrapped her in his arms and kissed her hard, making her giggle against his mouth. She swatted him playfully. "Be good."

Erin grinned at me and rolled her eyes while I screwed up my face in mock disgust.

After Dad left, Mom went upstairs to shower, leaving Erin and me to do the dishes. We chatted a little more about school before Erin's hazel eyes lit up.

"Oh, there's a new girl who started working at the coffee shop last night, Melanie Winters. She just moved here from Texas with her dad. I invited her to come over today." Erin paused before adding in a singsong voice, "And she's really pretty."

I narrowed my eyes, knowing where Erin was going with this. She was constantly trying to set me up with someone.

"Not even remotely interested."

She frowned at me. "You don't have to be like that all the time. I really like her. Would it kill you to be nice to her?"

It wasn't like I wasn't nice to her friends, but I suppose I wasn't exactly friendly, either. I couldn't imagine this girl was any different than the rest of them, easy with not a brain cell to her name. No, thank you.

Sure, I dated a bit here and there, but the girls I'd met never held my interest for long. They were all so superficial; all they cared about was how I looked, what I had, and what I could give them. So I didn't waste my time. It had earned me a reputation of being a dick who thought he was too good for everyone, but I really didn't care.

With only two years of high school left to prepare for college, I needed perfect grades since I'd finally decided I wanted to become a doctor. Dad never pushed me, but I knew he'd always hoped I'd follow in his footsteps. He said other than seeing his family happy, he'd never found more joy than in helping someone heal.

"Fine. I'll make an extra effort to say hi to her," I grumbled.

After helping Mom around the house, I went upstairs to my room to watch TV. I heard a car pull into the driveway and stop in front of the house. A door slammed and then the car drove away. Footsteps echoed on the wooden porch and distant voices seeped into my room.

I shook my head, trying to focus on the football game. I didn't care what was going on downstairs. I turned up the TV to drown out the sounds from below, but it didn't help. It was more as if I could feel the footsteps rather than hear them. When the front door opened and closed, I could ignore it no longer.

I slipped from my room and down the hall. When I saw her, I froze at the top of the stairs, unable to take my eyes off the girl standing in the middle of the living room, her intense emerald eyes staring back at me. We stood there for I don't know how long before I tore my eyes away from hers so I could take in the rest of her. Erin had said she was pretty, but her beauty was beyond words. She had long, brown hair that flowed in soft, thick curls all the way down her back. Her skin was pale and smooth like a porcelain doll. She didn't have Erin's hourglass figure, but her slender build was gentle with feminine curves, and she was maybe an inch shorter than Erin's five-foot eight. She wore tight jeans and an old band T-shirt that was a little snug, accentuating the perfection that was Melanie Winters.

In that moment, I knew I would never be the same.

Erin cleared her throat.

"Um, Melanie, this is my brother, Daniel. Daniel...Melanie." She gestured between the two of us, but it was unnecessary. I was already on my way down the stairs. It was as if there was a magnet drawing me to her. Even if I had tried, I couldn't have walked away. I reached for Melanie's hand, not to shake it but to hold it in mine. The warmth of her skin traveled through my body. It was relaxing, but exciting at the same time.

Melanie looked at our hands, then back to my face and smiled timidly. "Hi." The sound of her voice sent a shiver rolling through my body.

"Hi." I smiled back, still unable to look away.

"So, Melanie, are you hungry or anything?" Erin sounded cautious, almost awkward.

Melanie glanced at me, pensive, before slowly withdrawing her hand. "Sure."

For the first time in my life, I felt empty as I watched her walk away and trail Erin through the door and into the kitchen.

Not quite willing to return to my room, I dropped onto the couch, picked up the remote, and flipped on the game I'd been watching upstairs. Melanie and Erin's voices carried through the thin barrier of the kitchen door, muted, yet distinct of each other. Erin's laugh was loud and substantial, while Melanie's came soft and gentle, though not inhibited or shy. She sounded comfortable. Quietly confident.

It took me about five minutes to decide I was hungry, too.

Silence fell over the kitchen when I stepped in. Melanie and Erin turned to look at me from the small breakfast table where they ate potato chips and drank soda. Melanie's face spread into a warm smile.

God, she was so beautiful.

I held her gaze for a moment before I shook myself out of it and walked across the kitchen to get something to drink. I could feel her eyes on me as I leaned into the fridge and grabbed a soda, and they met mine when I turned to face her, unfailing as I took two steps toward the door.

I knew I should, but I just couldn't leave the room.

"Erin." I looked at my sister, my eyes pleading, hoping she would understand that I was asking her to leave Melanie and me alone.

She did. "I'm supposed to be at work at five. I should get ready." She stood up, looking awkwardly between Melanie and me. I flashed a thankful smile.

Melanie stood as if she were going to leave.

I almost panicked.

"Can you stay?" My voice came out sounding desperate.

What looked like relief swept over Melanie's face, and she nodded.

"I'll see you soon, Melanie?" Erin asked as if she were trying to gauge what Melanie wanted.

She turned to my sister, giving her a hug. "Yeah, I would like that. Thank you for inviting me over." Her voice was soft and kind, sincere.

Erin grinned at us, her eyes glinting with approval and just a little smugness as Melanie stepped to my side.

No doubt, I was going to hear it from my baby sister later.

The door swung closed behind Erin, leaving us alone.

I stood inches from her, staring into the warmth of her green eyes, feeling emotions I'd never felt before.

This time, she reached for me, her hand moving to grasp my index finger.

I closed my eyes, trying to make sense of what was happening between us.

My eyes flickered open to find hers studying my face as if she were memorizing every line.

Holding onto her hand, I led her out of the kitchen and upstairs, sneaking glances back at her to make sure she was real.

We spent the afternoon in my room just getting to know each other.

I learned she was fifteen and would be sixteen in April, ten months younger and a grade behind me.

I hung on her every word as she told me about her childhood, everything she had liked and disliked. I paid attention to what made her frown and what made her smile. I listened as she told me that her parents had divorced when she was young, but since both of her parents had lived within minutes of each other, she had grown up happy with what had felt like one big, extended family. Peggy, her mom, was married to her stepfather Mark and she had a little sister named Sarah.

Melanie had two stepbrothers from her father's second wife, Cheryl. It was her father's recent divorce from Cheryl that brought Melanie to Colorado. Steve, Melanie's father, had taken the divorce hard and he didn't want to stay in the same city as Cheryl. Melanie had moved with her dad, certain he shouldn't be alone in such dark times.

Clearly, her family was as important to her as mine was to me.

With a wistful smile, she listened to stories of my childhood, giggling as I told her of the trouble Erin and I used to get into together. She asked me what I liked and what I didn't like, and I knew she actually cared to know the answers. We talked about school and about how I hoped to become a doctor like my dad.

It was as if we already knew each other; we just needed to fill in the blanks.

We didn't need to make any declarations.

We just were.

The whole time we talked, we lay facing each other, our hands intertwined.

"Daniel, it's getting late. I'd better get home before my dad notices." Melanie stretched, obviously not wanting to leave any more than I wanted her to.

I said, "Okay," but didn't let her go.

Instead, I scooted closer, gentle as I took her face between my hands. My heart beat so hard, I was sure she could hear it, just as I could hear hers. I stroked her cheeks, hoping she didn't notice my fingers trembling.

She watched me with anticipation, clearly just as nervous as I was, but I felt no hesitation from her. She leaned in a little closer, and I pressed my lips against hers.

I kissed her softly and slowly for a couple of seconds. My hands found their way into her curls as I pulled her closer. I felt a tremor roll through her body when our tongues first met. Obviously, neither of us was very experienced as the kiss remained slow and tentative, our mouths gently moving together as we learned each other.

Her hands shook as they moved up my arms and onto my face, making their way into my hair and leaving that same trail of warmth I had felt earlier when we first touched. Her fingers created a desire I had never known. I clutched her to me as the kiss became urgent, the need to consume her overwhelming. She kissed me with as much intensity as I showed her, pressing her body into mine. My whole body sang with want for her. As desperately as I wanted to keep going, I knew it was too much, too fast.

I slowed the kiss, bringing my hands back to her face. I rested my forehead against hers and tried to catch my breath.

I looked into her eyes, seeing the emotion there, and I just knew.

I was in love with Melanie Winters.

Chapter Five

"Hey, Katie," I said, smiling as I climbed into her car.

"Morning, Mel." She leaned across the console to hug me. "All set?"

"Yep." As ready as I'd ever be to spend a day shopping with Katie.

I buckled in as Katie threw her silver Camry in drive. She sped back out of my neighborhood and jumped on the highway leading downtown.

If it were up to me, I would have grabbed the first thing I saw, but every time we went shopping, Katie insisted we try on everything. It was exhausting. It wasn't as if she didn't look amazing in anything she put on. She had a body any woman would envy.

At the third store, I found a dress we both approved of. It was dark green and fell to just below the knees, accentuating my slender waist and the modest flare of my hips without being too revealing. Nicholas always wanted me to look my best on these nights, and I had never let him down. I wasn't vain, but I knew the way people reacted to me. It was the very reason Nicholas wanted me on his arm when he entered a room.

At least shopping was a good distraction from the pain. It always fluttered around the edges, ready to burst through and send me spiraling. I'd learned long ago how to push the ache aside until I was alone.

By the time Katie had settled on a deep sapphire blue cocktail dress, it was nearing two.

"Hey, Katie, we'd better get home if we're going to have enough time to get ready."

She glanced at me as she slid her credit card back into her wallet. "I need to make one more stop at a little jewelry store up the street."

I hated jewelry stores. They all seemed to have a snobbish feel to them, a little like the house I lived in. I hated anything pretentious, yet somehow I'd managed to surround my life with those types of things and people.

With one look at me, she squashed all my objections on the tip of my tongue. "This one's different. They have an antique section. You'll love it."

Katie knew how to get me. I loved all things old. Old books, old furniture, old jewelry—anything somebody else had used and loved.

I could spend hours walking around in an antique store. I could imagine a mother with her son on her lap rocking him in a wooden rocker as she read him a bedtime story. I could picture a beautiful young woman in her wedding dress, holding onto the arm of her lover as they posed for a black and white photo. I could feel the anticipation as a man proposed, sliding his grandmother's ring onto his future wife's finger, asking her to be his forever. I could almost feel the joy and sorrow forever etched into each piece.

We entered the little store and I went straight for the antique section. I never bought anything but would immerse myself in another person's world for just a few moments. I fingered the rings worn into the shape of the owner's finger through years of use, feeling the stones set in gold. I smiled as I imagined all the places they had been. There were bracelets, some in perfect condition and others bearing the patina of age. Those were my favorites. I continued onto the necklaces, old pearls and diamond pendants worn with pride to the most formal of events.

I trailed my fingers along the display, gasping aloud at what I found next. Reaching out, I clutched the simple pendant in my palm as I was thrown into the past. Though it seemed impossible, it was the same.

April 1998

"You don't have anything to be nervous about," I kept telling myself over and over. "It's Daniel – my Daniel."

The last seven months had been indescribable. I would never have imagined that I could find a love like this, but I had known it that first day.

When I'd finished my freshman year of high school in Dallas, I'd never planned to leave. But when Dad decided to move to Colorado after Cheryl kicked him out and filed for divorce, I had to go with him. He was hurting. I'd never seen him like that, and I couldn't stand the thought of him moving out there alone. Mom had resisted at first but relented when I convinced her Dad needed me more than she did.

I'd never traveled outside of Texas before and was amazed by the beauty of Colorado Springs. In Dallas, I'd been surrounded by skyscrapers built on flat plains. Here I found myself surrounded by snowcapped mountains. Everything was green and lush, the opposite of Dallas. I loved it, though the fondness I felt for Colorado Springs may have been completely due to the people I'd met here.

I'd come for my dad, but it was here I'd found my life.

Erin had been so nice the day I had started work at the little coffee shop. I'd been nervous, but she'd shown me around, giving me advice, and at the end of our shift, she had invited me to her house to hang out the next day. I'd had no idea that accepting her invitation was going to change the course of my life.

Something had stirred in me the moment Dad had stopped the car. It had only intensified when I walked inside. It was as if the air around me was filled with a magnetism drawing me forward, urging me ahead. That call was met by hazel eyes, the outer portions lined in brown, melting into variations of green flecked in gold.

For an instant, I'd froze, my mind trying to catch up with what my heart was already racing toward. It was as if my heart jumped to life, not realizing it had lain dormant before that moment.

I was unable to look away while he remained motionless at the top of the stairs. His dark-blond hair was unruly, the loose, wavy curls coming down just over his ears and brow. He was tall and slim, every inch formed, from the toned muscles showing on his forearms to his well-defined chin. He was perfect. But none of that would have mattered because his eyes alone swallowed me whole.

And I hadn't been away from him for a single day since.

My heart fluttered again with thoughts of Daniel as I packed my bag for my sixteenth birthday. The rest of his family had gone to San Diego for the weekend, so we had the place to ourselves.

I rushed down the hall, preparing myself for Dad. I hated lying to him.

"Hey, Dad." He was on the couch drinking a beer, staring unseeing at the TV. He wasn't dealing well with the divorce, and I was starting to really worry about him. Not once in my entire life had I seen him drink, and now he did on a daily basis.

Pulled from his thoughts, he turned to me and forced a smile, setting his beer on the coffee table. "Happy birthday, Mel."

"Thanks." I felt nervous and was sure it was written all over my face. "Umm, Stacy's picking me up to go watch a movie, and then I'm spending the night at her house. Is that okay?"

"Well sure, honey, you have fun." He turned back to the TV and picked up his beer. I breathed a sigh of relief.

I raced out the door. Stacy was parked on the street, and I climbed into her car. "Thanks for doing this." I smiled at her, feeling guilty for involving her in my lie.

"No problem. Just have a happy sixteenth, okay?" She pulled into the grocery store parking lot where Daniel waited for me.

"Thanks," I said. "See you Monday at school."

She grinned and mouthed, "Have fun," as she drove away.

"Hey, baby." Two strong arms wrapped around my waist, and I turned to look at Daniel's face. "Happy birthday." He kissed me and led me around to my side of the car.

"Ready?" he asked as he climbed into the driver's seat. I fidgeted with the hem of my shirt, realizing the double entendre. Was I ready? I thought I was, but that didn't make me any less nervous. I didn't say anything, and I could tell the silence set Daniel on edge.

He reached over and brushed my hair behind my ear. "Hey, look at me. You know we don't have to do this, right? I don't want you to do anything you're not ready to do." He brushed his thumb over my cheek, and I knew he meant it. He would never do anything to hurt me.

"Are you ready?" I hesitantly looked at him, already knowing his answer.

"Of course I want to." He raised his eyebrow a little bit, and I knew exactly what he meant. He'd had a hard time holding himself back for the last seven months, but he'd never pushed. "But that doesn't matter. I'd wait for you forever."

That's why I wanted Daniel to have this part of me. I knew he loved me, and he'd wait for me no matter how long that was. It wasn't like we hadn't talked about it and planned for this day, but it didn't stop the butterflies. We'd committed our lives to each other; now it was time to commit our bodies.

I smiled softly at him, took his hand, and folded it into my lap.

"No, I'm ready, just nervous."

He nodded and pulled out onto the road.

When we arrived, he parked in the driveway and came around to help me out.

I couldn't help but notice how his hand trembled against mine. He was just as nervous as I was. This would be his first time too.

As soon as we walked through the door, he pulled me into his arms. We just stood there wrapped up in each other, neither of us saying anything. We didn't need to.

He kissed me again and then led me into the den. A fire crackled in the fireplace, warming the chilly April air. Candles glowed around the room, and blankets and pillows were spread out in front of the fireplace.

"Come here. I have something for you."

He led me to the nest of blankets and sat me down. I took off my shoes and threw them to the side, crossing my legs under me.

Daniel knelt in front of me, handing me a small box. "Happy birthday."

I unwrapped the gift, putting the paper aside and opening the lid to the black velvet box.

"Daniel," I whispered. "How, how?" I couldn't even get the question out. Emotions swirled, leaving me without words.

I had seen the necklace in an antique store on our first date, a flat gold pendant with delicate artwork etched on the front of it, but so worn, it was impossible to tell what it had been. I'd fallen in love with it, but hadn't said a word, simply admired it with a smile and moved on.

"Do you like it? I saw your face when you first saw it in the store, and I wanted you to have it. I know it's old, and I hope I didn't ruin it, but I wanted it to have a part of us as well."

He pulled the pendant from the box and flipped it over to reveal the cursive "D & M" engraved on the back.

"I love it." I pulled him to me, trying to show him in my kiss just how much it meant to me that he knew me so well. I had never received a better gift. "And I love you," I whispered against his mouth.

"I wish I could tell you how much I love you," he whispered, "How much you mean to me." He ran his nose over my cheek and continued down my neck, setting a fire across my skin, churning coals that burst into flames deep within my soul.

"Show me."

Tears welled up and spilled over, running down my face unchecked. My chest constricted as an intense mixture of love and pain broke through the walls I had so carefully put into place. I heard a strangled sob and realized it was coming from me.

I felt a soft hand on my arm.

"Mel, what's wrong?" Katie's voice was filled with concern as she took in the expression on my face.

I couldn't speak, my breathing rapid and strained, but I managed to wheeze out, "Daniel."

She looked down at my clenched hand. She pried my fingers loose, searching for what was within.

She studied the pendant for a moment and then ran her finger over the faded "D & M." A small, knowing smile formed on her lips, and she walked it straight to the register.

I stood under the hot stream of water feeling dazed. I still couldn't believe it had come back to me. My hand went to the chain around my neck. I could almost feel the energy radiating from it.

I breathed deeply, allowing that energy to comfort me.

When I'd come back from Colorado that last time, I'd tried to rid myself of every memory of the life I could no longer have. I'd packed everything he'd ever given me in a box and dumped it at Goodwill, leaving it there as if it would somehow make me forget.

The next morning I'd panicked, knowing I never *wanted* to forget. Those were the only memories that would ever mean anything to me. I needed them to survive. I'd gone to get it all back, but it was too late. The one thing I wanted most was gone.

Yet fate had brought it back to me, confirming what my heart had told me all along. Daniel loved me. That knowledge alone gave me the first true joy I had felt in years.

I finished my shower, surprised to feel refreshed. I always felt tired and worn, but there was something I didn't quite understand bubbling under the surface of my consciousness.

The door slammed downstairs, and all the comfort I'd felt evaporated. I replaced the towel with a robe, having no desire for Nicholas to see me so exposed. His feet pounded against the stairs.

"I'm late." He sounded frustrated as he kicked off his shoes, stripped, and stepped into the shower. I was surprised he hadn't been home earlier, but it was a pleasant surprise. At least I'd had the time in the shower to be alone in my thoughts. Now it was time to put on my mask and play my part. Nights like these were the whole reason I was here.

"I picked up your suit from the cleaners earlier. It's hanging in the closet."

He nodded as he shut the shower door behind him.

Nicholas was in and out of the shower, grabbing a towel from the cabinet.

"This night has to be perfect, Melanie." He looked at me with a warning in his eyes as he dried himself off.

I didn't know why he thought he had to instruct me about how to act. I'd never let him down before. I was there to make him look good, and that's what I did.

"Of course, Nicholas." I simply agreed with him, saying as little as possible.

After finishing my hair, I stepped into the huge walk-in closet attached to the bathroom to get my dress. Nicholas was already there, putting on his suit.

I rushed as I dropped the robe from my body, hoping to get dressed before he noticed. Of course, I failed. Nicholas groaned from behind me. I hurried to pull my underwear on, trying to ignore him.

"Turn around, let me see you," he demanded.

Shit. I hated this.

Slowly, I turned, my underwear my only source of cover. I kept my head down, refusing to make eye contact with him.

"You're almost perfect, *Melanie*," he sneered at me, hate dripping from his words. I wondered if he despised me as much as I did him. He looked me up and down, reaching out to run his fingers in a line from my neck, to my bellybutton, where he jerked his hand away. "You need to see a plastic surgeon. I'm sick of looking at those scars." He turned away from me to finish dressing, his use for me over for the moment.

Heat flared in my veins. I ran my fingers along the scarred flesh, remembering how I'd felt that day.

I'd *never* let Nicholas steal that from me.

"Never." The word was low, but clear and unwavering.

He wasn't facing me, but I could see the muscles tense in his back as he paused for the briefest moment.

It was the first time I'd ever told him no. Something was shifting within me. I was tired—tired of living a lie.

I'd known all this time that it was a mistake to come here with him, but I'd always just accepted it as my fate. Somewhere deep within me, something was beginning to fight that.

I didn't know how and I didn't know why, but what I did know was a change was coming.

Chapter Six

Finally, it was Thursday.

I couldn't wait to get this building project finalized. It had been wearing on me for so many months, and the thought of not having to think about it on a daily basis sounded like heaven.

The downside of it being Thursday would be dealing with Vanessa. That girl had control of my whole day, and the thought of sitting next to that bitch through two meals made my skin crawl.

"Well, that's what you get." I broke the rules and now I had to pay.

Maybe if this caused me enough grief, it would embed itself in my mind, ensuring that I never make that mistake again. Just the thought of talking to her made me ready to swear off women for the next century. It was just not worth it.

"Morning, Lisa," I said as I entered the lobby.

"Good morning, Dr. Montgomery." She looked up from her computer with a warm smile.

The morning was spent finishing the last of the paperwork that had to be turned into the bank while I tried desperately not to think of the meeting with Vanessa. I could only imagine the ways she would try to manipulate me, and all kinds of scenarios started to play out in my head as the clock neared noon.

I tried to concentrate on the sound of my breathing as I finished the last form and faxed it over to the lender.

Quarter to twelve—judgment time.

I took a steeling breath before I grabbed my coat and briefcase.

"Hey, Lisa, I'm leaving for my lunch meeting. I'll be back in a couple of hours. You can call my cell if you need me."

"Sure, Dr. Montgomery."

The drive to Tavalindo's was short, and I had a couple of minutes to sit in my car and gather my wits. This was going to be unpleasant no matter what, so I just needed to get it over with.

Getting out of the car, I walked into the restaurant foyer. I'd eaten here a couple of times, and it was good food, but there was no way I would be able to eat with my stomach twisted in knots.

"Such a pussy, Daniel," I muttered under my breath. This was ridiculous. She was just a girl. If I didn't like what she proposed, I would just tell her no. Simple as that. I didn't have to allow her control over me. Being in unfamiliar territory didn't mean I had to come out the loser.

Those thoughts gave me some courage as I scanned the restaurant. I spotted Vanessa sitting near a back window.

She really was a beautiful woman. Her strawberry blond hair and smattering of freckles across her face gave her a look that hinted at innocence, but the fire roaring behind her icy blue eyes and the way she held her impeccable body told you she was anything but. Yet she did nothing for me. Nobody ever did.

She gave me a nod from across the room, and I strode across the floor to her.

"Vanessa." I dipped a curt nod, deciding to go all business.

"Hello, Daniel." She leaned up from her chair, as if she expected some sort of embrace. I extended her my hand. She narrowed her eyes before returning the formal shake and then sat back down. She sipped her water and studied me.

I didn't want to be a complete dick to her. I still had to sit with her through dinner, but I didn't want her to have the upper hand in this conversation.

"So, how's everything going with the new practice?" she asked casually.

Nice way to start the conversation. She might as well have asked me to whip out my checkbook.

I struggled to sound normal. "Everything is going pretty well. That's actually what the dinner is about tonight. It's a meeting with the contractors I want to hire for the project."

The server appeared and took our order, and I was thankful for the few minutes of distraction. The moment the waitress walked away, an uncomfortable silence descended, Vanessa and I glancing around the restaurant and then back at the table—anything to keep from making eye contact. I began playing with my tie before deciding I'd had enough of the whole situation.

"Why am I here, Vanessa?"

Taken off guard, she jerked her head up. She pursed her lips together and then sucked the bottom one in nervously before looking me straight in the eye. "I'm pregnant." My brow furrowed as I tried to understand why the hell she thought that information would be important to me.

"Well, congratulations, I guess. But what does this have to do with me?" The whole conversation was uncomfortable. It took everything I had not to bolt from my chair.

"Daniel, I'm almost five months pregnant. Why do you think I've been trying to get in touch with you for the last three months?" she spat the words at me.

All the air left my lungs as her words clicked—Vanessa was pregnant, and she was telling me the baby was mine.

I shook my head. This could not be happening.

Blood drained from my face, and I felt lightheaded, the skin prickling on the back of my neck as sweat drenched my forehead. Hit by a wave of nausea, my hands began to tremble, and I grasped the table for support.

"Daniel. Daniel." Vanessa snapped her fingers in front of my face. "Have you heard anything I said? I was telling you I have an ultrasound next week—"

I put my hand up to stop her; I couldn't register a word she was saying right now over the roaring in my ears. "I have to go."

"What? You can't just leave. We need to talk about this, and our lunch isn't even here yet." She sounded desperate, begging me to sit back down, but I couldn't deal with her right now. It was as if every unhealed wound I'd harbored inside me had ripped open anew.

I could only shake my head and repeat, "I have to go."

As I stumbled away, I realized I didn't even know where she lived.

"Um...uh, we'll talk tonight, okay? I just have to go right now. Text me your address." She nodded, appearing frustrated and confused.

Somehow, I was able to walk out of the restaurant and to my car. Thoughts came fast and it was impossible to keep them at bay. Melanie was the only person in this world I ever wanted to have a child with. The thought of my flesh growing inside of another woman's body made me sick.

Starting the car, I raced from the parking lot.

There was no way I would ever make it back to the office this afternoon. I pulled myself together enough to dial the office.

"Montgomery Oncology," Lisa answered on the second ring. "How can I help you?"

"Lisa, it's...it's Daniel." I tried to keep my voice even, but it shook. "Something's come up. I'm not going to make it back to the office this afternoon."

"Daniel, what's wrong?" Uncharacteristic panic rose up in Lisa's voice. I could only imagine what I must have sounded like to her.

"Just something came up. Tell my father I'll see him tomorrow." I hung up as soon as I got it out.

Flying through the streets, I arrived at my condo only minutes later.

I ignored my phone as it rang, only for it to beep with a message and then start right up again. Looking at the screen, I saw it was Dad.

"Shit!" I raked my hands through my hair, trying to control the emotions that were threatening to explode.

He'd just keep calling and would probably send Mom to come and check on me if I didn't answer.

"Hey, Dad." I choked, trying to hide the pain that was ready to crush me.

"Daniel, what the hell is going on? Lisa called very worried about you." Dad was typically a calm, controlled man, but I could hear the dread welling up in his voice. "Where are you? Let me come get you."

"No, Dad. I'll be okay. I just need to be alone right now. I promise I'll explain it tomorrow at dinner, all right?" I just needed him to give me some space to pull myself back together before I told my family of the horrible mistake I'd made.

"Daniel..." He hesitated, trying to keep me on the phone.

"Dad, I promise. I'll be there tomorrow." I knew Mom and Dad always had the underlying fear that I was so depressed I would hurt myself, but I would never do something like that to them. I'd rather live in complete misery for eternity than cause them any more pain than I already had.

"Okay, son. But if you need anything, call."

"Yeah, Dad. I will."

I made my way through the hall to my apartment. I hung up the phone and slowly turned the key in my lock.

I knew it'd be all over once I walked through the door.

I swung it open and stepped inside. The barrier broke and the emotions came crashing down, bringing me to my knees.

I gasped as the sorrow took over—sorrow both for the loss of the baby girl I had so desperately wanted and for the guilt over the one that made me sick to think about.

October 1999

"I'm late."

I was so freaked out by the look on Melanie's face it took me a minute to comprehend what she was saying. Her intense green eyes were filled with so much fear and anxiety that I had started to think of every horrible thing that could have happened to her in the last two hours, so this took me by surprise.

"You mean, like late late?" I asked, moving my hands from her arms to her face, forcing her to make eye contact with me.

All she did was nod and try to look down.

"Hey, it's okay, baby. We'll be okay, no matter what." I gathered her back up in my arms, trying to ease some of her anxiety. It was hard to do with my own anxiety building in the pit of my stomach.

"No matter what?" she asked as she looked back up at me. So much emotion swirled behind her eyes it made me dizzy.

"No matter what," I smiled softly at her and nodded. "So, what do we need to do? I mean, have you taken a test or anything?" I didn't know if what she was telling me was a sure thing.

"No, not yet. I've kind of been ignoring the signs, but I couldn't exactly do that anymore after I puked up my lunch because Erin was eating a piece of pizza." I glanced at Erin's car in front of Melanie's house.

"Erin knows?"

"Yeah, she figured it out before I did."

"So, it sounds like we need to take a trip to the store?" I didn't want to start freaking out before I knew if I actually had something to freak out about.

"Yeah, I think we do." She squeezed my hand, clearly seeking comfort from me.

I felt shocked, but I knew I needed to be strong for Melanie. She was the one who still had to finish high school, and I couldn't imagine the amount of pressure something like this would put on her.

I mean, I always wanted to be a dad, and after I had found Melanie, there was no other woman I could even imagine having a child with. But right now, it was just so soon.

At the same time, there was some unknown feeling growing within me. A slight smile tugged at the corner of my mouth as I imagined my Melanie with her stomach swollen with our child. There'd never be anything more beautiful than that.

The front door opened and Erin walked toward us, tentative.

"Hey, big brother." Her words were soft and filled with emotion.

I couldn't help but reach for her and pull her into a hug.

"Thank you for taking care of her." I knew it was hard on Melanie with me being so far away, and it took some stress off me knowing Erin was spending time with Melanie.

I came down almost every weekend, but it was difficult at times, keeping up with school and making the almost two-hour trip from Boulder to Colorado Springs every Friday, but Melanie was more than worth it.

It was hard not seeing her every day, but it was only for the year. Once she graduated in May, she would join me at The University of Colorado, and we'd be together again. For the time being, though, I spent every extra minute either studying, going to class, or on the phone with Melanie.

It looked like we were going to need Erin even more.

"What does it say?" I took turns ringing my fingers together and then running them through my hair as I paced back and forth in the tiny space.

Melanie, on the other hand, sat rigid on the toilet lid and waited for the test to change. After what felt like an hour, she looked up at me. "It's positive."

Oh my God, it was positive. I was going to be a dad. Surging emotions sped through my veins, fear and anxiety and something that hinted at joy.

Melanie sat stunned, her face pale, unshed tears glistening her eyes.

I stretched my hand out and pulled her close to me. "Shh," I whispered against her head as I rocked us. "It's going to be okay."

"You're not upset?" she asked as she leaned back so she could touch my face, her fingers leaving a trail of fire across my skin.

"Mel, I'm not upset...I mean...I'm scared, yeah, but there's nothing I could ever want more than having a family with you." I had to let her know how committed I was to her and our baby. "You know the biggest desire in my life has always been to be a dad, even more than being a doctor." It was true. There was nothing more important in this world.

A timid smile crept to Melanie's lips and the tears broke free from her eyes. She had to be so scared. Hell, I was terrified. But together we would somehow make this work.

"Sure, it's sooner than we planned. So what? We'll just have to work a little harder. You'll finish your senior year before the baby's born, and then we'll get married. We'll make a home just like we've dreamed." I couldn't help the little grin playing at my mouth when I pictured Melanie sitting on a porch swing with our child on her lap.

Melanie had a faraway look in her eyes and a small smile on her lips, and I wondered if she was imagining something similar.

"Tell me what you're thinking, baby." She was tucked close to my chest, my hands moving in soothing circles across her back, her hands resting on my hips.

She shook her head as if she were trying to clear her thoughts. She looked up at me. "I'm scared to death, Daniel." She stepped back, resting her hand on her belly. "Our child is growing inside me, and I have no idea how we're going to do this, but I want her."

I smiled softly at this wonderful creature in front of me. She was perfect when I met her two years ago, and she was perfect today.

"Her?" I had to ask.

Melanie shrugged, and a small, soggy laugh escaped her. "I think it's a girl."

A baby girl. I could only imagine how beautiful she would be. I had to chuckle when I realized the picture in my head was a smaller, chubbier version of Melanie.

If I could only be so lucky to have two of them.

We moved to her bedroom, lying on her bed as we absorbed everything. We talked about all of our fears and the excitement that was beginning to build in us. Melanie eased every fear I had with a simple solution, and I did the same for her.

We could do this.

Melanie's face turned serious. "You know my dad's going to kill you, right?"

Shit.

Steve.

There was a very good chance he was going to cause me bodily harm. There were few people as intimidating as Steve. The guy was at least six foot three and probably weighed two hundred fifty pounds. I could never tell if he shaved his head or if he was bald, but either way, the effect was threatening.

"Oh, come on, Melanie. He's not gonna kill me…maybe just hurt me a little," I teased as I pulled her body on top of mine, holding her close. She felt so good. The days in between my weekend visits were complete torture. I woke up missing her and went to bed missing her. There was never a moment I didn't want her in my arms.

She kissed me, humming with pleasure as I pressed myself against her. Five days was much, much too long.

But that would have to wait, because just then, we heard Steve's truck pulling into the driveway.

I groaned as Melanie rolled off me, running into the bathroom to grab the test and put it in a garbage bag in her room.

"So, are we going to tell him right now?" I figured it was probably best to get this over with. Steve didn't show his emotions well, and I could see him ignoring my girl for the next six months just to make her feel bad. But I was confident he'd have some choice words for me.

"No!" Melanie shrieked at me as panic raced across her face.

"Melanie, we're going to have to tell him sometime. Better sooner than later."

"Don't you think we need some time to sort through all of this and decide exactly what we're going to do? I mean, Dad will handle this better if we have a plan in place and he sees we know what we're doing." I saw her point. We had some major decisions to make.

"Okay, we'll give it some time...but you don't plan on keeping this from my family, do you?" I was nervous she would feel the same way as she felt about her dad, but things were different with my mom and dad than they were with Steve. Yeah, they would be disappointed in us, but I felt certain they'd support us. Even if they didn't, we were all too close to hide something like this from them.

"No, of course we'll tell them. They'd want to know." She smiled tentatively and nodded.

Relieved, I held her face between my hands and brought my lips to hers. The kiss was filled with every ounce of respect and love I had for her. "Thank you." Her lips were sweet, her skin salty with tears. I pulled away when I heard Steve open the front door.

"Melanie?"

"Hey, Dad. Be out in a minute."

She smiled at me, giving me one last chaste kiss before grabbing my hand and pulling me down the hall.

"Hey, Dad." Melanie squirmed, averting her gaze to her feet as she stood in the middle of her father's small kitchen. I'm sure Steve had to know something was up just by the look on her face, but he was the best at being oblivious to everything around him. I didn't know if he really didn't notice or if he put a shield around himself so he didn't have to deal with anything.

"Hey, Mel." He looked her way as he reached into the fridge to grab a beer, snapping it open before glancing at me and looking away. He'd always hated me, barely acknowledging my presence anytime I was in his house. I tried not to let it bother me, but Melanie was going to be part of my life forever, and I hated that Steve and I couldn't be on better terms. Our current situation definitely wasn't going to help the relationship between us.

"Hey, Steve." The least I could do was try.

He grunted at me and turned his attention back to Melanie.

"Um, Dad, we were just headed over to Daniel's, okay?" She looked uncomfortable, fidgeting with the hem of her shirt. I hated that she was feeling ashamed of herself when she had no reason to.

"Not too late." With that statement, he looked in my direction. It was my responsibility to have her home "at a decent hour." I learned a long time ago that meant ten o'clock. Of course, that never stopped me from sneaking in the back door later after Steve had gone to bed.

"Okay, bye, Dad." She waved behind her as I took her hand.

I helped her into the car and went around to my side, feeling relieved to be away from Steve's scrutiny.

I studied her face. "How are you doing?" I didn't want her freaking out every time she was around her dad. She didn't need to be putting that kind of pressure on herself and the baby.

"Fine, I guess. That was just...uncomfortable?" It came out like a question. She sighed. "I guess I just was worried that Dad could see right through me, like I had 'I'm pregnant' written across my forehead or something."

"Let's just not prolong this, okay? You don't need to be feeling that much pressure every time you talk to him." I reached over and squeezed her hand to encourage her. She always tip-toed around her dad, worried that everything and anything would cause him more stress.

"He has a right to know, and yeah, he's going to be pissed." I softened my voice, hoping to soothe her. I knew Steve could be harsh, and Melanie didn't want to face that any more than she wanted to cause him added worry. "But we'll get through it. He loves you, and I think if we give him some time to deal with the shock, he'll be okay."

At least I hoped that's the way he'd react, but I didn't want my own fears troubling Melanie more. I mean, I was eighteen and, well, Melanie was not. Steve could have my ass if he wanted to.

There were so many things we needed to talk about, and I could see those questions and fears swirling behind her eyes. I couldn't even think straight when she looked at me like that. All the rest of this stuff didn't matter; we had each other, and everything was going to work out. It had to.

Closing the distance between us, I kissed her gently.

"I love you, baby," I whispered against her lips.

She giggled. "I think you're going to have to stop calling me that, because I'm not quite sure who you're talking to." She reached down and rubbed her belly as a sweet smile came to her lips.

I chuckled, reaching my hand down to cover hers. "Yes, I love you too, baby." It was true. Sure, I'd only known about "her" for the last two hours, but I did. How could I not be in love with something that Melanie and I had created?

My body trembled as all the regrets of my life washed through me, my heart feeling as if it were on the verge of failing. My soul cried out for her. It had never stopped its search for her in nine years, and I could still feel her calling out for me.

It was all I had left of her, this connection that could never be broken no matter how much time and space passed between us.

"Melanie, I don't want to do this without you. It was only supposed to be you." I dug my fingers into the carpet, praying I could feel her for just one second more. When my body had no more to give, I succumbed to the darkness that blurred the images in my mind.

Chapter Seven

My head spun as I slowly drifted toward consciousness. My body was stiff, muscles aching. My eyes fluttered, flashes of floor and eyelashes the only things visible as I tried to orient myself to my surroundings. Rays of sunlight filtered in low through the windows, an indication that the sun was just setting. My mind gradually allowed my body to come back to life.

I brought myself to my hands and knees, trying to gain enough strength to stand. My phone vibrated on the floor beside me, surely the trigger for my arousal.

I looked to the clock on the wall—five-thirty.

"Shit." I raked my hands over my face to rub the drowsiness away. I had to get moving or I would be late. Reaching for my phone, I ran my finger over the faceplate to read the message.

Vanessa's address.

Acid burned in my stomach. I couldn't believe I'd gotten myself into this mess. How could I have been so stupid?

I dragged myself to the shower and turned the water to as hot as I could tolerate, easing my body into the stream. It washed over me, somewhat easing the tension I felt. I breathed in the steam to try to clear my thoughts.

What was I going to do? I was so lost. Having a child had been so important to me, but that dream had died when she did.

First off, I needed to find out if this was even my baby. I mean, now after five months she tells me I'm going to be a father? I did not trust her. I never had, and I wasn't going to start now. But if the child was mine, what then?

Marry Vanessa?

Not a chance in hell.

The thought of living with that bitch put every fiber of my being on defense. There was no way I could do it. Yeah, it might be the right thing to do, but I was just not that noble—or stupid. I would have a responsibility to the child, but not to Vanessa.

After my shower, I put on the suit I'd picked up from the cleaners a couple of days before. I ran my hands through my wet hair and called it good.

I grabbed all the information I needed and stuffed the papers into my bag, praying I was organized enough to pull this off after ignoring the work I had planned to do this afternoon.

Locking my apartment, I headed down to the parking garage to my car and typed Vanessa's address into the navigation system. It was six-twenty—plenty of time to pick her up and still get to Cushing Grill on time.

I sat for a moment when I pulled up to the curb in front of her house. She lived in a little duplex in a nice area, nothing upscale, but it had a family feel. At least she'd have a decent place for the child to live.

I rushed up the sidewalk and rang the bell, nervously glancing around me and trying not to focus on our encounter.

Vanessa answered the door seconds after I rang. I was taken aback as she stepped out. I could see the obvious bump showing through her dress. In all the shock of the day, it had never registered just how far along she was. In four months, she was having this baby.

Nerves prickled across the back of my neck, and it was not a pleasant feeling.

"Hello, Daniel." She brushed my arm with her hand and started walking toward the car.

She let herself in, and I went around to the driver's side and slid into my seat, not hesitating to start my car and pull away. My hands shook against the wheel. I stared straight ahead while I struggled to find the right thing to say.

"Five months?" They were the only words I could find. I didn't believe she couldn't have found a way to tell me sooner. Suspicion boiled right below the surface.

From the corner of my eye, I could see her playing with the zipper of the purse on her lap, shaking her head.

Finally, she answered, "I just didn't know what to do. I called and you never called back. I got scared. I wanted to barge into your office and demand to see you, but I thought you'd just run. I figured if I kept calling, eventually you'd give in and call me back...just like you did." With the last statement, she looked my way, waiting for my response.

"I don't even know what to say to you, Vanessa. I met you one time five months ago, and now we're having a baby in four months?" The anger in my voice was obvious. "I just can't wrap my head around this right now. I don't have any clue what to do." I knew I was being harsh, but it was true. I had no idea how to handle this.

"It's a boy, you know," she said quietly into her lap.

I tried to guard myself from the memories her news summoned, but it was no use. They were all I could see.

January 2000

Melanie held onto my hand. I could feel her excitement and anxiety, as I'm sure she could feel mine. My stomach was in knots, my head sore from the number of times I had run my hands through my hair. I smiled down at her and caressed her cheek, looking into her green eyes that overflowed with emotion.

"Okay, Melanie, this is going to be a little cold." Dad squirted some clear gel onto Melanie's abdomen and held up the probe. "This is how we're going to take a look at this little one." He smiled at us, his joy evident. Mom placed both of her hands on my shoulders as she stood behind me.

Melanie was twenty weeks pregnant, and it was time for her first ultrasound. Dad had arranged to do it himself.

I had been so eager to see the baby, but I was still anxious. What if there was something wrong? The chances of that were low, but it didn't stop me from worrying.

Dad lowered the probe onto Melanie's stomach, and the monitor jumped around as he moved it to find the right spot. "There you are."

The fuzzy image on the screen cleared, and I saw my child. The moment took my breath away. Melanie squeezed my hand harder, and I turned to her. Tears ran down her face.

Melanie whispered to me, "Our baby."

I leaned over and kissed her, murmuring back the same, "Our baby."

Dad began to take measurements and talk about each body part. I was surprised at how big the head was, but he said it was supposed to be at this stage. We counted ten fingers and ten toes, and the heart was beating exactly as it should.

Relief swept over me as Dad assured us that everything was okay. He confirmed the due date as June seventh. We were halfway there.

"So did you two want to know the sex of your baby?" Dad grinned at us, knowing full well how much we did.

"Yes," Melanie and I said in unison.

He smiled a soft smile. "Baby girl."

We were having a baby girl. I looked at Melanie who mouthed to me, "I knew."

I took Melanie's face in my hands and kissed her. "Of course you knew," I murmured against her lips.

When Melanie and Mom left for the restroom, I pulled my dad aside. "Hey, Dad?"

He drew me into a hug, patting me on the back. "I can't believe you're making me a grandpa." He leaned away, his expression bittersweet. As disappointed as they'd been, they'd never failed to support us. Melanie still hadn't told her parents, and Mom had pretty much taken on the role of mother in her life.

"You know we couldn't have done this without you and Mom. I hope you know how much that means to me."

His brow wrinkled as he minutely shook his head. "You know we'd do anything for you, Daniel."

"That's actually what I need to talk to you about." I hated asking for more when they'd already done so much, but I'd thought this through and knew it was the best plan. "I need access to my money."

I had a trust fund from my grandparents that my parents had control of until I turned twenty-one. My intention had been to save it for my children for when they were older, but my child needed it now.

He nodded. "I was wondering when you were going to ask."

March 2000

It took two months of preparation. Mom had snuck up during the week to make everything perfect, and now that it was complete, I couldn't wait to show Melanie.

I smiled to myself as I dialed her number.

She picked up on the first ring. "Hey," she breathed into the phone. "I miss you."

"I know, Mel. I miss you so much." It was getting harder and harder to leave her each week.

"You're coming tomorrow, right?" Sadness weighed down her words.

"Well, that's what I wanted to talk to you about. Do you think you could tell your Dad you're staying with Stacy this weekend? I want you to come up here."

"Daniel, I don't think my car will make it." I heard her disappointment over the phone.

"Don't worry about that. I'll come get you. We'll just leave your car at my parents and drive back together. Do you think you could get out of school early?"

"Yeah. That'll be perfect!" she squealed into the phone. "I can't wait. We haven't had a weekend to ourselves since Christmas break. I really need to get away."

"So, I take it you're anxious to see me?" I teased her, knowing she was always as excited to see me as I was to see her.

"No, not at all," she laughed into the phone, her sarcasm evident.

I told her I loved her and hung up, counting the hours until I could leave.

I woke up early. I planned to be at my parents by ten so I could spend an hour with them before Melanie and I left.

When I arrived, I found Mom standing on the porch waiting for me.

"Hey, Mom!" I called out to her as I got out of the car.

"She's going to love it, Daniel." She beamed at me. She had put a lot of effort into this whole thing, and she was almost as eager for Melanie's reaction as I was.

"You think she will?" I wanted her to love everything and was sure she would, but I also didn't want her to be disappointed because she hadn't been a part of it.

"Of course she will, sweetheart. Don't worry, you'll see." That was all I needed to hear.

My parents and I spent the hour having a late breakfast.

"That was great, Mom" I smiled at her.

My baby girl was going to have the best grandparents. Sure, they were going to spoil her like crazy, but they'd also give her the same kind of selfless love they'd given me my entire life.

I jumped up when I heard Melanie's old car coming up the road. I flashed an excited smile at my parents before darting out the door. My heart burned with desire to hold her. The magnetism we shared was always there but grew stronger the nearer we were. I felt her spirit surge as she came into sight.

She pulled up behind where I'd parked, her face filled with disbelief as she looked between me and the car.

She got out giggling. "You didn't."

I descended the three steps to stand in front of her. "Do you like it?"

"Daniel, seriously, you bought a new car?"

"Did you think I was going to let my baby girl ride in that old thing?" I laughed as I pulled Melanie into my arms, feeling the peace that her touch brought.

Melanie's car was so old. It broke down constantly, so I bought a new car for our family. The four-door sedan was white and nothing fancy, but it was reliable and safe.

She hugged me. "Thank you for taking care of us."

I stood with her in my arms, swaying as I cherished her in our embrace. I grinned as I felt her stomach press against me, our baby now prominent between us. I never wanted to let her go. She was my home.

"Do you have any idea how much I love you?"

She grasped my hand from her side and brought it to her face, cupping her cheek with my hand. My whole arm burned with the fire that she set in me. "I feel it, Daniel, every time you touch me." She pressed her cheek further into my hand to demonstrate the power that held the two of us together, the energy flowing soundly between us.

A low "ahem" from behind caused me to pull away.

"We wanted to say hi to Melanie before you two took off for the weekend." Dad brought Melanie into a hug and kissed her on the temple. "How are my girls?"

Melanie grinned. "We're great, Patrick." She rubbed her belly. "Growing every day."

We loaded her bag into the trunk and said our goodbyes to Mom and Dad, promising we'd be back early enough on Sunday to spend some time with them.

The ride back to Boulder went quickly. We talked the whole way about our little girl, the plans we'd made, and how anxious we were for them to all come to pass.

A couple of months ago, we'd decided to get married as soon as Melanie turned eighteen, which was next month. Mom and Erin had planned a small wedding in our backyard, just family and a few friends. Melanie had never dreamed of the big wedding and neither had I.

Her parents still didn't know. I'd been pushing her for months to tell them. She was just over six-months pregnant and there would be no hiding this much longer. Rumors had already started, and Steve was either going to have to find out from us soon, or he was going to hear it from someone else. As it was, the man was blind if he hadn't noticed that Melanie was showing.

I didn't bring it up on the ride home; I just wanted us to be at peace.

Once the conversation died down, we enjoyed each other in silence as we traveled down the road. Melanie rested her head against the seat, her hand loosely entwined with mine.

Every time I glanced at her, my chest burned with the love I felt for her.

Trees became sparse as we neared town, the forest soon behind us. Buildings began to line the freeway, and before we knew it, we were in the city.

"Daniel, you just missed your turn." Melanie looked behind us as we passed the University of Colorado sign.

"We're not going to the apartment. I have a surprise for you." I made little circles on the back of her hand with my thumb as I took the second exit, making a left and heading north.

I pulled up in front of the little white house, the one I knew Melanie would love.

"Welcome home." I pecked her on the mouth before hopping out and running around to the passenger door. I helped her out, trying to gauge her reaction as she took everything in. We'd have to be here in Boulder for at least the next four or five years, and I wanted to be sure we had a home to raise our daughter.

"Daniel," she breathed out. Her eyes scanned the front yard, coming to rest on the front porch. Walking forward, she ran her hand along the railing as she ascended the steps, going directly to the swing suspended from the roof. She had tears in her eyes and a smile on her face, and I knew it was right.

"Home," she said the word and reached for my hand. "Thank you." She'd always said I felt like home to her, and I couldn't be happier than to give her one.

"Do you want to see inside?" I took her hand and unlocked the front door.

She stepped inside, and I heard a little gasp as both of her hands went to her face while she shook her head.

"Daniel, it's perfect. How?" She looked around our house, absorbing everything around her.

"Mom," we both said it at the same time. It was so clear my mom had a hand in this. Melanie loved old things, and I knew the house for her would be warm and comfortable, a place where we could be at ease while we watched our little girl play on the floor.

She walked around the family room, her fingers trailing over the photos my mom had so carefully picked out. Melanie picked up the picture of us right after my graduation. "I love this one." She turned it toward me so I could see it.

"It's my favorite, too."

"I can't believe your mom knows me this well, Daniel." She ran her hand over the fabric of the large suede couch, still shaking her head.

I led her to the kitchen, the room I was most excited for her to see. She was an amazing cook, and I wanted her to have her dream kitchen.

"Oh, my gosh," she gushed as she danced into the kitchen, running her fingertips along the butcher-block island that sat directly in the middle. "I want to make us dinner tonight!" Her eyes were wide with

excitement as she opened drawers and slammed cabinets, checking out everything.

"Of course, if that's what you want to do, but I don't want you to get too tired." I worried she put too much stress on herself, but the thought of Melanie cooking dinner in our kitchen made my mouth water.

She shook her head. "No, I really want to."

She slid her arms around my waist, pulling me close to rest her head on my chest. "You are the most perfect man ever created. Do you know how much this house means to me, Daniel? It's wonderful, but it would never be home without you. Do you understand? You're everything." She squeezed me tighter as she said the last words.

Her words left me awestruck. I knew with every part of my being, she'd been made specifically for me and I for her. My arms tightened around her, and I buried my nose in her hair.

Stepping back, I took her hand and whispered, "I want to show you something."

My heart raced as I approached the next room. I prayed Melanie would like it. I pushed the door open, and Melanie peeked in and froze. I was so afraid she'd be disappointed, but Erin had assured me Mel would love it. I placed my hands on her shoulders while she took it all in.

There was pink everywhere. Pink walls, pink curtains, pink bedding, all the way down to the pink teddy bear nestled in the rocking chair that sat beside the crib. There were little fairies painted in a mural scene against one wall and matching ones embroidered on pieces of the bedding. I thought I was going to hate it when Erin had started working on it, but once it was finished, I couldn't imagine a better room for any little girl.

Melanie was silent as she went to the crib. She reached inside and picked up one of the soft blankets, holding it to her nose as she continued her tour around the room. The closet was overflowing with enough baby clothes for the next three years. A changing table sat in the far corner stocked with baby supplies, and there were even books on shelves and toys in baskets. Erin had thought of everything.

I leaned against the doorjamb and watched as Melanie picked up little one-piece outfits and held them to her belly. She opened the bottles on the changing table and smelled each one. She looked through the titles of the books and the toys, acquainting herself with everything.

She finally looked at me and said, "She's going to love it."

"Yeah, I think she will too."

Melanie took one last look before we shut the door.

"Are you ready to see our room?"

She nodded and followed me in after I opened the door.

Mom had made it comfortable, not overdone. It was a place where we could come to be alone at the end of the day – a place of peace and love and commitment.

"Do you like it?"

"How could I not? It's ours." Her face radiated joy.

The combination of those words and the look on her face sent my heart racing, savoring the thought of our lives joined. No more weekend trips, no more sneaking in backdoors, no more hiding.

Ours.

Finally.

With the sun shining, we spent the afternoon out in the back yard, talking as we sat on the grass. Melanie looked at where her garden would be. It was barren now, but I knew it would be incredible as soon as Melanie was here and tending to it. We picked out the perfect spot for a swing set, imagining a time a few years from now when we would catch our little girl as she came down the slide or push her on the swing as she giggled and begged us to push her higher.

Evening approached, and Melanie still wanted to make dinner, so we picked up a few things from the store.

Dinner was amazing. Melanie reveled in her new kitchen. I think she used every dish we owned. I'd never seen her freer. Only three more months, and we'd be able to do this every day.

We ate at our little dining table, chatting and enjoying our food, the mood light between us.

When my phone rang in my pocket, and I pulled it out and glanced at the number before shutting it off and turning my attention back to Melanie.

"Who was that?" She smiled as she popped a piece of baked chicken into her mouth.

"Oh, just Stephanie. She's probably calling to remind me of our study group on Monday." She always called a couple of days ahead because one of the four of us in our group always forgot if she didn't.

A frown crossed Melanie's face, and she looked back down at her plate.

"Hey, what's wrong?"

"It's nothing." She tried to wave it off.

"It's not if something's bothering you." We had promised each other a long time ago that whenever anything upset us we'd get it out in the open.

"Honestly, it really is nothing. She just makes me uncomfortable." She shrugged her shoulders and took another bite.

Melanie had only met Stephanie once in passing. We were leaving a restaurant over Christmas break when Steph was coming in with her boyfriend, so I didn't understand where this was coming from. Melanie had never been the jealous type because she had no reason to be.

"You understand that I am only for you?" I squeezed her knee under the table, begging her to understand. "She's just my study partner."

"I know. She just gave me a weird feeling, but I trust you." She smiled, effectively closing the subject, because we both knew we didn't have to worry about that kind of thing. Nobody would ever come between us.

Later that night, we watched a movie on the couch, but Melanie never made it to the end. Her soft breaths were lulling me to sleep as well, so I picked her up and carried her to our room. I pulled the covers down and tucked her in, her brown ringlets falling all over her pillow.

"So beautiful," I whispered into her cheek as I kissed her good night. So unbelievably beautiful.

I don't think I'd ever even seen another woman's face since the moment I'd met her. It was as if my mind couldn't register anyone else.

Crawling into bed next to her, I tugged her back close to my chest so I could hold her as she slept. I rested my hand on her belly, content in this moment.

I felt a little thump against my hand, my other girl demanding my attention. I smiled into the back of Melanie's head as I continued to feel the little movements under my hand, wondering how it was even possible to feel this way.

ණ

We spent Saturday morning lounging around the house. It seemed we were always around somebody else, and we never had time to ourselves. It was great to be in our home just with each other.

Around noon, we decided to go into town to shop a little. We browsed around, taking our time as we looked in store windows, holding hands as we strolled together.

Melanie held up a baby name book with a questioning look, and I grinned and nodded. It was definitely time to start thinking about naming our little girl.

The afternoon came and went, and sadness began to creep in as I thought of having to take Melanie back to her dad's tomorrow. I had thought about asking her to come up here to finish school, but I knew that would be selfish of me.

When Melanie's feet started hurting, we went home to relax, but I felt anxious. We needed to talk about her parents. We couldn't put it off any longer.

Melanie had her back propped against the headboard with her feet up on a pillow as she flipped through the name book. I crawled beside her, pulling her against me.

"Melanie, baby, we need to talk."

She frowned, set the book down, and straightened up a bit.

"We have to tell your dad."

She sighed. "I know. I'm just so scared. Every day I leave my room promising myself that I'm going to tell him, but as soon as I see him, I lose my nerve. It was like I wanted to spare him the worry, but now I've let it go on for too long. How am I supposed to tell him he's going to be a grandpa in three months? He's going to lose it." She clenched her fists in agitation.

"I know he is, but we can't wait any longer. You're showing and people are starting to notice." I raked my hands through my hair and breathed out heavily, the sound hanging in the air. "I talked to Erin. She said the whole school is talking about it. He's going to hear about it, if he hasn't already...we need to tell him tomorrow."

She bit her lip, fighting tears. I knew she was scared, but there was no way around this.

I wiped the solitary tear that ran down my girl's cheek, and she nodded against my hand, giving her silent promise that we'd get this out in the open tomorrow.

"So what are we naming this little thing?" I affectionately rubbed her stomach, trying to lighten the mood. We had tonight left, and I didn't want to ruin it with the worry of tomorrow.

We flipped through page after page. There were so many names it was overwhelming. "Daniel, look at this." She pointed to a name.

I read it aloud, "Eva." I let the name run through my head and it clicked in my heart. "It's beautiful, Melanie."

She sat up a little further. "It means life in Hebrew. It's perfect."

She placed both of her hands on her stomach and looked at me, an almost sad smile on her face. "I can't wait to meet her."

"God, I love you, Melanie." I kissed her, tasting her sweetness as I ran my hands over her belly, down to her hips.

Melanie whimpered against my lips. She shifted and pressed her body against mine.

I made love to her softly, slowly – carefully, her body still perfectly fitting with mine. Every touch was like fire against my skin, her love for me undeniable in the wake of her fingers.

"Melanie, my love. You're so beautiful," I murmured against her cheek.

Her breath tickled against my ear as a low, "Daniel," tumbled from her mouth.

The energy that bound our souls together was suffocating, her fire roaring through my veins.

"Melanie, you feel so good."

Never could I desire another. There would never be anyone who could make me feel this way, anyone who could bring me complete ecstasy in one passing touch or ease my soul with the warmth of their eyes. There was only Melanie.

⸙

Sleep was difficult, only coming in short bursts throughout the night. I felt anxious about meeting with Steve. Telling him that Melanie was six months pregnant, and we'd been hiding it from him this whole time, was not going to go over well. If he had a real temper, this was sure to bring it out in him.

Melanie stirred next to me in the early morning hours. Turning, she wrapped her arms around me, fingering the hair on the back of my neck, her simple touch soothing my nerves.

"Hey, you awake already?" Her voice was raspy and low.

"Yeah. Couldn't sleep."

She sat up on her elbow facing me, her hair falling over her shoulder and pooling on the bed below her. Her skin was paler than normal in the muted morning light, her green eyes intense as they searched mine.

Moving to cup my cheek, she ran her thumb beneath my eye to smooth away the stress. I had tried to hide my own fear about telling Steve, but it was obvious I was not looking forward to this any more than she was.

I turned my head into her palm, kissing the tender skin there.

Sadness washed over me once again at the thought of taking Melanie back. This was her home now, and I wanted her to be here with me. These next three months were going to feel like an eternity, and the worst was yet to come. After we got married in April, I knew it was going to be awful coming back to this house and our king-sized bed while she was alone in the small room at the end of the hall in her dad's house. It was just so wrong.

We lay together for what seemed like hours without saying a word, simply showing each other our love through touch. The morning slipped away and, as much as I didn't want to, it was time to put an end to the procrastination. Melanie got up to take a shower while I packed her things.

With reluctance, I started my car and drove us in the direction of Colorado Springs. Traffic was light, so at least we'd save a few minutes of worry.

Melanie hadn't said anything in the last half hour as she stared out the window. "Are you ready for this?" I asked, hoping to break her out of the worried silence she'd fallen into.

She jumped, startled. "Oh." She blinked a couple of times. "I guess as ready as I'll ever be." She bit her thumbnail. "I just don't know what he's going to say. I'm really scared."

I glanced at her. Tears ran down her face, the moisture on her cheeks reflecting the sun shining through the window.

She groaned aloud into her hands, shaking her head at the thought. "What if he has you arrested or something?" she whispered, the true fear she'd been harboring coming out. It dawned on me then that she hadn't been hiding this from Steve to protect herself from his wrath, but to protect me from it.

"Melanie..." Reaching out, I brushed her hair aside, cupped the back of her neck. "I'd never let him keep you away from me." I tried to reassure her with the promise in my eyes, a promise that no matter what, we would never be apart. She stared back at me, the fear that mingled with the devotion in her green eyes melting my heart.

Suddenly, she jerked under my hand, every muscle in her body tensing as she screamed, "Daniel!"

My head snapped forward, but there was nothing I could do. My vision barely registered the streak of red before my head filled with the sound of crumpling metal and shattering glass. Searing pain sliced through my chest as a desperate cry for Melanie fell from my lips. Her name pounded against my ears as blackness washed over me and forced me into darkness.

Gripping the steering wheel, I gasped for air. I couldn't tell if my chest was caving in against my heart or if my heart had ruptured through my chest.

"Daniel, are you okay?"

I squeezed my eyes shut, trying to shake off the panic attack, and forced myself to speak. "I'm fine."

Minutes later, we arrived at the restaurant and I pulled up to the valet. I tried to regain my composure before I went in there and ruined everything. Today had been the single hardest day I'd had since coming back from Dallas, and it seemed thoughts of Melanie would not be kept at bay. I would have to smile and fake my way through this night. I prayed they'd do all the talking and I could just sit there, nod, and sign on the dotted line.

I groaned when I caught my reflection in the mirror. Hair sticking up in every possible way, not one strand in accord, eyes puffy and red from this afternoon, hands visibly shaking—I was a complete disaster.

I grabbed my bag when the valet opened my door. He gave me my tag, and I went around to gather Vanessa.

We entered, greeted by a hostess wearing a black cocktail dress and heels. I hated places like this.

"Do you have a reservation, sir?"

"Yes. I have a business meeting with Nicholas Borelli and Shane Preston. I'm not sure if they've arrived yet." I glanced around the restaurant. Never having met either of them, I had no idea who I was looking for.

Studying the black book on the stand, she shook her head. "No, they haven't arrived yet, but we can show you to your table."

She led us to a round table for six near a large bank of windows. Vanessa and I sat on the far side, facing the room. "This is very nice, Daniel." Vanessa pretended to appreciate the room and then looked back at me through her eyelashes.

Was she trying to flirt with me? I uttered a barely audible, "Mmm hmm," before turning my attention to the menu, wary of making eye contact with her. This had been a complete mistake. I should have just come alone. It was becoming much too obvious that Vanessa thought this dinner meant more to me than just a need to have somebody accompany me to a dinner meeting. The *accidental* brush of her leg against mine under the table confirmed that.

"*Shit*," I swore at myself. This day just got worse by the minute.

When a waiter arrived and asked what we'd like to drink, Vanessa gave him an exaggerated smile and ordered a water.

"Whiskey, no ice." I was in dire need of a drink.

Vanessa began to make comments about the menu, trying to draw me into conversation, but her words didn't register. I couldn't think straight. My head started to spin, my skin prickling all over. I felt the hairs on the back of my neck rise up and stand on end.

I tried to shake it off.

Apparently, I had thought too much about Melanie today because my body was reacting as if she were near.

Rubbing the back of my neck, I tried to brush off the feeling but couldn't stop the panic from setting in when I realized I was finally going to lose it. My hands started to tingle with the palpable energy that connected Melanie to me, what made us one, and an intense longing filling my chest.

I had to pull myself together.

I stood to take a few minutes to clear my head when a strangled sob grounded me to the floor. My head jerked up, my eyes desperate to find what I so longed to see.

My knees went weak, and I grasped the table for support when my eyes met with the emerald that owned my soul.

Chapter Eight

The ride to the restaurant was tense.

My outright refusal had set Nicholas on edge and I didn't think he knew how to deal with it.

Nicholas pulled up to the restaurant valet. Katie and Shane waited on the sidewalk as the attendant helped me from the car.

"Hey, Mel." Shane's smile was infectious. I could never resist it, my own spreading across my face as he brought me into a huge hug and gave me a quick peck on the cheek. If I hadn't known him, I might have been a little leery of him, given that he resembled a younger version of my dad. He was just as tall and shaved his head, though his eyes were green where Dad's were brown. He was muscular from years of hard construction work and so tanned it nearly washed out the sleeves of tattoos covering his arms.

"Hey, Shane. Are you ready for this?" I patted his back as I hugged him, giving him encouragement for the evening.

"Yep, I have a good feeling about it." This would change everything for them. It was ironic that the one thing Nicholas thought was going to bring him power and recognition would actually bring him to his knees if everything went as planned.

Katie and I exchanged knowing smiles as we stepped in for a quick hug.

"Let's go take care of some business." Nicholas took charge, leading us inside. He held the door as Shane and Katie entered in front of us, placing his hand on the small of my back as I followed.

Once inside, I felt that pull, the energy that bound my soul to Daniel's, and I smiled as I brought my hand to the pendant. I fingered it, knowing it had somehow been brought back into my life to give me comfort.

As the hostess led us deeper into the restaurant, the pull grew, expanded my chest. Goose bumps popped up all over my arms as my skin began to tingle.

I ran my hands up each arm trying to chase away the feeling, hugging myself across my middle. Something was wrong. I'd never felt Daniel like this unless he was actually nearby. Maybe finding the pendant had brought too many memories to the surface and my mind had lost touch with reality.

With each step, the feeling grew, almost suffocating.

"Get it together, Melanie," I scolded myself, trying to snap myself out of it.

As I rounded the corner, my eyes landed on the head of hair that could only belong to one man. A wounded cry escaped my throat.

Energy surged, and I could almost see it connect with him. His head snapped up and my eyes locked with his soul.

I couldn't look away. Every emotion I'd had in the last nine years flowed between us—the pain, the longing, the desire, the lost love, each one crashing and washing over us in waves.

My fingers dug into Katie's shoulder as I willed myself not to lose it in the middle of the restaurant. I couldn't tell if I wanted to dive over the table and devour him or if I wanted to scream and pound his chest, releasing all the anger and hurt that he'd caused me in the last nine years.

I don't know how long we stared at each other before Nicholas finally tugged on my elbow. Anger burned on his face—a warning.

Tilting her head, Katie studied me with concern. That concern grew when she watched me pry my trembling fingers from her shoulder. Shane looked between Daniel and me, seemingly clueless of its source, but not ignorant to my distress.

Taking control of the situation, Nicholas extended his hand across the table to Daniel who had risen as we approached. "You must be Daniel. It's nice to finally meet you. I'm Nicholas Borelli." Daniel barely acknowledged him as he halfheartedly shook Nicholas's hand, never taking his eyes off of me for more than a second.

Nicholas frowned, shrouded in annoyance at Daniel's obvious dismissal of him. Still, he continued. "This is Shane Preston and his wife, Katie." Nicholas gestured to them, and Daniel tore his eyes from me. "Nice to meet you both," Daniel said and nodded, unease evident in his every move.

"And this is my beautiful wife, Melanie." Nicholas presented me like the trophy I was.

Daniel's eyes came back to mine, sadness pouring from them as he reached across to take my visibly trembling hand. A whimper escaped through my lips as my fingertips grazed his before he took my hand. Too long—it had been too long since I'd touched him. A flash of energy burned up my arm, my wounded heart pounding with its first true beats in nine years. Relief at the contact swept over my body, making my head spin and desire throb in my belly as his warmth sped through my veins.

Neither of us seemed to be able to let go.

"Hello, Melanie." The words were soft but laden with need, each tumbling from his lips like a song. My cheeks burned red, the heat rising up my body and settling on my face.

I could only nod and swallow.

A slight "ahem" from beside him caused him to reluctantly drop my hand. My arm felt heavy with loss. I glanced to the left at the extremely beautiful woman sitting in the chair beside him. Bile rose in my throat at the sight of her. She wasn't even the same girl who'd taken my place.

Confusion clouded my head. My knees went weak as a keening shiver rolled down my spine, and I grabbed the back of the chair to steady myself, trying to remain coherent. I'd never passed out before, but I was sure I was only seconds away.

My legs wobbled as Nicholas pulled my chair out for me. For once, I was thankful for the false chivalry as I stumbled into my chair. Taking the chair to my right, Nicholas situated himself directly between Daniel and me.

To my left, Katie kept glancing my way. She placed a worried hand on my thigh to get my attention. "What's going on?" she mouthed.

Through a grimace, I shook my head. I'd tell her later. She frowned, but turned away.

I kept my head down while the waiter took our drink orders, but the pull wouldn't allow it for long. My eyes traveled up until they rested on Daniel's face.

God, I missed him.

So many emotions raged inside me. I didn't know how I was going to make it through dinner. Either I needed to run to Daniel or run from him, but I could do neither, so I sat and stared at the one person my heart cried out for every day.

I tried to pay attention to what was going on around me as Nicholas and Shane began to present their proposal to Daniel.

"So Daniel, I'm sure you'll find..." Nicholas's voice was a distant sound in my head, everything other than Daniel a haze around me. I still had never seen a more beautiful man, but he was so different from the carefree boy I once knew. His hair was in utter disarray, the color darkened with age, but still with natural light blond streaks. I longed to run my fingers through it the way I used to. His body was still firm, muscles toned and smooth, though now maybe even thinner than he had been before.

But it was his eyes that broke my heart all over again.

No longer did they glimmer with the joy that used to radiate from them. Instead, the intensity was gone, the life sucked from them. There had been a faint flicker of it when our eyes had first met, but it'd passed in almost the same instant.

His cheeks were sunken and there were dark bags under his eyes.

The sadness surrounding his presence was sickening, like a disease had taken over his body and he had given up his will to live.

Never had I wanted to comfort anyone more. I wanted to call his name, to touch his face, to taste his lips. I wanted to assure him that my love for him was unending. I wanted to promise we could heal together. I wanted to forgive him, to forget about the past, to move on. There was one simple fact that held me back.

He didn't want me anymore.

But seeing him now—my spirit couldn't believe that. I could feel he loved me. But sometimes love just wasn't enough. He needed more than I could give.

I looked at the woman beside him and jealousy surged through my whole being.

Had he pledged his life to her, to love her forever? Did he go to bed with her every night and pull her body against his, holding her the way he used to hold me? Did they have children waiting at home?

If he had all these things, why was he so broken? He had the same look on his face that I had every day when I looked in the mirror. He was nothing more than a shell of a person.

Daniel seemed to be struggling to listen to what Nicholas was saying. His gaze would travel to me and then snap back to Nicholas as if he was in a constant war with himself. I could almost feel his body drifting in my direction even though it stayed in place.

Nicholas's attention darted between Daniel and me, suspicion thick on his brow. While he had no idea who Daniel was, he was no fool, just as aware of the tension in the room as any one of us.

"So, Daniel..." Nicholas handed him another sheet of paper. "If you take a look at this, you'll see that we have the building permit outlined here. We should be able to get it through the city in four to six weeks." Nicholas pointed something out on the paper, but Daniel did little more than glance at it before his eyes came back to me.

His possessive nature getting the best of him, Nicholas reached his hand out to stroke my face. I cringed away. He ran his hand down to rest on the side of my neck, his fingers digging into my skin. He leaned in near my face as if he were going to kiss me beneath the ear. Instead, he whispered, "Bitch," low enough that only I could hear.

Daniel's hands tightened into fists upon the table. His face burned, and his eyes, dead only moments ago, flamed with hate.

Rarely had I seen that expression on his face, but I knew it—Daniel was absolutely dripping with rage. He looked as if he were going to rip Nicholas's arm off. I could see him restraining himself in his seat, holding himself back, his fury threatening to explode.

I just didn't understand it. He didn't want me. How could he sit there and be angry that I was with somebody else when he had let me go? I wanted to scream at him, to beg him for an answer. Why? Why did he do this to me? Love and hate warred within me, tearing my soul apart.

Daniel's date sat silent, fidgeting with her napkin, leaning in further and further toward him. He ignored her. She sighed every few seconds, seeking his attention, but it seemed as if he didn't even know she was there.

Nicholas had grown frustrated with the situation, his voice commanding attention as he tried to force his presentation on Daniel. There was an edge to his voice that no smart businessman would ever direct toward a potential client, but I knew Nicholas. He was jealous that I was receiving what he thought he deserved. I was supposed to be there to win him more attention, not to take it from him.

Poor Shane seemed to have no clue what was going on, only that things were spiraling out of control. He jumped in and tried to salvage the evening. I felt awful that my presence had ruined this for him. I looked at him, offering a weak smile of apology when he cut in and began speaking for Nicholas.

Katie stared at Daniel as he stared at me. Clearly, she was trying to sort everything out. It was apparent in the squint of her eyes and the furrow of her brow.

Shane seemed to have drawn Daniel in. I could still feel the tension radiating from him, but he was at least having a serious conversation with Shane. Daniel still had never so much as glanced at Vanessa, who sipped her water, appearing bored or maybe even annoyed.

Shane made quick progress, putting all of Daniel's concerns to rest when he offered a solution for each one. From his seat, Nicholas seethed at Shane, jealous, once again, that his younger partner had the charisma he lacked.

Relief washed over the table when dinner arrived. They put talk of business on hold for the moment as our server placed our food in front of us.

Katie gave me a cautious glance as she started to speak. "So, Daniel, you just recently moved here to Chicago? Where did you come from?" Her head tilted to the side, waiting for his answer, her eyes sliding to mine for the briefest moment before they went back to Daniel's.

He cleared his throat, frowning. "Uh, I'm from Colorado." He turned his attention back to his plate, obviously trying to avoid Katie's questions. I tried to warn her by clenching her thigh to stop but knew she'd continue until she got her answers. I was sure she'd already figured out who Daniel was.

"Mmm." She took a small bite of her baked potato as she nodded and then turned her attention to Vanessa. "So how do you know Daniel?" She played it off as small talk, but it was anything but.

Vanessa's face brightened, and she reached for Daniel's hand and squeezed it. "Daniel and I are having a baby!"

I choked on my steak. Tears filled my eyes as another part of my heart was ripped away. I knew that was the reason he didn't want me, but it was devastating to have it paraded in front of my face. I covered the sob in my throat with a cough. Nicholas glared at me—another warning to get myself under control.

Daniel's eyes flew to me, pain etched deep in the lines of his face, and he jerked his hand from Vanessa. I didn't understand what was happening between the two of them. He should be thrilled. All he'd ever wanted was to be a father and now he was going to get it. Part of me wanted to be angry that he had that without me, but deep inside, all I wanted was for him to be happy even if it killed me to watch it happen.

Katie was relentless. "Oh, I guess congratulations are in order then?" It was almost a question as she looked at Daniel. He turned his head to the opposite wall, raking his hands through his hair the way he always had done when he was worried or upset.

When he said nothing, she pressed on. "So, is this your first child?" It was clear she wanted Daniel to answer, but Vanessa spoke first. "Yes, it's a boy. We're so excited."

I felt as if a knife had been thrust into my stomach, the air knocked from me as I clutched my torso and squeezed my eyes shut.

I couldn't listen.

Chapter Nine

I still couldn't believe Melanie was here.

It was all I could do to keep myself from jumping over the table to get to her, to fall to my knees, to plead for forgiveness, to beg her to take me back. In her brief touch, I'd found everything I'd missed for the last nine years, and I knew then what my heart had known the whole time—she was mine. Even with her husband sitting between us, I knew she was mine.

I'd never told anyone about Eva. It was my loss and I couldn't bear to have a stranger pity me when it was impossible for them to even begin to understand the way her death had destroyed me. But I knew it'd destroyed Melanie too, and there was no way I'd sit across from her and not acknowledge the child we'd created. Swallowing, I cleared my throat and tried to gain enough courage to verbalize it in front of these strangers. "I had a baby girl. But she passed away."

March 2000

What was happening?

Everything was a blur. Voices murmured too low for me to hear or the pain drowned them out, I wasn't sure which. I hurt everywhere and I felt as if I was suffocating. I gasped against the burn in my lungs as I fought to take in a breath. Suddenly everything shifted as my eyesight came into focus, as my surroundings became clear.

"Melanie!" I struggled to sit up, but I was strapped onto a stretcher. "Please, I have to get to her. Please!" My voice cracked with the sob that erupted from my chest as I begged them to free me. I had to find her.

"Sir, you need to calm down. We're trying to help you." A paramedic leaned over me, shining a light in my eyes.

"I have to help her. Where is she? Please." My eyes darted around. Dense trees lining the road rushed past the windows of the speeding ambulance. I caught sight of my blood-soaked shirt.

Oh my God.

I thrashed against the restraints as fear gutted me. A scream rushed up my throat, but no sound came.

"Sir, you need to relax. She's already on her way to the hospital in Denver."

A needle was jabbed in my arm and warmth spread through my veins, but it wasn't the warmth I desired. A fog trapped me in my mind, my heart screaming, but the rest of my body went numb as darkness raced in.

❧

"Daniel." The voice was soft and drew me in. "Sweetheart." Tender fingers ran through my hair, caressing me, giving me strength.

"Mom?" I blinked.

She leaned over me, one hand holding mine while the other stroked my head. Her eyes filled with tears.

I tried to sit up, but the pain tearing through my chest forced me back down.

"Just relax." She tried to soothe me, but her voice trembled and it had the opposite effect.

"Melanie?" I rasped. Sensing movement, I turned to find my dad standing on the other side. He cleared his throat, his face tormented. His mouth opened and closed, as if he couldn't find it in himself to speak the words. Dread twisted itself deep inside me, in a place I didn't know, and I braced myself for the news that would shatter my life.

"She's going to be okay, Daniel." He placed his hand on my shoulder, looking me in the eyes.

Relief flooded me, and I breathed in a painful breath, tears breaking free and running down my face.

"She's still in surgery right now and she's doing well."

I choked, the relief I felt moments before gone. "Surgery?"

"She had some internal bleeding, but they have it under control." He tried to reassure me, but that same dread burrowed deeper.

I felt my heart breaking as I forced myself to ask the next question. "The baby?" They were less than words and more like a strangled sound in the back of my throat, sticking to my tongue as they tried to pass.

Dad grimaced. "It's not good, Daniel." He closed his eyes, trying to get himself together to play the doctor, before he looked back up at me. "They took her by C-section, and she's on a ventilator." He paused and looked away from me, his voice cracking when he whispered, "It's very early, son."

Overwhelming grief shook me as I realized what I'd done. "It was my fault...oh my God...I wasn't paying attention...I…" Guilt tumbled from my mouth as an incoherent, tangled confession.

"No, Daniel." Mom clutched at my hand, releasing the words in a desperate whisper, "The other driver crossed into your lane. There was nothing you could have done."

Mom could say anything she wanted, but I wouldn't lie to myself. Even Melanie saw that car before I did.

I closed my eyes, allowed the guilt to come.

Dad's hold tightened on my shoulder, his voice low and firm. "You don't have time for this, Daniel. Melanie's going to need you to be strong for her...and blaming yourself isn't going to help anyone."

"Can I see them?" The need to see Melanie was just as powerful as the guilt I bore. I had to feel her heart beat beneath my hands, to see for myself that she was okay.

And Eva.

The thought of my baby girl nearly made me crumble.

"You should be able to soon. I have to warn you, Daniel," his voice softened, "Melanie's going to be on a ventilator for a few days until the swelling goes down around her brain. You need to be prepared that she's not going to look very good. She also has some other injuries..." he said, trailing off as his focus drifted to the floor.

"What? Dad...please?" After everything, I couldn't handle him hiding anything from me. "You have to be honest with me."

He sighed. "I know, Daniel, it's just a lot for you to take in all at once, and you have to take care of yourself too. You have three cracked ribs and a pretty bad cut above your eye."

I shook my head. "No, I'm fine."

He pulled up a chair next to me and I did the best I could to prepare myself for what he would say. He ran the palm of his hand back and forth over his mouth, tension rolling from him as he began to speak.

My heart fell as he described Melanie's injuries. She was going to be devastated. But we could get through that. I just had to be thankful she was going to be okay.

"Tell me more about the baby," I asked, unable to keep my voice from shaking.

His head dropped into his hands, and when he looked back up, unshed tears clouded his eyes. His words were barely audible and I strained to hear. "She's in bad shape, Daniel. She only weighs a little over a pound and a half and she can't breathe on her own. All we can do is wait."

It just didn't seem real. But I knew what would make it real.

"I need to see her." I sat up, struggling to right myself against the physical pain trying to hold me down. "Please, take me to her. I have to see her."

"I'll go out and check. Your doctor was already having your paperwork drawn up to have you discharged."

It seemed like the next hour dragged on forever as I waited to be released. We received word that Melanie was out of surgery and in recovery, and they'd let us see her in about three hours. They said I could see the baby anytime. I almost got up and left, but Dad wanted to make sure I was cleared before I started walking around. I couldn't bring myself to care about my injuries. All I cared about was seeing my girls.

"Daniel, sweetheart," Mom cooed to me as if I were five again, but somehow I didn't mind. Instinctively, I knew she needed to take care of me as much as I felt the need to take care of my own child. "It's going to be okay." Worry lines were set deep on her face. I couldn't imagine the fear my parents must have felt when they got the call.

"Mom, does Steve know?" I couldn't even imagine how angry Steve was going to be. He didn't even know Melanie was pregnant, and now he was a grandfather.

"Your dad just called a few minutes ago after Melanie got out of surgery. But, Daniel..." She hesitated before she continued. "He doesn't know about the baby. We thought it would be best if you told him face-to-face." I was certain that would be the most difficult conversation I'd ever had.

Dad poked his head through the door. "You're all cleared. Are you ready to go?"

I nodded pensively, both eager and terrified to meet my daughter.

Cautiously, I stood, the ache searing through my chest.

Mom wrapped a supportive arm around my waist as we followed Dad to the elevator. The gesture wasn't enough to keep my anxiety from boiling over.

It was hard to breathe as the elevator door opened to the floor below. I reached out to the wall for support as the window came into view, the one displaying the perfect, healthy babies. Families stood with smiles on their faces, excited to catch their first glimpse.

Dad stopped me at the sign directing us to the neonatal intensive care unit. "Daniel, do you need a few minutes?"

I shook my head. I needed to see her now, no matter how scared I was.

We walked farther down the hall to a window with a woman behind a counter. In a very low voice, Dad said, "Baby Montgomery."

"ID's please." She began to go through a list of the rules, but Dad cut in. "I'm a consulting physician on the case. I'll go over the details with them." He took out his ID and the woman verified it.

Even though infants were not his specialty, I took comfort in knowing my father would watch over her care.

Once the nurse buzzed us through double doors, we scrubbed our hands at a sink. I washed beside Dad, my gut twisted in knots, unable to grasp what I was preparing to face. Finally, we entered through a second pair of double doors, the light dim and the room quiet. It was as if I had entered another world. Little incubators sat between curtained walls, nurses quickly and silently moving around the room. Couples sat in rocking chairs next to some of the incubators, a few of them with babies in their arms.

Fear traveled up my spine and settled in my neck as it all became real. A lump formed in my throat. Swallowing over it, I followed Dad across the room.

My knees became weak when I first saw her, and Dad reached out to steady me. Placing all my weight upon him, I tried to rid myself of the apprehension I felt so I could focus on my daughter.

Wires were everywhere—in her legs, in her arms, running through her nose and mouth. I couldn't hold back the sob when I saw just how small she really was. Her legs and arms were not much thicker than one of my fingers, and her whole body was not much longer than my hand. Her skin was almost transparent, as if I could see every vein in her body. Her eyes were taped closed, and her little chest rose and fell with the machine that kept her alive.

It was simultaneously the most horrifying and beautiful thing I had ever seen.

She was so broken and yet so perfect.

My daughter.

My heart swelled with love for her and broke all at the same time. "Eva," I whispered to her, hoping she could hear me.

"What did you say?" Mom asked, a small smile on her face and her cheeks wet with tears.

"Her name is Eva. We decided last night." How long ago that perfect moment seemed now.

"It's beautiful." Mom reached a tender hand out to me, once again, giving me comfort.

"Can I hold her?"

Could I? I was terrified, but I'd never wanted anything more.

"Give me a minute and I'll check" Dad walked to one of the nurses, talked to her lower than I could hear. She followed him back and pointed to the single chair that was in the enclosure.

"If you'll sit there, I'll bring her to you."

Obviously she was adept at her job as she shuffled wires around and wrapped Eva in a blanket at the same moment she lifted her. Carefully, she transferred my daughter to my arms. I cautiously held my little girl, her chest resting against mine.

Precious.

I closed my eyes against the fear and the pain and just loved her.

It was the only thing I could give her.

Breathing her in, I committed her unique scent to memory. She smelled almost sweet, like her mom, but something altogether her own. I smiled against her head and cradled her to me, rocking her, murmuring my adoration to her.

"Please, baby girl, you have to be strong."

In silence, my parents stood by my side, each with a hand on one of my shoulders, their support complete and unending.

I flinched with the flash of light as Mom snapped a picture of us. "Sorry," she mumbled. I shook my head. I didn't mind.

I'd only held her for a few minutes when the nurse said it was time to return her to her incubator. I watched as the nurse settled her back and checked her monitors. As much as I hated the thought of leaving her, it was time to go to Melanie.

When I reached in to touch her little hand, Eva wrapped it around my finger. I smiled as I felt her against me. I whispered, "I love you," as I caressed the back of her hand. Longing filled my chest when I turned to walk away.

The second we were in the hall, Mom pulled me into a hug. "I'm so proud of you, Daniel. You've grown into the man I've always prayed you'd become." Swollen and red, her eyes shimmered in the light as she looked at me.

I hugged her back, needing her support now more than I ever had. "Thank you, Mom." My voice was strained with the fatigue that quickly set in, the unrelenting pain in my chest absolutely killing me as I sagged against my mother.

Dad joined in our embrace, drawing us close as the three of us grieved together. He pulled back first. "I think Melanie should be in her room by now."

Taking Mom by the hand, he led us upstairs to Melanie's room. When Dad reached for the latch, I stopped him. "Can I go in alone?" I just needed to be with her by myself for a while. With a nod of understanding, he opened the door and stood aside.

The room was quiet and dark as I entered, and all air escaped my lungs in an audible rush when I saw her lying in that bed.

Melanie.

She was white against the already white sheets, except for the huge purple bruises beneath her eyes. An IV bag hung near her head, the tube trailing down and attached to her wrist. Her mouth was slack and covered with tape that held the tube in her throat, her chest rising and falling at a constant rate. The heart monitor with its rhythmic beeping and the soft, steady sound of the ventilator were the only background noises. A blanket was pulled up over her chest and tucked under her arms, her body a silhouette beneath it.

Everything else was completely still except for the energy flowing between us. It was all the reassurance I needed to believe that she was really going to be okay. My relief was almost palpable as I released a weighted breath.

Moving to stand beside her, I took her hand in mine. Her fingers twitched, and I knew she was aware I was there.

"Hey, Mel." I placed a soft kiss on her temple and ran my fingers over her cheek, whispering near her ear, "My love. You're going to be okay." I settled into the chair next to her, her hand still in mine.

"We have a baby girl." I smiled at the image of Eva in my head. "You have to get better quickly so you can meet her." How much I wanted Melanie to see and hold her, but all I could do was tell her about her. "She's amazing, Melanie. So beautiful, just like you." I choked on the emotions, knowing Melanie would understand them better in my touch than with any words I could say.

I sat by Melanie's side for hours before Mom and Dad finally insisted I get something to eat.

"I'll be right back, baby." I glanced at her one more time as I stepped outside the room, praying she would be fine until I returned.

When I turned down the hall, I came face-to-face with Steve. His face was red and contorted, chest heaving with rage.

"You fucking coward!" I barely registered Steve's arm cock back before a stinging pain tore through my head as his fist connected with my face. The force knocked me to the ground. My hand went to my eyebrow, fingering the wound where the stitches had been ripped open.

"Are you insane? Don't you dare come in here and make this any worse than it already is," Dad hissed at Steve. I looked up at Melanie's father. His face full of bloodlust just moments before now looked down at me in horror.

"No, Dad. He should be angry," I sputtered as blood flowed down my face and over my lips.

"Steve, I'm so sorry." I swayed to the left as I tried to get to my knees, my body threatening to collapse at any moment. "We never should have kept this from you. Please understand. We were on our way to tell you." I shuddered as memories of the accident flashed in my mind.

The remorse evaporated as he seethed and leaned toward me, his hands resting on his thighs, his face close enough that I could smell the alcohol on his breath.

"You expect me to believe anything you say, Daniel, when I get a phone call two hours ago that my baby girl," he ground out, gesturing to himself with his thumbs and exaggerating the words, "was in a car accident on the way back from Boulder when she was supposed to be staying the weekend with a friend?" His breaths came heavy, and I could actually hear his teeth grinding together. "Then I show up here and ask for her room number, and they want to know if I also want the room number for her baby. Do you have any idea how that feels?"

I jumped as he abruptly stood and swung around, smashing his fist against the wall, crying out in both pain and fury.

"Steve, you have to calm down. I know you're angry, but this isn't the time or the place for this." Dad tried to temper the situation, but Steve's rage only grew.

"You!" Steve shouted as he pointed a shaky finger at Dad. "You knew the whole time, didn't you? Every time you passed me on the street, you fucking knew, didn't you?" Dad's silence served as confirmation. Steve rubbed his hands over his face, his eyes wild. "Were you taking care of her?"

Dad's patience finally hit its end, his cheeks red and his voice low, but sharp and stinging. "Of course I was taking care of her. Would you expect me to do anything different? She came to me!" He jabbed himself in the chest with his forefinger. "Maybe she would have come to you if you paid her a little attention instead of spending every free second drowning in your own self-pity. Did you really not see it, Steve? That girl," Dad said, pointing at her door, "has been showing for two months! And what did you do? You turned your head the other way."

A crowd had gathered, visitors peeking out from cracks in doors, two nurses watching nervously at the front end of the hall. A security guard rounded the corner, and Steve stepped back, raising his hands in surrender.

"Sir, we're going to have to ask you to leave."

The hostility bled from him as his shoulders slumped, and Steve turned his face to the floor, his brow twisting in torment. "Please...I just...I need to see my daughter."

"Let him stay. Steve, you need to go to her," I said. Steve seemed unwilling to look at me while he waited for consent from the security guard. The guard gave Steve what he said would be his first and only warning.

Dad helped me to my feet, and we left Steve to stand in the hall in front of his daughter's door.

"Come on, Daniel, we need to get your eye fixed." While my eye was resutured, Mom brought us dinner from the cafeteria. We ate in silence, exchanging nothing more than the occasional apprehensive glance. It was so hard to just sit and wait, each of us subject to the hands of fate.

"I'm going to go back upstairs." I finished my food, tasting none of it, anxious to get back to Melanie. "Dad, could you check on Eva?" I felt an impossible pull between my two girls, wanting to be with both of them at the same time.

When I returned to Melanie's room, I found Steve sitting next to her bed with unshed tears in his eyes. He didn't acknowledge me as I came in, but I didn't feel threatened by him, either. We both sat in silence, neither of us regarding the other, each of us just there for her.

I turned when I heard subdued footsteps. Dad came up behind me and placed both hands on my shoulders.

His voice was muted. "I just left Eva. Nothing has changed since this afternoon."

I nodded, both thankful and discouraged at the news. At least she was no worse.

A few seconds passed. The room was quiet except for the sound of the ventilator.

"Eva?" Steve whispered.

My heart broke as her name came from his lips, his heartache unbearable.

"Yeah, your granddaughter's name is Eva. Melanie and I picked it yesterday." I hoped giving him this information wouldn't remind him of where Melanie had been, but rather help him focus on the fact that he had a granddaughter. I wanted him to talk to me, to ask me about Eva. Instead, he stood and strode from the room.

ꟹ

Dad left for the night and I tried to settle in, falling into fitful bouts of sleep that didn't last for more than a few minutes at a time. Nothing changed, though I woke often just to make sure Melanie was okay, to feel her skin under mine. Then my eyes would flutter closed once again for a few moments.

My eyes fought against rays of sunlight coming in through the window. I must have fallen asleep. The last time I looked at the clock it was three in the morning. Hushed voices wrestled in the background; I could discern one was Mom, the other familiar, but unidentifiable. They were quiet, but not friendly.

"For six months? How could you?"

"What else was I supposed to do, Peggy? She didn't feel she could come to you. Maybe if you focused a little bit more on your daughter, you would have realized what was going on. She needed you. Instead, she had to come to me. I didn't mind, of course, I love her like my own, but she needed her mother!" Shifting in my chair, I rubbed my face to get rid my fatigue, before I stood and walked to them.

"It's okay, Mom." This wasn't a battle she needed to fight; if Melanie's mom had a problem, she needed to take it up with me. Mom had only done what was right.

"Peggy," I started to speak to her, but she held up her hand.

"Don't give me any excuses, Daniel. This is all your fault. I can't even stand to look at you. You make me sick." She shook her head, turned, and walked to Melanie, shutting us out. I wanted to resent her for her words, but how could I? I already knew I was to blame.

"I'm going to see Eva. Call me if anything changes, okay?" It was the right time to go. Peggy needed time alone with Melanie, and I needed to see my daughter.

I hurried to the NICU, checked in, and washed up, this time not hesitating as I went to her. She looked the same as she had the day before, yet somehow, I loved her more.

They let me hold her for a short time again, stating that it was good for her to feel me, but she also needed the warmth of her incubator. It was so frustrating. I wanted to hold her all day, but I also wanted what was best for her.

That's how I spent the next day and night – dividing my time between my girls. I felt like the go between until the three of us could be together. It was as if I were carrying a piece of one to the other, making them whole, as if we were part of the same soul.

Just as I had the night before, I slept in Melanie's room. Mom woke me with breakfast that she had picked up from the diner near the hotel.

"Good morning, sweetheart." She kissed me on the head, her smile soft, but her body weary. "Did you sleep okay?"

I shrugged. How well could you sleep in an uncomfortable chair in a hospital room? But I wasn't going to complain. I was the one who had gotten off easy.

Pursing her lips in transparent worry, she pulled my food from the bag, setting it before me. She looked as exhausted as I felt, drained from days of stress and far too little sleep.

I glanced at her and then the Styrofoam container. She really was an angel. "Thanks, Mom...for everything." I hoped she understood how much I appreciated her.

Her mouth twisted, her expression serious as she lifted my chin. "Your my son, Daniel. You know I'd do anything for you."

Nodding, I mumbled, "Yeah...I know."

Her face brightened as she seemed to push aside the heaviness. "I'm going to head down to check on Eva. Why don't you finish your breakfast and then meet us down there? Your dad took Peggy and Steve over to meet her, so you might want to give them a few minutes alone with her."

"Yeah, I'll come down in half an hour or so." Yesterday they'd sat vigil over Melanie for the entire day, refusing to leave her side. I just hoped that meeting Eva now would finally soften their hearts toward her.

As I ate, I talked to Melanie, knowing she could feel my presence. I finished and sat by her for a few minutes more, letting her know how much I loved her.

"Sweetheart, I'm going to see Eva now." I kissed her head, and her pulse quickened beneath my touch.

"I love you too, Mel." I smiled. Finally, I felt like everything was going to be okay – that we were going to make it.

I ran downstairs, now familiar with the routine. I jogged down the hall and to the elevator. I rushed past the newborns and turned into the hallway leading to the NICU, stumbling over my feet when I turned the corner. Mom clutched Dad, sobbing as he held her up, her legs slack beneath her.

My eyes scanned, finding Peggy in a similar position against Steve.

My heart stopped.

My feet that were frozen seconds before broke flat out into a run. Racing the rest of the way down the hall, I passed my parents and gripped the handle to swing the door open.

I had to get to her.

Two strong hands yanked me by the shoulders, holding me back.

"Daniel, stop." Dad's voice cracked. His hands slid from my shoulders to wrap around my waist, dragging me back. "Daniel," he grunted through his tears. "Look at me." I struggled against him. I had to see her.

"No, Dad! Let me go!" I screamed at him, but he wouldn't release me.

He couldn't keep me from her.

"Daniel, please," he choked, his words like poison as they came from his mouth. "She's gone. It was just too soon."

"No." I shook my head. "No!"

"Daniel, it's too late." Hands restrained me, but my body pushed forward.

"No! Please. Save her. You have to save her!" I begged. "No!" If I said it enough, I could make it true. She couldn't be gone. I just saw her.

"God, no. Please!" Why weren't they fighting for her? Why were they all standing here doing nothing?

"It's too late," Dad said the words again, their sharp finality ringing in my ears, his arms wrapping around me tighter. They were no longer trying to fight me, but trying to provide me some form of comfort.

"It's too late." His repeated words, now soft, crushed me, bringing me to my knees.

I wept on the floor on my hands and knees. Dad's arms remained around my waist as he knelt with me, the sound of Mom's torment stinging my ears.

Eva.

My baby girl.

Gone.

Chapter Ten

God, it hurt so bad.

Worst was that Melanie had to sit there while Vanessa bragged about how we were going to be parents.

Never had I wanted to hold her more, to tell her she was the only mother I wanted for my child, to tell her that what had happened with Vanessa was a mistake.

A second later, Melanie's chair protested against the floor, the legs squeaking as she mumbled, "I need to use the restroom," to Nicholas before she fled, tripping over her feet.

I watched her rush away. All of me ached for all of her—her mind, her soul, her body.

Something close to a growl came from Nicholas, my rapt attention on Melanie broken by his anger. "Who the fuck do you think you are?" He leaned in close, his voice low.

Turning to him, I wished for nothing more than to tell him who *I* was.

That *I* was supposed to be Melanie's husband, not him.

That *I* adored her more than any other creature that had ever lived and always would.

That *I* had every intention of taking her away from him.

But I couldn't do that. I knew Melanie still loved me.

What I didn't know was whether she still *wanted* me.

Besides, based on the way he acted toward her all night, it was apparent that it would not be in Melanie's favor to anger this asshole. If he treated her like this in public, I couldn't imagine how he must treat her in private.

Once again, my fury toward him set in. What if he hurt her? My stomach clenched and my hands curled into fists, every piece of me wanting to protect my girl. I wanted to hide her away. I wanted to keep her safe from him. I wanted to see life in her eyes once again. But that had to be Melanie's choice, not mine.

I swallowed down the need to beat the shit out of the guy and forced words out, making them as true a statement as I could. "She just reminds me of somebody I used to know." That was the most he was going to get from me.

"So, Daniel," Shane cut in, his voice clear, though you could hear the tension in it. "What do you think? Do you have any more questions about the proposal, or are you ready to get this thing started?"

I ran my hands through my hair, trying to focus. Did I want them to build it? Could I be this close to Melanie's husband and not go completely insane? Would it allow me to see Melanie again?

Katie watched me knowingly. I was sure she could read every question I'd just asked myself as if it were written across my forehead.

"Uh, it's a lot to take in, Shane. Just give me a minute. I need to clear my head before I can decide." I stood, and Shane nodded at me.

Hands that I never wanted to feel again grabbed my arm. "Where are you going?" Vanessa whined.

I shook her arm off. "To the men's room. Is that okay with you?" My tone was hard and condescending. I didn't give a shit. There was no way I was going to let her have any control over me—ever.

Her face contorted, as if she was offended, which I hoped she was. Maybe then she'd accept I would never want her or her baby. I turned on my heel, and as I walked away, everything clicked.

"Daniel and I are having a baby."

She'd done it on purpose. Vanessa wasn't trying to further her career, to find an easy way to get ahead. She had wanted it all. The name, the money—everything. I knew then that there was no question whether the baby was mine or not. Thoughts of her in my drunken stupor, assuring me she was on the pill when I had insisted we needed to use something, distracting me, spurring me on. I was always careful, always—except for that one time with her.

I had every intention of going to the men's room, but as I neared it, the pull intensified, drawing me to *her*. Placing my hand against the men's room door, I tried to push it open, but I just couldn't do it. I could feel her heart beating against my chest, her body begging mine to find hers. Dropping my hand, I stepped back and looked between the two doors. She was only feet from me; I could walk right in there and ask her everything.

My steps were slow as I approached the women's restroom, my breaths shallow and hard. Setting both hands flat against the door, I prayed she'd let me talk to her.

If I could just tell Melanie that I was sorry one more time, would she finally forgive me? I could never take back what I had done, but did she love me enough to see past it and allow me to love her and adore her the way she should be? Would she let me take care of her, allow me to try to breathe life back into her? Was I being selfish because I knew if she allowed me that, I'd become whole myself? That if she allowed me to touch her, my heart would beat again?

God, I wanted to touch her.

That thought alone gave me the courage to push the door open. I froze when I heard her cries coming from a closed stall. The sound nearly brought me to my knees. I had never heard so much pain coming from one person. It made it so much worse that it was coming from the one person who meant everything to me. I wanted to comfort her, but I knew my presence was what had caused it to begin with. I retreated to give her privacy, though I couldn't go far.

I just waited. I'd been waiting for her to return to me for nine years. I could be patient.

When the faucet ran, I knew she'd be coming out soon. I braced myself to face her. What would she say to me? What would I say to her?

I didn't have time to contemplate it before the door swung open, her sweet scent filling the air. My heart leapt at the sight of her. Her brown hair was a disaster, her face blotchy and red, green eyes glistening from her tears.

My beautiful, broken girl.

None of the times that I'd imagined being near her again could have prepared me for this. Our connection was stronger than it had ever been. In that moment, just the two of us existed. The air crackled with our need. I could hear her heart speed up in her chest and her breathing become erratic, and I felt her fingers twitch toward me.

She wanted me.

I had to touch.

Slowly, I brought my hand to her face, and I swore I could actually see the electricity travel between us. I traced my fingertips across her cheekbone, unsure of how much contact I could take.

"Melanie." Everything I felt about her came out in that one word, my voice cracking as the emotions tumbled from my mouth.

"Why?" I whispered.

Of course, I knew why. What I didn't understand was why she didn't tell me herself. Why she left me waiting for months when I didn't even know she'd left me for someone else. Searching her face, I prayed I'd find the answer there. Almost imperceptibly, her head tilted to the side, her eyes filling with—confusion? The expression on her face left me with more questions than I'd started with.

She gave me no answer, and I didn't push her. Perhaps the reason she'd never told me herself was she couldn't bring herself to say the words to me. It didn't matter anyway. All that mattered was the love flowing between us right now, and I knew I only had a few moments more. I couldn't waste them.

Her neck was flushed, wrapped in the same gold I'd given her the first time I made love to her, tangible evidence that she still thought of me.

Slowly, I dragged my fingertips from her cheek to her neck so I could touch the chain, running my fingers along it. It held an energy all its own. I reached for the pendant, needing to feel our initials intertwined together, a promise of forever resting over her heart. I couldn't hold back the smile tugging on my lips as I rubbed it between two fingers, the inscription worn but unmistakable.

"My love." I had to say it out loud. I'd been telling her all night with my body, hoping she'd understand. Now she could make no mistake.

Her whole body shook, and I was afraid she was going to break down or run from me. Instead, her hand reached for me, her movements jerky. My mouth watered when she finally touched me, her thumb running across my bottom lip. Our bodies drifted closer, every second bringing her nearer to me. I had to taste. I leaned in, her lips inviting mine.

"Melanie." Katie's voice cut through the air.

I jumped back.

Shit.

Jerked back into reality, I realized I'd nearly kissed a woman whose husband was sitting twenty feet away. Katie stood guard over her friend, pulling her away, defending her from me.

It stung. She was mine, not his. But only in soul and not in body. My girl would leave with that man. The weight of our circumstances crushed me as I tore myself away from her. I felt on the verge of death as I forced myself to turn and walk away.

I nearly ran the rest of the way to the table, my decision made. How could I not sign this contract? Shane knew what he was doing, though none of that was even a consideration. I would do anything it took to be near Melanie.

"Okay, Shane, let's do this." He nodded agreement, his grin wide as he pushed the papers toward me, using his finger to indicate everywhere I needed to sign.

My heart rate sped up when I felt Melanie approach from behind. I reveled in the satisfaction that I *knew* her; no one could take that away from me.

With the last signature in place, we all stood to leave. Shane reached out and took his wife's hand.

Nicholas grabbed Melanie's hand, dragging her through the restaurant as she struggled to keep up.

Watching it was torture, and all I could do was follow.

I quietly muttered, "Come on," to Vanessa, gesturing for her to walk ahead of me. I would have to deal with that situation soon enough, but it would have to wait. I had to get one more glimpse of Melanie before she took my heart with her once again.

Outside the restaurant, we gathered on the sidewalk, waiting for our cars. Once again, that uncomfortable tension set in. Resentment rolled off Nicholas. I couldn't tell if it was directed at me or Shane or Melanie—most likely a combination of us all.

Shane extended his hand to me. "It's going to be great working with you, Daniel. I promise you will not be disappointed."

Positive it was going to be a good experience working with him, I returned his handshake. "I have faith in you, Shane. We'll talk again on Monday when I bring the information from the bank to your office." I didn't even acknowledge Nicholas. As far as I was concerned, he had no bearing in this decision.

Katie was at Shane's side, regarding me with unabashed curiosity. I still didn't know what this woman was up to, but somehow I believed she was on Melanie's side.

I reached my hand to hers, taking it. "It was a pleasure to meet you, Katie." Her tender glance at Melanie confirmed her love for my girl, and I relaxed at her touch, squeezing her hand lightly.

"Nice to meet you, too, Daniel." Katie flashed a knowing smile, her blue eyes twinkling. No question. She knew exactly who I was.

I cringed when Nicholas's voice broke through the calm that had settled in the air. "Let's go, Melanie." I turned just in time to see him shove her into the car. His grip was rough, and I didn't miss the grimace on Melanie's face as she was thrown into her seat.

It was the last I could take. I wouldn't stand by and watch him treat Melanie like that.

With my hands in fists, I mentally prepared for a fight. I had taken no more than a step when a firm hand tugged on my shoulder. Katie's face was solemn and hard, expressing her disapproval with two sharp shakes of her head. I nearly ripped her hand from me, stopping only when she leaned in and whispered urgently in my ear, "Daniel, you're just going to make it worse."

Resigned at her words, I shoved my hands into my pockets. It killed me to allow Melanie to go with that creep, but the last thing I wanted to do was cause trouble for her. I'd done enough of that to last her a lifetime.

I couldn't tear my eyes from her as she waited in her seat for her bastard husband to run around to the other side of the car.

"Bye," passed from her lips as the car sped away. I could only hope she could see it when I mouthed "my love" to her. Instantly, my chest burned with the loss. Giving me a sad smile, Katie squeezed my arm. She leaned in, her mouth close to my ear.

"She loves you too." In confusion, Shane watched our interaction. With one last small smile, she turned away from me and wrapped her arms around Shane's waist, speaking to him under her breath.

Shane's expression quickly shone in understanding. He nodded a couple of times before a smile took over his face. They bid us goodbye when their car pulled up to the curb.

"What the hell was that?" Vanessa stood behind me, irritated, her hands on her hips.

"Just get in the car, Vanessa." This was not going to be a pleasant conversation.

I knew it was better to just get it over with—the sooner the better. I ran the back of my hand across my lips as I pulled out onto the road, glancing in her direction. She stared straight ahead, pouting.

"What exactly do you want from me, Vanessa?"

"What do you mean?" She'd turned toward me, her posture defensive, her voice feigning innocence.

"You know exactly what I mean. I'm not here to play games. Tell me what you want from me." I had no intention of giving her what she wanted, but I just needed to hear her say it.

"Well, Daniel, we *are* having a baby. Don't you think we should get married?"

Holy shit. I was right. I just hadn't expected her to come straight out and say it. She wanted money. And she wanted my name. I laughed out loud as I shook my head; she was indeed insane.

"Why are you laughing? There is nothing funny about this situation, Daniel."

"Oh, I disagree. I find this utterly fucking hilarious." Did she really think she could get away with this? Yeah, I had been stupid enough to fall for it the first time, but that night would be the one mistake I'd make; there would not be a repeat.

"Daniel, we're having a baby. We need to...find a way to work this out." She tried to sound confident, but it sounded more as if she were pleading.

"No, Vanessa. There will never be anything between us." I looked directly at her. "Never." Even I hated the sound of my voice, but I had to be clear on this point.

"What? Is this about that bitch at dinner that you couldn't stop staring at? She's married for God's sake!" she screeched.

That bitch? I couldn't believe she had the nerve to talk as if she knew anything about Melanie or me. I ran my hands through my hair, trying to rein in the outrage consuming me.

"You don't know me, Vanessa, so I'd appreciate it if you'd stop talking like you do." Getting my temper under control, I forced myself to keep my tone even. "I don't want anything to do with you." I squeezed the steering wheel as I said the words, trying to keep myself from spitting them at her. "I know that baby is my responsibility, and I'll accept that. I'll pay child support, but I expect to have joint custody."

Inside the car was silent except for the short breaths I could hear Vanessa taking as she chewed on her lip, her hands clutching her purse. I looked around, surprised we were already approaching her house.

"You'll hear from my attorney tomorrow. Other than that, I don't want to hear from you unless it is directly related to the baby. Do you understand?" I sat in my seat and waited for her answer.

"What? W…wha…why?" she stammered, gawking at me.

"Because I don't appreciate being taken advantage of." I glared at her, daring her to deny it.

"I...I..." Her words twisted together, unable to form a lie quickly enough.

That's what I thought.

I would never have treated her like this if this had been an accident, if the two of us had been irresponsible and had the consequences to face. What I wouldn't tolerate was being manipulated.

She mumbled under her breath, "You're an asshole," as she opened the door and got out, running up the sidewalk to her house.

Yeah, probably so.

"But you are a whore," I muttered to her retreating form.

Mom would kill me if she ever found out how I'd treated Vanessa. She'd remind me that everyone deserved to be respected, even if you didn't feel like giving it to them. But I was in full defense mode because Vanessa was most definitely a threat.

Leaving Vanessa allowed the emptiness to suck me in, and I drove aimlessly, my only companion the burn on my skin Melanie had left behind.

I'd missed her so badly all these years, haunted by the memories of her face, agonized by the loss of her comfort, plagued by the grief we should have shared. All of that was still there, strong and growing, except there was something else building with it. I wasn't sure what it was, but it felt—good?

Even though I knew I should stay away, there was not a chance in hell I would. I had to see her again even if it was only from a distance.

I pulled off to the side of the road, dust flying as I came to an abrupt stop. I searched for Nicholas Borelli on my phone. Numerous results popped up on the screen, but there was something specific I was looking for. Scrolling through, one caught my eye—his personal address. I saved the site and threw my phone onto the seat next to me as I took off toward home.

I knew I'd never fall asleep tonight; I didn't even think I wanted to. I entered my apartment, an expanse of desolation only because she wasn't there, but tonight it was different. Instead of climbing into the shower and giving myself over to my pain, I walked out onto the balcony and gazed upon the city lights, knowing she was there. Leaning against the railing, I closed my eyes and allowed myself to feel all the love, hurt, and longing she had shown me tonight. My chest filled with my love for her, and once again, I called upon the power that somehow held us together. I prayed she was safe and felt loved, by me.

Chapter Eleven

I glanced back up to see Daniel watching me with his hands in his pockets, defeat in his eyes. I mouthed a silent *bye* to him as Nicholas slid into the driver's side and pulled away. I almost missed the words *my love* form on Daniel's lips. As we drove away from the restaurant, my heart broke all over again as I watched him disappear from sight in the side mirror.

A thick silence descended over the car as Nicholas sped through the streets. His knuckles strained against the steering wheel, his chin taut and teeth clenched. Not a word was uttered in the twenty-five minutes it took us to get back to the house.

He pulled into the garage and climbed from the car. Fear ran up my spine. I'd never been afraid of him before, but the expression on his face told me it was time to start. He said nothing as he opened my door, waiting for me to get out. The only sound was that of my heels clicking on the concrete floor as he followed me into the house.

"You fucking whore." The words were controlled and menacing, making me stop mid-stride, and I slowly turned to him. He stared at me, and I felt the threat in his eyes. I didn't know where the courage came from, but I didn't back down. I was done. I would no longer allow him this control over me. My face must have told him that very thing, because I heard the crack before I felt the sting on my face.

My hand went to my face, my hate growing with each rise and fall of my chest.

"Melanie." With a sneer, he brought his face close to mine. "You're very lucky that guy was as fucked up as you are, otherwise I would beat the shit out of you right now." Purposefully, he unbuttoned the sleeves of his shirt and rolled them up his arms, quiet fury on his face as he waited for me to succumb.

That was not going to happen.

I leaned in close to him, exhaling into his face. I felt the words form, knowing my response would change everything.

"Fuck you." The words slowly slid through my lips. He froze, his shock evident, and I turned and left him standing in the foyer.

I went upstairs and got a pair of pajamas. When I got back downstairs, Nicholas still stood in the same spot. I didn't acknowledge him as I retired to the guest bedroom. There was no way I would lie next to that man.

As sleep neared, I could feel myself racing toward the usual dreams of love and loss. But tonight, I could also feel something new. It was the same feeling I couldn't quite put my finger on earlier in the day.

Hope.

Yes, change was coming.

I jolted upright, unaware of where I was while the events of last night seeped into my consciousness.

Daniel.

I smiled as I looked around the guest room, running my hands over the soft sheets, remembering the dreams I had had of him last night. It was the best sleep I'd had in years. Even though he wasn't lying there beside me, his presence was never far.

Distant rapping echoed from the front door, while my phone buzzed at the same time.

I glanced to the clock.

"Nine thirty-four?" I mumbled to myself.

I couldn't believe I'd slept the morning away. Nicholas would have left for the office hours ago. Never in nine years had I not gotten up to make him breakfast. I was still shocked that I'd finally stood up to him and refused him that control I'd so willingly given.

I felt so—free.

My phone buzzed again, and I grabbed it, seeing seven missed texts from Katie. The last demanded that I hurry up and open the front door. Grinning, I got up and padded barefoot across the tile floor, anxious to see my friend. I wasn't sure what would have happened had she not been there last night.

I looked through the peephole before twisting the lock and opening the door. "Katie!" I launched myself into her arms as she stood in my entryway.

She was the only one who understood, and right now, I had never been more confused in my entire life. My heart was soaring with the palpable love I had felt from Daniel last night. It finally beat with true life, my dead soul resuscitated by his mere touch. At the same time, my chest had been torn open, old wounds gaping with fresh memories of our lost love, thoughts of what could have been—what should have been—and now what would never be. But he loved me. I knew I could go on knowing that. The thought of him crawling into bed next to another woman nearly killed me, but I could accept it.

I would never attempt to come between him and his family.

She had his body, but I had his soul.

"I thought you were going to need me today." Katie hugged me, rubbing my back as I buried my face in her shoulder.

She pulled back to look at my face, an audible *hiss* coming from her lips. "That bastard." Her hand came up to my chin, tilting my head her direction.

I touched my cheek, wincing at the slight soreness. Turning to the mirror on the wall, there was a purple bruise that marked my cheekbone. I ran my fingers across it, the sight of it stirring my hatred once again.

Katie stood behind me, concern on her face. "Are you okay?" I could see she was trying to control herself, but there was rage brewing in her.

I shook my head as I turned to her. "This," I said, gesturing to the bruise, "is as far as the asshole got." I felt sick to my stomach as I recalled the look on his face last night as he had tried to put me in my place.

"I can't believe he actually hit me, after all these years of playing this part he wrote for me, fitting it perfectly. I've hated myself for so long. I'd allowed him to treat me like garbage because I didn't feel like I was worth anything." I chewed on my bottom lip, trying to keep the tears from coming. "I don't know what came over me. I was just...done. I finally stood up for myself, Katie...I slept in the guestroom last night." A small smile crept over my face as I waited for her reaction.

She stared at me for a few moments before she gently touched my shoulder. "I'm so proud of you."

"You don't know what it means to me that you're here, that you knew I'd need you."

"Of course I knew, Mel." A moment was spent in knowing silence before her serious expression shifted and she smirked.

"Besides, did you really think I'd miss getting the scoop on what the hell was going on last night? You know me better than that."

I laughed and shook my head at her.

"Come on." She inclined her head in the direction of the family room. "Go sit down, I'll make us some coffee. We need to talk."

She turned toward the kitchen, and I headed to the family room. Goose bumps popped up over my arms when I walked by the window. I could feel Daniel everywhere, the energy now a constant reminder of just how near he was.

Minutes later, Katie came into the room carrying two coffee cups. She handed one to me before settling onto the couch and drawing one leg up under her to face me. My back was propped against the armrest, my legs drawn to my chest. I brought the cup to my lips, taking the first sip. The warmth traveled down my throat and into my belly as I mulled over the events of the last twenty-four hours. It was almost as if it had all been a dream.

Katie took a sip of her coffee and seemed to search for the right words. She looked me in the eyes, shaking her head. "I almost can't believe it, this whole *fate* thing you've always talked about with Daniel, as if there were something magical between the two of you." She inhaled deeply, scrunching up her nose. "I've never believed in stuff like that, but first the necklace and now last night…" she said, trailing off and waving her hand in the air as if she were trying to dismiss the whole concept.

"I know, Katie. The whole idea seems so cliché, but there was always more to us than normal. Erin called us soul mates, but I...I've always known it was more than that." I was almost embarrassed to describe it, but I needed Katie to understand. "It's like we share the *same* soul, and when we're apart, each half is looking for the other." Katie'd probably think I'd lost my mind, but it was the truth.

"I miss him so much. Seeing him with that woman...it just...tore me apart," I swallowed the lump in my throat as I stumbled over the words. "But he loves me. He loves me just as much as I love him. I know it." Tears began to fall. So many conflicting emotions had rocked me last night that it was hard to decipher them all. But there was one emotion that I couldn't question, and that was his love for me.

"Well, that much was very obvious, Melanie. I couldn't tell what he wanted more...to rip Nicholas's face off or to take you against the wall." She raised her eyebrows at me, clearly referring to what she'd interrupted in front of the restrooms last night. "Sorry about that, by the way. Nicholas was getting ready to come looking for you, and I insisted I would check on you."

"Thanks." I could only imagine what would have happened had it been Nicholas who found us rather than Katie.

I groaned in frustration, remembering Daniel's words—his *why* and the hurt on his face as if I had somehow put it there.

"Katie, I've never been so confused. He's the one who left me. He didn't want me anymore, but he looked at me as if I was the one who broke his heart. I don't understand."

"Yeah, I definitely picked up on that too." Katie sucked in her bottom lip as she thought back to last night, her eyes narrowing in concentration. "I mean, there's something missing, Melanie." Her eyes darted back to mine. "You told me what happened when you went back for him, but why did you leave him in the first place?"

I took a deep breath, preparing to tell a story I wasn't sure I'd be able to get through without completely breaking down.

"It's just so hard," I choked through my tears.

March 2000

It was excruciating – the pain. Where it was coming from, I wasn't sure. I lay in the darkness, for how long I couldn't tell. Voices, faint beeping, the shuffling of chairs came indistinct against my ears. I was so scared, though somehow I knew I would be okay, only because I could feel him. Daniel was there. Then there were times when he was not.

When I'd hear whispered words and could feel the touch of his lips against my skin, I would relax. Then cold would descend, fear rushing in and threatening to take me away forever when he was gone. And just when I'd begin to despair, he would suddenly be there once again.

I wanted to open my eyes to see him, and I fought so hard to. They'd flutter, the light stinging them, but I was unable to focus on anything.

"Melanie." I heard Daniel's voice as he shifted toward me. I tried to call to him. I could barely make out the shape of his face before I drifted back into darkness once again. Finally, the fog began to fade. Voices became clearer, the pain became worse. I was suddenly aware of how difficult it was to breathe.

"Melanie, my love," he whispered against my hand. His lips caressed my skin.

A cloud surrounded my head when I was finally able to keep my eyes open, like there was a haze hovering in the room. Everything was a blur – except for the hazel eyes staring down at me.

They were filled with complete anguish.

Everything became clear, confusion turned to clarity. Fear raced through my veins. "Eva?" I struggled to form the word, to ask about her, to call to her. My mouth was dry, my tongue thick, and no sound came. My hands searched for her, clawing at the emptiness of my belly in panic.

"Shh...shh. Baby, please calm down. You're going to hurt yourself." Daniel's hands restrained mine as he leaned over me and spoke against my ear. I calmed against his touch, unwilling to fight him, feeling his tears roll down my cheek and into my hair.

I swallowed, saliva wetting my mouth as I licked my lips and found enough moisture to form the word. "Eva?"

All of his breath left him as he stilled against my face, finally pulling away to look me in the eye. No words were said as he shook his head with tears running in a continuous stream down his face.

No?

His meaning soaked into my soul like poison. Soundless sobs racked my body as I fought to deny the truth. My baby girl. How could she be gone?

Unbearable sadness consumed me and I was sucked back into the darkness, the pain too great to face. In moments of utter blackness, I struggled to find her, to go to her, but Daniel's soul called me back to him, willing me to survive. When I could resist him no longer, I opened my eyes, once again, to meet his. Our grief poured between us as we silently mourned her.

He spoke first, his voice cracked and strained. "Melanie, I'm so sorry."

Of course he was sorry. I was sorry, sorry for our pain, sorry for our loss. But the tortured look on his face told me that he blamed himself.

Shaking my head, I reached out for Daniel's cheek, wiping the tears from under his eyes. "I love you," I said as I weakly tried to smile at him. He squeezed his eyes tight as more tears fell, and he shook his head against my hand, his body trembling.

"I don't deserve you, Melanie. You can never understand how sorry I am. If I could change it..." His chest heaved with his escalating anguish.

I ran my hand through his hair in an attempt to ease him. "Look at me." I cupped his cheek. His face contained more pain than any one person should ever bear. "It wasn't your fault. You can't blame yourself for this." I didn't know all the details of what had happened, but what I did know was that the car had come out of nowhere. "It hurts me even more to think of you blaming yourself for this. Please, I need you to forgive yourself for whatever you think you're responsible for." I rubbed the back of his neck, looking him in the face, making sure he understood and accepted what I was trying to tell him.

He sighed and nodded a silent promise to move on.

"Tell me what happened," I pleaded.

"Melanie, I...I…"

"Please," I choked out. As much as I knew he wanted to shield me from any more suffering, he had to tell me. I didn't want to know, but I had to know.

"Are you sure you're ready to hear it?" The devastation on his face tore me apart.

I nodded, and he gripped my hand tighter. He stared at his feet for a few moments before finally looking at me.

"Eva…she lived for two days."

I gasped, struggling to get air in my lungs.

"What?" I rasped out.

Wetting his lips, he swallowed hard. "She was so beautiful." His face was so sad, but there was a light in his eyes when he spoke of her. "So small. God, Melanie, you can't imagine how small she was. So perfect." He talked about her with a reverence and love I'd never seen before, and I smiled as he described her, my tiny baby girl.

"Did you hold her?" I bit back the sob that threatened. He nodded, rubbing my arm. "A few times, but not for long. I would have held her all day if they had let me, but the nurses wanted her to be in her bed as much as possible." I realized where he'd been all those times when I'd felt his absence. He was taking care of our baby girl.

"Thank you," I whispered through my tears as I held him close to me. "Thank you for taking care of us." I kissed his dry, chapped lips, unable to imagine the pain he must have felt over the last – days? I wasn't sure how long it had been. There was still so much I didn't know.

I pulled away, my hands on his chest. "Are you hurt?" I asked, for the first time able to focus on more than just his eyes. A huge bruise covered the left side of his face and a small row of stitches sat just above his eyebrow. But he was dressed in normal clothes and sitting beside my bed, it was obvious his worst injury was a broken heart.

He shook his head. "No, I'm fine. A couple of cracked ribs," he said as he pointed to the stitches on his brow, "and this."

Cracked ribs? "Does it hurt?"

"Honestly, Melanie, I really haven't even thought about it. It's not a big deal."

"How badly was I injured?" I asked. I hurt – everywhere.

He took in a deep breath, slowly blowing the air out through pursed lips as he ran his free hand nervously through his hair.

"You were on the ventilator for three days. They kept you on it until the swelling went down around your brain," Daniel grimaced as he described the reason I'd been out for so long. I followed his gaze down my

body. "Your right leg is badly broken. You're going to need some pretty intense physical therapy when you get out of here, but Dad says you'll heal fine. You have a lot of bruises and cuts all over..." he said as his voice trailed off. He broke eye contact as he looked away.

He was hiding something from me.

"Daniel, everything," I demanded. Unease raced through me when I saw his face again filled with agony, his jaw held tight in an attempt to hide the obvious trembling. I was terrified at what would cause him this reaction, but I pressed him. "Everything."

He closed his eyes, his beautiful face weary and broken. "Baby." He tried to keep his voice soft, but it cracked. "You were bleeding." He paused, waiting for my reaction. I blinked at him, not understanding what about that could cause him so much pain. He cleared his throat, swallowing. "What I mean is..." He stalled.

"Melanie." He gathered up my hand in both of his. "The cesarean...there was too much bleeding..."

He didn't have to say the words because I knew by the expression on his face what he was trying to tell me. I couldn't have more children.

Never would I give Daniel the family he wanted.

Never would I be a mother.

I gasped against the pain, clutching my chest as I tried to breathe, a full panic attack taking over my body. I was devastated. We lost our baby girl and now we couldn't have another – well, not we. Me.

Would Daniel still want me?

He shushed me, rubbed the back of my neck, and rocked me. I looked at his face, filled with his love and compassion for me, and I had to believe that he would always want me. In one day, all of our dreams had been shattered, but we still had each other, and we would make it. My tears finally subsided and I began to accept what life had dealt us. It was going to take a very long time to heal from it, but Daniel and I would do it together.

A constant stream of nurses and doctors came and went over the next few of hours.

After the latest round of nurses left, Julia walked into the room, Patrick following close behind. Her voice was soft, always motherly. "Hey, beautiful girl." She came near and leaned over me, kissing me ever so softly on my forehead. I loved her so much.

"How are you feeling?"

How was I feeling? I honestly didn't know. I smiled weakly and didn't answer because I couldn't. Anything I said would have been a lie.

"Can we get anything for you?" Patrick had the same concerned look on his face as he always did, radiating kindness.

"Um, no. But thanks, Patrick." I smiled at him and reached for his hand, and Julia placed hers over both of ours.

"Did...did you get to meet her?" I hoped they did. I looked at their broken faces and my heart broke a little more. The loss of Eva wasn't just Daniel's and mine; it was also theirs. They'd lost their granddaughter, the one they'd planned for, taken care of, loved.

Julia whimpered, her eyes bloodshot and her forehead wrinkled with lines that had never been there before. "Oh, Melanie, honey. She was so beautiful, just like you. She had your mouth." Through tears she told me everything she remembered about Eva. It was heartbreaking and wonderful at the same time. I wanted to know my daughter. But somehow I already did. Even though I had never seen her face, I felt her, knew her soul, and it would always be a part of me. Patrick stood in silence behind Daniel, his face weary, but his love and support unwavering.

When the door creaked open, we all turned to see a flash of brown, frizzy hair.

Mom.

Chapter Twelve

March 2000

Mom was here. Of course she was. Guilt overcame me. This was how my parents found out about Eva. Slow and hesitant, Mom walked into the room. Black, heavy bags drooped under brown eyes so red, it was hard to tell their normal color. She had always been thin, but her cheeks were sunken in, the skin sagging. Her hair was up in a messy bun, pieces falling out and sticking to her face where her tears had dried. For the first time, she looked old. She stood at the foot of my bed, nervously straightening her shirt against her stomach.

"Mom," I breathed out, not having a clue what to say to her. Anxiously, I glanced at Daniel, trying to gauge his reaction to her. He was already standing to kiss me on the forehead, and he and his parents excused themselves. When they reached the door, Daniel mouthed, "I love you," before following his parents out. Mom still fidgeted, standing in the same spot.

"Mom?" I asked. Would she even talk to me? She had to be so disappointed – so angry.

"Oh, Melanie," Mom cried, rushing around to take my cheeks in her hands.

"Mom, I'm so sorry." I cried into her shoulder, hugging her to me as we grieved for Eva and for the wall we'd unknowingly built between us.

"It's okay." She shushed me and swept my hair behind my ear. "We have a lot to deal with, but we'll do that later, okay? Right now, I just want you to get better."

"Mom...I" I needed to explain everything to her now, to tell her why I'd been scared to let her know, but the door opened.

Dad.

My stomach twisted in knots when I saw his face. Lax, deceptively void of emotion, he looked as if he felt nothing, though he couldn't hide the disgust he felt for me. My voice trembled, shaky and barely audible as I called to him across the room, "Dad?" My voice implored him to talk to me. He shook his head and looked down, leaving the room without saying a word. It was exactly as I had feared. He would never forgive me for this. I could only imagine the way he had treated Daniel. Mom narrowed her eyes as she watched him leave, turning back to me with a tight smile.

"Don't let him bother you, sweetheart."

"I knew he was going to be so disappointed." Looking at the empty spot my father had just taken up, I couldn't help but wish I'd listened to Daniel when he'd insisted we tell him. "I'm not ashamed, Mom." I looked at her, needing her to understand I would never regret Eva.

"I know, sweetheart. I know." She patted my arm to soothe my nerves from the non-confrontation with my dad.

"Did you get here in time?"

A wistful smile lit her face.

"She was so beautiful." Mom seemed to be lost in her thoughts before she spoke again. "You're so young." I started to protest, but she stopped me, shaking her head. "No, let me say this. You're young, but you don't love as if you are." She swallowed. "You would have been the best mom." She wiped her tears with the back of her hand, sighing as she looked

away. "I just wanted you to know that I truly believe that, for whatever it's worth."

It was worth everything.

With a subdued knock, Daniel peeked in the door.

I smiled and he came into the room and sat across from Mom. The tension between them was palpable. It was clear that the forgiveness she had shown me had not been extended to Daniel.

I knew my parents would see it as if Daniel had taken advantage of their little girl. It sickened me that anyone could even begin to think of him that way, but I had to be patient. Eventually they would realize how much he really did care about me. Time would just have to prove that.

The rest of the evening people filtered in and out. Nurses came and went, Mom left to get coffee at least ten times, and Erin and Julia ran back and forth to get people whatever they needed. Patrick continually checked to be sure I was being well taken care of while Dad stared at me from across the room.

And Daniel – he never left my side.

He was so exhausted, yet he stayed. I could never love him more than I did right then.

When night fell, everybody left but Daniel, who attempted to sleep in the chair beside my bed. I asked him to go with his parents and get a good night's sleep. Of course, he refused. We both slept restlessly. How people ever expected to "rest and get well" in a hospital, I'd never know. Nurses came in and out at least five times during the night, poking and prodding me. I was convinced if they'd just let me sleep, I'd be well in half the time. Daniel and I gave up when the first rays of light came through the window. Neither of us felt any better than we had the night before.

"Are you up for any more visitors?" Erin popped her head through the door, her eyes glistening. Daniel and I welcomed her in. She hugged me and then wrapped her arms around Daniel.

Erin convinced Daniel to go take a shower and get something to eat. He looked to me and I could see how hesitant he was to leave.

My chest constricted at the thought of him walking out the door, an irrational fear taking hold. I wanted to beg him to stay, but I forced myself to assure him I would be fine. I was going to have to get over that.

After what had happened, I didn't think I'd ever want to be away from him again, but I still had to go back home to Colorado Springs. I still had two months of school left.

Erin settled in beside me and took my hand. "Hey, sister." She smiled at me and I smiled back. I loved when she called me that. "How are you? And don't give me any of that bullshit that you're fine, either."

I laughed, thankful that she always forced me to be honest with her. She wouldn't have it any other way.

"I really can't say, Erin. I mean, I can't even begin to describe the heartbreak I feel over her. It's like this huge piece of me is missing and I don't think I'll ever stop feeling that way. But when Daniel's nearby, I know everything is going to be all right." Her lip trembled as she nodded in understanding.

"Erin, what happened? I can't ask Daniel because he blames himself."

She took a deep breath. "Yeah, I know. He really does, Melanie. I don't know if he'll ever stop, but there was nothing he could have done. The guy hit you, not the other way around." She shook her head and picked at her fingernails before looking back to me. "They charged him with manslaughter this morning. He'd been drinking—all night—and was on his way back to Denver. Apparently, he fell asleep at the wheel. His blood alcohol level was more than double the limit." She paused to give me time to absorb what she'd said.

Anger welled up from a place inside me I didn't know, a foreign hatred that I didn't understand. I fought to push it aside. I knew that would be something I would have to deal with over time, forgiving someone I didn't even know. For now, her news was too much for my broken heart to deal with.

"What about my parents?" Daniel told me everything was fine, even when I knew it wasn't.

"Well, I think your mom is okay. She was really upset when she first got here and got into it with Mom. She hadn't slept all night on her way here. When she came in and saw you in this bed, I think she just...snapped. She didn't really talk to anyone that first day, but once she saw…Eva," she said, hesitating on Eva's name as tears filled her eyes.

"Oh, Melanie, that little girl could soften anyone's heart. Peggy apologized to Mom. She hasn't really spoken much to Daniel, but she stayed beside him that whole morning after Eva passed. She's hurt, Melanie, but she loves you and is willing to forgive you."

"And Dad?"

Anger flashed across her face.

"Erin, what did he do?"

She finally spoke. "He, uh...hit Daniel."

"What?"

"Melanie, he really messed Daniel up. He broke open all the stitches on his face." She groaned, putting her hands over her face. "I don't want to feel so angry at your dad, but how could he do that after everything you guys had been through? And now, he just hovers outside your door, not saying anything to anyone. It's kinda creepy."

He did exactly what I'd feared he'd do all these months. He'd hurt Daniel. If I could, I would have taken any punishment to prevent this, but I knew Daniel would always be the bad guy in my dad's eyes no matter what he did.

"So, what are you going to do now?" Erin asked, ringing her hands together. "Are we canceling the wedding?"

Right. I was supposed to get married in three weeks. All of my insecurities were back. Would Daniel still want me to be his wife? I wanted it more than anything. Tears started to stream down my face.

"Melanie..." Erin released a sympathetic breath as she leaned in closer. "You don't have to, you know. We can wait until you've healed."

"No, it's not that, Erin."

"Then what? Do...do you blame him?" The hurt on her face told me she had been fearful I would.

"No..." I shook my head. "Never." Relief swept over her face before confusion took its place.

"But?"

"Erin," I spoke barely above a whisper. "What if he doesn't want me anymore? I can't give him a family."

I felt ashamed – I wasn't whole – and Daniel deserved someone who was. He told me he wanted me, but what about in five years? Or ten?

Would he still feel the same when he realized he would never have a normal life with me?

"Melanie..." Her stern voice took me by surprise. "Are you insane? That man loves you more than anything. He can't even look at another woman. What could possibly make you think that?"

Even though I knew she was right, I couldn't help but feel as if I was no longer good enough for him.

"I just want him to have everything...everything he's ever wanted."

"You realize that's you, right?"

My heart did know that. Now I just had to convince my stupid head of it.

"Yeah, Erin. I know. I think we should wait though, maybe until summer." Daniel at least deserved that time. I forced a bright smile to wash the disappointment from her face. "You know, I'd like to actually be able to walk down the aisle to marry your brother." As I gestured to my leg, we laughed, dispelling the tension in the room. And for the first time, I felt real hope for the future.

I spent the rest of the day figuring out what to do from there. Privately, I'd asked Patrick if I could come and stay with them while I finished school. There was no way I could be in the same house with my father.

Patrick seemed thrilled and said he'd been thinking the same thing. Daniel's face glowed when I told him of the plans.

I dreaded being separated from Daniel. Really, I just wanted to go back to Boulder with him, but I was going to need care he couldn't provide if he was in school. I knew he'd take the rest of the semester off in a heartbeat, and there was no way I could allow that.

Mom fretted over me, trying to make up for the time we'd been apart. I loved her even more for it. It made me sad that Julia seemed to feel she had to step back. She was a mother to me too, and I wanted them both. I didn't want one to replace the other.

The day came and went. Daniel gave up trying to sleep on the chair and snuggled beside me on the bed instead. The nurses were not happy about it. It was, of course, against the rules, but it was the only way *either of us could sleep. Friday morning I actually felt rested and I could tell by the look on Daniel's face he did too.*

Today I had to tell Mom my plans. I figured it was going to be a fight, but I was tired of hiding things from her.

I found my opportunity when she was cleaning up my area after lunch.

"Hey, Mom?"

Pausing, she smiled as she glanced my direction. "What is it, sweetie?"

I had to wipe the sweat from my palms I was so nervous, but it was time I grew up and told my parents what I wanted from my life. "I, uh, wanted to let you know I'm not going back to Dad's. I'm going to stay with Patrick and Julia until I finish school. It just makes sense. Patrick will be able to monitor my therapy, and Erin can bring me my school work until I can actually go back to class."

Disappointment clouded her face.

"Honey, I thought maybe you'd come home with me."

I didn't want to hurt her more than I already had, but I couldn't go with her. That wasn't my home anymore.

"Mom, I can't. I love him."

She needed to understand my home was with Daniel now. She was quiet as she stared at her feet before looking up at me, grimacing. She pushed a lock of hair from my face. "Honey, I think you and Daniel should take some time away from each other."

"What?" I looked at her in confusion and hurt.

She sighed and seemed to struggle with what to say. "It's just...it might be the right time for the two of you to take some time to decide what you want to do with your lives. You both moved so quickly in this relationship, and I think it would be wise for you to take a step back."

I shook my head. "Daniel is what I want."

"But are you sure this is what he wants, Melanie? He's an eighteen year old boy. Can you be certain he's ready to decide who he wants to spend the rest of his life with?" Her face was sympathetic, but her words stung.

"Yes," flew from my mouth, though her words brought questions – doubt. I pushed them aside and reiterated, "Yes."

She closed her eyes and exhaled. "Just think about it, Melanie."

I didn't want to think about it. "No, Mom. I'm staying here."

She nodded and hugged me for a long time, her nose in my hair before she whispered, "Okay," against my head.

When Mom left to get some rest, Daniel took her place. He was trying to give me time with her, but my heart hurt every time he walked out the door. He was never far and always returned the moment she left. I wanted to talk to him about the things my mom had said, her suggestion eating at me as every hour passed. But every time he smiled at me and kissed me, I'd convince myself I was just being foolish.

We were both exhausted, and as soon as the sun set, Daniel crawled in beside me, holding me close as we drifted to sleep.

I woke up Saturday feeling anxious to get out of there. Only one more day. I could tell that everyone else was excited to get out of there, as well. Julia's eyes were brighter than they'd been all week, Patrick stayed busy preparing for me to come home with them, and Erin was bouncing with excitement for her "sister" to come and live with her.

Daniel stepped out with his dad so they could discuss the details, and Mom came in. When I saw her face, I knew something was very wrong. She was nervous, not making eye contact or saying anything. My heart sped up as her anxiety filled the room.

"Mom, what's wrong?"

She stood beside me, all the compassion she'd shown over the week wiped from her face. "Melanie, you're coming home with me."

"What?" I shook my head.

"You're coming home with me."

"No, Mom. I'm not."

"You don't have a choice, Melanie. You're still a minor, and I'm telling you that you're coming with me." She still wouldn't look at me.

"What? You can't force me. I turn eighteen next month."

"Melanie, you either come freely with me, or we're pressing charges against Daniel."

Pressing charges? Against Daniel?

"How could you? After everything we've been through, you'd do this to us? Just yesterday you told me you wanted me to be happy! Please, Mom, don't do this!" I begged her.

I jumped when I noticed my father standing against the wall. Fear raced up my spine. I could see it on his face; he was here to destroy – not me – but Daniel.

My eyes darted between the two of them, silently begging them not to do this. Mom turned her back to me, unwilling to face me. She kept her voice cool, but wasn't able to hide the way it shook. "Just be ready to go tomorrow. I'll be here at nine. I'll speak with Daniel's parents to let them know I'm taking you home."

"Mom, please!" I cried, but she walked from the room, never turning back. Dad didn't say a word. He just pushed from the wall and followed her out.

I sobbed against my pillow. How could they do this? For months, I'd hidden my pregnancy from my father to protect Daniel, and now he'd done what I'd feared most. He was taking Daniel from me. I was terrified of being away from Daniel, but I would do anything to protect him. I'd just have to stay away until I was eighteen. Then my parents could do nothing to stop me from going back to him.

But would he still want me? Would the time away make him realize he was better off without me?

Gasping against the pain, I accepted that I at least owed him that time to decide, reasoned that this was all meant to be.

"Hey." Daniel smiled as he walked through the door, his face dropping as soon as he saw mine. "What happened? Are you okay?"

This was going to be the hardest thing I'd ever done.

"I'm just having a really hard time, Daniel. I think I need some time away to heal." How could I sit here and lie to him? The last thing I wanted was time away from him. But I'd never allow my father to hurt him, and beyond that, I owed him that time

"What do you mean?"

"I'm going home with my mom for a few months. I just need to deal with this on my own."

Lie, lie, lie.

"No." He shook his head adamantly. "No, Melanie. You need me as much as I need you. Please, don't leave me." Tears flooded his eyes as I broke our hearts just a little bit more.

I didn't know how we would get through this. I needed him more than anything, and I couldn't imagine life without him, even if it were only for a month or two.

"Please, Daniel. Just let me go, just for a little while. Then I'll come back to you. I promise. I love you more than anything. I just have to go now." At least this time my words were the truth. I touched his face, praying he could feel my love, praying he'd understand that the last thing I'd ever want to do was to be away from him. I was doing this for him.

"I...Melanie..." he cried, his voice shaking. "Is this because you blame me?"

"No!" I yelled. How could he possibly think that? My voice softened to a whisper. "No, Daniel. Never."

He moved forward and took my hand in desperation. "Then stay."

Tears poured down my face, and in my selfishness, I wanted to agree. I shook my head, knowing this was for the best. I was too tired to fight my parents and loved Daniel too much to take this option from him. "I can't."

He took a step back, his mouth twisted in despair, and he turned to leave the room.

"Please, Daniel. Wait for me," I cried out in my own need.

He paused at the door and looked over his shoulder. "Forever."

Then he walked from the room. For the first time ever, he needed to escape from me, running from the pain I'd inflicted on him. I held it together long enough for the door to close before I let go. I could hear myself sobbing, but I couldn't stop.

"Melanie, what the hell happened?" Erin grasped my shoulders, shaking me. Reaching out, I clung to her, weeping into her shoulder.

"You're going home with your mom?"

I pulled back from her and realized she wasn't trying to comfort me. She was pissed. Her face was hard, her eyes narrowed and filled with accusation.

"You just broke him, Melanie."

This sent a new wave of guilt over me, more tears pouring down my face.

"Erin!" I wailed, clutching her to me. "I love him. I promise. More than anything," I said, gasping as I tried to make her understand. "Promise me you'll never say anything, but you're the only one I can tell," I begged her as I sat up, digging my fingers into her arms.

She shrugged off my arms and sat back, waiting for an explanation.

"My parents are going to press charges for statutory rape if I don't go with Mom. I have to protect him, Erin."

"What? That's total bullshit, and you know it, Melanie. It doesn't even apply. You're seventeen." She shook her head, still not understanding why I would do what they said.

"I know it's just a threat to pull us apart, but there's something about the way my dad's acting, like...I don't know. I'm scared, Erin, for Daniel."

"That's crazy. Your dad's just mad."

"It kills me to go, Erin. I'll go for a few months until things cool down. Besides, it'll give Daniel a chance..." I pressed my lips together when I realized I was about to voice it aloud. Erin caught it immediately.

"What, Melanie? Give him a chance to what?" she spat angrily.

"You know what, Erin."

"Decide if he wants you?" she yelled. "Just stop it, Melanie. He's devastated right now, and you're sitting here thinking there's a chance he doesn't want you? This is all so fucked up!" Her hands flew up in the air.

"I know." I groaned and grabbed my head with my hands. Nothing was right.

"You're really going?"

"You know I'd stay if there was any other way. I can't risk him, Erin. Promise me you'll never tell him. If he knew why I left, he would confront my dad and I can't handle another fight between them."

Hesitating, she seemed to waver, nodding when she gave in. "I don't agree with this at all, Melanie...this is just..." She shook her head before she looked me in the eye. "I'll do it for you."

She brought me in for a tight hug, whispering in my ear. "Don't leave him waiting long. Promise me. He's dying right now, and I don't know how long he can handle it."

I didn't know how long I could handle it either, or if I could at all.

The expression on his face when he returned hours later killed me. He looked dead. The light had disappeared from his eyes and there was no joy in his smile.

Unsure of where he stood, he looked uncomfortably around the room. Reaching for him, I drew him to my side. Uneasily, he climbed into my hospital bed, lying behind me and pulling me to his chest. How we had tears left to shed, I didn't know. Neither of us slept as we said goodbye the only way we could, holding each other through the night. He kissed me softly as the sun began to rise, our time coming to an end.

At nine, Mom came as she said she would, standing by the door while she watched Daniel cling to me, refusing to let me go. Julia stood crying at the back of the room while Patrick tried to convince Daniel that it would be all right. Two aides brought a wheelchair in to take me from my room, and Patrick had to physically pry Daniel from me as he begged me to stay.

I couldn't breathe as I felt my life being torn from me. "Daniel, you have to let me go." The words stung, tasting foul in their untruth; it was the last thing I wanted him to do.

Finally, he released me, and the two orderlies helped me into the wheelchair.

Soon my things were loaded into the trunk of the taxicab that sat waiting to take me away from my home. Daniel stood and watched, silent tears streaming down his cheeks, his arms slack at his sides.

Patrick and one of the orderlies helped me into the cab. The pain was excruciating – not the one they were trying to shield me against as they gingerly placed me in the car, but the one created as I was torn away from my life.

"Melanie," Daniel cried one more time before my dad shut the door in his face.

I reached for him through the window, just needing to touch him one more time, and his fingers reached out for mine.

"My love," he mouthed, and the cab pulled away.

"His face," I sobbed into Katie's chest as she held me. "It was devastating. I knew right then it was a mistake. I had to go to him. I begged my mom to take me back, but she refused." How could I have been so stupid? To let them take away the one thing that mattered to me? To force him from my life without giving him the choice? But in the end, I'd done what was best for him.

Katie's face was stained with tears. "Was that the last time you actually talked to him?"

I nodded.

"I just can't believe he would do that to you. I could see it on his face last night. He still loves you just as much as he did that day."

"I know he loves me. But I always knew he deserved more."

"Hmm, I don't think so, Melanie. I'm pretty sure you're the more."

She sat with me a long time, both of us saying nothing, deep in thought.

Sniffling, I glanced up at her. "Please, tell me what you're thinking."

She grimaced and held me closer. Her voice was soft. "I think you broke his heart."

I cried harder as I pictured Daniel's face last night, finally accepting that in some way I had.

She held me until my tears finally subsided. I sat up, wiping my face with the back of my hand.

"Katie?"

"Yeah?"

"You know when you offered to help me the other day?"

She nodded.

"When you make your break, I think I'm ready to make mine."

She exhaled a weighty breath and smiled. "Thank God."

Chapter Thirteen

I finally gave up. The anticipation was just too great. Rolling to sit up on the side of my bed, I rested my elbows on my thighs and buried my hands in my hair. I fought futilely to calm the raging of my nerves, my heart still pounding just as hard as it had been since the moment I had seen Melanie last night. I'd crawled into bed around two in the morning, hoping to find sleep. But I'd only found her. I had dreamed of seeing her face again, but had never allowed myself to believe it could actually happen. Now I couldn't rest until I saw her again.

Last night had given me a newfound reason to live. What I'd seen in her eyes, felt in her touch—I couldn't question it any longer. Melanie loved me.

Everything I had believed about the life she had left me for and the picture I had always imagined was so wrong.

I had never been so confused. The way she looked at me as if I had broken her heart. It haunted me. I thought she'd found someone to love, someone to make her happy, someone who wouldn't remind her every day of what I had taken away. Instead, seeing her was like seeing a reflection of myself, a mirror of my pain, my loss, my regret. A mirror of what stirred within me now—this love that had refused to die. She had found me. I had always felt her heart calling to mine just as mine called to hers, this power bringing us together once again.

What was I supposed to do about it now? She was married, and I didn't even know if she wanted me. Well, I really didn't believe that. I felt her—there was no denying her desire for me. The pull was just as strong as it had been the first time I had met her.

How could we ignore this? Even if she could, I couldn't.

I stood and made my way to the shower, relieved to know it was almost time. Standing under the steaming water, I allowed it to relax me as I anticipated seeing her once again.

I put on a dark blue T-shirt and pulled on some jeans, unable to control the way my fingers trembled as I tried to button them.

Because I was unwilling to call, I sent a text to Dad, letting him know I wouldn't be in the office today, but I would see him tonight. I was not ready to face his questions. Once I made it to my parents' house, I would have a lot of explaining to do, but none of that concerned me now. All that mattered was Melanie, and I was determined to at least catch a glimpse of her today.

I didn't know what time Nicholas left for work, but I thought it would be safe if I waited until ten. It was only seven-thirty and I was positive I would go insane for the next two and a half hours.

Grabbing some coffee at the downstairs café, I began walking, allowing my thoughts to take over. For the first time in nine years, my memories didn't completely crush me. I was able to think of her and just…love her. I loved every broken piece of her and was determined to make her whole again.

After forcing myself to wait a couple of hours, I made my way back to my complex, this time getting into my car and entering the address into the GPS. This was probably stupid, but I didn't care. The directions popped up and I shook my head as I read them on the screen. What kind of asshole had a house in this kind of neighborhood and then made his address public? Exactly the kind of person Melanie had always run from—one who wanted to be seen. I just couldn't understand it. Why did she want him? The thought of him made my stomach turn. And the thought of him touching her—I shook it off, refusing to think of it.

I slowed as I turned onto the quiet street. Tall maple and ash trees lined the sidewalks and manicured lawns framed the massive houses set back from the road.

Nearing the address, my heart fluttered in my chest. The closer I got, the more I could feel her. I passed by once. Turning around, I parked on the opposite side of the street but not close enough to be seen. At least I had a car that wouldn't set off any red flags in this neighborhood.

Melanie has to hate this house. I shook my head, once again clueless as to what would lead her to this life. Did I hurt her so badly that she would do this to herself? Yeah, from the outside, it looked like she had everything: The perfect husband, the perfect house, more money than anybody could ever spend. I knew firsthand none of that mattered to her. And after seeing her last night, there was no question. Nothing about this lifestyle made her happy.

A silver Camry was parked out front. I glanced at the clock. It was just past ten. I settled into my seat. I was willing to wait forever to see her.

And even if she never came out, I was happy to just sit there and feel her. It was as if I could sense her as she moved around her house, pulses of energy slamming into me, each one Melanie.

Finally, more than an hour later, the door swung open, and Melanie and Katie stepped out, embracing each other. My heart ended up in my throat when she came into view.

I groaned, my fingers twitching toward the door handle. My girl—so close. I wanted to run to her, but I couldn't. What if she rejected me? Yes, she'd almost kissed me last night, but what if she regretted it? What if she remembered what I'd done, how I'd ruined our lives? What if she told me to leave? I didn't think my heart could take it, so I did the only thing I could—I admired her from afar. That would have to be enough for now.

I watched as she and Katie exchanged their goodbyes, and Katie jumped into the silver car and drove away.

Quietly, I called to Melanie when she turned her back to go inside, murmuring, "I love you, my beautiful girl." I knew she heard, or rather, felt me. Her back stiffened and she stopped. Her hand clutched the door as she caught her breath. I felt her love radiating back to me. I leaned into the wheel, clutching it to keep from going to her. Every part of me longed to hold her, to comfort her, to make her mine once again. I watched as she stepped inside and shut the door behind her. I released the breath I didn't know I'd been holding as she disappeared from sight.

Now what? I knew I should leave and let her continue with her life, but I couldn't bring myself to.

Shit.

I was officially a stalker. But I'd take any title in order to be near her. So once again, I waited—and waited.

Hours later, a little before three, the garage opened, and a small black four-door sedan backed out. It was newer, but didn't even begin to look like it belonged in the garage that housed it.

I laughed. Only Melanie would be surrounded by all this wealth and drive a car like that. I took comfort in knowing she was the same girl I'd fallen in love with so many years ago. None of this had affected her. So *why* was she here? Because she loved him? No, I didn't believe that, did I?

Shit. My mind was so messed up. I had no clue.

She pulled onto the street, leaving in the same direction I had come. I was almost ashamed of what I was doing, but I just couldn't resist the pull. I prayed I wouldn't scare her. I just needed to be near her.

I was nervous I'd lose her. Instead, it was easy, as if I could anticipate her every move, my body naturally trailing hers. We drove back downtown and the surroundings became increasingly familiar.

"Holy shit," I muttered aloud. We were on the street in front of my office. She was doing the exact same thing I had done all day.

I pulled in several spaces in front of her. Through my rear-view mirror, I could see her trying to peer into my building.

She looked nervous. Her door opened and her foot touched the ground before she hesitated, pulling it back inside.

"What are you doing, baby?" I asked as I watched the panicked look on her face. Her hands came up and obstructed my view. When she brought them down, I could see she was crying.

I couldn't handle anymore; I had to go to her. I reached for the handle to get out, but faster than I could comprehend, she jumped her car back into traffic and sped away. I punched the steering wheel in frustration. How many times would I have to watch her drive away from me? I sat in my car, not knowing what to do from here. Clearly, neither of us did.

Easing my car back onto the road, I headed back to my apartment to get ready for dinner with my parents. Tonight was going to be hard. I was going to break Mom's heart again. I dreaded seeing the disappointment on her face.

And Dad, I didn't even want to face him. I'd been so reckless. He had so much faith in me, inviting me into his practice right out of my residency, and I repaid him by doing something completely unethical.

At seven, I pulled up in front of their house, my movements weighed down with the dread I felt. The huge 1890s mansion was about forty minutes outside of Chicago. Mom had spent the last six months remodeling it; the result was beautiful and comfortable, just like everything else she touched.

As I stepped from my car, Erin squealed from the doorway, ran down the steps, and threw herself in my arms.

"Hi, big brother." She squeezed me and I hugged her close.

"Hey, baby sister." I kissed her head, reluctantly setting her down. Her arms stayed firmly around my shoulders, her eyes wide as she tried to read everything in mine.

"Daniel, what's wrong?"

Averting my eyes, I tried to hide my guilt.

"Can, we…uh," I stammered, "I'd rather tell everyone at the same time, okay?"

Erin's eyebrows furrowed, accentuating the first hint of wrinkles on her forehead, and she nodded. "Okay." She took my hand and led me up the walkway.

Dad stood at the door, trepidation clear in his posture. He grabbed me and pulled me to him, whispering against the side of my head, "I don't know what's going on, son, but we're here for you. Always remember that."

I grimaced as I took in the unwavering love and support he gave me, his respect, knowing I deserved none of it. I'd thrown everything he'd done for me back in his face.

Mom stood at the entryway to the family room, anxious and ill at ease. Reaching her hand out for mine, she silently led me to the brown leather sofa and took the seat beside me. I watched warily as Dad and Erin sat across the room.

"Daniel, please, honey. What's happened?"

I sucked in as much air as I could, feeling as though I might pass out. Every regret of my life sat heavily upon my chest, each pressing down, digging into my skin. I rubbed my hand over my shirt, trying to soothe it away.

"I'm going to be a father." The words made me sick, and I was ashamed that they did.

Mom gasped beside me. She took my hand and ran her thumb over my knuckles.

"When?" she asked.

Words tumbled from my mouth in a rush. "In four months. It's a boy, I just found out yesterday."

"With who? Are you seeing somebody?" Her brow drew up in confusion.

I wondered whether she thought I'd never been with anyone since Melanie.

Dad sighed from across the room. "Dad, I'm so sorry. I..." I stalled as he shook his head, assuring me I had nothing to be sorry for when I knew I did. "I really messed up. Do you remember that mixer we had when we first got to town?"

"Sure," he said as if it didn't mean anything.

"I slept with one of the reps that night."

Silence fell over the room as Mom and Erin stared at me. But it was Dad's expression that told me how disappointed he actually was.

"What? How could you do this, Daniel? Do you realize the position you've put us in? This could ruin our reputation before we even have a chance to get started...damn it." He stood and paced as he ranted.

"Dad...I..."

Pausing, he blew the air from his lungs, raked a hand through his hair. His voice was low, but no longer filled with anger. "Can I speak with you in private?"

I nodded, following him to his study. A strange, twisted *déjà vu* came over me as I sat across from the same desk he had sat at when Melanie and I told him of our child.

"Who is it?" He was calm, now just wanting information.

"Her name's Vanessa."

"And I'm to assume this was one of your usual one-time flings?"

I didn't answer. I didn't need to.

He breathed heavily out his nose, looked away as he muttered, "Damn it, Daniel."

"I know, Dad. I'm so sorry." I would have done anything to take it back. How ironic it was that I'd sat on this same sofa with my seventeen year old girlfriend, never ashamed, and now I was here, almost thirty, begging for forgiveness?

"So, what does she want? I mean, you said she's five-months? Do you even know if it's yours?" I told him everything that had happened with Vanessa the day before. He remained silent as I voiced all my fears, regrets, and anger.

He rocked back in his black leather chair, tenting his fingers. "It sounds like you're probably right."

Leaning forward, he tilted his head as he raised an eyebrow. "So, what are you going to do? You're going to be a father, Daniel. You are responsible for this baby, you know, even if this Vanessa did try to trap you."

"I know. I just..." I swallowed. "This wasn't supposed to happen. It used to be the thing I wanted most, and now...it was only supposed to be with Melanie." I felt so guilty. I should be ecstatic right now, sitting here with the woman I loved, telling my family we were having a baby. Without Melanie, that wasn't possible.

I was reluctant to get back up and face the rest of my family, but I couldn't hide in Dad's office all night. I opened the door, halting when I found Mom waiting, tears wetting her face.

"I'm so sorry to disappoint you, Mom."

She shook her head. "No, Daniel. You never could. I always knew you'd be a wonderful father."

Could my heart break any more? Mom was telling me I was going to be a wonderful father, and I couldn't even stand the thought of it. I didn't respond, just forced a tight smile, before I left her and walked down the hall.

Dinner was tense. Nobody knew what to say.

Erin finally broke the tension.

"Um, guys, this feels kind of inappropriate right now, but I have some good news. I got the transfer I wanted, and I'll be moving here next month."

Real joy lit my face. For the first time in ten years, my entire family would live in the same city. Mom was so happy I couldn't help but forget the problems I was faced with right then.

And Melanie.

It was as if everyone I loved was being drawn back to me.

I looked across to Dad, his smile wide and uninhibited, and I couldn't help but return the same to him. Yeah, I'd disappointed him, but we'd be okay. I swore to myself right then that I'd never do anything to jeopardize his trust again.

Erin quirked an eyebrow at me as she caught the smile on my face. I shrugged. How could I explain to her what I was feeling right then? I didn't even know, but for the first time, it wasn't the complete hopelessness that had filled me every single day for the last nine years.

The conversation became loud and excited as they talked about Erin's move and where she planned to live. She hoped to find a small place she could afford near our parents, and she and Mom started making plans to look for a house.

It occurred to me then that I hadn't even told Dad about the building. It was crazy how something that had been so consuming less than two days before hadn't even entered my mind since I signed those papers last night.

"I can't believe I forgot to tell you. I signed a contract last night with Borelli & Preston Contractors for the building. We should be able to break ground in the next two months."

"Really? That's great, Daniel." As he asked me details, he looked at me as if he was proud of me once again.

Looking around the table at my family, their faces filled with joy, I couldn't help but feel it was a...good day. Did I really feel that? I didn't think I had the ability to feel good about anything, but

I did. I met Erin's stare across the table, and a million questions ran across her face.

She stood up, grabbing her plate. "Why don't you two go for a walk? Daniel and I are doing dishes." She smiled sweetly at me, a gleam in her eye.

I followed her lead, gathering the rest of the dishes, and trailed her into the kitchen. Erin leaned against the island, arms crossed over her chest.

"Spill it."

I frowned at her as I walked past, placing the dishes in the sink. "What are you talking about, Erin?"

"Oh, don't give me that, Daniel. Something's up. I haven't seen you this happy—or happy at all, I should say—in nine years. And I'd venture to say this happiness isn't related to the news you just dropped on us a couple of hours ago."

I turned to face her, once again thankful she knew me so well. Exhaling, I leaned against the counter and crossed my arms over my chest. "Erin, I can't believe I got myself into this situation." I ran a hand through my hair, trying not to get upset. "What am I supposed to do? This girl completely screwed me."

She scowled at me. "No, Daniel, I'm pretty sure it's *you* who screwed *her*."

While I could always confide in Erin, she never hesitated to set me straight, either.

"I told you you'd end up getting yourself into trouble. Your whole no-strings-attached lifestyle doesn't always end up working out in real life. You should have known it was going to catch up to you one day." She fell quiet, suddenly appearing uncomfortable.

"Are you scared?" She took the couple of steps to come beside me, leaning on one elbow so she could look at me.

"I can't even think about a baby...or that one, at least." I hung my head. After losing Eva, I just couldn't ever feel the same. "So yeah, I am scared. Scared I'll never love him. It's so unfair to him, Erin. This poor kid...you know, I told her I wanted joint custody. It just came out my mouth, and I don't even know why."

"Don't count yourself out quite yet, big brother. You might just surprise yourself."

I wished she was right, but the only thing I felt was regret.

She nudged me with her shoulder, smirking up at me. "So, now that we've got the bad out of the way, tell me what it is that has lit that fire in your eyes again. That flame's been out for a long time now."

Turning, I gestured toward the sink. I dug my hands into the soapy water, and Erin grabbed a hand towel to dry. I started on the first plate and glanced down at Erin, giving her a small smile. "You know how I signed those papers last night?" She nodded. "Well, it's with a company Borelli & Preston Contractors. I met with them at a restaurant to go over their proposal, and they brought their wives." She bit her lip and narrowed her eyes, unsure where I was going with this story. It was absolutely *not* what she was thinking, while at the same time being *exactly* what she was thinking.

Shit. It really was complicated.

I handed her a plate to dry and started on another. "*She* was there. One of the wives," I said as I looked directly at her, "was Melanie."

Her face paled and the plate she was drying slipped through her fingers, shattering against the marble floor.

"What?" Her breathing quickened and escalated out of control as the pain she'd repressed all these years came to the surface.

"Melanie found you?" she rasped out, her hand digging into my arm as tears started to roll down her cheeks. "What happened? What did you say to her? Is she okay? Is she happy?" Questions poured from her, each one coming faster than the last. Erin's heart had been broken too; when Melanie had left, Erin had lost her best friend and the only sister she'd known. Still, Erin had never stopped loving her.

I brought her to my chest, holding her to me. "Can you believe it? Melanie is here in Chicago. I can't even explain how I felt last night, sitting across from her. I could still feel her, Erin. That power." She nodded against my chest. Erin was the one person I could talk to openly about it; she was the one who helped us understand what it was in the first place. "It was like it had grown, like it had worked all these years to bring us to that very spot last night. She still loves me, Erin. I know it...I could feel it. She wanted me."

I rocked her against me, not sure who was comforting who. "I've never been so confused. I always believed she found someone better, someone who could make her happy since I couldn't do that. But her face…she was anything but happy." I pulled back, searching Erin's face, trying to make her understand. "She was just like me."

Erin tensed and her body shook against me.

"You!" She pounded on my chest with her fists, rubbing her nose in my shirt at the same time. "So fucking stupid, Daniel." I tried to restrain her as she continued to beat her hands against me. She cried again and again, "So stupid, so stupid!"

"Erin, stop. Please!" She was killing me, breaking my heart all over again.

"No, Daniel. I've kept this in for too long, and I'm done! I'm done sitting aside while you blame yourself for something that wasn't your fault, done keeping secrets that only hurt the people I love!" she screamed, her fists balled in my shirt as she unleashed her anger on me.

"What the hell are you talking about, Erin?"

"You let her go, Daniel! That's what I'm talking about! You made me promise to never contact my best friend...my sister!"

"You know why I had to do that, Erin! She didn't want me anymore. You would have run after her to try to change her mind. You would have made her feel guilty for leaving. I wanted her to live the life that *she* wanted, to have a chance to be happy. I couldn't stand in the way of that, and you running after her definitely would have!"

How could Erin blame me for wanting Melanie to be happy? Every day I had wanted to find her. But if being away from me was the one thing that made her happy, that was the one thing I could give her.

"Right there, Daniel! Right there! Where in that screwed up head of yours would you get the idea Melanie didn't love you anymore? That she didn't want you?"

"Oh, I don't know, Erin, maybe when I killed our daughter!" Anger rolled off me as I hovered over her, my hands in fists at my side.

"She never blamed you, Daniel!" she yelled back. "It wasn't your fault!"

"You don't know what you're talking about, Erin."

Erin kicked pieces of the shattered plate across the floor.

"Daniel, I've kept this in for nine years. Nine fucking years!" She sobbed as she held her stomach with one arm. "I made promises to both of you, and I should have broken them a long time ago. All they did was ruin your lives, both of you trying to protect the other. You were both fools, and I was a fool to agree!"

"Erin, please, what are you saying?"

"She never blamed you, Daniel." As her unexpected anger seemed to wane, she stepped forward, spoke softly. "She was protecting you. Her parents threatened that if she didn't go back to Dallas, they'd have you arrested. It broke her heart to leave, Daniel. She was crushed. She made me promise to never tell you because she knew you'd go straight to her father. At that time she was terrified of him, terrified of what he would do to you."

What? Her parents did this to us? How could they?

Erin bit her lip and averted her gaze as if in guilt. "And she kept making these comments." She looked up at me, her expression tortured. "She said maybe she wasn't good enough for you, and she needed to give you time to decide.

My knees went weak, and I reached to Erin for support.

She didn't blame me? All of these years, I'd always believed what everyone had insisted wasn't true. Erin was right—I was a fool.

"Why then, Erin? Why, when I went after her, had she married somebody else? Why?" I begged, praying she knew.

"I don't know, Daniel." We swayed, clutching each other, our anger released and washed away, now replaced with questions and what-ifs. "That's why I was so angry that you wouldn't let me go to her. I always knew we were missing something, and the only person who could answer that question was Melanie."

All these years, everything I had believed was a lie—a lie I had told myself.

I clung to my sister and let go of the blame I'd held onto for so long and just accepted it.

It wasn't my fault.

Chapter Fourteen

The smell of coffee filtered through the kitchen. I stood in front of the pot, willing it to brew faster, my eyes heavy with fatigue.

The last three weeks had not been easy.

The foundation I'd built my life on for the past nine miserable years had been shaken, cracks rippling through the concrete. I had no idea what side I'd end up on when it finally broke apart.

I hadn't come face-to-face with Daniel since that night, but I knew he was always near.

I could feel him, sense his eyes upon me in almost everything I did. My nerves bristled as I walked down the street, my body calling to him, begging to be touched.

I knew why he had to stay away. I'd never want to be that kind of person anyway, one who would break apart a family, a home. As badly as I wanted him, I would never be responsible for that. Yet, it didn't stop me from driving by his office each day, hoping to catch just a glimpse of him, though I never did. And it definitely didn't keep away the black car, barely visible from where it sat down the street. That car was there in those moments when the weight of his presence nearly brought to my knees, when the pull was almost too great to ignore. It was in those moments I almost didn't care if it'd make me a bad person if I went to him. Still, I held back. I didn't have room for one more regret in my life, so we loved each other from afar.

I heard movement upstairs and braced myself. Things with Nicholas had been…interesting.

I'd never gone back to his room after that night. I'd made the guest room my own and refused to allow myself to be used in that way again. I knew he had no qualms about getting what he wanted elsewhere. When I first came to Chicago, I'd made an effort to do the normal things I thought a wife should do, thinking if I had a role to play, then I should play it well. I'd packed the chicken salad and the bread I'd baked and headed to Nicholas's office. I'd opened his office door to find a naked woman in his lap, his pants pooled around his feet. He'd acknowledged me by coolly telling me, "Close the door, Melanie." He'd come home that night and never said one thing about it or acted any different. I'd felt nothing but relief in finding them, hoping it meant he would come to me less often. I learned quickly it didn't.

But that didn't matter now. I'd promised myself that night three weeks ago that I'd never let him touch me again.

Footsteps thudded down the stairs as I poured my first cup of coffee. I ignored Nicholas when he came in the room.

The air surrounding us was tense. We'd said very few words to each other since that night. He'd crossed a line when he hit me, and he knew it. Never would I let things get back to the way were, even though I sensed he expected it to. I could feel his anger simmering, always on the verge of exploding.

I knew it was just a matter of time.

"Melanie." I looked up in shock, surprised he'd spoken to me. "Shane is coming by to pick up these papers. He'll be here in about a half an hour. I was supposed to take them, but I'm running late for a meeting." He flopped a legal-sized manila envelope down on the counter.

I nodded but otherwise continued to ignore him shuffling around the kitchen as he gathered his things. Only when I heard his car back out of the garage did I begin to relax. Curious, I reached over and grabbed the envelope, nearly dropping it when I saw what was written across it. "Montgomery Oncology." Daniel. These papers were for Daniel.

My palms became sweaty as I contemplated.

It was true I'd driven by his office every day for the last three weeks, but I'd never stepped foot inside. Could I bear to be that close to him? To maybe catch sight of his wavy hair as he walked down the hallway, hesitation in his step when he felt me? To possibly see his eyes filled with love for me, even if it were only for a second?

I dialed Shane's number before I allowed myself to think of the consequences. Shane dithered over the idea, but ultimately conceded and promised he would tell Nicholas he had dropped them off himself.

"Just a glimpse, Melanie," I promised myself as I ascended the stairs. I still hadn't moved all of my things out, resigning myself to showering and dressing after Nicholas had gone.

I rushed through my shower. Trying to relax would be futile. My stomach was in knots, protesting against the anticipation igniting a path through my veins. I dried quickly, slipped into my robe, and wrapped a towel around my head.

"Humph." I hesitated when I walked into the closet, before I settled on a white-collared blouse with the sleeves rolled up and a black skirt that barely passed as business casual. It was snug at the hips and tapered out to flow loosely down my thighs, coming to rest right above my knees. I slipped into some black round-toed pumps and stood in front of my mirror. It was conservative but cute, and it would just have to do as not a single emotion swirling through me even came close to resembling one of confidence.

I walked down the stairs, tension building with each step. My body knew each one brought me closer to him.

I took the now very familiar path to his office, my fingers kneading the steering wheel as I tried to give myself reassurance for the reason I was doing this. Was I trying to torture or comfort myself?

It was blatantly clear that seeing him this one time would never be enough or fulfill my need for him. Every time I felt him near, I only wanted more. Right now, though, I was willing to fool myself into believing anything.

The first wave of energy hit me as I turned onto his street, the pull seeking me out and drawing me near. He was here. When I reached the front of his building, I pulled into the first space I could find, and I gave myself a minute to compose myself. How was I going to walk in there as if this was nothing and I was simply handing the receptionist a pack of papers?

"Come on, Melanie. You can do this." I breathed in as I coaxed my nerves to settle.

I just needed to get in there and get out. I would take with me a visual, a picture of where he spent his days so I could place him there in my mind as I thought of him each day.

Gathering my last bit of courage, I stepped out, something I'd tried once, the day after first seeing him, but my feet had been unable to carry me. I hadn't tried again since. This time I pressed forward, my steps loud in my ears as I crossed the street. Daniel's presence was a dull buzz in the back of my head, growing each second, becoming a steady throb. I inhaled, closed my eyes, and swung the door open, immediately overwhelmed by the energy in the room. There was no oxygen to breathe, only Daniel, the one who supplied life to my lungs.

I stumbled as I entered the room, and I struggled to maintain some sort of composure. The room was silent except for the clinking of a keyboard and the pounding in my head.

Tentatively, I walked forward. The woman behind the desk halted her strokes to look up and smile at me. "May I help you, dear?" I braced myself on the counter, finding it difficult to make my mouth work. My jaw locked in restraint against every part of me that demanded I seek Daniel out, but I controlled myself and handed the woman the envelope. "Um, yes. I have a delivery for Dr. Montgomery from Borelli & Preston Contractors."

Okay. Job done. Now it was time to run. I couldn't handle being here. He was just too close. I had promised myself weeks ago I would keep my distance and allow us to love each other through that space, and it was clear now I'd crossed that line.

I whispered, "Thank you," but before I could turn to leave, she pushed the envelope back to me.

"Dr. Montgomery asked that I ensure he was able to speak with the person who delivered this, if you don't mind?" Her eyes were kind.

I gulped for the nonexistent oxygen in the room. I knew I should run, escape, but secretly I'd been hoping this would happen. To see him, talk to him. Just once. He'd never told me goodbye, and somewhere inside me, I wanted that resolution. I wanted him just to say it, to end the confusion I felt. But was I really ready for that rejection? To hear him say I wasn't enough? And what would it change anyway? My soul would always belong to him just as his belonged to me, no matter what words he said.

The longing to see him ultimately won. I nodded and took the envelope back in my hands.

She pressed a button on her headset. "Dr. Montgomery, your delivery from Borelli & Preston is here."

She bobbed her head and said, "Yes, doctor."

"He'll see you now." She stood and started around her desk, when the front door opened and somebody came through. She had a look of apology on her face. "He's the first door on the left. Can you find it okay?"

"Sure," I muttered mostly to myself as she turned to help the other person. I stared down the hallway. Both fear and longing consumed me. I willed myself to walk, but every footstep was heavy, dragging with what I feared would soon be regret. I stalled outside his door, my heart listening to his. I could feel it pounding, drawing me forward.

I didn't even knock. I turned the knob and pushed the door open. My feet locked in place when I saw him. Daniel. I blinked several times as I took him in. He was leaning over, bracing himself with his palms flat on his desk. He must have realized that it was me just before I opened the door. His head was cocked, his hazel eyes wide.

I couldn't move. I felt as if I were caught in time and the second hand was unable to tick on.

Finally he rose, cautious and slow. His eyes were fierce and desperate, a fire that I'd never seen before burning behind them. My feet moved of their own accord and my arm dropped from the door. Silently it closed behind me. Everything in the room was still except for the energy roaring between us.

"Melanie," he called to me, a whisper directly to my heart, pumping it with life. I was mesmerized as he wet his dry lips. His shoulders were held rigid, his chest trembling with his staggered breaths. I felt it all—his longing, his desire, his hunger. And I knew he could feel mine. Quivering under his intense stare, my muscles twitched in anticipation. My knees went weak when I saw him snap, undecided no more.

I could barely register the movement before he rounded his desk, and his lips crashed against mine. His hands sank into my hair, pulling my body roughly against his.

It felt as if my body had burst into flames with his sudden touch. Everything about him was overpowering, consuming, dominating. Rough and gentle at the same time.

I pressed into him, my chest against his, our hearts beating in rhythm. Digging my fingers into his neck, I struggled to get closer. We were desperate as we clung to each other. We needed to feel, to heal the scars disfiguring our hearts, to erase some of the hurt. His hands rushed with need, twisted through my curls, down my back, and then into my hair again. His kiss was forceful—too intense—ice and fire and sweet—all Daniel. I breathed him in, touched him, memorized the way he smelled, the way he felt.

His hair was so soft between my fingers. A shiver traveled down his spine.

With a sudden slant of his head, he swept his tongue across my lip. I opened to him, drawing him in. There was no teasing or testing. Aggressively, he moved his mouth with mine, sucking in my bottom lip at the same time he bit at it. Rough. Hard. Perfect. He pushed me back against the door, his body flush with mine. A moan escaped my mouth.

Oh, how I had missed this body.

I ran my hands over his shoulders and down his arms, his muscles firm under my touch. His lips were incessant, his tongue hot and wet.

Fisting a hand in my hair, he pulled it tight, exposing my neck. His movements slowed as he licked down the sensitive skin, seeking out the spot behind my ear he knew would ruin me. He sucked, tugging with his lips, lingering at the delicate hollow below my jaw. I drew in a ragged breath, and my emotions caught up with me. He remembered.

He kissed his way back up, found my mouth again. Fingertips caressed and massaged the back of my neck, the skin afire with his touch.

When he grabbed the back of my knee and hooked my leg over his hip, I gasped. His palm traveled up the exposed flesh of my thigh, his thumb rubbing circles, coaxing, persuading, demanding a reaction. I pushed back into him, my body deprived of his for far too long.

"Melanie, my love," he whispered, the words vibrating against my lips.

"Daniel," I breathed into his mouth.

He pulled back, hooded eyes flaming in their intensity as they sought mine. I couldn't look away as I peered deep into his soul. The love I found there was never ending, but shrouded in vast regret, grief imprinted on his heart. He ran his nose along my cheek, murmuring in my ear, this time the words dripping in sadness. "Only you."

Those words resonated in the air, and as much as I knew he wanted to convince himself that they were true, they weren't.

The weight of what I was doing crushed me. Thoughts of his wife and child lay heavy on my heart, and I remembered how we had gotten here in the first place. He hadn't chosen *me*. He didn't want *me*.

With trembling hands, I shook my head, trying to keep my insecurities from pouring out. It was impossible. The feelings of complete rejection I'd swallowed down and harbored for all these years came bubbling to the surface and spilled over, erupted as tears rushing down my face.

"You didn't want me." My words were barely audible, but I knew he heard them. I pulled back, desperate to remove myself from the spell he had me under. He jerked his head back, meeting my gaze, his eyes clouded with confusion.

I pushed against his chest with my hands. "You didn't want me!" It was hard to speak. The words stuck in my throat and came up between sobs. "You have her!"

He had chosen a different life, and he couldn't take it back.

"What?" He released my thigh and stepped back. "Melanie, please...don't say that. I've always wanted you. Only you."

Desperate to remove myself, I squeezed my eyes and flattened myself further against the door. I had to get away.

I had promised myself I would never become this person—someone who would steal the same thing that had been stolen from me. Daniel had a family, and as much as I would always love him, that had to come before my need for him.

I turned to flee, unable to be in his presence a second longer.

If I stayed, I'd only take more of what wasn't mine.

I flung the door open, and Daniel tried to grab my arm and pull me back. "Please, Melanie! Please...don't leave," he begged.

I refused to look back. I hit the hallway, pushing myself forward and forcing myself away.

He was right behind me. "Melanie...please...just listen to me." I shook his hand from my arm when he grabbed me again. My heels slid across the tile floor as I raced through the lobby. In my periphery, I was aware of his secretary jumping to her feet, shock freezing her face in a small gasp as she watched the scene unfold in front of her. Tears fell faster when I realized what I'd put Daniel through here in his office. I couldn't even remain professional for five minutes.

My steps didn't falter as I flung the glass door wide open, never slowing when I darted across the street. There was only the sound of car horns blaring and the echo of Daniel's pleas fading into the distance.

I jumped into my car and slammed the door, chanting over and over, "You didn't want me. You didn't want me. You didn't want me."

July 2000

"Melanie, hurry up! You're going to be late again," Mom called up the stairway, her voice stressed.

"I said I was coming!" I yelled back as I tried to bend over to tie my shoes. My right leg was tight, the constant dull ache now a sharp pang in my thigh as I strained to reach my foot. I wiped the single tear that slid down my cheek. It was impossible to separate the physical pain from the emotional.

Physical therapy again. I hated it. Hadn't they tortured me enough? I'd spent three days a week, every week, for nearly the last four months in a gym, stretching, pushing, basically learning to walk again, and I was so sick of it. My mood was sour, and I definitely didn't feel like cooperating as somebody "encouraged" me to push just a little bit harder.

"Melanie, now!" I cringed at Mom's tone of voice. Things had not been going well here, and each day just got worse.

I had been so angry when my parents had forced me to come to Dallas. I resented them and I let Mom know it. I'd spent three full weeks in bed, unwilling to speak to her or look at her, and I'd barely eaten. The third week my new doctor demanded that I start physical therapy, telling me I'd never walk again if I didn't. So I spent my eighteenth birthday at my first appointment, discovering just how grueling my recovery was going to be.

As painful as it had been, I'd done everything with a smile on my face. Even though my parents had demanded he not contact me, that he give me some time, I had been convinced he'd call that day. I was eighteen and free to leave. But there had been nothing. It was the day I felt the first real flicker of fear that maybe he didn't want me anymore. Shrugging it off, I'd told myself he was just being respectful, giving me the space my parents had insisted I needed.

So I continued on, obligingly attending my therapy sessions every Monday, Wednesday, and Friday and silently crying through the abuse. Diane, my therapist, tried to be kind, her own eyes usually damp by the end of the hour, promising it wouldn't always hurt this bad. What she didn't understand was that the physical pain had nothing on the pain in my heart. It seemed that as my body became stronger, my mind became weaker, a cloud settling in around me, heavy and ominous.

I missed Daniel so much. Each night I'd crawl into bed alone, succumbing to the ache I'd felt all day. I'd bury my face in my pillow to try to drown out my sorrow as I begged him to come to me. My body longed for his, needing to feel his love for me. For the better part of a month, Mom had rushed into my room each night, running her hands through my hair as she promised it would be okay. I'd cursed at her. Blamed her. She'd beg me to stop, saying she'd only wanted what was best for me. I had insisted that that was Daniel. She stopped coming the night I told her I hated her.

The days that passed only made it worse, each one a reminder that he still hadn't called. I was in a constant state of despair, weeping behind closed doors and a total bitch to anyone who crossed my path. I never wanted to act this way, but I found myself unable dig myself out of the depression I was in. It had gotten harder to go to my appointments, harder to do my schoolwork, harder to live. It would have been okay had he done anything just to let me know he still loved me and wanted me. I would have happily lived out this sentence until I could go back to him. But he didn't.

Four excruciating months, and still nothing from Daniel.

"Melanie!"

Didn't she have any idea how hard it was just to put on my freaking shoes? I stood, the first step always the most painful. I winced as I began down the stairs, descending them as quickly as possible while Mom waited impatiently at the landing. Thankfully, I no longer needed Mark to carry me up and down. I hated being dependent on anyone, even though it was clear my step-dad didn't share in my parents' view of Daniel. He'd taken the moments of my vulnerability as he carried me up the stairs to tell me I'd be better soon and then I could go to Daniel. The only hope I had was Mark and the energy that pulled me back to Colorado, the tug on my heart that told me where I belonged – with Daniel.

And that was exactly my plan. I'd made up my mind that as soon as Diane discharged me, I'd go back to him. There was always an underlying insecurity I felt that Daniel might not want me anymore, but that wasn't what I truly believed. I could still feel his love for me, traveling all these miles over all this time, and I had to believe in that.

Mom fumbled with her keys in her agitation, dropping them twice before finding the right one to bring her small red car to life. She looked over her right shoulder as she backed down the driveway and caught my eye.

"This is getting old, Melanie. You need to stop acting like some petulant little child and grow up," she huffed as she braked in the street, switching the car into drive. Staring straight ahead, she held her jaw rigid as she chose her words carefully, her tone softening. "It's time you moved on."

"What do you mean by that?" I spat back at her.

She almost imperceptively shook her head. "Melanie, Daniel hasn't even tried to contact you in four months. That isn't exactly the kind of behavior you'd expect from someone who says he cares about you. He hasn't even checked to see how you're doing. You could still be in a wheelchair for all he knows."

Anger burned, fueled by my fear that her words might be true. I could feel my face flush, my fists curling around the sides of the seat. "If you remember correctly, Mom, I'm here because of you, and you know exactly why he hasn't called."

She was quiet for a moment before breathing out heavily through her nose. "If you want to blame me for all of this, Melanie, then fine, you can do that. But being angry with me doesn't change the fact that he hasn't called or...or even had one of his parents call to check on you. Doesn't that seem a little odd after all of this time?"

She looked at me, but I refused to meet her gaze, staring into my lap. Of course I thought it was "a little odd." I was tormented by it, but I wasn't about to admit that to her.

"I just don't want you to get hurt any more than you already have, sweetheart."

I squeezed my eyes tight as an exasperated yelp escaped my pursed lips. She didn't want me to get hurt anymore than I already had? How dare she?

"Now you don't want me to hurt, Mom? Was the pain you caused me just enough, and now you want to protect me from any more? Is that how it works? Was it okay for you to take me away from the one person I love the most, right after our baby died, so I had to grieve for her without him? Was that just the right amount of pain for me? Tell me, Mom, because I'd like to know just how much pain you think I should have!"

As if my words were suffocating her, she struggled to catch her breath. I knew they stung, but I refused to take them back. "Melanie...I...I never meant to hurt you." She sniffed and her chest jerked as she tried to hold back her cries. "You'll never understand how sorry I am."

"Sorry doesn't take away what you did to me...to us."

Maybe someday I would forgive her, but not now. I'd always been quick to forgive and never hold a grudge, but what she'd done was cruel, especially after giving me her blessing. I still didn't understand her reasons.

Neither of us spoke as we drove; the only sound was Mom's whimpering. I felt guilty for upsetting her so much, but she needed to understand how much she'd hurt me.

She pulled into the parking lot, and for the first time, she didn't get out. She just stared straight ahead as I struggled to stand from the seat. Then she left me standing alone, watching her drive away.

Another pang of guilt washed over me, before I pushed it away and subjected myself to one more day of Diane's torture.

Diane assured me that I was doing great and that I probably had maybe three or four more weeks of therapy left before I could do the exercises on my own. I really didn't think I could wait that long.

After the session, I pushed the door open, not sure how I was going to get home. Mom was waiting outside. Through the windshield, I saw that her face was flat and void of all emotion. The only evidence of our argument was her red, splotchy cheeks.

Neither of us acknowledged the other the entire way home. Slowly, I took the stairs to my bedroom, feeling terrible for ignoring my little sister who tried to talk to me, and locked the door behind me. I'd already had enough of this day and it wasn't even noon.

It went against my nature to say such nasty things to Mom. I was so angry with her for putting me through this. And if I was being honest with myself, I was angry with Daniel. Angry that he had forgotten me.

No.

I didn't want to allow myself to think that, but couldn't extinguish that deep-seated fear.

Falling to the floor, I clutched my chest and buried my face into the carpet. What if Mom was right? Had he moved on? Had he decided I couldn't give him what he wanted in life?

But Daniel loved me. I knew he did. I could feel it, even here in my old room a thousand miles away from him. But just because he loved me didn't mean he wanted to be with me.

I sobbed on the carpet for what seemed like hours, releasing everything that had built over the days and months we'd spent apart.

Curled into a ball, I tried to comfort myself, rocking as I shed every tear I could find. When they finally started to slow, I turned to wrestle myself to my knees, when I saw the little box tucked under my bed.

It was the same box I'd seen on the counter in the hospital. I'd noticed it once but forgot it right away. I pulled it out and sat up, propping myself up against the side of the bed. I lifted the lid and peeked inside, unsure of what I'd find.

Cards.

A lump formed in my throat when I realized what they were. I picked up the first that wished "Get Well Soon," and the tears began again, this time not from my heartbreak and anger, but from the love I felt. Opening it, I saw it was from Stacy. The next was a sympathy card from all the teachers at Springs High. Through misty eyes, I read through all of them, each one reminding me of all the people who cared about me – loved me – and I knew I wasn't alone.

I gasped as I pulled the last item from the box, dropping it as I clapped my hands over my mouth to stifle a cry. My hands trembled as I reached for the picture that had fallen upside down onto the floor.

I couldn't breathe.

Eva.

I'd never seen her, my baby girl, but there she was, tucked in her daddy's arms. She was the smallest thing I'd ever seen. Even though Daniel had told me, I never could have imagined how tiny she really was. I knew she was broken, but I saw none of that. All I saw was how perfect she was. My heart rejoiced to have this piece of her, this moment in her short life captured forever.

And Daniel. I couldn't see his face – he was looking down at her. But I could feel it, how he tenderly held her, loved her, took care of her while he could. I could also sense his pain, how his heart had broke as he held her in his arms, and I realized how badly he needed me.

I couldn't wait any longer.

Chapter Fifteen

July 2000

I paid little attention to what I packed as I stuffed clothes into my small suitcase. Where was it – that simple red dress Daniel always loved? I would go to him in that. Pulling it from the closet, I quickly changed into it and slipped on my black flats.

My hands trembled with excitement. Rushing out, I dragged the suitcase behind me. I made it down the stairs faster than I ever had before, going straight for the phone in the family room and calling a cab.

"Melanie?" I tensed when I heard Mom behind me, her voice strained. "What's going on?"

Slowly, I turned to her, bracing myself for what was sure to be a fight. "I'm leaving."

"What?"

"I'm going back to Colorado. I can't stay here any longer. I have to go back to Daniel." I pushed past her, looking out the window for the cab, even though I knew it wouldn't be here for another ten minutes.

"You can't...you...you still have to finish therapy," she stammered, searching for a reason to make me stay.

"I'll do it there." I turned back to the window, peering out at the heat radiating from the asphalt.

"Melanie, please don't do this. You need to stay here a little longer. Please, for me. I'm begging you." She clutched my arm. She seemed so – desperate and scared?

"I'm eighteen now, and I'll do what I want." I shrugged her off, unwilling to allow her to sway my decision. Right then, I couldn't care less what she thought. It was obvious how badly she hated Daniel, and I refused to listen to anything she said. The cab pulled up and I made for the door, dodging her as she tried to block my path.

"Melanie, you don't understand. Please, we need to talk. Just wait!"

Anything she had to say should have been said months ago if it was so important.

Throwing my suitcase into the backseat, I jumped in. "Airport."

The driver hesitated, unsure of what to do with the woman yanking at the door and pleading with me to get out.

"Just go!" I yelled at him. He looked back at me before shrugging and driving away.

As he sped down the freeway, I couldn't sit still as I fidgeted in my seat. I really was going.

"I'm coming," I whispered to Daniel, promising him I would be there soon.

The first leg of my flight to Denver boarded, and soon we were taxiing down the runway. When we landed, I had to rush to my meet my connecting flight to Boulder. When the plane landed, I was still soaring. I nearly pushed through the aisle as everyone stood to exit.

I couldn't remember one time in my life when I'd felt this excited – this happy. I couldn't wait to see Daniel's face when I surprised him.

I hailed a cab and gave the driver the address.

The closer we got, the faster I tapped my key on my thigh, the faster my foot bounced.

It was nearing dusk when I stepped from the cab. I breathed in.

Home.

My heart swelled with the few precious memories I had of this place.

I stalled when I noticed the little white, beat-up car parked out front on the street. I hoped he didn't have company; I wanted this homecoming to be just between the two of us. Dragging my suitcase behind me, I climbed the two steps to the porch. I slipped my key into the lock and swung the door open.

I was prepared to run into his arms, but the room was empty – and filthy. Daniel had always been meticulously clean, but the house was trashed. A feeling of unease swept through me as I stepped inside. I tried to focus on the pull, relying on it to lead me to him. Everything was silent except for the distant sound of the shower running and pots rattling in the kitchen. The smell of canned spaghetti sauce stung my nose.

My attention was drawn down the hall – Daniel's soul called out for mine. I started for him. I didn't know why, but I hesitated, my curiosity winning out, and walked toward the kitchen. My kitchen.

At the archway, I froze when I saw the blonde girl in a tight red tank top and a very, very short skirt. Her back was to me as she stood in front of the stove. It took a second before I recognized her.

"Stephanie?" I whispered. Something tightened my stomach, the high from just moments ago knocked out of me. What the hell was she doing in my kitchen?

She whipped around, startled, her hand grasping her chest as she caught her breath.

"Shit! You scared me!" Her face went from stunned to irritated to determined in a second flat. "What are you doing here, Melanie?" She had her hands on her hips as she glared at me.

Was she – mad?

"Daniel." It was the only word I could form – it was the only one that mattered.

She turned and stirred the pot.

"Did you really think he'd just be sitting here waiting for you, Melanie? After all this time?"

My head spun.

She turned back toward me, her voice patronizing, soft and sarcastic, as she tilted her head to sneer at me. "He really was heartbroken. You should be thanking me I was here to pick up the pieces you left behind. But it didn't take long for him to realize what he really needed."

From somewhere deep within, from a place where souls connect, a voice screamed that her words were impossible. He needed me as much as I needed him.

Not her.

I watched her standing there in my spot and I knew she could never replace me. She didn't fit him the way I did. I was made for him. My head shook of its own accord. "I don't believe you."

She let out a small, condescending laugh, and my body recoiled. "Then why do you think I'm here, Melanie, in your kitchen, making dinner for your boyfriend?"

Had she been staying here? Visions of the two of them in our bed flashed through my mind before I could stop them. They nearly brought me to my knees. I braced myself on the counter.

She laughed is if I were stupid and naive. "What do you think, Melanie." Maybe I was.

I choked back the sob that crawled its way up my throat, my fingers trembling where I pressed them against my lips. Slowly, I backed away, my attention darting around the room, landing anywhere but on Stephanie.

Would Daniel really do this to me? I could still feel him, and I didn't believe I would still feel the pull on my heart if he had given up on that love. He had to love me. But what if it wasn't enough. What if he wanted more? I had to get away from Stephanie and…just clear my head.

Think.

I fumbled out onto the porch, curling in on myself, clutching my stomach as I fought the dread the welled up inside me.

Shaking my head against it, I murmured, "He loves me," just as I was hit a rush of energy, his presence wrapping its arms around my body. "He loves me."

Slowly, I turned. He stood in view of the window, his sandy blond hair dark from his shower. A midnight blue T-shirt clung to his toned body, his jeans hung low on his waist.

"Daniel," fell from my mouth as a whispered plea, my knees weak with relief. I reached for the door, but stopped short when I caught sight of his face as he turned toward the kitchen.

It was beautiful and perfect, and it broke my heart because he was grinning as he gazed into the kitchen. My stomach turned when just her hand came into view, extended to him.

He was happy – with her.

I had to look away, to protect myself from the image that would surely sear itself into my mind forever. Still, I couldn't seem to move, my feet glued to the peeling wood beneath me.

How could I just walk away from him forever?

The notion made me physically ill. I almost didn't make it to the railing before I vomited over it. My fingers curled around the handrail as I willed myself away from this place. I squeezed my eyes and tried to ignore his pull and deny my need for him as I forced myself down the steps.

All I'd ever wanted was for him to be happy. Of course, I wanted to be the one to make him that way, but I had to accept that I couldn't anymore. He needed more. He deserved more.

Leaving him was the hardest thing I'd ever done, but I had to because I loved him. I'd give up everything to make him happy.

My heart died as I walked away. My blood felt stagnant, soured, poisoned, no longer filled with life. I was numb. The only feeling left was the distant tug calling me back to him.

Blindly, I walked the streets, having no idea where I was going. I found myself in a shopping center and called a cab to take me to the airport. I bought a ticket for the first available flight – L.A. – stared straight ahead as it took me away from my home, from my love, from my life. Only now, my life was over.

We landed in L.A., and I eventually found myself in the airport lounge, sitting alone at the bar and sipping on a soda that burned as it traveled down my dry throat. It was the only thing open, and nobody seemed to care that I shouldn't be there. I was so tired. All I wanted was to find a place where I could fall asleep and never wake up.

I ignored the movement beside me as a stool slid back, its legs creaking against the floor. I continued to stare into my drink. Words were exchanged, but I was unable to care enough to listen. A shoulder nudged me, partially pulling me from my daze.

"Having a bad night?"

I looked up to see a man grinning from the seat beside me. He was older than I was by probably twenty years. His black hair was meticulously combed against his head, his cold, almost black eyes curious as they took in my expression. Grimacing, I gave him no response, just turned away.

"You're awfully pretty to be sitting here all alone."

I cringed. I knew I was – pretty. Daniel used to tell me all the time. It was sweet and had made me feel good. But something about the way this guy said it made me feel dirty.

"What are you drinking there?"

Couldn't he see I didn't want to talk to anyone?

"Um, a soda."

He chuckled beside me before calling to the bartender, "Can you bring us another of these?" The ice clinked in his glass when he lifted it in the air. The woman set a short glass down in front me, the dark liquid somehow suddenly appealing. I'd never drank liquor before, but I figured this was a really good time to start. I brought the glass to my lips and tipped it into my mouth, taking in more than anticipated. I choked against the terrible taste, my gag reflex kicking in as I tried to swallow. I finally forced it down, chasing it with some of my soda.

Again, the chuckle beside me. He was amused.

I refused to acknowledge him as I brought the glass to my lips again, this time carefully, and I sipped a small amount. It tasted awful, but I found comfort in the warm trail it left in my throat. I knew it was wrong to drink to feel better. I just couldn't make myself care. I finished the first glass before he handed me another.

"That's a good girl," he whispered near my ear.

My skin prickled against his breath on my face, warning me, telling me something wasn't right, but the mixture of alcohol and despair clouded my judgment.

I glanced at him. His left elbow was propped on the bar, his head resting in his hand, his face hard and curious.

"So where are you headed?" He squinted as he waited for my answer, bringing his glass to his lips once again.

I shrugged. I had nowhere to go.

Laughing under his breath, he tilted my chin and looked over my face. I got the impression he was inspecting me.

I knew I should shrug him off, probably even run, but I just sat there, unable to make myself care.

"You have nowhere to go?" he asked, his tone harsh, doubtful. I shook my head. He snorted through his nose, his chest shaking, no sound coming from his mouth.

"How old are you?"

"Eighteen." It was only a whisper.

His eyes narrowed, and he looked me over again. He stood and put out his hand. "Come." It wasn't a request. It was a demand. Somehow I knew it was a test to see if I would obey. I felt nauseous when I touched him, my body repulsed by his. Yet, I followed him out of the airport and into a cab, knowing I was giving away the only part of me I had left. But the alcohol in my system argued I had nowhere to go, no one to turn to. It insisted I couldn't run back to my mother; she would only laugh in my face and tell me she'd been right all along.

Daniel didn't want me.

So I convinced myself I had no other choice. I sat in the back of the cab as he ran his fingers up and down my arm, the touch eliciting chills, revulsion clamoring through my veins.

"Are you excited?"

My dead heart quickened at his words, and I felt scared and ashamed. Never in a million years would I have dreamt I'd give myself away like this.

The trip to the nearest hotel was short. In silence, I followed as he led me into the hotel, and I let the numbness take over while he arranged for a room and led me to the elevator.

I tried not to feel as he explored my body, declaring it as his own. His hands were rough and hard. I'd never been touched this way. Daniel had always worshipped—adored—but this was something I didn't understand. It made me ill. I lay frozen under him as I tried to seek comfort in my mind, tried to retreat to another time and place, but I couldn't block him out completely. Tears streamed down my face and I prayed for it to end.

When he finally rolled away from me, I rushed for the bathroom. Slamming the door behind me, I spilled the contents of my stomach into the toilet. The alcohol burned as it made its second pass through my throat. I curled into a ball on the cold floor, my leg hurting worse than it ever had. I welcomed the pain. I deserved the punishment for what I'd done.

My soul called out for Daniel, begging him to comfort me, to take it all away. I prayed he'd know, no matter what I'd done or what I subjected myself to, that he would always be my only love.

Using the toilet to brace myself, I pulled myself up, reaching for a towel to clean my face, hoping it would wipe away some of the shame. I stared at my reflection in the mirror, my dead eyes haunting me. I allowed myself to shed one last tear for the girl I once knew before accepting what I'd now become.

I flew back to Dallas the next day. Nicholas Borelli sat next to me in first class, his posture relaxed as he read the paper.

He'd offered me an escape. I could leave everything behind and not have the constant reminder of the life I'd once had.

Of course, I knew I'd always carry Daniel with me. I could never completely escape him. I felt him as Nicholas and I touched down in Dallas. I felt him when we went to city hall and signed papers that made us husband and wife. I felt him when we went to Mom's and I sat and I lied and told her I'd fallen in love. I felt him as I tore through my room, trying to rid myself of every reminder of Daniel and Eva. And I felt him three days later when I boarded the plane to serve my sentence in Hell.

"You didn't want me!" I cried over and over. Daniel's rejection was fresh, the scars ripped open.

I wanted him so badly. I'd almost given in and become that person I refused to be. I didn't know how I'd torn myself from his arms.

I had to be strong.

I had to be strong.

And the only way to do that was to stay away from Daniel Montgomery.

Chapter Sixteen

Once again, I stood helplessly and watched her drive away. Would this torment never end?

I knew I'd pushed her too far. We'd needed to talk first, get everything out, and I'd given in and allowed my desire for her to drive me. Her words still echoed through my mind, distinct and utterly untrue. *"You didn't want me."*

I shook my head. There wasn't a moment in my life when I didn't desire her. How could she have ever believed I didn't want her?

I wasn't going to allow her to walk out of my life again without knowing the truth.

I turned on my heel, yanked the door wide, and rushed through the lobby.

"Was that who I think it was?" Dad stood at the end of the hallway, panting, almost seeming disoriented from the shock. He leaned one hand against the wall for support, the other clutching the front of his jacket. I nodded, unwilling to take the time to explain the situation to him. I had to get to her.

Rushing into my office, I grabbed my keys from the desk. Frantically, I searched for my wallet, strewing papers across the floor as I pushed them out of the way.

Dad appeared in the doorway, his eyes wide as he surveyed my office, trying to put the pieces together. "Daniel, what the hell is going on? How did she find you? "

"She's married to Nicholas Borelli," I mumbled as I continued rummaging through my desk.

He stared blankly; the name meant nothing to him.

"Borelli & Preston." I raised my eyebrows at him while I continued my search.

His body stiffened, his eyes wide and disturbed. "Shit," he cursed under his breath, looking around anxiously. "What happened? What did she say?"

"Not a whole lot was said." And I wasn't about to go into detail about what did happen. "She just kept saying that I didn't want her. How could she believe that? I'm going to find her and make some sense of this craziness." I finally spied the black leather lying beside my chair on the floor. I whipped it up, grabbed my jacket, and made for the door.

Dad stepped in front of me, blocking my way. "Whoa. You need to take a step back, son. You're agitated and irrational. It's quite obvious she was upset and wanted you to give her some space, so that's what you need to do." His hand was firm against my chest, though his face was compassionate.

"The last time I gave her space, I didn't see her for nine fucking years, and there's not a chance in hell I'm going to let that happen again." This time I was going to fight for her, and I was going to win.

"I'm not saying to stay away from her forever, but you need to give her some time to calm down."

I ran my hands through my hair and took a step back, trying to let go of some of the tension coursing through my body. He was right. I needed to think this through before I scared her away forever.

"I can't pretend to understand what you're feeling right now. I've watched you suffer more in the last nine years than any one person should ever have to. But you need to realize the seriousness of this situation. I know you love her..." He hesitated, waiting for me to look him in the eye. "But have you even considered the fact that she's married? I've always hoped and prayed she'd come back to you, but breaking up a marriage..." He winced as he said the last words, probably thinking his words would cut me, but where they should bring me shame, I felt none. He hadn't seen her with *him*.

"She doesn't love him." Retreating to my desk, I sank into my chair. "I'm scared for her, Dad. If you saw the way he looked at her." My body rippled with an involuntary shudder as I thought back to their interaction that night. "He was so controlling, so cold." I snapped myself back, looking directly at Dad. "You know I've never gone after her all these years because I thought I was allowing her some amount of happiness. If she was happy, or even satisfied, I'd leave her alone. But, Dad, if you looked into her eyes and saw her face, you'd understand. She can't live without me any more than I can live without her. I just can't believe it was an accident that we both ended up here in Chicago. She loves me. She needs me." I stressed the words. "I know she does."

Dad inhaled deeply and sat on the edge of my desk. "This is really complicated, but I can't doubt you. You know Melanie better than anyone else. You do know this could get really ugly, right?"

I nodded. Of course I knew it, but she was more than worth it.

"Then I want you to give her a few days to think things through." He looked at the wall, seemingly focused on some nonexistent object, then suddenly looked down at me. "And then go bring my daughter back."

ঌ

My eyes fluttered opened, a faint glow of light barely illuminating the room. My arms were wrapped around my pillow, her presence still surrounding me.

I smiled into the cotton as I rolled myself over. I glanced at the clock—six thirty-seven in the morning.

I'd dreamt of her again. Beautiful visions of Melanie replaced the nightmares that had plagued me for the last nine years. Instead of waking to the crushing pain, I woke to the memory of her soft skin beneath my hands, my fingertips ghosting trails over her cheekbones, her body reacting to mine. It had been a long time since I'd felt so alive. The dreams were more real than the agonizing reality I'd faced without her. For two days, I had waited. Those days had been spent longing for her, unable to concentrate on anything except her, just biding my time. Today that time was up. Today I wouldn't stop until it was all out. I wouldn't rest until I knew everything. I wouldn't give up until Melanie Winters knew I would love her forever.

July 2000

Four months without her. I had been lying in bed for three days, consumed with nothing but Melanie. Every thought was of her and what she was doing.

It was as if I'd been living for months without my soul.

Overwhelmed with grief, I lived day-to-day, just waiting for Melanie to come back to me.

She had gone back to Dallas with her mom. I had begged her to come home with me, but she insisted she needed time alone to deal with everything that had happened. I couldn't begin to understand how she thought it would be better if we were apart. Without Melanie, every second would be torture.

But I had to respect her wishes. After all, it was my fault, and even though she'd never admit it, I knew it hurt her to even look at me. I'd caused all of this, and I feared she would never totally forgive me.

That thought alone nearly killed me. I longed to hear her voice, just one phone call to hold me over until we were together again. I picked up the phone a hundred times a day to call her, just to tell her I loved her and that I couldn't wait to hold her again. It was the memory of Melanie's father whispering misery near my ear just after Melanie's cab pulled from view that made me hang up the phone each time, how he'd reminded me that I'd killed Eva, that I'd almost killed his daughter, how he'd threatened me to stay away.

Still, I clung to the promise Melanie had made that she would come back to me.

So I waited, going through the motions each day, waiting for my heart to return to me.

I was ready to crack. I couldn't continue like this much longer. I hadn't been to class in a week and had barely made it out of bed in the last three days. I just wanted to lay here until Melanie came back to me. I didn't have the strength to do anything else.

A knocking on the door jarred me from my thoughts. I pressed the pillow over my head, trying to drown out the incessant noise, but the pounding continued, growing louder.

"Go away!" I shouted as I threw the pillow across the room. Couldn't people understand I just wanted to be alone? Obviously not, because whoever it was just kept knocking. Groaning, I stood up, my body aching from disuse and weak from lack of food. I dragged myself down the hallway, sure I looked as near to death as I felt. Ready to take all my frustration out on whoever was at the door, I swung it open, but stopped when I saw who it was.

Stephanie.

Shit.

"Daniel Montgomery." She let out an audible breath when she took in my appearance.

She'd been leaving messages for the last three days, wondering why I'd missed all of our study sessions, and I'd never replied. We'd forged somewhat of a friendship over the last year as study partners, and she'd convinced me to take physics over the summer session, insisting it would help get my mind off things. Last week, I had decided to blow it off. I just couldn't focus on school right now. I guess I should have let her know.

"Why didn't you call me back? I was getting worried about you."

She seemed relieved. I'm not sure what she expected to find when she got over here.

"Sorry, I'm just not doing so great right now." I stood there in nothing but my boxers, feeling a little self-conscious.

"I figured as much, so I came to make you dinner." She held up a paper sack. "I thought you might need somebody to take care of you." Reaching up, she caressed my cheek with her fingertips. Something about her touch felt too intimate. My instincts kicked in, telling me only Melanie should touch me that way. I eased back, not wanting to offend the only friend I had, but not wanting to encourage her. Hurt flitted across her face before she scrunched up her nose.

"Ew! Daniel! Seriously, you smell. I bet you haven't had a shower in days. Go get cleaned up while I make us dinner." She grinned at me, nodding her head toward the hallway. "And hurry up before I lose my appetite," she teased, trying to lighten my mood a little bit. For a moment, it felt good to have a friend that cared enough to check up on me.

It was hard being up here in Boulder all alone. Mom and Dad tried to visit often, but with Dad at the hospital working long hours, it was hard for them to make it up more than every couple of weeks, and Erin wouldn't get home from her trip backpacking around Europe for another two months. She'd been adamant that she cancel her trip, but I'd insisted that she go. There was no reason for her to stay here when she could do nothing for me anyway.

And it wasn't like I was the best of company.

But Steph came to take care of me.

I forced a smile and headed to the bathroom. I turned on the shower and stepped into the steam. When I breathed in, it hurt. The slight pressure in my ribs served as a constant reminder of what I had done, of the damage I caused. I welcomed the pain; God knew how much Melanie had suffered.

I missed her so much.

"Melanie, come back to me." I prayed that she could hear me – feel me.

Stephanie was waiting for me, so I forced myself to hurry and finish my shower. Dried and dressed, I walked out to the kitchen. I stopped in the entryway and watched Stephanie working at the stove. I pictured my girl making us dinner. I grinned when I thought about how excited Melanie had been as she explored her kitchen for the first time, remembering just how happy it had made her.

"Hey you," Stephanie said as she stepped toward me, holding out her hand. "Dinner's almost ready."

"Thanks for doing this, Steph. You don't know how much it means." This was what I needed, somebody to force me out of the fog I was living in.

Sitting there eating the spaghetti Stephanie had made, I realized I couldn't stay here and wait for Melanie much longer. I needed to bring her back to me, and I couldn't do that if I was wasting away in bed.

We had to move on. I would go for her, and soon.

July's End 2000

I couldn't see through the tears as I tried to find my way back to the Dallas airport. It poured rain outside, coming down in sheets, lightning flashing through the sky every few seconds.

"Fuck!" I screamed, punching the steering wheel. I screamed again as I rammed my head into it this time, trying to feel something other than the unbearable pain tearing through my chest. A horn blared behind me. I was stopped in the middle of the road, disoriented and unaware of anything around me.

Blindly, I pulled over to the side, curling in on myself, gasping through my tears. "Melanie, how could you? Please, God, no," I begged. Vomit pooled in the back of my throat as images of Melanie touching another man flooded my mind. I pushed the door open and purged. Rain poured down on my head and everything spun. I felt as if I was drowning.

She'd blamed me after all.

I couldn't remember getting back to the airport, but somehow I found myself standing at the ticket counter, handing the woman my credit card. Her lips moved, but I heard nothing she said.

I didn't feel the plane take off or land, only being jostled into action by the man next to me, gathering his things to depart.

My parents had called relentlessly over the last twenty-four hours. My phone constantly beeped, urging me to answer. I couldn't deal with them right now. That meant acknowledging my Melanie was gone, and I was not ready to do that yet.

I drove home, dazed, but all too soon the emotions welled up within me, ready to burst.

"You have to get home before you lose it, Daniel." I could make it. I just had to get home. Our home.

As I pulled into the driveway and stumbled out of my car, the first wave of grief overtook me. A bitter laugh escaped my lips as I thought of her telling me this was the only home she'd ever know.

I grabbed the picture of us at my graduation and threw it against the wall, shattered glass fell to the floor. "You fucking whore!" I screamed at her as my heartbroken rage boiled over. As soon as the words left my mouth, I regretted them. I knew they were a lie. I could never blame her.

I just didn't understand how she could do this. I knew she loved me. I had always felt it and never questioned it. I tried to hold on to that knowledge; it was the only thing I'd ever have.

Picking up the broken frame from the floor, I looked at my girl, her beautiful face filled with so much joy. I'd taken that all away.

I hadn't slept the last two days, and I collapsed onto my bed. I pulled my pillow into me, seeking some form of comfort, imagining it was Melanie holding me.

In the other room, my phone alternated between buzzing and ringing, but I couldn't bring myself to get out of bed to answer it. The pain was too great.

I tried to will myself to die, to just fall asleep and to never wake. Instead, I would drift off to a sleep filled with nightmares that should have destroyed me, waking to a reality I prayed would finally end me.

Had it been minutes or days? I couldn't tell.

"What?" I mumbled to myself, lifting my head when the front door clicked. "Shit." I hadn't locked the front door when I had come home. I couldn't deal with anyone right now. My parents would be worried, but I couldn't face them.

My bedroom door opened, and Stephanie peeked through the crack, allowing a stream of light into the room.

"Daniel?" she called.

Damn it. Stephanie.

"Steph, just go. I can't talk right now."

She hesitated.

"Please!" I croaked, my voice rough from crying.

I should have known Stephanie would never leave. She pushed the door open and climbed onto the bed. I turned away from her, but she was insistent, reaching out to rub my back.

"Daniel, you know I'm here for you. What's going on? I mean, I've been worried sick about you. I left you at least ten messages."

I couldn't answer her questions. She ran her fingers through my hair.

I wasn't facing her, but I'm sure she could feel my body tremble as I tried to hide that I was crying.

"Daniel, look at me."

I wasn't sure if I wanted to allow her to see me like this or not, but I gave in, turning around to face her.

"Oh, Daniel, what happened? You look awful."

"Melanie left me."

She looked at me for a few seconds, still running her hand through my hair. I thought she was going to say something else, but she leaned forward and kissed me instead.

I tried to pull away, but she pressed herself closer and whispered, "Please, let me make you feel better," as her lips moved against mine.

Part of me wanted to push her off, but another part just wanted to feel anything other than the ache. Maybe if I gave in, it would mask it, even if it was only for a few minutes. So I kissed her back – hard.

Everything came pouring out of me, and I gave it to her as if she could somehow take some of the burden from me. Tears began to spill from my eyes as I held her body roughly against mine, pressing myself into her. I tore her shirt over her head, not caring what was underneath.

Her hands felt wrong against my skin as she ran them up under my shirt to remove it. But I let her anyway.

"Please, just for one minute, let me forget." I spoke to myself, trying to will it all away, unaware I'd said the words aloud.

"Yes, Daniel, forget," she pleaded with me as she removed the last barrier between us. I slammed into her, praying it would fill some of the void I felt inside.

It only grew.

"Why am I doing this?" I shook my head against the crook of her neck, trying to will the guilt away. All I could see was Melanie's face.

My heart cried out for her, "Melanie...Melanie...Melanie," longing for the only thing that could make it complete.

"I'm not Melanie," she said, her voice bringing me back. "It's Stephanie." She reached out and touched my face. "Let her go. Don't you see it? Now we can finally be together."

I pushed her away. What had I done? I quickly gathered her clothes and tossed them at her. Guilt assaulted me from every direction.

"I'm so sorry, Stephanie...I can't believe I did this..." I raked a hand through my hair. "I...you know I will never love anyone but Melanie. I'm sorry if I gave you the wrong impression." I couldn't believe the mistake I'd just made. I dug through the pile of clothes on the floor to find my boxers.

"No!" She shook her head, vehement. "I can feel it, Daniel. This all happened for a reason. It was the only way for us to find each other."

I felt sick. I had trusted her and thought she cared about me as a friend, but now it was clear. How could I be so blind?

Fear consumed me during the drive to Melanie's house. Every doubt I'd ever had about myself came to the surface, insisting I wasn't good enough, reminding me of what I'd done. I tried to shove it down, to stamp it out, to allow only the assurance of Erin's revelation and the promise of the pull from within Melanie's house to guide me. Yet my stomach was still in my throat. I gathered all of my courage, bracing myself against the possibility that Melanie could, once again, reject me. But I was through living with the questions; it was time to get answers. I would deal with the consequences later.

My palms were sweaty from gripping the steering wheel. I'd been sitting outside her house for more than twenty-five minutes. I swallowed hard, wiping my hands against my jeans. When I opened the car door, her presence intensified. My feet no longer felt heavy, but quickened in anticipation. This was it. I bounded up to her porch, standing in front of her door. Another wave of uncertainty washed over me, leaving me unsure of myself again. I felt like I would go crazy with the constant surge of emotions, each one pushing me forward or dragging me back.

Lifting my hand, I hesitated before rapping against the heavy wooden door. The bell somehow felt too formal. Why I even bothered, I didn't know. Melanie would have already known I was near.

I ran my hands incessantly through my hair as I waited for her, dread creeping through my veins. The house remained completely still. I banged against the door, this time louder. "I'm not leaving until you talk to me, Melanie." I leaned my forehead against the door and pounded my palm against it. Her presence was so strong, I felt as if I could touch her. I realized then she was leaning against the other side, the door our only barrier.

"Please, Melanie," I whispered against the wood, my heart begging her. There was a shift in the air and the sound of metal sliding. The door cracked open, but only a lock of her brown hair was visible.

"You shouldn't be here, Daniel." As much as she wanted me to be believe what she said, I knew she was lying. The pull was overwhelming, and even if I'd wanted to, I could never have walked away.

I pushed against the door, nudging it open a little more. "We have to talk, Melanie, and I'm not leaving until we do."

I felt her give in and the door swung open wide. I tried to gather myself as I stepped forward.

I stood in a massive living room, the furniture pristine, unused, and completely uninviting. I cringed, thinking of Melanie living in this place. There was no hint of her in it whatsoever. The house was devoid of any warmth.

Slowly, I turned back to her, mentally preparing myself. My breath hitched and a lump formed in my throat when we came face-to-face. She was so beautiful; it made it impossible to think straight. She appeared to be in her pajamas, pink sweats resting low on her waist and a pink tank top. Her creamy shoulders were exposed, accentuating her brown curls that fell over them.

But I only allowed myself to focus on her face. Her expression was so sad and guarded, her emerald eyes glistening as she fought to hold back tears.

It was hard to breathe with the weight on my chest. Everything rode on this one moment.

"Melanie." How did I even start? The pull to hold her was so intense, it made it difficult to form words, but I fought it. We had to talk.

She stood feet from me, her breathing even, though she couldn't hide the tremors rolling through her body. She looked so scared, so broken, but even that couldn't mask the love shining in her eyes when she looked at me. I couldn't help but voice my own.

"I love you."

Her lip quivered and she sucked it in, her eyes never leaving mine. Tears broke loose, running quickly down her face. "I know."

I swallowed and allowed the pain to come. I wouldn't hold back. She had to know how deeply she'd wounded me.

"What you said in my office the other day…I couldn't live another day with you believing that I don't want you. You have to understand, nothing was more devastating than finding out you'd left me."

The painful memory flashed in my mind. "She's not here." Peggy looked at me in confusion as if she thought I should know exactly what she was talking about. "Melanie got married, Daniel. Didn't you know?"

"What?" Melanie's forehead wrinkled, her voice suddenly high. "What are you talking about...the day you found out I left you?"

"When I went to Dallas to get you, Melanie. The day your mom ripped my heart out."

Peggy's voice filled my mind. "She's happy, Daniel. Let her go. Find someone that makes you happy like she has."

"For almost five months, I hardly slept or ate. I spent every minute worrying about you, dreaming of you, longing for you. I tried so hard to respect your wishes to stay away and let you heal, but it was too much. I had to come for you." Each word became more heated than the last as the anger I'd always ignored was released. It was never my intention to come here and hurt her more, but it was time we were honest with each other.

"Do you have any idea what that felt like? Finding out that the one person I loved most in this world had left me for someone else, and she never even had the decency to tell me goodbye? Even then, I never stopped loving you, wanting you—ever."

Melanie's face twisted in rage.

"How dare you," she seethed, inching closer, her hands balled in tiny fists, "come in here and lie to me after all this time! If I wasn't good enough for you, you should have just told me. It would have broken my heart to hear you say it, but you know I would have respected it...accepted it." She stood inches from my face. "But to find her in *my* house...it was cruel, Daniel." I could feel her anger dissipate, hurt taking its place. Her hands that had been fisted at her sides fisted in my shirt.

I stared down at her, my mouth hanging open as I tried to process what she was saying.

"Who?" I stuttered.

"Stephanie!" Melanie screamed.

My hands trembled at the mention of Stephanie's name.

How the fuck did Melanie know about Stephanie? I reached out and grasped her upper arms, forcing her to look at me.

"Melanie, please." I was begging, pure and simple. "That meant nothing. I was so broken after you left...I...I—"

"Broken after I left? I left?" she cried. "I never left you! I could never leave you...ever." Her voice softened as she reached out and caressed my cheek. "You were everything to me, my life, my soul." She removed her shaky hand, taking a step back, withdrawing from me.

Pacing, I desperately tried to remember every detail of that time. What the hell was she talking about? Stephanie? I fiercely rubbed my palm over my face. I spun back to her, speaking to her from across the room. "Did you know I came to Dallas for you, Melanie?"

She shook her head and my heart sank. She never knew I came for her? Is that why she thought I didn't want her? Did she feel rejected because I waited too damn long? I knew I should have gone. Every part of me had insisted I go.

That still didn't explain how she knew about Stephanie.

God, I hated having this conversation with her, but we had to get it all out. No hiding.

I tried to phrase it so I didn't sound like the asshole I knew I was. "Did...did you know I was with Stephanie after I came back from Dallas?" Even now, that memory made my skin crawl.

Melanie shook her head, her lips pressed together. Her face was agonized as she forced herself to say it. Squeezing her eyes shut, she refused to look at me. "No, Daniel. I found out about Stephanie when I got to Colorado."

I sucked in the air I couldn't seem to find. Reeling, I tried to wrap my mind around a fact I had never thought possible. Melanie had come back to me.

"When did you come to Colorado?"

She didn't hesitate, having no need to search for the date. "July seventh."

I choked. July seventh. I didn't go to Dallas until the sixteenth. I tried unsuccessfully to control my shaking as everything clicked. From across the room, I stared at my beautiful girl, realizing what I should have known all along. She didn't leave me.

My heart rejoiced and broke at the same time because Melanie had believed something very, very wrong, believed something so wrong it was powerful enough to destroy two lives—our lives. The possible scenarios ran through my head, each of them leading back to the same person.

"Melanie, what happened when you came to Colorado?" I closed my eyes against her words, bracing myself for the rage I knew was sure to come.

I squeezed them tighter when a loud sob erupted from her. Her pain echoed around the room. "Stephanie," she forced out, her voice choppy, "told me you were happy...with her."

I bit back the growl that rumbled in my chest. How could someone be so cruel, so selfish to look an angel in the eye and lie, the intent only to steal and destroy? And how could Melanie have believed her?

I looked back to Melanie. Her eyes were still shut as if she were trying to block the memories.

I called softly to her, coaxing her eyes to meet mine, desperate to reveal the truth, "Melanie." I took a tentative step forward when she opened her eyes. "I would never choose her over you. I don't know what she said to you, but whatever it was, it was a lie."

Swallowing, I took another step, narrowing the gap between us.

"It's true, I slept with her, but not until I'd found out you were married, and even then, it wasn't because I wanted her," I whispered through a pained confession. "I've only ever wanted you. Every second since the moment I first felt you when your dad dropped you off in my driveway and every day since, it was you."

Her face went white, the light reflecting the tears on her face. "She lied to me." Such a simple statement, but I knew those words meant more to her than anyone could ever know. She struggled against her tears as she painfully ground out the words, "Nine years, Daniel. Nine years, and now it's too late."

"No, don't say that," I commanded. "Do you really think it's an accident that I'm here, Melanie? You know as well as I do that we were brought together again. I can't live without you. I haven't lived a day without you," I pleaded as I risked another step forward.

This couldn't happen. I wouldn't let it. We'd been through too much, and it was time to make it right.

She shook her head, looking at the floor. "I won't come between you and your family. As much as I love you, Daniel, I refuse to be that person."

Of course she thought I was with Vanessa. I should have realized what she'd meant when she said I had *her*. She had always been one of the most honorable people I knew. This was yet another thing that proved to me she was still the same girl I loved. She would give up what she wanted in order to do what was right.

Exhaling, I ran my hand through my hair, searching for an explanation. "I've never cared about anyone since you, Melanie, but I've *been* with a lot of women," I stressed the word, praying she'd understand without having to go into all of the sordid details. I wasn't proud of my exploits, but I refused to hide them from her. "Vanessa and I aren't together. We've never been. It was one night, just like all the rest. She caught up with me the very day I saw you again. That was the day I found out about the baby."

Melanie stared at me from across the room, her eyes intense as she absorbed everything. My stomach was twisted up in knots, my body rigid as I waited—waited for her to decide. We both knew what this was. She had to make the choice.

Neither of us said anything. The room suddenly felt small, as if the ceiling had dropped and the walls closed in, drawing us together. Energy swirled around us, her breath so heavy I could taste it. Our chests heaved as we realized how much we'd lost, how much we'd suffered, and how we'd been robbed of so much time. Stronger than all the regrets, though, was the force churning in the air, boiling, surging in our veins. It reminded us of where it had led us, standing mere feet from each other, insisting we didn't waste another minute.

Chapter Seventeen

He'd always wanted me. Somewhere deep within me, I'd always known. Always. He'd lived the last nine years exactly as I had—alone—each of us in our own way. The energy built as we both stood staring, unable to move as our minds rejected the lies we'd once believed. It was all so clear. Part of me felt foolish, so naive to have fallen for another's envy. But really, it'd had much less to do with Stephanie than with the insecurity I'd allowed to control my life. But now was not the time for regret.

"Daniel," I called to him softly and without hesitation. I raised my hand, my fingertips hovering in the air as I beckoned him to me.

Relief washed over his face, and he closed the space between us. Our fingertips met, our spirits rejoicing in the contact.

My heart stuttered as his eyes traveled from our fingers to my face. His mouth turned up in the saddest, sweetest smile I'd ever seen. "I missed you," he whispered.

I nodded, never agreeing with a statement more. Tears continued down my cheeks as I returned my own small, sad smile.

Wiping my tears away, his smile grew, true joy finally shining in his eyes, but his words were still filled with grief. "I missed this face." He dropped my fingers to hold my face in his hands. His touch was soothing, filled with a love that stirred every nerve in my body. "And this mouth." His thumb ran over my bottom lip before his mouth captured mine in a slow, adoring kiss.

I clung to him for support, my legs weak as I stared into his eyes. His love was so intense, yet his soul held so much sorrow. I wondered if his hurt went so deep that he could never heal.

"And these eyes," he choked out the last as he gently brushed his lips across each of my eyelids. He pulled back, his hands gripping my shoulders. "I missed nine years." With trembling hands, he held me, his anguish apparent, and I could hold back no longer.

Taking his face in my hands, I pulled his mouth down to mine, the desperation in my touch demanding that he never let me go.

His reaction was instant.

One hand found my lower back while the other dove into my hair, pulling me even closer. His lips were fervent, but gentle and sweet—always sweet. My body caught fire, desire coursing through me as I fully gave myself over to him. This time I wouldn't hold back.

"Melanie," he murmured as his mouth overtook mine. Surging warmth spread over my body as his hand traveled down my spine to join the other at the small of my back.

I pulled back, gasping for air.

It was hard to grasp that less than an hour ago, I'd roamed this house, sinking deeper and deeper into a depression I was sure I would never recover from. The incident in Daniel's office had undone me—in a devastating way—sending the failing grip I had on my heart spiraling out of control.

But now.

Now he was mine.

Scorching eyes searched mine, filled with need. He must have found his answer in the flush of my face, because his hands abruptly moved to my thighs, lifting. Instinctively, I wrapped my legs around his waist.

I whimpered as he pressed into me. I longed to feel all of him. He crashed his lips back to mine and began to walk, whispering against my lips, "Where?"

I nodded toward the guest room. "There."

His eyes darted behind me, and he carried me to the room, never breaking our kiss. Kicking the door shut behind us, he carried me across the floor to the end of the bed. The sheets were still twisted and tangled from my night of sleep.

Carefully, he laid me down, taking a step back to stare down at me with intense eyes. I'd never felt more loved, more cherished. Wetting his lips, he swallowed hard, his words thick in his throat. "I love you, Melanie."

"I love you...more than anything."

He stood above me, his body visibly trembling. "This is forever."

Propped on my elbows, I looked up at the beautiful man standing before me, his statement simple as he promised we'd never be apart again.

I whispered back, "Forever."

I would take nothing less.

The room was dim, the windows covered, the sun a faint glow through the slats of the shutters. His face softened and he slowly crawled up the mattress to me, kneeling between my legs. His hands rested on either side of my head, his body hovering above. Dipping down, he lightly grazed his lips over mine.

"How did I ever stay away from you?" Gentle fingertips caressed my cheeks, my lips, ran over my chin and down my neck. His palm came to rest on my chest, his fingers splayed out over my heart. It thrummed in devotion against his hand.

"I heard this calling out for me every day." His breath whispered across my face, his words so sad, filled with so much regret. "Did you hear mine?"

"Yes," I breathed out as I began to tremble beneath him. His eyes swallowed me, drawing me deeper into his soul, his beautiful soul that held so much sorrow and so much loss.

I covered his hand with my own. "It was the only thing I had."

A wistful smile arched his mouth as his hand slowly pressed into my skin through my shirt. He brought his mouth back to mine, his lips smooth, his tongue sweet.

Exploring the body they'd missed so badly, my hands roamed his chest and his arms. Where I touched, his muscles twitched, jerked in recognition.

Snaking his hand under my back, he drew me close, pressed his body into mine. "Daniel," escaped as a moan from the back of my throat.

My whole body ignited when he began to slowly move against me.

He wet my neck with open-mouthed kisses, and tingles shot down my spine when he traveled across the sensitive skin to the back of my ear, licking and sucking the whole way. He moved down my neck and over my shoulder, kissing a trail across my collarbone.

I found the hem of his shirt and tugged. He sat back and I ripped the fabric over his head, tossing it to the floor, leaving his heaving chest exposed. When he threw himself back at me, his mouth was urgent. His hands were everywhere as he ran them up and down my body.

"I wish I could tell you what I'm feeling right now," he whispered against my lips, his voice hoarse with desire. "How many times I fantasized about this."

"Yes..." I whispered back, unable to voice my own emotions—too many, too strong.

Above my head, he gathered both of my hands in one of his, skimmed down the exposed flesh of my arm with the other. He grazed past my jaw and neck, ran his thumb across my breast. He released a heavy breath when he found the band of my pants, his fingers trembling as he tugged the drawstring loose.

He pulled back, looking me in the eye as if to ask permission. Slowly, I lifted my hips, and he slid his hand between the fabric and my skin, pushing my pants down inch by inch until they fell to the floor. His fingers caressed my bare skin, awakening the desire I'd always held for him but never thought would find release.

His face was so close, his forehead against mine, his shaky breath mixing with mine. Gentle hands pushed my shirt up and over my head, his gaze never leaving mine.

Cool air hit my bare skin and combined with the heat radiating from Daniel. Thrilling shivers raced through my body.

His eyes swept over me. There was an audible intake of air as he looked down upon my naked flesh. "So beautiful," he murmured, more to himself than to me as his eyes traveled farther down. I heard a small gasp and his body stiffened.

Chapter Eighteen

My eyes roamed her body, taking in every change and remembering all that was the same. I froze, my breath gone as old sorrow took its place. *Eva.* Her face filtered through my mind when I saw the scarred flesh, tangible evidence of my baby girl. Our baby girl. I looked at Melanie. Her face filled with understanding, her love and pain for Eva mingling with my own. My fingers shook as I reached a tentative hand out to touch them, to run my fingers along the skin marred in perfection, the deformity a treasure. I ached to embrace my baby girl as I left small kisses along the long-healed wounds, praying Eva could somehow feel my love for her.

I found Melanie's face, desperate to tell the one person I knew would understand. "I miss her." Gentle fingers reached out to run through my hair, her expression soft as we shared in a loss I was certain neither of us had ever healed from. No words were needed as we mourned for our daughter, our heartbreak freely given to each other. And for the first time since I'd lost Eva, my thoughts of her were not completely unbearable.

I'd never stop missing my baby girl, never stop loving her, but as Melanie and I clung to each other, I knew I could finally allow myself to heal.

The intensity of the moment was overpowering in the quiet stillness of the room. The tension grew as our energy surged in the air. Finally, it was too much.

"Daniel, please."

Simple words, words I was all too happy to heed.

Hooking my thumbs around the edges of her panties, I pulled them slowly down her legs. "Beautiful," tumbled from my mouth as I looked down upon her fully unclothed and waiting for me.

I scooted off the bed and removed my jeans and boxers in one quick movement. Slowly, I crawled back between her legs. I showered her in adoration, hands and words and mouth.

I pulled back, just a fraction, so I could focus on her face. Never had I felt more loved—more complete. Green eyes stared back at me, filled with so much emotion. Melanie's spirit swam behind them, promising me that I was everything.

I took her hands in each of mine and pressed them into the bed at either side of her head, hugging her body close, the energy so intense it almost burned.

"Are you ready for me?"

"Yes," she whispered, her mouth a breath away, her body trembling as she anticipated me. Her eyes held mine and I pushed into her slowly, every nerve aflame in expectation of the greatest pleasure I could know. Melanie's skin was flushed and radiant. Her face told of ecstasy and life, a spirit roused, two souls rejoined, marking it the most significant moment in my life as she became one with me.

Sweat shone across her forehead, her mouth twisting with a hint of satisfaction. I nearly cried when she began to move beneath me.

I fought to maintain control, focusing on the beat of her heart and the warmth in her eyes. I caressed her face and kissed her mouth. Intuition took over and I began to move with her.

The memories I had of making love with Melanie could never compare to the real thing. This physical gratification was greater than any other. Ever. Nothing could possibly feel better. But it went so far beyond that, this connection we shared. I almost wept as she clung to me, digging her fingernails into my skin as we shared the most intimate of embraces. I was filled with awe at being able hold this precious woman again, the one who had invaded every thought of mine for more than eleven years. Eleven years.

"Promise me," I grunted in desperation as I moved against her. "Promise you'll never leave me."

Sweet, soft hands stroked away my worry, and Melanie uttered the only word I would ever accept. "Never."

"I'll never let you go again, Melanie. Never. Nothing will come between us...nothing." I would destroy anything, anyone who tried to take her from me. Being away from her was no longer an option. She was mine, only mine.

"Never," she promised again, unwavering, unshakable.

I finally gave myself over to her, my body rushed against hers. I was lost in soft murmurs of love, our heat building and breaking. Waves of release rolled from Melanie's flushed body, beckoning, coaxing me. Words of love and need and devotion came indistinct as I cried out in pleasure, a pleasure that had no comparison. It was a pleasure that went deeper than physical. It was a pleasure attained by a heart made whole. It was a pleasure found only in this beautiful, perfect girl.

Heaven.

There was no other way to describe it. Melanie laid wrapped in my arms, her head on my shoulder as she ran soft fingers over my chest.

My hand trailed up and down the soft, creamy skin of her shoulder and arm, the other wrapped around her back holding her close.

We'd lain silently together for more than an hour, basking in each other's touch. We had so much to talk about, but we couldn't seem to let go of this quiet moment.

I still couldn't believe I was lying next to her—next to my life. Long ago, I'd accepted I would never truly live again, that I would merely exist. Then when she'd reached for me, I'd been reborn. I glanced down to find her eyes. The pain, so evident this morning, had been wiped away. Her mouth spread into a radiant smile. She looked so—happy.

I beamed down at her. Melanie's cheeks immediately reddened, and she buried her head in the crook of my arm, mumbling into the skin, "You have no idea how much I missed your smile." She propped herself on her elbow to look at me, running her fingers over my bare chest.

I quirked an eyebrow. "That's what you missed?"

She released a small giggle before turning serious, her voice low and laced with sadness. "I missed you, Daniel. Everything about you, including that smile."

"You have no idea how much I missed you."

"I think I do." She shifted to recline against the headboard and tucked the sheet under her arm. I mirrored her, trying to relax through the sudden unease that filled the room. It was apparent our quiet time had come to an end.

She took my hand, holding it between us. "How did this happen to us?"

I shook my head. We would probably spend forever asking the same question and never find an answer. "I don't know,

Melanie." I pulled her closer, hating the distance. "How could you believe I would choose Stephanie over you...or anyone, for that matter? Had I ever shown anything less than commitment to you?"

She grimaced, her body stiffening. "I was *eighteen* and heartbroken, Daniel. I didn't how know to deal with everything that had happened. In one moment, it seemed like I'd lost everything—Eva, my ability to have children. I was depressed and insecure. In that frame of mind, it was easy to believe you'd been stolen from me too." She sighed and closed her eyes, before opening them to me, contrite and guilt-ridden. "I never should have doubted your devotion to me. Deep inside, I always knew you wanted me, but those thoughts just kept creeping up on me. I felt I wasn't good enough for you anymore and that you deserved more."

I closed my eyes, realizing everything she'd sacrificed because she thought it was what I wanted. I hooked my index finger under her chin, pulling her beautiful, distraught face back to mine. "Melanie, there's no such thing as family without you."

I wiped her tears that flowed down her face. She shook her head in my palm, her hair hanging over her shoulder and brushing across the sheet.

"You said you kept having those thoughts. When? What made you think that?"

Her voice was small, hesitant, but necessary if we were going to deal with this and put it behind us. "When you told me in the hospital that I couldn't have more children, it was the first thing I thought."

I clutched her to me, whispering reassurances as I ran my fingers through her hair. "Baby, I wanted to call you every day, every second. You were all I ever thought of. I should have, I know. I was so stupid, but you told me not to and..." I said, trailing off. If I had dialed once in the thousand times I'd picked up the phone, none of this would have ever happened.

"And what?" she pressed, not letting it go.

I was aware she already knew, but somehow it was hard to admit it aloud. "And...I blamed myself." My guilt was probably the biggest factor in all of this. I sighed and ran my hand through my hair in an attempt to calm myself.

"When you went back to Dallas, I was devastated, Melanie. I was convinced it was because you thought it was my fault and needed to get away from me. When you didn't call me in all that time, some part of me started to believe you couldn't forgive me."

She shook her head. "I don't understand how you could have ever believed that."

I looked at her, incredulous. "What did you expect me to believe, Melanie? One minute you're moving in with my parents, and the next you're *leaving* me...telling me not to contact you. I just assumed you'd finally realized the truth."

She cupped my face, searched my eyes. "Daniel, never, not for one day, did I ever blame you. You have to believe that."

"I know that now, Melanie. I'm just trying to make you understand what I felt then. Honestly, it's what I felt up until three weeks ago when Erin finally told me your parents forced you to leave."

Melanie grimaced. "She told you?"

I nodded as I ran my fingertips over her cheek. "You should have told me."

"I was just trying to protect you," she whispered urgently.

"I know, but it was wrong to hide it from me." Really, I should have figured it out myself, the way her father had acted, the things he'd said. Grief and guilt had left us both irrational, vulnerable to our own thoughts and insecurities.

"I'm so sorry, Daniel. I needed you so badly."

I shushed her, whispering how badly that I had needed her too, that I wasn't angry, that neither of us was to blame—that maybe we'd both just been too young and naive to handle the circumstances we'd found ourselves in.

I breathed her in, thankful that in spite of the disaster we'd created, she was here in my arms.

She took a deep breath as her tears slowed. "You were always in my thoughts. Every night I'd pray that you could hear me."

How had we spent these years apart feeling exactly the same? How had one of us not broken down and sought the other out?

"I know," I murmured, hugging her closer, "You invaded...everything. I wanted you every day. I stayed away thinking you had found some kind of happiness in your new life."

A sound that would be impossible to recreate came from deep within Melanie's throat. "I was anything but happy—I never could have been without you—but I still managed to end up in the most miserable place possible."

Eventually, I'd have to ask her how she'd gotten involved with an asshole like Nicholas. I really didn't think I could stomach it at this point. We'd dealt with enough today without evoking the jealousy that conversation was sure to bring. The thought of anyone else touching my girl had me nearly homicidal.

"It's all behind us now." I pulled back so I could smile down at her.

Melanie fidgeted for a minute. "How's Erin?" She flinched when Erin's name passed through her lips. It hadn't occurred to me before then that Melanie had missed Erin as much as Erin had missed her.

"She's really good. She misses you."

She eyed me skeptically.

"She loves you, Mel. Believe me when I say you've been a sore spot between us all these years."

"What?"

I sighed, not looking forward to this revelation. "She had gone to Europe after graduation and didn't get back until after I'd gone to Dallas for you. When she found out what happened, she was dead set on finding you but I wouldn't let her. I made her promise to leave you alone and never contact you."

Melanie recoiled as if she had been slapped. "Why?"

Why? Because I thought it was a really fucking bright idea at the time, that I was doing you a favor, that it would be easier for you that way.

I groaned, once again disgusted with myself. "I thought you'd feel guilty for leaving if Erin confronted you about it. Melanie, baby, I thought you wanted me...us...out of your life. You and I both know how Erin is. She would have had you packed and on your way home, even if that wasn't what you really wanted. I couldn't allow that. I wanted you to live, to be happy, and I thought that meant removing my family from the picture."

"I thought you all had abandoned me." Melanie shook her head.

"I'm so sorry. I hurt you, all the while thinking I was protecting you." I drew her close, praying none of the shit we had to hash out would drive a wedge between us.

Closing her eyes, she pressed her lips together, seemed to be trying to accept what I'd revealed. "I understand what you were trying to do. I was just so alone. I had lost everybody...everything...you, Eva, Erin." I flinched at her words, realizing I had no idea how much she had suffered. "Your mom and dad had been like parents to me, and they were just...gone." She hesitated. "You know, I haven't spoken to my father since leaving the hospital nine years ago. And things with my mom, well, they were never the same. I've seen her a handful of times since then, but I just could never completely forgive her for taking you away from me."

Alone.

I knew how empty I had been, how alone I had felt. Still, I'd had my parents who had supported me, made sure I survived each day, and a sister who loved and encouraged me. Without them, I would never have been where I was today. In the beginning, they had kept me sane and breathing, but Melanie—she'd had no one.

"You'll never be alone again." I could promise her that.

Truly, I was a little shocked that she didn't have a relationship with her parents. Yeah, they messed up our lives, no doubt. But they were her parents and Melanie was always the first to forgive. I just couldn't fathom that she'd spent all of this time hating them. On the other hand, I would never forget they were the ones who set in motion the chain of events that ultimately took my girl from me.

"I can't believe you haven't talked to your dad since you left the hospital."

She pursed her lips, shaking her head. "I never even knew what he was most angry about, me getting pregnant or the fact that I hid it from him. Either way, he disowned me. I was hurt at first, but over time, I realized just what a jerk he was. I mean, who would do that?"

I shook my head, at a loss. I was positive it was me he was angry with, not Melanie.

"What about your mom?"

She tucked a strand of hair behind her ear. "I don't really know," she said, shrugging, " I guess she knew I'd never completely forgiven her and she kept her distance because of it." She smiled a little, glanced up at me. "She called a few weeks ago...I could just tell things were different. She's coming the week of Thanksgiving. I think we're going to be okay." With that, her mouth spread into a real smile, and while it would not be so easy for me to forgive Peggy, it was obvious Melanie needed her mom in her life. There'd be no way I'd stand in the way of that.

I rolled onto my back, pulling her with me. I reveled in the feel of her naked body pressed against mine as she lay against my chest. Slowly I caressed her back, her shoulders, her head, relishing the feel of her hair as it fell over her shoulders and onto mine.

Loving fingers ran through my hair, traced my jaw, played across my lips, perfection across my skin. She seemed thoughtful as she played with a lock of my hair. Her eyes finally locked with mine, filled with some unknown emotion. "You're going to be a father."

I stiffened under her, unable to stop my reaction as I rolled away and sat up on the side of the bed. Thinking of Vanessa's baby made it hard to breathe. Melanie crawled up behind me, wrapping us up like a cocoon in the sheet. She leaned into me, holding me tight. "Daniel...what's wrong?" Calmed by her touch, I ran my hand over my face and through my hair, drew in a shaky breath.

"I...I..." I looked down, unable to face her, but unwilling to lie. "I don't want him." I knew that statement was wrong in so many different ways. And honestly, I was terrified of Melanie's reaction to him.

Melanie remained silent as she continued to soothe me, never faltering in the rhythmic movements she made on my shoulders and neck. With her mouth close to my ear, she spoke quietly, "Do you want to talk about it?"

Did I? Not really, but I couldn't hide from it much longer. In three months, I would have a son, whether I liked it or not.

I turned to her. My lips were tight as I studied her face, looking for any indication of how she felt about the fact that I was going to be a father. All I found was concern for me. "I messed up. I was careless and stupid, and now there's a child who's going to suffer because of a mistake I made."

"Suffer?" Her voice was soft, confused.

And this was where I failed.

"Because I can't love him."

Her hand stilled for a brief moment before resuming its calming reassurance, the slight shaking in her fingertips my only clue she was disappointed in me, just as she should be.

"Daniel, I'm so sorry. I can't imagine what you're going through, but I'm here for you—whatever you need."

Okay, not disappointed, just understanding and sympathetic.

I was afraid to voice the words. What if this was all too much for her? Could I ask her to deal with all of my baggage?

"I'm going to have joint custody." I looked at her, hoping she'd understand what this would mean.

Her mouth gaped. "I don't understand. I thought you didn't want him?"

I exhaled heavily, wishing I knew the answer to that question. "I don't know what I was thinking when I told Vanessa that's what I wanted. I'm not sure if it was out of spite or obligation." I cringed as the words came out my mouth, appalled at my own admission, but I couldn't be anything other than straightforward with Melanie. "I guess probably a bit of both."

I was positive it weighed a little heavier on the spite side, demanding that control, doing anything to take some of it from Vanessa. As it was, Vanessa had been completely up my ass lately, texting and calling continuously, trying to get me involved in the pregnancy and, no doubt, with her. I'd almost recanted my claim to the child and offered just to cut her a check. But paying her off would give her control and would do nothing to stop her from hounding me in the future. I refused to allow that to happen.

I waited, giving Melanie the opportunity to digest all of this information. I grew restless when she said nothing. Finally, unable to take her silence any longer, I pleaded, "Please…say something. Tell me what you're thinking."

"I'm thinking that I love you, and anything you have to deal with, I have to deal with."

I turned and pulled her to me, tugging her onto my lap, breathing my relief onto the top of her head.

"Thank you." What more could I say?

I glanced at the little clock on the nightstand. It was already past two. We'd been in this bed for almost four hours.

"Come on...let's get your stuff." Gauging what little I knew about her marriage, I was betting that Melanie had very few possessions of her own. What we couldn't fit in the car, we'd just replace.

Her head jerked back to meet my face, panicked as she scrambled to sit up. "I can't leave yet."

What?

After everything we'd just shared and promised, she was going to say she couldn't leave?

"No way, Melanie." The thought of leaving her here with Nicholas—I didn't even try to hide my disgust. "I will not share you with that asshole."

"Stop. Listen to me." She gripped my shoulders. "You'll never share me. I'm yours. If you look around," she said as she gestured around the room, "you'll see that this is where I sleep. I haven't shared his bed since the night of the dinner. I knew then I was yours, even if I couldn't have you. I'll never again give myself to anyone else, especially Nicholas." I relaxed a little, not because I was conceding but because of the relief from knowing that Melanie hadn't been sleeping with him.

"This isn't just about us, Daniel. What about your building?" she said, as if that somehow could be more important than she was.

"I couldn't care less about the building, Melanie. It means nothing."

"Maybe not to you, but what about Shane and Katie? They're the only family I've had this whole time. I owe them this for everything they've done for me. I honestly don't know whether I would still exist if Katie hadn't been there for me, and I'm not going to do something that would jeopardize Shane's freedom."

"What are you talking about?"

"Shane hates Nicholas almost as much as I do. With the profit from the building, he's planning to break from Nicholas and start his own company. He *needs* this. We have to at least figure out how to do this without putting the deal in jeopardy."

It was so frustrating—Melanie always thinking about everyone except herself. I didn't see how Melanie leaving Nicholas would affect the building. I had a signed contract. Nicholas had to stick to it, didn't he? Honestly, I hadn't even looked at the contract when I had signed it, so I had no idea.

Okay, so maybe I needed to talk to Shane—and my lawyer.

Melanie's hands were back on my face, forcing me to look at her. "And my mom, I need to try to work things out with her...to know her again. I miss her." She looked away, deep in thought, whispered, "You know I'm not ashamed of us, Daniel, but I think she and I need to resolve the past before I tell her you and I are back together."

I groaned with frustration. I couldn't imagine walking out that door without her.

"If you think I want to stay here, you're wrong. There's no other place I want to be than with you."

I drew her close, murmured against the soft skin of her neck, "It absolutely kills me to leave you here."

She tightened her hold and exhaled softly, knowing I'd surrendered.

I knew a little part of her wished I'd refuse and throw her over my shoulder and carry her out the door.

"I know," she said, "but we have to."

She pulled me down on the bed beside her, her face at peace as she smiled at me. Even though it had been hard revisiting all of our issues, we had come to the place where our questions were answered and we were confident about our future.

Our future.

Melanie kissed me solidly on the mouth, humming in contentment as she snuggled in close to my side. "Besides, was this afternoon so bad?"

I grinned back at her and trailed my nose down her jaw. "No, no, not bad at all," I agreed as my hands began to roam her body.

As I came to her for the second time that day, the desperation of our broken hearts was gone, replaced with the security of what would be.

Chapter Nineteen

I watched as the black car slowly drove away. It took all the power within me not to run after him. I stood there in silence as he disappeared from view, wondering if this qualified as breaking the promise that we had just reiterated, the one that bound me to tell him everything I was feeling, what I feared, and what I needed.

Yeah, probably.

But I couldn't voice it to Daniel.

He didn't know Nicholas like I did.

I was the one who bore witness to the highly questionable things that had taken place in my *home* over the past nine years, things that Nicholas did without a second thought if it benefitted him in any way. I'd seen him lie and cheat and steal. He would go any distance to keep something from damaging his reputation—his self-importance.

When Daniel nonchalantly told me to get my things so we could leave, he'd caught me off guard. It was as if being with him hadn't been real, that the afternoon was a figment of my imagination, and soon I would wake up to live my non-existence.

Realizing what Daniel planned had solidified the reality of what we'd experienced, and I'd panicked. I was seized with visions of the punishment Nicholas would impose upon me when he dragged me back here. Most of them centered on Daniel being harmed in some form or another because of me. So I'd searched for reasons to stay, and well, they seemed likely enough because they were, in fact, true. We had to make sure the building went through and it was high time for me to reconcile with Mom. I had to see that through. The fact was, though, one way or another, those situations could have been resolved without my being here.

Deep inside, I was probably being irrational. In all probability, Nicholas would do nothing to me, but I had to have time to think about how to leave him. He would take it a lot better if he didn't come home and just find me gone. If I gradually withdrew from him, he wouldn't be shocked when I finally did leave. He'd expect it. It was what I'd initially planned to do when I had made plans to leave with Katie, so this wouldn't be any different.

I just needed a couple of weeks to make it clear to Nicholas that he did not own me. Then I would leave. I would stay through Mom's visit, and ensure Daniel and I didn't hurt Shane and Katie with any rash decisions. Then I would be free.

A contented smile spread across my face at the thought. Free—with Daniel. I'd spent nine years here. I could somehow endure a few more weeks.

I withdrew back into the house, filled with emotions that had so long been lacking from my life that I almost didn't recognize them.

I padded barefoot across the cool floor, my feet light as if I were no longer weighed down. I hummed quietly to myself as I stood in front of the refrigerator, pulling out the ingredients for the salmon I'd planned to make for dinner. I sealed the salmon in foil and placed the packets in the oven before dancing across the kitchen to start water for rice. When I caught my reflection in the arched window overlooking the backyard, I stopped short.

And grinned.

I ran into the bathroom to get a better look. The mirror confirmed what I'd seen in the hazy window.

Yes, my hair was a mess and my clothes were wrinkled and disheveled. But my face—it was flushed and pink and glowing.

It was me. The real me—not broken Melanie, but my mother's little girl. The girl who'd run carefree and climbed trees in her daddy's backyard. The one who'd stayed up late giggling with her friends in sixth grade as we'd dreamed of our first kiss. The fifteen-year-old girl who'd fallen in love with Daniel Montgomery. The same one who'd love him until the day she died. I'd almost forgotten her, but there she was, staring straight back, her eyes alight and alive.

I traced the outline of my face, touching the heated skin of my cheeks and fingering the creases at the corners of my eyes as if I had to confirm that what I was seeing was real.

I smiled once more at my reflection before heading back into the kitchen. Joy surrounded me like an aura, hovering in the air, dense and thick, but unlike the weight of pain, it provided comfort and warmth.

Daniel loved me, wanted me, had me. The experience was euphoric. It was as if we had been taken to another realm, to a place where only the two of us existed.

My hands worked with precision as I sliced tomatoes and onions for a salad, fingers wet from the lettuce as I ripped the leaves from the head piece by piece. My body hummed with excitement, right along with the humming that came from my mouth.

There was nothing that could touch my mood. Well, except for the sound of the garage opening and the purr of the car pulling in. I vowed that I wouldn't even let Nicholas steal this feeling from me. Instead of focusing on the sound of his footsteps echoing through the house, I focused on the warmth still covering every inch of my body from Daniel's touch.

Heat flooded my cheeks.

I averted my face as Nicholas entered the room, concealing myself by stooping to retrieve the silver salad bowl from under the island. I waited until the refrigerator door snapped open to stand.

I said nothing to Nicholas when he turned, simply ignored his presence as I filled the bowl. He twisted the cap off the beer bottle and crossed his arms over his chest. Sighing deeply, he rested against the refrigerator door and took a deep drag of the yellow liquid. I moved across the room and poured the rice into the boiling water, careful to keep my head down as I made my way back to the island to keep from drawing attention to myself. It took everything in me to stay focused on the task in front of me.

The intensity of Nicholas's dark eyes burned into the side of my face, and anxiety steadily built within me. I'd been so successful in avoiding him for the better part of a month. Neither of us had said anything more than was necessary to the other. Now there was something very different and very unsettling about the way he stood silently drinking me in.

Did he know?

I struggled to control my escalating breaths as fear set in. My stomach twisted in knots. My mouth became dry.

He couldn't know. There was no possible way. Could he?

Keeping my eyes focused in front of me, I spent an exceeding amount of time arranging the salad in the bowl. Still, I couldn't keep myself from glancing at him through the veil of hair that had fallen over my shoulder.

The fear I'd had that he knew about Daniel was put at ease. For the first time, Nicholas's face held no anger or disdain, only complete curiosity. My hands trembled as I continued to work. He took another swig of his beer before stepping to the island. He placed the bottle on the counter and pushed my hair from my face. I cringed away from his fingers, desperate to escape the scrutiny. "You look different." His shook his head, trying to put his finger on the change.

Oh, if he only knew.

I scowled at him, tried to brush him off. "That's ridiculous."

We both jumped when the buzzer went off, effectively giving me an out. I took the long way around the island, pulled the salmon out, and went to the cabinet to get the plates. The heat of his intense gaze never left me for a second. In my shaky hands, the plates clattered, and I clipped the edge of the cabinet as I pulled them down, thankfully not hard enough to break them.

I took a deep breath to steady myself. I had to get myself together. I needed to stay here for at least another month, and I was raising suspicion the first day.

Collecting myself the best I could, I turned and cautiously placed the plates on the counter.

I should have known Nicholas would not let this go. As much as I hated him and would have liked to believe otherwise, he was an intelligent man and never easily deceived.

He was suddenly behind me, breathing down my neck as he looked over my shoulder. My hands visibly shook as I tried to tear the foil packets open and dump the salmon onto the plates. I went rigid when his fingers ran up the length of my arm, my chest quaking as I held down the sob forming within.

"Not ridiculous, Melanie." His voiced oozed an unknown tenor, intrigued and searching, unlike anything I'd ever heard from him before, but more frightening than any threat he'd ever made. "Something's different." He swallowed, the sound loud against my ear. His words came rough and needy as he whispered into my jaw, the complete foulness of his being washing across my face, "And I like it."

My fingers dug into the countertop as he ground himself against me, his mouth aggressive on the skin of my neck. I tried not to whimper as tears sprang to my eyes.

No.

I couldn't let this happen. I had just promised Daniel I was his, that I would never allow myself to be touched by another man, and here I stood, enabling it, just like I'd done those nine, miserable years. But there was more. *I* didn't want to be touched. I wanted to keep that promise I'd made to myself, not just because of Daniel, but because I deserved to be respected, to respect myself. I didn't have to subject myself to this.

Though I was scared, the need to be free was so much greater than that fear. Somewhere within me, I found the same courage I'd found the night I'd successfully removed myself from Nicholas's bed, because there was no way in hell I was going back to it.

I wrestled out of his grasp and he released me in his surprise. His eyes first widened, then narrowed as his anger flared.

I rounded my shoulders and turned back to him, praying I looked much more confident than I felt. Truly, I was terrified. My whole body rocked with the fear coursing through my veins. The pumping adrenaline was my only salvation.

Amazingly, my mouth spilled the words I'd dreamt of saying every day for the last nine years. "Don't ever touch me again."

Nicholas's face twisted in fury, indignant at being defied for the second time. It became clear in his expression that I needed to get away. I turned on my heel to flee, but he wrapped his hand around my wrist and jerked me back, digging his fingers into my skin.

"Don't forget who you belong to, Melanie." His words were sharp, deep with implication.

I was tempted to end it all right there and tell him exactly who I *did* belong to, but I was certain that it would push him over the edge. Instead, I remained still, never backing down as his eyes bore into mine.

He squeezed harder, his hold becoming increasingly more painful, but I could see the uncertainty swirling in his thoughts. "I've had about enough of you." He constricted his hold on my wrist, and I bit my lip to hold back the cry before he dropped my arm in frustration, glaring at me before turning and stalking from the room.

The breath I'd been holding escaped in a loud, audible gush, leaving me gasping. I braced myself on the counter for support, my knees weak and threatening to give way.

I did it.

He'd backed down, and I'd done it almost unscathed, all except for the throb in my wrist. I cradled it against my chest as I massaged it, fingering the band of red, swollen skin. It was definitely going to bruise.

Once my breathing returned to normal and my body began to relax, I realized I was exhausted—and starving. It seemed days since Daniel had come. So much had happened since then, so much had changed. I just wanted to eat and then curl up in bed so I could relive today.

I tore open the intact foil packet. Steam rose as I dumped its contents onto a plate. I added a healthy portion of salad, skipping the rice that sat overdone and dry on the stovetop. By second nature, I began to pack up the other serving but stopped myself. That wasn't my job anymore. The bastard could fend for himself. I took my plate and left the kitchen, leaving the rest of the food on the counter. I just hoped he would get the message I was sending him.

❧

I yawned as I lay my head against the pillow. My stomach was full and satisfied, my body pleasantly tired and seeking respite. I curled onto my side, burying my face in the sheets, breathing in Daniel's scent mixed with mine. My muscles twitched as I relaxed and slowly drifted to sleep. Daniel's face was the only thing I saw from behind closed eyes. I murmured, "Good night, Daniel. I love you," into the darkness, certain now that he always sensed my distant thoughts and words.

My eyes darted open from my half-conscious state, jarred by the sudden buzzing coming from somewhere deep within the bed.

I had a text.

Frantically, I shuffled through the twisted sheets, searching for the offending object. I hadn't called Katie today, so she was probably worried, and Katie worried translated to Katie being just a little bit pissed. The red, blinking light served as my guide, and I reached deep into the covers to grab the missing phone. I pressed the roller ball to retrieve the message.

Not Katie.

My stomach did a flip-flop and suddenly I felt like a teenage girl again, butterflies making an appearance for the first time in nine years. The sender was unknown and the message simply asked if I was there, but I knew it was Daniel.

He told me he missed me and loved me, that he couldn't wait to see me again, and then he bid me goodnight. Knowing that tomorrow we didn't have to wake to feel the same emptiness and hopelessness we'd felt for nine years, I knew it would be a very good night.

≈

I was soaring.

I had awoken rested, refreshed, feeling loved and wanted. There had been a text patiently waiting for me when I woke, one sent hours before that wished me a good morning.

Yes it was.

I replied, telling him I couldn't wait to see him again. I had no idea when that would be, but I knew we wouldn't be able to stay apart for long. Carefully, I erased all of our messages, feeling a little guilty about doing so. Every single one of his words was precious to me, but I knew I was going to have to be cautious if I was going to pull off this ruse. My phone immediately vibrated and I grinned, expecting his reply. Instead, a snarky message from Katie illuminated the screen, demanding to know what was going on.

Crap.

That's where Daniel had gotten my number.

I'd had every intention of calling her this morning, but she beat me to it. Instead of explaining myself on the phone, I asked her to meet me for lunch. Three hours later, I arrived at our favorite deli.

As I walked through the door, I found Katie already seated. Her eyes flooded with relief when she caught sight of me. It lasted only moments before a whole lot of curiosity washed it away. Apparently, Nicholas was not the only one who'd noticed the difference. I smiled as I crossed the white and black-checkered floor and slid into the red vinyl booth opposite her.

"Look at you." She shook her head in disbelief, reaching both hands across the table to take one of mine. Then she muttered, "Unbelievable," under her breath, making me uncertain whether she'd intended for me to hear it or not.

Our regular waitress greeted us, and we ordered our usual chicken salad and iced tea. The moment she walked away, Katie assaulted me with questions.

"What the hell happened? I've been freaking out all night! Did Daniel call you? I mean, obviously, look at you." She waved her hand at me, exasperated, before continuing. "He called Shane and asked for your number and then asked to have a meeting with him." She was nearly panting by the time she finished. To the casual onlooker, it would have appeared that she was upset with me, but I knew she was just dying to know what was going on. She did not like being kept in the dark.

"I was busy yesterday," I spoke softly and slowly, communicating to her more by tone than with actual words. I watched as comprehension flickered in her features.

"So, he didn't...just...call."

I looked down and shook my head, redness working its way up my neck and onto my cheeks.

"Tell me everything."

As I told her of what happened the day before, I was unable to keep myself from crying, once again, when I went into detail about how we'd been cheated out of the last nine years.

"That's...awful." Katie reached across the table to grab my hand with hers, gently squeezing. "See, I told you that you were his *more*."

I nodded, this time without doubt.

"So?" Katie prodded, bouncing in her seat, impatient for me to get to the good part. She gaped as I described the most incredible day of my life. I thought I'd be embarrassed, but there was nothing embarrassing about what Daniel and I had shared.

"I'm so happy for you. All I've ever wanted is to see you happy, and I can *see* it. It was obvious when you walked through the door. I almost didn't recognize you."

She might not have recognized me, but I definitely did.

"So, what's the plan?" She hesitated, lowering her voice. "I mean, what are you going to do about Nicholas? That asshole isn't going to take it very well when he finds out you're leaving him for another man."

"Yeah, I know. Daniel was all set for me to leave with him yesterday, but I just couldn't do it. Who knows what Nicholas would have done if he'd come home and found me gone. I need some time to think about the best way to get out of there." I leaned in closer, hyperaware that the people around us could hear our conversation. "I feel terrible, but I misled Daniel. I told him we had to talk to Shane first and make sure it wouldn't affect the building in any way. If I had told him the real reason, I know he would never have let me stay."

"Oh, thank God, that's what the meeting must be about. Shane's been pissing his pants since Daniel called. He was convinced Daniel wanted to cancel." She grimaced, stopping short. "Sorry, I didn't mean it like that...you know we'd happily let the building go if it meant your freedom."

I shook my head, dismissing her worry. The building was a really big deal, life changing for them. Of course they would be worried about it. "You guys have been there for me more than you could ever know, and I want the building to happen, too. Regardless of whether I stay in that house or not, I can't see Nicholas letting that kind of money go."

Katie took a bite of her salad, thinking about what I'd said. "Yeah, you're probably right. I just don't know what it's gonna take for him to let you go. I don't see him taking subtle hints. I mean, look what happened the last time you told him no. The guy's a tyrant."

I sighed, shifting uncomfortably. "It wasn't the last time." I pushed my sleeve up to reveal the very green and blue ring wrapping around my wrist.

"I'm going to kill that asshole," she said, her voice a low rumble as she carefully inspected my wrist. "What led to this?"

I couldn't contain the smug feeling I got when I described the altercation I'd had with Nicholas the previous evening. It'd left me feeling in control. Yeah, I'd been scared—really scared. But I'd won.

We ate in silence for a few minutes. Katie would pause every few moments, chewing more on her lip than on her food.

"What?" I asked. She was making me nervous.

She exhaled heavily, sitting back in her seat. "I just know this must be really hard on you."

I looked at her, puzzled.

"The baby," she clarified, "How do you feel about that whole situation?"

Oh.

How did I feel about the baby? Jealous? Yes. Scared? Yes. Sad? Very. Very, very sad. Truly, it was devastating. Every single insecurity I had was wrapped up in the fact that I couldn't give Daniel a child. It was the reason that for nine years I had believed he didn't want me. More than that, *I* wanted a child. I desperately wanted to be a mother. Yeah, they'd cut me open and removed the ability, but they couldn't remove the ache, the need to hold, feed, and nurture. The pangs of envy I'd feel as I'd walk through a store and hear a child call mommy as if no one else in the world existed. The way she'd pick up that precious little person and ease his or her fears. The way she loved and coddled. I wanted to be her, and I would never be.

What troubled me most was the way Daniel felt about it. I'd never allowed myself to really consider how broken he was over Eva. It was as if when I lost the ability to become a parent, he did too. That scared me because he was actually going to be one, and I wasn't sure he could handle it.

But if I put everything together, that question was easy to answer.

"I wish he was mine."

ණ

After lunch, I sat in the office checking my e-mail when that welcomed tingle ran down my spine. My phone vibrated with a text, asking if it was clear.

Daniel was here. I bounced in excitement. Yep, officially fifteen again.

I skipped out of the office and raced to the front door, swinging it open the very moment he topped the stairs. As soon as the door closed behind him, he swept me into his arms and buried his face in my hair as he breathed me in, my heart thrumming in contentment.

"Hi," I whispered into his chest.

"Hi." He pressed his lips to the top of my head. "Look at us, sneaking around again."

"We can't win, can we?"

He pulled back, just enough so that I could see his gorgeous face, his hazel eyes brilliant and filled with fire, the sorrow of yesterday gone. "We already won, Melanie."

He was right. Maybe the battle wasn't over, but it was already won. We had each other, and that was the only thing that mattered.

"I can't stay, but I had to see you."

I squeezed him tighter. "No...stay with me."

He groaned, lingering as he held my face and kissed me. "You have no idea how badly I want to take you up on that, but I have a meeting in a half hour that I can't miss. Can you get away tomorrow night? I want to take you to dinner."

"Like on a date?" I laughed at the absurdity of the whole situation.

He grinned down at me, red-faced. "Yeah, like on a date."

He was too adorable. And truly, there was something really appealing about pretending we were just a normal couple for a few hours.

"Well, in that case, I'd love to."

He finally tore himself from me when our chaste kiss goodbye evolved into five minutes of much, much more. His voice was low and rough against my ear. "I love you."

In the middle of the living room, I stood gasping, trying to bring myself down from the high I was riding as I watched him walk out the door.

I scrambled to my phone and fumbled through the numbers with trembling fingers. "Katie, I need your help."

I stood in front of Katie's full-length mirror, appreciating the way the simple black jersey dress hung on my body. The scoop neck revealed just a modest amount of cleavage, and the three-quarter length flared sleeves brushed against my forearms. The only problem was the skirt; it was a bit too tight and a bit too short—really short. Of course, Katie paired it with four-inch heels.

"I don't know, Katie. It might be a little much." I turned and peeked over my shoulder at the back.

"Are you kidding me? You look amazing." The doorbell rang, declaring that the time to worry about my appearance was over. Katie pushed me toward the door. "Go. Have fun." Her smile was warm, encouraging. I hugged her, thanked her for taking care of me, and moved to follow her from the bedroom. I stopped short when I reached the threshold, reaching for her arm.

She looked at me over her shoulder, confused.

I mouthed, "Wait."

Something didn't feel right.

We both stood silently, straining to listen as Shane unlocked the door. A very familiar voice cut through the air. My fingers curled into the tense muscles of Katie's arm when we both realized Nicholas was here.

"Yeah." Shane sounded irritated. "No, that's fine…Yeah, she's here, that *is* her car...I don't know, they rented movies or some shit...Why don't you just cut her a break for once?" Shane was arguing with Nicholas—over me. I desperately fought to hear the other side of the conversation, but couldn't with Nicholas's hushed tone. I'm sure my expression verged on terrified, because Katie squeezed my arm, reassuring me it would be okay.

Tonight was the first time I'd ever simply left Nicholas a note saying I was going out for the evening. In my mind, this was just one of the painful steps I'd have to take in order to extract myself from his control. Little by little, I would free myself.

Finally, after what felt like hours, the door slammed, and Katie rushed down the hallway.

"What the hell was that about?" she demanded.

Shane exhaled, his body tense. "He knows something's up."

I wrung my hands to calm my flaring nerves. "What do you mean? Is he suspicious about Daniel?"

He shook his head and strode into the kitchen, Katie and I close behind. He pulled a beer from the fridge and downed half of it. "No, I don't think so. He just knows something's changed."

When bell rang again, I knew who it was, but Shane told us to stay in the kitchen. Seconds later, Daniel trailed Shane to where we waited. He was visibly shaken and full of apologies. "Baby, this is so messed up. I'm so sorry."

I cut him off by pressing my lips to his. We couldn't let it ruin our night. He returned the kiss, though I could feel the despondency in his touch. He rested his forehead on mine, his eyes strained as he looked down at me. "I don't know how long I can take this."

"All right you guys, get out of here," Katie urged, trying to pull everyone from the heaviness threatening to suck us under. Daniel nudged me, breaking our embrace.

I shrugged into my jacket and reached for Daniel's hand.

We thanked Shane and Katie and bid them goodbye. This night would never have happened without them.

Tension rolled off of Daniel as he scanned the yard and road. I hated that the choices I'd made had left us with Nicholas haunting our every move. Desperate to ease his nerves, I touched his arm. His face was gentle when he smiled down at me, colored with his own regret.

"We're going to be okay," I said.

"I know."

The mutual reassurance was all we needed for the mood to lighten. A cool breeze rustled through the trees, blowing through the sparse yellow and orange leaves that still clung to the branches as winter approached. Daniel wrapped his arm over my shoulder and led me down the steps to the walkway. I sighed, relishing in his warmth against the crisp, night air. A feeling of contentment settled into the depths of my bones.

I giggled when he opened the passenger door and helped me inside, careful to keep my dress from riding up as I sank down into the low seat. I whispered a breathy, "Thank you," against his lips when he ducked inside for a kiss.

He rushed around, jumped in, and leaned over the console to kiss me again. I was not going to get tired of that.

"Chinese okay?" He started his car and pulled away.

"Yeah, that sounds great." It was my favorite.

He traveled farther out of town than I normally would have ventured, I'm sure out of fear of running into somebody who would recognize us. Twenty-five minutes later, he pulled into a half-full parking lot. "I ate here a few weeks ago. It's quiet and has the best Mongolian beef I've ever eaten." He smiled at me, touching my cheek. My chest swelled with the love I felt as he showed me that he remembered *me*, not just taking me for my favorite type of food, but for the exact dish we'd shared many times before.

"Thank you."

Dinner was perfect. There was no awkwardness, only complete calm as we talked for what seemed like hours. We teased and loved. His lips were never far, and we shared gentle caresses beneath the table, whispered tender words that had been silent for too long.

Laughing, we reminisced about our high school days. When Daniel's phone chimed, he was making fun of Erin, his words still flowing as he casually ran his finger over the face of the phone. The shift in his demeanor was instant, his jaw clenching when he read the message.

I watched as he tried to play it off as if nothing had happened. He turned back to me and continued with the story though his words were forced.

I sat back, feeling unsure of myself. Where did we stand here? Before, I wouldn't have hesitated to ask him who it was and what was wrong. We had told each other everything—shared everything. That was the way it should be.

He trailed off mid-sentence when he noticed my pained expression. He grimaced and ran a frustrated hand through his hair before answering the question I'd never voiced.

"It was Vanessa."

Tentative, I asked, "What did she want?"

He stared down at the table, struggling with what to say.

"Daniel, look at me," I prodded, making him look up. "Please, don't hide from me. You can tell me anything. We have a lot of stuff to deal with, but we have to do it together."

Shaking his head, he looked away before cutting his eyes back to me. "She just...she's constantly calling...sending these little messages...anything to get my attention."

I swallowed hard, trying to rid myself of the insecurity I felt. That little voice had piped up again, telling me he should be with her. "How...how do you feel about her?"

His immediate, malignant response took me by surprise. "I despise her."

I blinked, failing to understand. "Why?" Maybe he didn't want to have a child with her, but it didn't make him any less responsible for their situation than she was.

Lines set deep in his forehead as he took a deep breath, and I felt the undercurrent of hatred as he spoke of her.

"She got pregnant on purpose, Melanie. I made it clear I have no interest in her, but she won't leave me alone. She wants money, and she's using this baby as a pawn." He grimaced, his eyes pained as they searched mine for understanding.

I was horror-struck. Did people really do stuff like that?

Suddenly, any trace of envy I had for her was gone.

The only way I knew to give him comfort was to draw him closer, to murmur that I was sorry. In our separation, we had both made such destructive choices.

He held me, his voice urgent as he whispered against my ear, "She's going to try to tear us apart. Don't let her."

I shook my head buried in the crook of his neck, reminding him of the promise I'd made to him two days ago when I'd pledged him my life. "Forever."

His breath washed across my face as he placed a small kiss below my ear. "Forever."

With our confidence restored, the stress dissipated, and we settled back into our easy conversation as we shared a bowl of vanilla ice cream and a pile of fortune cookies.

Daniel smiled at the weathered Asian woman who dropped off our check, wishing her a good night, before he slid from his chair, watching me intently as I followed suit. The moment I stood, he stepped to me and placed a hand on each of my hips, drawing me to him. His kiss was no longer sweet and playful, but filled with a hunger that set me off kilter. I suddenly wished we were somewhere a little less public. His hands traveled farther down my sides until they found the heated, bare skin of my legs, and he hooked his thumbs under the hem of my skirt. His voice came low and pleading as he asked, "My place?"

Chapter Twenty

That dress.

I sped down the street, failing to keep my eyes on the road. Instead, they continually traveled back to the place where Melanie's creamy, white flesh flowed from *that* dress and met my black leather seats. She was trying to kill me. I'd nearly had a heart attack when I'd seen what she was wearing.

Thankfully I'd parked two houses down from the Preston's when I'd arrived to pick her up for our date. When I'd stepped from my car, I'd almost not seen the car speeding down the street. But as soon as I had, I'd recognized Nicholas immediately and retreated to my car, ducking down in the seat. I'd felt so helpless. I'd wanted to confront him, to protect Melanie from him, to jump from my car and tell him she was mine, but I could do nothing. So I'd hidden like a coward.

He probably wouldn't have noticed me anyway. His only concern was Melanie's car parked in the Preston's driveway. I couldn't see his face, but even from a distance, I could see the anger rolling from him. I had no idea what he intended, what Melanie had told him, or what he knew. All I could do was wait, helpless, while someone else protected my girl. It sucked.

I'd watched while he stood on the porch and talked to someone for a few minutes before leaving, angrier than when he had arrived.

When I'd finally made it inside their house, I was shaken. The only thing on my mind was Melanie's safety, and it wasn't until she'd stepped away from me to get her coat and purse that I'd noticed what she wore. It was single-handedly the most arousing thing I'd ever seen.

Melanie had always been breathtakingly beautiful, but she'd grown into the most stunning woman I'd ever seen. I'd spent the evening dueling with my self-control. My body was hyperaware of her every move, the way she'd cross and uncross her legs under the table, her leg brushing up against mine as she did. My blood slowly simmered, building to a rolling boil. I'd managed to keep myself restrained until Melanie slid from the booth, and then it was all over. I had to touch, to feel where light met dark. Her skin was like fire against my fingertips. I'd never left a restaurant so fast in my life.

Now I found myself trying to focus on the road in front of me. It was nearly impossible as Melanie tried to inconspicuously rub her thighs together. Her fingers kneaded the leather, her breath still heavy as she unabashedly stared at me from her seat. I glared at the hem of her dress, silently cursing it for taunting me all night.

She pulled the hem down. "Don't look at me like that. I had to borrow something from Katie."

I couldn't help but grin at her, a small laugh escaping as I shook my head. She couldn't be more off base.

"No, baby, I like the dress." I was just going to like it much, much more in a pile on my bedroom floor. "You look...really good." *Too good.* She relaxed when I reached out and gently tugged a fistful of the material to show her just how much I liked it.

Pulling into the parking garage, I swung the car into my spot. I jumped out and rushed around, nearly dragging Melanie from the car in my excitement to get her upstairs. A shiver ran up my spine with the sound of her pealing laughter as she raced to keep up with me. Her face was radiant. She giggled and her brown curls bounced against her shoulders as she struggled to keep up. Absolutely exquisite.

In one fluid movement, I spun her into a little half twirl, guiding our arms over her head before I drew her back to my chest. I nuzzled my nose in her hair as we slowly swayed to the rhythm of our pounding hearts in an impromptu dance.

The elevator chimed and we stepped forward. The resounding energy bounding between us was nearly insufferable in the tight quarters. My hands were firm on her stomach as I drew her to me. Reaching up, she grasped me by the back of the neck. Soft fingers played, pulling, tugging, massaging. My sudden lightheadedness had nothing to do with the elevator ride to the twenty-first floor. The door opened, and I took her hand to lead her out. "Ready?"

My nerves flared as I prepared to show her where I lived. Would this be our home? I unlocked the door, and she stepped in. Her face was thoughtful as she assessed the large, open space. Her words from long ago rang out, *"It would never be home unless you're here in it with me,"* and I knew it didn't matter. Wherever we lived, it would be home simply because we were together.

I watched as she explored my apartment, running her fingertips along the throw pillows on the couch, inspecting the art on the walls. Whenever she recognized the few things from our house, a faint smile would grace her lips. She pulled one of the photo albums from the bookshelf, gasping when she saw most of the pictures were of her.

In a blink, a tear rushed down her cheek. I cautiously came up behind her. "I told you I never let you go."

"I know. This was just unexpected." She flipped through the pages, smiling through her tears, every few seconds glancing at me when she'd come across one that seemed to provoke a particularly fond memory. "This is amazing, Daniel. I can't believe you have these..."

Her hand froze when she came to the last. "You have this, too?" She looked up at me with shocked wonder as she asked about the one picture I had of Eva, the one Mom had snapped the first time I'd held her. I nodded before realizing what Melanie had said.

"Wait, you have this picture? How?"

"There was this box from the hospital; it was filled with a bunch of get well cards and stuff. I found it under my bed in Dallas. I have no idea how it even got there." She shook her head. "Anyway, this was in there. I found it the day..." She closed her eyes, her voice tapering off.

"What day?" I reached out to stroke her cheek, encouraging her to open up to me.

"The day I went back for you...I saw it and knew I had to go."

"Melanie," I breathed out as a whisper. I took the album from her and set it aside, wrapped her up in my arms. She buried her head in my chest.

"It's okay, Daniel. I'm just thankful to have had it...to have a face to put with Eva's memory."

God, I couldn't even imagine what she must have felt when she found it. I could remember Eva's face, the way she felt in my arms, the way she smelled, even the little sounds she made. But Melanie only had the small picture. "I'm so sorry, sweetheart. I wish you would have seen her."

"Me too."

"Can you believe we would have had a nine-year-old by now?" I barely choked out the sentence, and Melanie's arms tightened around my waist.

"She would have been amazing. Smart and sweet. She would have had your eyes," she said as she pulled back to look at me with glistening eyes and a wistful smile.

"And your hair." I ran my hands through her hair, twisting my fingers through the curls as I imagined it on a little girl with my eyes.

It felt so good to comfort her, to talk to her, to finally feel like the man I was supposed to be—one that was there for his family. This was what Melanie needed—what I needed—to mourn together over our lost daughter. Yeah, it was nine years late, but it was necessary and surprisingly welcome.

Melanie stepped back, released a heavy breath, and shook herself off. Squeezing my hand, she whispered, "Thank you."

I tucked her hair behind her ear, touched her face. "I needed that as much as you, Melanie."

Her face lit in understanding, and she graced me with a small, peaceful smile. Somehow that heavy moment had left us feeling light and free.

"Would you like a glass of wine?" I asked.

"Please." She nodded.

I kissed her on the corner of her mouth before making my way to the kitchen where I selected a bottle of red wine and dug through the drawer to find an opener.

Melanie sank into the couch. She relaxed against the plush pillows, her legs drawn up under her.

"So, what do you think of the place?" I gestured around the room, watching closely for her reaction. I knew it was nice by most people's standards. The kitchen was sleek and modern, sharp lines and high ceilings making a perfect flow into the attached living room. Brown leather couches sat almost intrusively on the beige carpet, situated around the flat screen TV that rested on the entertainment console in the corner. She hadn't seen the rest of it, only missing the bedroom and a small office. Her gaze went almost immediately to the view of the Chicago lights glinting through floor to ceiling windows that opened to the balcony. To me it was the most inviting part of the whole place.

"It's beautiful," she said.

I didn't know if she was simply referring to the view or the apartment. Even after all the work Erin and Mom had put into it, I had found it cold and hollow. But with Melanie on my couch, it suddenly felt warm. A place I would look forward to coming home to at the end of the day only because she would be here, waiting for me. Her eyes still focused outside, and her brow creased as she continued to think. She turned back to face me expectantly, as if I should know what she was thinking.

I had no clue.

"I'm thinking you're going to need to move."

I should have expected that. This place was nothing like the little house I'd bought for us. It had been perfect for her, for us, but that was when we were going to have a family. I just didn't know if she still wanted something like that.

"That's fine. We'll move wherever you want." I grabbed two glasses on my way back and settled in beside her. Pouring each of us a glass, I handed Melanie hers before taking my own. I mirrored her pose, my elbow perched against the back of the couch and one leg tucked up under me, our knees overlapping.

"Maybe a little house out by my parents?" If I knew Melanie, she'd want to be near them. I couldn't contain the excitement I felt at that thought—Melanie and my family. I could hardly wait for them to be together again, but I would need to give that some time. Sneaking around was proving hard enough, let alone adding my family to the mix.

"Not for me, Daniel. I would be perfectly happy here just because I'm with you." She shifted and reached out to brush her fingertips along the top of my knuckles. "I meant you're going to need a different place for your son."

My son. Who could imagine two words could sting so much? My son. Not our son. But Daniel's son. Vanessa's son. Would I ever be able to think of him and not feel sick?

The worst part was that Melanie was the one making me aware of my responsibility to him. Moving had never even crossed my mind, but as I looked around my apartment, I couldn't imagine a child being here.

Really, though, could I see that child anywhere? In any aspect of my life? Not at all. And that terrified me.

"Will you help me?" It was clear I was asking a lot more of her than help finding an acceptable place for us to live. I hated putting so much pressure on her, the responsibility I was asking her to take on, passing my mistake on to her. She'd promised that whatever came our way, we'd deal with together, but this was different; I wasn't just asking her to tolerate it, I was asking her to be a part of it.

Her muscles tensed slightly. If I hadn't been watching her so closely, I would have missed it. The sorrow that invaded her passed just as quickly as it had come. When it was gone, an expression of determination took its place. "You know I'll be here for you."

"You are the most remarkable person. Do you know that?" I didn't wait for an answer, knowing she was likely to disagree. I lightly brushed my lips against hers and silently thanked her for being an amazing woman.

She rewarded me by unfolding her gorgeous legs and leaning against me. I turned to recline against the arm of the couch and stretched out my legs so she could settle between them.

It was perfect, her hair bunched up over my shoulder, her fingertips playing along my pant leg, her body draped over mine as we shared the bottle of wine. I mindlessly twisted a lock of her hair around my finger, the curl eternal as I wound it round and round.

She glanced back at me, her eyes alight with joy. "I'm so proud of you, Daniel. I always knew you were going to be an amazing doctor."

I squeezed her hip, kissing the top of her head. "It's Dad who made it all happen. I'm just glad he asked me to be a part of it."

"What's it like having all of these sick people come to you? I mean, is it what you thought it would be?"

"Hmm...I don't know. Sometimes I love it, sometimes I hate it. There's so much pressure. It can be very sad and very rewarding all in the same day."

She nodded. "I can only imagine."

We continued to drink and laugh as she asked me questions about my job, what school had been like, and the things I'd done with my family over the years. She giggled as I told her of all the mistakes I'd made along the way and the crazy things I'd witnessed on my ER rotation in New York City. So much had seemed insignificant through the haze of nothing I'd lived. Now, with my girl in my arms, her body shaking as she laughed, I could almost see what life would have been like had she been there. As she experienced my life through the stories I told, it felt as if I was experiencing it for the first time myself.

By the time she'd told me about the important events in her life over the last nine years, the bottle was polished off, and we were both totally at ease. We grinned from ear to ear, neither attempting to hide our bliss.

Melanie suddenly rolled, bringing us chest to chest, her lips on mine. The movement rekindled the fire that had been smoldering the entire night. Her mouth was hot and a little bit sloppy. Her hands pressed firmly into my shoulders as she held herself over me. She straddled my legs, the energy consuming, forceful, pushing us together. I dove my fingers into her hair, kissed her hard. She fumbled through the buttons of my shirt, unwilling to break our frantic kiss.

I pushed her back, and Melanie groaned in protest. I stood and pulled her with me, my mouth immediately taking hers again as we stumbled blindly to my room.

The light from the bathroom shed a faint glow across the room. I spun her, edging her back, anxious to see her lying across my bed.

I watched as she scooted back, her creamy skin in perfect contrast to the thick, black comforter. Her hair spilled all around her face as she lay back against my pillow, the gold chain around her neck a reminder of our forever.

There was no hesitation as I climbed onto the bed, losing the shirt hanging from my shoulders in the process. I devoured her mouth, neck, arms, anything I could find, my hands as greedy as my mouth.

Snaking my hand under her dress, I pushed it higher, revealing her inch by inch. With her arms outstretched above her, I pulled it over her head and tossed it to the floor where it belonged.

"Make love to me, Daniel."

Those words shot straight through me. Quickly, I shed the rest of my clothes. Her fingers sank into my back as I sank into her. Our bodies moved unhurried, slow and hard and absolutely perfect.

I was in complete ecstasy until I saw her wrist, the skin contused and so carefully concealed behind the large silver cuff.

He hurt her.

My beautiful girl continued to move beneath me, her eyes closed, lost in a sea of pleasure while I looked down at her in horror, the reality hitting me hard.

She had stayed because of him. Not because of her mom. Not because of Katie and Shane. Not because of some stupid building. But because she was scared of *him.*

I couldn't make sense of the emotions running through me, emotions that I poured out on Melanie as I abruptly wrapped her up in my arms. I fought to erase any space between us, my arms urgent as I mashed her chest against mine, unable to get her close enough.

I was consumed with jealousy and hatred, the need to destroy. It all mixed with my love, my need to protect, to keep her secure. Both of those desires melted into one. All I knew was that he hurt my girl, and he was going to pay.

"Hey." A delicate hand brushed back my hair, stroking, easing, calming. "Come back to me." Melanie's eyes burned into mine, searching the storm, caressing the creases that had gathered on my forehead. Her expression washed in relief when my eyes came back into focus.

I kissed her gently, struggling to keep the rage at bay. I wouldn't let Nicholas take this moment, too.

All the hate and fear and dread I felt were channeled into my love, my desire, my need to make her whole. I allowed myself to hear every contented sound that dropped from her lips, every whimper, every tiny moan. I allowed myself to feel every tremble, every twitch, every roll of pleasure traveling through her body.

With each one, I silently promised to keep her safe, to protect her, and to never allow that bastard to hurt her again.

❧

I rolled to the side and snuggled behind her, reaching down to drape the sheet over us. I kissed the exposed skin of her shoulder and back. Shivers rolled down her spine as she relaxed into me.

"I love you." I hugged her tighter, stressing how much I meant it. She let out a satisfied sigh, and she drew my arm more firmly around her. I took a deep breath, preparing myself for what was sure to be a battle. "I can't let you go back there, Melanie."

I couldn't see her face, but I could feel her muscles tense. Running my hand down her arm to her wrist, I brought it to my lips, placing gentle kisses along the bruised skin. "He hurt you," I said against the black and blue.

Her pulse quickened under my palm, and I knew she was going to resist. "Daniel," she said as she released a heavy breath, "you have to."

I shook my head into her hair. "You're not safe there."

"You have to trust me on this. I know what I'm doing." Her voice was strong, completely unexpected. She rolled over to face me, her body flush against mine. "This is the best way."

My mouth opened and closed as I struggled to find the right words to argue her logic.

"You don't know him like I do." Her expression was intense, pleading. "Please...just...*don't*."

What was I supposed to say to that?

In frustration, I raked a hand through my hair. Why did she have to be so stubborn? She was placing herself at risk. And for what? She was afraid he was going to hurt her, so she put herself in the very position where he *could* hurt her. It didn't make any sense.

"I know what you're thinking, Daniel. It's not stupid. I have a plan."

I opened my mouth to tell her just how stupid it actually was, when the doorbell rang. Melanie's eyes widened with fear, and she jerked up in bed, pulling the sheet higher and tighter around herself as if it were a shield.

I took her face in my hands, forcing her to look at me. "Baby, it's okay. Just stay here and be quiet."

On the inside, I was terrified. If he found her here, I could only imagine what would happen.

Sifting through the clothes on the floor, I found my underwear and pulled them on as fast as I could. I tossed Melanie my button up, figuring it would provide more coverage than her dress. I pressed my index finger to my lips before I walked from the room and shut the door behind me.

Whoever was there impatiently knocked on the door, spiking my nerves. I tentatively crossed the floor, peeking through the small hole.

Erin.

I breathed a sigh of relief, before a whole new set of worries flooded me. Was Melanie ready for this? Today had been such an incredibly draining day, filled with so many emotions and issues, and we still had a ton to work through. Surely it was best we resolved some of those issues before we faced our families.

Not to mention that Melanie probably wouldn't want to be discovered under these circumstances.

Resolved to tell Erin I was busy and get rid of her as quickly as possible, I swung the door open before she could use her key to unlock it. Grinning, my baby sister flung herself into my arms. "Daniel."

"Hey." I hugged her tight before taking two steps back and planting my feet to block her entrance. "What are you doing here? I didn't even know you were in town."

"I came in at the last minute. A couple of houses came on the market this week that my realtor wanted me to see. I wanted to stop by to say hi before I went to Mom and Dad's." She stepped forward, but I didn't back down.

Glancing up and down at me, she frowned as if just noticing that I was standing there in nothing but my boxers. Her voice lowered as she studied me, "You're not alone, are you?"

My lips tightened into a line, and I pushed out a sigh as I shook my head.

She scowled and narrowed her eyes, hissing under her breath, "What the hell is wrong with you, Daniel? Haven't you learned anything? God, you're so stupid. Look at what happened..." Erin's face paled, and she clapped her hand over her mouth as her other reached out to push me aside.

I glanced over my shoulder. Melanie stood in the doorway to my bedroom, clad in nothing but my dark blue shirt.

Erin looked at me, her eyes wild, shocked, confused—hurt. For some reason, I felt that I had to confirm the obvious, silently nodding as I allowed a small smile to spread across my face. Erin dug her fingers into my arm. I couldn't tell if she was angry or faint. They remained silent as they studied each other. Slowly, they advanced toward one another, cautious, each unsure of where the other stood.

All it took was Melanie reaching out a shaky hand for them to end up in an embrace.

"You two have some explaining to do."

⁂

I clutched the steering wheel, willing myself to breathe as I watched her drive away.

We'd spent more than an hour with Erin. She wanted to know everything, bristling as we told her about the events that had driven us apart. It was obvious their wounds would easily heal. There would be no grudges kept, no resentment over what the other had not known.

Erin finally left, but only after receiving a promise that I would join her and Mom in the morning for breakfast. I agreed, both anxious to spend time with my family and to get her out the door. All I wanted was to continue the earlier conversation with Melanie.

As it turned out, I was weak and incapable of standing my ground when Melanie insisted she needed to see through what she'd started. I didn't want to let her go, yet I realized that if I made her stay, it would be against her will, and I didn't want to be anything like that asshole. I refused to be the guy who wouldn't let her make her own decisions. It left me stuck between doing what I *knew* was right and what she *felt* was right.

In the end, I had relented with the stipulation that if he hurt her again, that would be it—and that we wouldn't drag this shit out. She promised it was already working as proven by his sudden presence at the Preston's this evening. She was positive she would only need to stay a few weeks.

The moment she was gone, fear saturated my every thought. Would he be waiting up for her when she got home? What if he hurt her? I mean, really hurt her. I couldn't fathom it.

I was on the road to her house before I even realized what I was doing. I had to ensure she was safe. If she felt as if she had to stay there, fine, but she didn't have to do it alone.

I must have driven faster than Melanie, because the garage door had just touched down behind her car when her house came into view.

Hopefully, Nicholas was already asleep. It was late—the green glow from the dash displayed "two-thirteen."

Only the trees rustled in the wind and a dog barked in the distance. Other than that, it was complete and total silence. My mind buzzed as I listened for Melanie. I strained to feel her as she moved around the darkened house. Two dim lamps illuminated the porch, casting black shadows across the face of the white mansion.

A light flickered on in a downstairs window. I reasoned it was the same room we'd shared just two days ago. Somehow, that gave me a bit of comfort.

I reached for my phone and typed a quick message to let her know I was right outside if she needed me. She responded only seconds later that she was safe and bid me a goodnight. I wished her the same, pressed send, and sent my heart with it. I waited until darkness swallowed the house before I forced myself to drive away.

Erin and Mom tried to keep me sufficiently distracted after they'd coerced me into joining them in their search for a new house for Erin. I just couldn't say no, not after how unbelievably happy Mom had been when Erin *accidentally* let it slip about what she'd walked in on last night. It was as if the worry of years had been erased from Mom's face in one passing moment. Of course, when I had to explain our circumstances, a completely new set of concerns faced her.

I spent the morning as a backseat passenger, only offering my opinion when asked as I followed Mom and Erin house-to-house and room-to-room.

After what seemed like hours, we were finally headed to the last place on the list. We were exhausted, and Erin was no closer to a decision than when we'd first started. I blocked out the conversation happening ahead of me as we followed a path across a small grassy yard and ascended three steps. My thoughts were twenty miles away, wondering what Melanie was doing. I stared at my feet as I crossed the wooden porch, wishing she were here. I collided into Erin's back. My mind was so far away, I didn't even notice Erin and Mom had stopped in the doorway. Startled, I caught her, muttering an apology. I became aware they were both wide-eyed as they looked back at me, their mouths slightly agape. I frowned and glanced around the room. My heart stuttered as I processed the sight in front of me.

I braced myself against the doorframe to keep myself from falling.

It was so similar to our little house, but more than that, it *felt* the same.

Erin fidgeted beside me, and Mom stood there in silence, giving me time. Both knew what that house had meant to me. They knew I had wanted to raise a family there, had wanted to fill it with laughter and love. Instead, I had tainted it with my mistakes—left the bed defiled. I had simply walked out the front door and never returned. Mom had dealt with clearing out my things. She'd kept what she knew I would want—what I would eventually treasure—even if I couldn't bear to look at them at that time. Then she sold the house to the first person who made an offer. I'd just wanted to be rid of it. It had held all of the hopes of a life that was shattered, and I couldn't bear that it had become a reminder of what would never be.

Mom's soft, warm hand slipped into mine, and I glanced down at her as she nodded her wordless encouragement.

ಯಾ

The rest of the weekend proved to be tortuous, simply because of Melanie's absence. With Nicholas home through the weekend, we were left with texts and one quick call spread out over too much time. By the time Monday morning rolled around, my spirit was rumbling, demanding hers.

I glanced at the clock. Still two hours before lunch. Plenty of time to finish what I needed to do at the office before I could take off for the rest of the afternoon.

I dialed Melanie's number, praying she could get away. It only took one ring before my body buzzed. Even the sound of her voice had a physical effect on me.

"Hey," she whispered in a breathy voice.

"Hey, baby. Can you get away for a couple of hours?"

"Of course." Her answer was immediate, always as anxious as I was.

"Meet me at my office at noon?"

"Yeah...I'll be there…love you."

"Mmm, love you, too. See you soon." I hung up smiling, eager to see my girl. I settled into work to square things away so I could enjoy the afternoon with her. So wrapped up in work, sorting through the seemingly endless piles of paper, I jumped when my phone buzzed in my pocket. I chuckled when I saw the name on the screen for the tenth time since Saturday.

"Hey, Mom." She was thrilled, beside herself with anticipation, wondering if I'd talked to Melanie and when I was taking her to see the house. I laughed, saying I hoped I'd be able to take her there this afternoon, yes, I was nervous, and no, I didn't regret it—yet.

I just hoped it wouldn't be the wrong kind of reminder, one that would take Melanie back to the place where we had lost each other. I prayed it would be a reminder of the hope we'd had for our future, the future that we would now be able to share. I knew there would be a gaping hole where Eva should have been, but it still felt right. The energy had been there, working in full force, and I had to take the chance.

The direct line from Lisa rang, and I asked Mom to hold on a sec.

I picked up the receiver on my desk. "Yes?"

"Hi...Dr. Montgomery. You have a visitor." I glanced at the clock. It was eleven minutes to twelve. Melanie was a few minutes early.

"Send her in." I grinned and hung up. Turning my attention back to Mom, I smiled as I anticipated my girl walking through the door. "Hey, Mom, I have to go..."

My mouth seized mid-sentence and sweat gathered at my forehead. I should have been paying more attention, but I'd been distracted by the conversation with Mom and thoughts of Melanie. My body hadn't kicked in fast enough to tell me she wasn't there.

But Vanessa was.

I hadn't seen Vanessa since that fateful night. I had relied on correspondence from my attorney and ignored all her calls and texts. I didn't want to talk to her, see her, or deal with her.

She apparently didn't get the picture, because she entered my office and closed the door behind her. She turned to me, her chin held high as she eyed me with confidence.

I desperately tried to avoid looking at her stomach. The large protuberance seemed to mock me. Vanessa's tight white T-shirt clung to the swollen mound, demanding I acknowledge what I'd done, but my entire being rejected it.

My voice cracked when I regained enough mental function to speak, leaving me with a strangled stream of words. "What...what the hell are you doing here?"

Vanessa's blue eyes flashed fire, and then she forced a smile, artificially sweet. "You weren't returning my calls, so I decided to stop by and pay you a little visit."

I stared at her, willing myself to control my temper. "I told you I didn't want to hear from you unless it was something directly related to the baby, and for that, you can go through my lawyer. I trust you have his number?" My voice took on a condescending edge as I watched her resolve waver, her eyes darting to her feet before she looked back at me.

"Daniel." She sighed, disheartened. "Why can't you give us a chance? Let's be friends and see where it goes. I don't want to raise this baby alone."

Was she serious?

"First of all, I don't want to be your friend. Second, you're not going to be raising him by yourself. He's going to be with me half the time. This," I said, pointing back and forth between the two of us, "isn't going to happen."

"Well, Daniel, in case you'd forgotten, *this* already happened!" She rubbed both hands over her belly, emphasizing the biggest mistake I'd ever made. "And you really didn't seem to mind it then, did you? Don't you think it's time you stepped up and acted like a man instead of leaving me alone to deal with all of this by myself?"

A brief wave of guilt roll through me before remembering her that night. I wasn't the selfish one. She had made a choice for me, a choice that would affect me for the rest of my life.

I pointed at her stomach, my disdain wiping away every trace of sympathy I'd had. "That was your fault," I hissed, the pent up hatred and blame I felt for her pouring freely, "You did this." I shoved my finger closer. "And I never wanted this...so don't you dare come in here and tell me how I should be handling it! I don't want anything to do with you, Vanessa." I stormed across the room and flung the door open. "Now get out of my office and don't come back." I leveled my eyes at her, the threat clear in my voice.

Chapter Twenty-One

As soon as I walked through the door, I knew something was wrong. The feeling was just…off. I could feel him—the energy—but it was frenzied and distressed.

I looked toward Daniel's secretary for some kind of indication. Her eyes grew wide when she recognized me. We both turned when we heard Daniel's heated voice. I'd *never* heard him speak like that to anyone. I rushed to his office, panicked and unable to comprehend what would draw a reaction like that from him. My feet felt momentarily disconnected from my body, and I fought to stay upright when I saw Vanessa. The sight of her was like a punch in the gut, a knife to the chest. In a fleeting moment, it all came upon me, crushing, crashing, pulsing—uncertainty, resentment, jealousy, the baby—*his* baby.

I couldn't see, couldn't breathe. Anxiety rippled through me, nipping my nerves, tearing me down, taunting me with what I could not have. Would it always be there, lurking and begging for release? How could I still feel this way after everything we'd been through? After what he'd said and what he'd shown? How could there be any lingering doubt?

"This is why you don't want me? I knew it. You're really going to take this slut over me? *I'm* the one carrying your child."

Somehow her spiteful words that were meant to cut me down offered me a reason for conviction. Suddenly, it became clear. Those destructive thoughts and words had no place in me, because I knew he would take me over her, over anyone else. For the first time, I truly believed it.

"You know nothing about me...nothing about Daniel." I reached for him, drawing strength. "You know nothing about us or what we've been through. Now I believe Daniel asked you to leave."

I didn't back down as she looked between us, her eyes imploring as they raked over Daniel, probing for any uncertainty.

I could almost feel her blood run cold when she found none. Her face grew pallid as her resolve faded, her body sagging in defeat when she realized she'd lost the game she'd been playing. I couldn't take my eyes from her as she walked away, taking with her every last trace of insecurity I'd ever felt. My heart nearly stopped when I saw Daniel's face. He looked at me as if he had just found the treasure he'd spent his life searching for, his mouth reverent as his lips traveled over the back of my hand. He was proud of me.

"Come on, I have something to show you."

"What?" I grinned.

I followed him into his office. He grabbed his keys and jacket and led me back down the hallway.

"It's a surprise." His eyes gleamed.

I snuggled into his side, relaxing as I looked forward to time with Daniel. As long as I was with him, I didn't care what it was. It could only be good. Wrapping his arm around my shoulder, he drew me closer. I glanced up just in time to anticipate his kiss, his smile wide when he pulled away.

Daniel introduced me to Lisa, his office manager. I was a bit mortified to meet her after the behavior she'd witnessed the last time I was here, but her welcome was genuine, and I couldn't help but return her warm smile. Daniel gave her a few instructions for the rest of the afternoon before taking my hand and pulling me out the door.

I sank into the warmth of the heated seats, relishing the soothing pulse of our energy as Daniel and I traveled. He kept stealing glances at me, a contented smile on his face. We rode in an easy silence with only the sound of soft muted music and the purr of the engine as we sped down the open road.

"That's my parents' exit." He lifted his hand from my leg to point to the road we passed. I peered out the window, imagining what it was going to be like to see them again. Reuniting with Erin the other night had been healing. Losing her had been devastating, only eclipsed by the hole Daniel's absence had left. It was as if when each of them came back into my life, a piece was put back into place, filling me, making me whole. I couldn't wait to fill the spot forever reserved for Patrick and Julia.

"You miss them?" His voice was soft, concerned, his soul attentive to the ache coming from my heart.

"Very much." I didn't realize I was getting emotional until I heard my choppy voice.

"Melanie, sweetheart, I don't want to pressure you. Say no if you're not ready for this yet...but they really want to see you."

"They know?"

"Yeah." He nodded, watching me apprehensively.

Daniel told me of how Patrick had seen me the day I had come to the office and the conversation they had had afterward. And of course, now that Erin knew, Julia knew.

"I'd thought it would be better to wait..." The sudden break in his sentence allowed me to fill in what was left unsaid, *Until you're not married anymore.* He raked a hand through his hair as if the very thought seemed to cause him distress. "But I just can't see keeping you from them. Erin is coming back this weekend, and she's kind of made...plans." He looked across at me, both hopeful and scared of my reaction. "She wants us all to have dinner at my parents' house."

I guess I had thought it was better to wait, too, but really it just didn't make sense anymore. Everyone knew about Nicholas. Did I wish I were coming back into this relationship under different circumstances? Absolutely. But they loved me and I loved them, and a legal document couldn't change that, not any more than it could change what Daniel and I had. In my heart, he'd always been my husband and they'd always been my family. My marriage was nothing more than a sham, a cover for an indentured servant.

"I'd like that."

He blew out a sigh of relief and squeezed my leg in a silent thank you.

I looked back out at the road when he slowed for the next exit. I felt a vague sense of *déjà vu* as we pulled up in front of a small white house framed by tall expansive trees. Winter had left the branches bare and they scraped across the pitched roof of the house. The porch jutted out into the yard as if in greeting. Welcoming. Everything about the house was simple and plain, completely unassuming.

It was wonderful and perfect and heartbreaking, because I knew what Daniel felt when he saw it. I had told him he needed to get a new house for his son, but he hadn't. Instead, he'd gotten a new house for me.

A black-haired woman in her mid-forties, dressed in a business suit, stepped from a silver luxury SUV parked in the driveway. She shielded her eyes with her hand, squinting as she looked toward Daniel's car and waited for us to get out.

"It's okay if you don't want it, Melanie." Daniel's voice broke through the silence in the car, soft and uncertain. I turned to him. His hazel eyes burned into mine, searching my soul. I allowed the emotion to come, didn't fight the moisture that filled my eyes. I looked back at the house, drawn to it and terrified all at the same time. I forced myself to—just—get out of the car.

The realtor introduced herself before taking a step back when she saw the expression on my face. She seemed relieved to switch her attention to Daniel as he shook her hand. Silently we followed her up the walkway. I braced myself as she slid the key into the lock and turned the knob. My breath escaped me when the door slowly drifted open. It was not the same—not at all—but it *felt* the same.

And it would have hurt if it hadn't have felt so right.

Silent tears ran down my face as I felt the pull bounding around the room, insisting that I stay. I knew I looked as if I was breaking down, falling apart, but it was completely the opposite. I was coming together. It was as if I had ended up in the same spot I'd been torn from so long ago.

At the same time, everything was so messed up. It made my head spin.

From behind, Daniel wrapped his strong arms around my shoulders and pulled me against his chest, his heart pounding against my back as he rocked us. He leaned in and whispered his remorse near my ear, "Baby, I'm so sorry. It was stupid. I should have thought. I should have known. It just felt...*right*."

I wanted to tell him so many things. I wanted to tell him how wonderful he was. I wanted to praise his extraordinary heart, his perfect soul. I wanted to tell him that this meant as much to me as it did to him. Instead, I whispered the only thing I could manage, "It *is* right."

He exhaled heavily, his rigid muscles easing as his arms slid down to my waist. Intertwining our fingers, he hugged me tightly, never letting go while we continued to sway.

Neither of us wanted to move, the moment sublime. Daniel reluctantly pulled away when we realized how awkward it had to be for the realtor. Her back was to us as she stared blankly out the kitchen window into the backyard.

Daniel brushed his lips along my ear. "I love you." I nodded, and he walked away to speak with her.

I ran my hands through my hair, dried my eyes, and pulled myself together, feeling strong enough to explore this house that had taken hold of me.

It was perfect, except for the glaring void it held because Eva wasn't here.

And I desperately tried to see *him* here, to picture a crib in the corner of the small bedroom or a highchair beside the dining room table. I strained to hear the laughter of a child as he ran down the wooden floors of the hallway, to see him playing in the backyard. Instead, there was nothing.

I wanted to feel—needed to feel—because I had promised Daniel I would do this with him, but I didn't think I'd even begun to grasp how that child was going to rip my heart out.

ණ

My nerves were out of control. With shaky hands, I stuffed a pair of pajamas and change of clothes into an overnight bag.

I'd seen Daniel every day this week. Every morning I'd anticipate his call to meet him for lunch, and I'd race to meet him as soon as I got word. We'd hold hands as we walked the streets, sharing all of our favorite places, telling stories we'd forgotten we had. And at the end of the day, we'd always find ourselves back at his apartment.

I was playing a dangerous game of cat and mouse with Nicholas, teetering on the line between accomplishing the goal I'd set and exposing what was going on between Daniel and me. I knew Nicholas would eventually find out about us, but I hoped that I would be long gone before that happened.

Nicholas had been watching my every move, studying me as I moved about the house. I knew that I wanted him to see a difference, to feel the change that was coming. Still, I couldn't control the instinct to hide it from him. On some level, I'd always been fearful of Nicholas, though I'd never really cared because I'd thought I had nothing to lose.

But now I had to admit to myself I was terrified of him, terrified of what he might destroy. Yet, I pressed on, determined to do this.

I slung the overnight bag over my shoulder and headed downstairs.

It was only five-fifteen and Nicholas was already home. Never in nine years had he been home this early unless he had a real reason to be, and I knew that reason was me. But there was no way I was going to allow his presence to deter my plans for the night. He narrowed his eyes when he noticed the bag draped over my shoulder. "Going somewhere?"

I prayed that he didn't notice the way my muscles flinched under his menacing tone, and I raised my chin to look him straight in the eye. "Katie's. I'll be back in the morning."

I saw the rise of his chest as he breathed in and held it. Anger made a visible ascent up his neck and settled on his reddened face. I could see the war in his eyes as he decided how to best deal with my insubordination. The way his lip twitched and his fists curled—he wanted to tear me apart. Instead, his mouth spread into a cocky, arrogant grin. He cocked his head to the side. "Mmm, I see."

I was pretty sure "I see" meant he could see right through me, but I didn't wait for him to clarify. I escaped the room and his knowing eyes, threw my bag in the car, and left as quickly as possible.

I was suddenly very thankful for the arrangement Katie and I had made earlier. I'd go to her house and change for dinner with Daniel's family, leave my car at the her house, and then she'd drive me to Daniel's to drop me off. I really didn't think I could stomach another near miss with Nicholas.

ꕥ

I rode in Katie's car, hoping I wouldn't be late. My knee bounced as I watched the clock draw nearer to six. Of course, Katie wouldn't allow that. She pulled up in front of Daniel's building at five minutes till. "Thank you so much, Katie. I'm so sorry I have you involved in this." I waved toward Daniel's building, feeling guilty that I was putting her in this situation once again.

"Pssh." She shrugged my concerns off, turning and giving me a quick hug. "You have no idea how happy it makes me to see you like this." She laughed. "Plus, Nicholas is pissed, right? I mean, how much better could this night get?"

I chuckled and shook my head as I gathered my things. "Yeah. Let's just pray he doesn't show up at your house tonight." I stepped onto the curb and leaned in to thank her again before she took off.

I rushed upstairs and rang the doorbell. Almost immediately, Daniel swung the door open as if he'd been waiting on the other side. He wore black dress pants and a maroon button up, the sleeves rolled up his forearms. He never ceased to take my breath away. Smiling, he didn't hesitate to pull me into his arms.

"Hi." I pulled back to see his face, grinning at the joy I found.

"Hey, beautiful." He tugged at one of the curls that brushed against my shoulder as he raked his eyes down my body. He grinned as he took in my charcoal gray cowl neck sweater and black skinny pants. They rested a beat longer on my favorite stiletto boots. "You look stunning."

"Thank you." I loved that he noticed. He was the only one I'd ever wanted to impress.

He grabbed his keys and wallet from the small table beside the door and tucked me into his side. "Ready?"

"Yeah." Really, I couldn't wait.

With Daniel next to me, the forty-minute drive passed faster than I could have imagined. We pulled up in front of the most beautiful house I'd ever seen, both grand and humble. Only the group of people waiting on the portico were more captivating.

I'd anticipated being timid and unsure of myself, insecure of what my place would be, but as soon as I saw their faces, I was gone. My hand was on the door handle before the car came to a complete stop. I hurled myself out and raced into Julia's waiting arms. We crushed each other in our embrace, barely aware that we were both crying and laughing at the same time. It felt amazing to hold this woman who meant so much to me—this woman who had long ago become my mother. We pulled back, just enough to look at each other, to take in the change.

She was every bit as beautiful as she'd always been, her age only adding to her grace. She stepped back and took both of my hands in hers, inspecting me. It reminded me of the way a new mother would take her baby and look her over, count her fingers and toes to make sure she was complete. She pulled me back into a hug. "I'm so glad you're here," she whispered.

I nodded against her and squeezed her once more before turning to Patrick, who'd been standing patiently at her side. I grinned up at him as he reached for me. "Hi, Patrick." I wrapped my arms around his waist and he wrapped his arms around my shoulders. He placed a gentle kiss on my forehead. "Welcome home, Melanie."

As I stood up, I wiped the tears from my eyes before focusing on Erin, who stood behind us. I knew it was taking everything she had to not to rush me and to give me a moment to reunite with the rest of the family. As soon as our faces met, though, neither of us could wait any longer. "I can't believe you're really here," she said, holding me close.

"Shall we head inside? Dinner will be ready in about ten minutes." Julia brushed her fingers over the back of my hand and turned to lead everyone inside, smiling at me over her shoulder as she walked through the door.

I hugged myself as I watched my family follow her inside. Sometimes *this* still didn't seem real.

I dried the last of my tears as I prepared to share a table with them. I sensed him, and I turned to meet the hazel eyes that were burning into the back of my head. Daniel's face was indescribable—breathtaking—as if he'd just seen paradise from where he stood at the bottom of his parents' steps. I reached out to him, my fingers extended, the energy flowing freely in the space between us. His mouth twisted up at the corners as I silently asked him to be by my side. I turned to walk inside, but he stopped me, taking my face in his hands.

He stared intently at me, placing a firm, closed-mouth kiss against my lips. "Thank you."

I beamed up at him and ran the back of my hand over his smooth cheek and down his neck. I nodded in slow acceptance, because while I could object and tell him that I should be the one thanking him, that I was the one benefitting from it all, I knew he was every bit as grateful for my return to this family as I was.

We stepped inside, and I couldn't help but stand in awe. The house was incredible, a perfect flow of past and present as if a person could walk through a museum and still feel at home. I absolutely loved that Julia shared my penchant for antiques. Daniel chuckled and pulled me forward when the particularly charming sideboard in the foyer distracted me. "We'll explore later," he whispered.

I smiled meekly. "Sorry."

The others had already found their seats when we entered the dining room. The conversation was loud and carefree as dishes were passed and plates were filled. When I saw that Julia had made my favorite chicken dish, I cast her a meaningful look across the table. She shrugged though she couldn't hide her smile, clearly gratified I'd noticed her display of affection.

My attention darted back and forth over the table. Everyone took turns sharing stories and filling me in on everything I'd missed in the last nine years. The table was filled with near constant laughter and mirth. The mood only darkened for a few moments when Patrick told of how he had lost his beloved aunt two years before.

I never felt uncomfortable—not once. I'd thought perhaps I would feel somewhat like an outsider, like the second-wife who'd never quite fit in. Instead, it was as if a place at this table had been sitting empty while they awaited my return.

Daniel's touch was never far—his hand on my knee, intertwined with my own, woven through my hair, resting on my neck.

I didn't miss the way his family watched his every move. Patrick's eyes widened when Daniel offered up a different version of the story Erin told, teasing that she could never tell a story without exaggerating it. Patrick's contented expression only grew with each story that they told. Whenever Daniel laughed, Julia become nearly delirious as if she were hearing music for the very first time. And Erin, while she'd always been one of the happiest people I knew, I'd never seen her like this. She absolutely glowed.

It was then I realized this dinner wasn't just welcoming me back but Daniel as well.

For dessert, Julia served coffee and her homemade apple pie. We all fell into a relaxed state, our bodies sated. The easy conversation continued as we sat and sipped our coffee.

Daniel leaned in and whispered in my ear, "You ready for that tour now?"

I grinned, and he stood to help me to my feet. He led me from room to room, giving me time to explore everything. I loved all that Julia had done to create such an amazing home, but I honestly was more drawn to the photos in each room. Some were familiar, ones of Daniel and Erin as children, and it was heartwarming to see them again, jogging old memories of stories I'd heard about their youth. Then there were those I'd never seen, ones of things I'd missed—family vacations, Daniel's graduation from medical school, past Christmases—each a glimpse of a time that had simply stood still for me.

What struck me most was the expression on Daniel's face in every single one, each depicting an empty, hollow man.

Daniel was patient while I examined everything, each piece holding a story that he was happy to share. It was obvious Julia never purchased anything unless it touched her in some way.

Daniel stood behind me with his chin resting on my shoulder, telling me about the painting his parents had acquired on their last trip to Europe for their thirtieth anniversary. It hung proudly on the wall in the upstairs study. It was mesmerizing, capturing the life-long love affair of an aging couple. "I guess Dad saw it and looked at Mom and said, *we're half way there,* and she had to have it."

I couldn't imagine a better anniversary gift, one that was a testament to the love they'd shared and a promise of what was still to come.

The energy swelled between us, both of us caught up in the hope of that kind of love, the kind that Patrick and Julia shared, the kind that lasted forever.

"You about ready to go home?" He pressed a small kiss into my neck, nuzzling his nose into my hair.

I nodded, both reluctant to leave my family and eager to be alone with him.

The night had grown late. Erin bid everyone goodnight and went upstairs, tired from the long day of travel. We told Patrick and Julia goodbye after promising them we would be back soon. Daniel helped me into my jacket before we stepped out into the chilly night air. The second he started the car, I found myself thinking I couldn't wait to get back to his apartment.

The only thing better than falling asleep in Daniel's arms was going to be waking up in them.

Chapter Twenty-Two

"Okay, see you tomorrow. Bye."

"Bye, Melanie."

I hung up with Mom, ringing my hands together, trying to calm myself as it sank in that the day had nearly arrived. The past three weeks had been nothing short of amazing. I had spent every minute I could with Daniel, but I wasn't blind; I knew it was starting to wear on him. It seemed as if he held me a little tighter and kissed me a little longer each time we said goodbye. I took comfort in knowing it was almost over. I'd decided to leave as soon as Mom left after her visit for Thanksgiving.

It had given me the time I needed to put a closure on my previous life and afforded me a week with my mom, one without interruptions, a time when she and I could get to know each other again.

Even though I was incredibly excited to see her, I was nervous and unsure of how to handle things with her. I still carried resentment, even more so now that I'd learned Daniel had gone to Dallas and she'd never let me know. But I was going to do everything in my power to see past all of it and repair our relationship. I knew it was going to be hard dredging up old issues and memories, but it was necessary if we were ever going to get past this. We both needed forgiveness and we both needed to give it. It wouldn't be easy on either account.

The rest of the day was spent transforming the downstairs den into a second guestroom for my mom. Until that moment, I hadn't really even considered the fact that I'd be sleeping apart from Nicholas while she was here. If this didn't give her a clue that my marriage was on the eve of its demise, then nothing short of telling her would, and I wasn't planning to do that until the day she left.

I figured we'd have the beginning of the week to talk—maybe reminisce a little about my childhood. I felt as if we needed to reestablish our connection, reform our mother-daughter bond, and build a belief in our love for each other. Otherwise, I would never trust her enough to go back to our past issues and just ask her why. She could never take back what she had done, but at least she could *explain* why, apologize, and take some responsibility for what she had done. Then maybe—just maybe—I would trust her enough to tell her about Daniel.

I spent the night in a fitful sleep, nodding off only to jolt upright in bed, my body in constant upheaval. I'd study the clock to find only minutes had passed between each unwelcomed arousal, and I was never able to settle into comfort. I'd hoped to sleep away most of the morning, or else I'd be pacing the floors awaiting her arrival. Finally, I gave up and hauled myself out of bed at six-fifteen. The sky was still dark, the roads silent on this early Sunday morning. I wrapped myself in my satin robe. Thanks to the lack of sleep and my frayed nerves, I was all too eager for my morning pot of coffee. It was going to be a very long day.

After Nicholas left to play racquetball, I busied myself with small chores around the house. I hated feeling so agitated. I mean, my *mother* was coming to visit. I should have been thrilled—not weighed down with so much worry and apprehension.

At just after four-thirty, the doorbell rang. I raced across the living room, only to stop in front of the door to give myself an internal pep talk. *It's going to be okay. She wants this as much as you. She's your mother.* My hand trembled against the knob. *Open the damn door, Melanie!* I screamed at myself. I inhaled deeply, finding enough strength to turn the knob, and stood back to allow the door to swing open. I stifled a sob that gathered in my throat when I saw her. My feet were frozen, unable to move as her gaze met mine.

Mom.

I had missed her more than I ever understood until that very moment. She stood in front of me, her hair piled on top of her head and streaked with gray, her waist noticeably thicker, her eyes sad.

"Melanie," she whispered. I could feel her probing, penetrating through my exterior, searching me. There was a peculiar expression on her face as she drank me in.

"Mom."

That was all it took for her to drop her luggage and throw her arms around me. She moved to hold my face in her hands, wiping away my tears produced by the sudden onslaught of affection with her thumbs. It was an affection I'd craved, missed, needed. An affection that came only in a mother's touch. An affection I would never outgrow.

Her words bled heavy and penitent as she told me over and over, "I missed you...I missed you."

"I missed you so much, Mom." I hugged her back hard, clinging to her.

"Sweetheart, I'm so sorry."

I pulled back, shaking my head as I squeezed her hands in mine. "Not yet. I know we need to talk, and we will before you go, but can we please just enjoy each other for a little while?"

She nodded and pulled me to her again. "Whatever you need. But I'm not leaving here until you and I are okay."

I laughed through my tears, nodding, thankful she was here for the same reason I wanted her to be.

I sniffled and shook myself from the overwhelming emotions. "Here, let's get you settled." I helped her gather her bags, handing her one, slinging the other over my shoulder, and pulling the large suitcase behind me.

"Are you tired? I can go and start dinner while you take a little nap."

"Yeah, that sounds great. Are you sure you don't need help with dinner?"

I shook my head. "No, just get some rest. I'll come get you when it's ready." I gave her another quick hug and left her in the makeshift room.

During my day of mania, I'd made meatballs, and now I only needed to make the sauce and noodles for the spaghetti I'd planned. I figured I'd let the sauce simmer for a while to give Mom enough time to recuperate from the long flight.

I found myself at ease in the kitchen, my unrest settled the moment I'd seen Mom. Every worry I'd allowed to work me into a frenzy had been soothed by her very presence and the promise she would stay until we worked things out.

My phone vibrated in the back pocket of my jeans. I smiled because I already knew who it was, his sweet words asking if I was okay.

I looked over my shoulder just to ensure that it was clear, my fingers quick across the small buttons as I told him everything was perfect and I couldn't wait to see him again.

It was surreal just how perfect everything was.

I quickly deleted both messages and tucked the phone back into my pocket. After adding the noodles to the boiling water and stirring the sauce, I set the table and pulled the salad from the fridge. I waited until the last minute to wake Mom.

I popped my head in the door, and she stirred under the blankets when I called to her, "Hey, Mom, dinner's ready."

She looked up, still sleepy-eyed and tired, but her mouth turned up into a wide smile when she realized where she was. She rubbed her palm over her face and through her hair, yawning as she threw back the covers. "Coming."

She excused herself to the restroom to wash up while I went in and placed the food on the table. Nicholas had come home about a half an hour before and I reluctantly went upstairs to call him to dinner. I hadn't made him dinner in weeks, but I couldn't see sitting down to eat without him while Mom was here.

"Peggy." Nicholas walked into the room wearing his carefully crafted façade, the one he wore for those he wanted to impress, for those who he wanted to think more of him than he really was. He pulled her into a condescending embrace, patted her on the back, kissed her cheek. My muscles recoiled as I watched him delude her into believing he was something he was not. I knew it shouldn't bother me that she thought so much of him. She didn't know him, and why should I expect her to? I'd kept her away all this time. Why would she not believe I was happily married, that Nicholas was a good man, and that I wanted to be here?

"So nice to see you again, Nicholas." She forced a smile as she halfheartedly returned his hug, withdrawing quickly to find her seat.

My mouth dropped open as I looked between the two of them. Could I really have been that blind? Had my pain left me in such a haze that I really hadn't seen? All these years, I had believed that Mom loved Nicholas, thought he was perfect for me, thought he was better than Daniel.

But it was clear now that my perception had been skewed because my mom's feelings for Nicholas were unmistakable.

She hated him.

ଓ

"Could you hand me that, sweetheart." Mom pointed to the measuring cup closest to me.

"Sure." I smiled and passed it across the island to her. I turned back to stir the milk into the potatoes and pulled the mixer from the cupboard to whip them. We both moved effortlessly about the kitchen. It was clear that cooking had been a love I'd inherited from my mother, and we'd done a lot of it this week. We'd baked and laughed and talked, finding refuge in the best room of the house. We'd start our day off in here over coffee and breakfast and cap it off with dinner, the two of us growing closer with each meal. We still hadn't had *the talk*, but we knew it was coming. Instead, we savored our time together as mother and daughter, not as two strangers, but as we had been years ago.

She knew something was up. That first night after we'd wished each other goodnight, I'd gone into the bathroom to brush my teeth and get ready for bed, only to find her lingering in the darkened living room. I'd stood fidgeting with the hem of my pajama top, not sure what to do. I'd realized then she was asking me to give her a glimpse into my life—asking me to trust her. I'd walked quietly across the room, my face trained on the floor, and stopped to look back at her as I opened the door to the guestroom. She'd simply given me a single nod of understanding and withdrawn into her room, closing the door behind her. She'd never mentioned it once, though over the week, she'd watched. It was not because she was judging me, condemning me, or finding some fault in my actions. Her eyes were soft and tender as they followed me through the room.

"How's that turkey coming?" Mom grabbed a towel and patted her hands dry, leaning down to peer into the oven over my shoulder.

"Looking pretty good. I'd say we have about another half an hour before we can pull it out."

"Smells good." She placed a loving hand on my shoulder, offering a gentle squeeze as she went back to the green beans simmering on the stove.

I basted the turkey before closing it in the oven, then crossed the kitchen to begin pulling the china from the hutch. Even facing away, I could feel her become rigid, her muscles tighten, her back stiffen.

"Will you ever be able to forgive me?" Her voice was soft—so soft I almost wondered if she'd wanted me to hear. I stilled before lowering the plates to the counter. Resting my hands flat on either side of them, I searched for a way to answer her question. I was still so angry. But after this week, the time we'd spent, the things we'd shared, everything had changed.

"I think I already have."

I felt her release the breath she'd held, and we turned at the same time, ready to finally face the past, only to be interrupted by Nicholas rushing in through the door from the garage. Flashing a fake smile, he declared how delicious everything smelled. My face flushed red, angered by his mere presence. Mom saw my frustration and smiled weakly before she mouthed, "Later," as Nicholas left the room and headed upstairs. I nodded and continued to pull the rest of the dishes out and took them into the dining room to set the table.

"Melanie, sweetie, could you come and help me in here?"

I followed Mom's voice back into the kitchen, finding her struggling to pull the huge turkey from the oven. I giggled at how ridiculous it had been for us to pick such a large turkey for three people.

"Here, let me get that." I nudged her aside and took her mitts. I strained to pull the pan out and wrestled it to the counter. We both fell into a fit of laughter at our physical inadequacy. Mom chuckled as she whispered conspiratorially, "Well, that was the first time I actually wished Nicholas was around."

I looked at her, stunned, before I clapped my hand over my mouth and cracked up all over again. I quickly composed myself when I heard Nicholas coming down the stairs, but I was still snickering under my breath.

"Nicholas." Mom's voice still hinted her amusement. "Would you be a dear and carve the turkey for us?"

Nicholas was far from a dear, and it would have made me cringe had I not known of Mom's contempt for him. She was apparently just a little bit better at hiding it than I was.

"I'd love to."

I couldn't keep from rolling my eyes. Nicholas was the ultimate charlatan.

We all took a seat and filled our plates.

The mood was surprisingly light, even with Nicholas at the table. Mom and I were on a high because of the week we'd spent together and the small breakthrough we'd made earlier that evening. Even Nicholas seemed to enjoy himself, adding small bits to the conversation and acting as if he were a halfway-decent person. Mom had said very little to him the entire week, but with the light climate, she engaged him, chatting about his well-known love of the game of golf.

"So, how's work, Nicholas?"

I choked on the wine I'd just tipped into my mouth, forcing it down my throat, suddenly very uncomfortable with the change of subject.

"It's great...perfect really. You know I've been quite successful in the past, but this year we've exceeded all our goals." His face glowed with pride, his eyes gleaming as he told her of the prosperity soon to befall him. "We just landed the largest contract we've ever had."

God, no. Please, I silently begged as I twisted the fabric napkin tightly around my fingers in my lap.

Mom smirked, Nicholas oblivious as she patronized, "Well, that is quite impressive, Nicholas."

He nodded vigorously, shoving another bite of turkey into his mouth before continuing, "Yeah. It's this huge medical complex."

I closed my eyes, praying for him to stop.

"A new oncology center. It's pretty extravagant...going to make us a ton of money."

"Oh, what kind of oncology?" Mom feigned interest, simply keeping up the conversation, unaware of the trap she was setting for me.

Mom, please, stop. I struggled to think of some way to portray the words to her, but nothing would come.

"Breast cancer. Some big shots that came up with some new treatment..." Nicholas sneered, not covering his distaste, "The Montgomerys."

Mom sputtered, whipping her head around to look at me. "Daniel?" Her eyes were wide from the impact of the name, growing into sheer panic when she took on my expression. Her throat bobbed, and she swallowed hard as if she were trying to reel his name back in.

Nicholas froze, momentarily dumbfounded by her words. He looked back and forth between the two of us before understanding dawned on his face.

"And just how do you know Dr. Montgomery, Peggy?" Nicholas demanded, his face red as he glared at her from across the table.

Her eyes darted to mine, and she quickly shifted them to her lap and said nothing.

Nicholas jumped to his feet, his hands flat on the table as he leaned forward, his attention now directed to me. "How the fuck do you know Daniel Montgomery?" he growled.

I was going to throw up. I squeezed my eyes shut, trying to find some sort of acceptable answer to give him.

He couldn't find out—not like this.

He slammed his fist down on the table. "Tell me!"

I recoiled into the chair, muttering the words into my lap, "He was my baby's father."

I didn't look up until I heard the mocking chuckle. "Well...isn't that sweet."

He looked away, rubbing his fingers over his mouth as he gathered his thoughts, before he turned his attention back to me, trapping me with his eyes while he spoke to Mom. "Peggy, I think you need to give me a moment with my *wife*."

I sat rigidly except for my hands that shook uncontrollably under the table. I stared at the half-eaten plate of food in front of me. Mom's eyes burned into me, pleading for direction on what to do. I was too terrified to acknowledge her. I felt her give up and rise from her chair, her footsteps soft as she walked from the room.

An overwhelming feeling of dread consumed me, my chest convulsing in waves as I tried to hide my fear.

Right then, all I wanted was Daniel. I wanted him to break through the door and save me, to swoop in and rescue me. I wished I'd just listened to him when he'd begged me to leave in the first place. I was so stupid. Now, I'd placed us both in more danger than we ever would have faced otherwise.

I flinched when Nicolas suddenly moved, stalking around the table and grabbing my arm. He dragged me into the kitchen and pushed me up against the wall.

Tears sprung to my eyes, and I fought to hold them back. Showing him weakness would only make it worse.

"Suddenly that night makes a whole lot more sense to me. The way you fumbled all over yourself and acted like a complete fool...made me look like a fool." He dug his fingers into my arm. I bit my lip to keep from crying out.

It was as if he could taste it—my fear. His mouth twisted up in a malicious grin as he pinned me to the wall with one hand by the neck.

"It would be a shame for something to happen to such a young, promising doctor, wouldn't it?" His mock concern turned my stomach. My blood ran cold and my mouth suddenly went dry when he brought both hands to my neck.

"Besides, do you really think he'd want you? You and your worthless body?"

Panic worked its way through my body, my legs beginning to flail and my fingers clawing at his hands as I sucked in enough air to produce the lie. "He didn't want me then, why would he want me now?"

He cracked a menacing smile. "That's right." He increased the pressure of his hold, but he had enough of my weight pinned against the wall that he didn't completely obstruct the flow of air.

It was a warning.

"I was beginning to think maybe you'd forgotten who you belong to." This time when he squeezed, he stole my breath. "Don't fuck with me, Melanie."

"Oh my God." My mother's gasp echoed over the tile floor of the kitchen, leaving me feeling both relieved and ashamed at having her find me like this.

Reflexively, Nicholas glanced over his shoulder at Mom, releasing his hold. I crumbled and landed hard against the floor. He turned to her, his voice hard and without remorse. "I was just reminding your daughter of her place."

He leaned down close to my face, his breath making me sick as I gasped for air. "Until *death* do us part." His voice lowered as he came in even closer, his mouth pressed into my cheek. "Don't forget it."

I struggled, finding enough strength to whisper the thing I wanted to say most. "I hate you." It was hardly a defense, but I couldn't go another second without him knowing exactly how I felt about him.

"Oh, I know..." he sneered, his mouth twitching up as if he experienced some sort of morbid pleasure in my misery.

He stood and strode from the room. He brushed past Mom as if she wasn't there, leaving me in a pile on the floor trying to piece myself back together.

My hands fisted as angry tears flowed down my face. How had I allowed it to come to this? Allowed him this control? I was worse off now than I had been when I'd started. The worst part was that Mom stood just ten feet away, her face pale, trembling, frozen in fear.

I felt the break, the way her mind snapped into action, and she rushed to me. "Melanie..."

I tried to pull myself from the floor, but it was harder to do than I had anticipated. My feet wobbled beneath me, and I had to reach out to steady myself on the wall. I was having a hard time making my limbs function.

Mom reached to help me, her face stricken. "Melanie," she said again, "Are..."

I put my hand out to stop her, feeling horrible for doing so, but I couldn't handle talking about this with her yet. I had to figure out what I was going to do. I had been thrown back to square one, and I had no idea where to go from here.

Chapter Twenty-Three

The door silently clicked behind me, I fell onto the unmade bed and buried my face in the pillows in an attempt to drown out my cries.

I snaked my arm under my chest and up to the fiery skin, bruised at Nicholas's hand, a concrete warning that his threats were more than just idle. I'd never felt so helpless.

I tried to ignore the light tapping against the door, but then Mom called softly, "Melanie? Sweetheart? I'm so sorry."

I took in a breath, tried to hide my tears and the hoarseness of my voice. "Not tonight, Mom. Please. I'm okay, I just need some time." She was probably blaming herself for what had happened, but I couldn't bring myself to talk to her yet.

She patted the door, a soft, soothing sound that promised she was there if I needed her, followed by the sound of her retreating footsteps.

I fell into a restless sleep filled with nightmares, ones where I searched but could never find, where he called and I could never answer—where I would never be free to live my life with Daniel.

❧

The sky was still dark when I awoke, the house silent except for the distinct sound of the shower running upstairs.

I swallowed, bringing my fingers up to touch the sensitive skin at my neck, and I fought against the angry tears that pricked at my eyes.

I hated him so much.

The shower shut off, and Nicholas's footsteps moved heavily on the floor in the room above. Soon, the sound traveled down the stairs. I waited, tense. After what seemed like hours, the garage door opened and closed, and silence fell over the house once again.

I released the terrified breath I'd been holding.

Standing, I stretched my sore muscles and tiptoed across the floor to open the door a crack and peeked into the living room. Mom slept on the couch, hugging the blue blanket from her room to her chest.

A wistful smile played at my lips as I realized she'd slept there to protect me.

I closed the door, unwilling to interrupt her sleep, and crawled back into bed, knowing I'd never get any more sleep.

About an hour later, I heard rattling in the kitchen. I shuffled into the kitchen, embarrassed and unable to make eye contact with Mom when I entered.

I had no idea what to say to her or how to explain how I'd ended up like this.

She filled two green coffee mugs as I took a seat on a barstool at the island, and she slid the mug to me across the smooth surface of the countertop. I mumbled a quiet, "Thank you," as I rubbed my eye with the back of my hand, trying to clear my head. Lifting the mug, I inhaled deeply and brought the cup to my lips.

Neither of us wanted to have this conversation, especially after last night, but we were out of time. I just had no idea where to start.

Apparently, Mom did.

"Daniel?" she asked, her voice soft.

A little choking sound escaped my mouth, my eyes wide as I jerked my head up. She waited patiently while she stared at me. Finally, I nodded, my voice cracking when I spoke. "I love him, Mom."

"I know, sweetheart." She sat on the stool across from me, watching me sip my coffee. Her expression was understanding and without judgment.

"Will you tell me?" she asked.

I hesitated only for a second before I nodded. "Yeah. I need you to know."

Without interruption, she listened while I told her of the fateful evening that had brought Daniel and I face-to-face and everything we'd learned since. Her eyes grew wider and I could see her guilt grow with each account. She seemed to stop breathing altogether when I got to the part where Daniel had gone to Texas.

"I'm so sorry, Melanie. I can't tell you how badly I wanted to let you know that he came, how many times I picked up the phone to call. I just *couldn't*. It seemed that every time I tried to intervene in your life, I just messed things up more."

"Like forcing me to go home with you?" I tried to remain impassive, but there was a bite to my words. It still made me so angry.

She sighed and nodded, looking out the window at the still morning before looking back at me. "I never meant to hurt you."

"But you did."

This was getting hard. No wonder we'd so carefully avoided it the whole week.

"I know I did, and I take responsibility for it. But please believe me when I tell you it was never my intention."

"Mom, you were going to have him *arrested*! How did you think that wouldn't hurt me? You treated the one person who loved me more than anyone else like a criminal. And why? Because he was ten-months older than me? What you did was...was cruel. At one point I would have said unforgivable."

She blanched, and I knew it hurt her to hear it, but she needed to understand what she had done.

"Melanie..." She looked down as if in shame. "Part of me really did believe that the two of you needed some time apart, but I'd never planned on keeping you from Daniel forever. Your father..."

Anger flashed hot across my skin with the mention of my dad.

"He was so angry with Daniel. When I first got to the hospital, he was obviously furious about the whole situation and hurt at being deceived, but not any more than I was. Then when Eva passed..." She paused as if saying her name hurt. I'm sure the expression on my face reflected the way she felt. "He just snapped," she went on. "He blamed Daniel for...everything...you...the accident...Eva's death. He was set on making Daniel pay, and he figured the best way to do that would be to take you away from him. I tried to make him understand that it would punish you just as much as it would Daniel, but he wouldn't listen. I'd just thought it would be best to take you home with me and let things cool off. It didn't mean that decision didn't come with a ton of guilt, but I figured everything would work out the way it was supposed to in the end."

She chuckled humorlessly, shaking her head. "That was where my plan fell to pieces. I couldn't believe that Daniel hadn't called you in all of those months. It ripped my heart out to hear you crying in your room and there was nothing I could do. When you were set on going back, I knew you were getting ready to get your heart broken all over again...that Daniel had betrayed you in some way."

She glanced away, before turning her attention back to me. Her eyes glistened with unshed tears. "Then you showed up at my door with Nicholas...it made me sick to see you with him. I knew you were running from whatever you'd found in Colorado. But by then, I'd realized part of that was my fault, and I made the decision right then that I was done interfering in your life." She looked away, her mouth trembling. "That was the worst decision I've ever made."

"Why now, Mom? Why did you wait so long to tell me this?"

A tear broke free and slid down her face. "Because I hated myself, Melanie. Do you have any idea what it feels like to watch your daughter fade away and know it's your fault? I stayed away because I couldn't stand to see what I'd done. I went through so many years of depression, carried so much guilt, especially for never telling you Daniel had come to Texas. When he'd first shown up, I figured he was just there to beg you back after he'd had enough of whatever girl he'd hooked up with while you were away. But inside...I *knew*...I saw the same thing in his face that I saw in yours. It haunted me, and the longer I hid from it, the stronger it grew."

She dabbed at her eye with a tissue, sucked in a shuddering breath, attempted to smile. "Mark convinced me to get help about a year and a half ago. I went on medication that helped me to think clearer, but it was the counseling that made the difference. The day I called, I'd just been to see my therapist. She finally made me see that I had to tell you."

Resting my elbows on the top of the island, I buried my head in my hands, trying to deal with everything she'd said. I looked up, meeting her bleary eyes. "You should have told me," I whispered.

"I know that now, and that's why I'm here. I wish I could take it all back, but I *can't*. All I can do now is ask for forgiveness."

I put my hand over my mouth and tried to block the sob that built up in my throat. They'd stolen so many years, Stephanie, my dad, my mom. But when I looked at my mother now, I couldn't find the anger that part of me recognized should be there. "I just wish we hadn't lost so much time."

She pressed her fingers against her mouth, a harsh sound of relief escaping through them as the tears she'd been holding back began to fall. "Oh...Melanie." She wiped at her face with the tissue.

Inhaling, she straightened and inclined her head to capture my eyes. "I'm done with turning my cheek, Melanie...I'm not going to stand aside and watch you live like this." She glanced around. "You have to get out of this house."

"I know, Mom." Somehow I had to get out of here. I just couldn't hide the fear of actually doing it.

Chapter Twenty-Four

I was done.

Her concern was clearly for me, but my safety was the least of my concerns.

I released the blind, allowing it to fall back into place, cutting off the stream of natural sunlight from my office once he had driven away. It was the third time I'd seen him, twice in front of my office and once outside my apartment building the day I moved to the new house. He was just sitting, watching, waiting. He wasn't even trying to hide himself. It seemed that just as Melanie had been trying to send him a message, he was sending me one in return.

After what had happened on Thanksgiving, everything had changed. I'd only seen Melanie four times in the past three weeks, only in those rare moments when we were certain Nicholas was busy, relying on Shane to let us know when it was safe to steal away for a little bit of time.

Melanie insisted that she continue to stay in his house. As hard as she tried to convince me otherwise, I knew it wasn't about the *plan* anymore. She was scared.

I'd promised to give her the time she needed, but not if giving her that time put her in danger. The whole thing had backfired, and I wasn't about to stand by while she was forced back into that hopeless life.

Never in a million years would I have thought Peggy would become my ally through all of this. I'd not even known what to say when she'd called and explained everything to me, apologizing for what she'd done. Melanie had freely forgiven her, as if I would ever expect anything less from her. I wanted to have the capacity to do the same, but I still couldn't get over how Peggy had let it go on for so many years. She knew we still loved each other and had seen what Melanie had become and she'd never done a thing.

Her intentions had never been cruel, though, and it seemed she wanted Melanie out of that house almost as much as I did. In fact, she had flat out begged me to get Melanie out of there. As hard as it had been to do, I pushed back the resentment I had for her and asked for her help.

I knew that as long as Melanie faced Nicholas's scrutiny on a daily basis, she would never be able to see how effective he had been at keeping her just where he wanted her. I needed Melanie to step back and see that if she stayed on this path, she would never be free and nothing would ever change. Nicholas still had the control, and he always would until she finally walked away. I was going to take her away and make sure she never went back.

I looked over the tickets that arrived this morning, one for her and one for me. These two tickets would allow us almost two weeks of sanctuary. I would spend that time getting Melanie to accept why I could never allow her to go near Nicholas again.

Another ticket had been delivered to Nicholas's house. Peggy had called him directly and told him she'd purchased a ticket for Melanie to come to their house for Christmas, convincing him Melanie would be spending time between Christmas and New Year's with them. She insisted Melanie had to be there because Melanie's little sister, Sarah, would be home from college. I didn't believe Nicholas would care anything about that, but he'd surprisingly relented. Maybe he liked the idea of her being farther away from me.

When my phone vibrated against my desk, I emitted a heavy sigh of relief. I hated our new routine—waiting for Melanie to call me so there would be no chance that my calls would occur while Nicholas was around.

My heart sped up just in anticipation of hearing her voice. "Hey, baby."

"Hi." I could feel her smile, could picture her curled up on her bed as she squeezed the phone to her ear. "Is it Wednesday yet?"

I chuckled, warmed at her eagerness, never agreeing with a sentiment more. December twenty-third could not come fast enough.

"Two days, baby, and then you're all mine. Are you all set?"

"Um, I think so. Do I need to pack anything special?"

"Just pack warm, okay?"

"Hmm, I need to dress warm, huh? I guess Hawaii's out, then? Should I even try to guess where we're going?"

"Nope."

She giggled, sighing through the phone. "I can't wait. I miss you." Her voice softened, colored with a hint of sadness.

I knew she hated what she was putting herself through. She just felt trapped. I wanted to tell her it was all about to end, but I didn't want her to know my intentions until she was safely with me. "I miss you so much, baby. It's only two days away."

"I know...but these next two days are going to be very long."

We both fell silent, wishing we could somehow erase the distance.

"I love you, Daniel."

"I love you more than anything. Now go pack some sweaters. You know, it's supposed to be freezing in Dallas this Christmas."

She laughed. "Right."

"I'll see you at eight on Wednesday, okay?"

"Okay. Love you." She was obviously as reluctant as I was to hang up the phone.

"Love you. Bye, Mel."

"Bye."

I sighed and set my phone down, running my hands through my hair as I sank back into my chair. I would have lost it before now if I hadn't already have known how close we were to the end of this mess. My phone vibrated again and Vanessa's number flashed across the screen again. I dutifully rejected her call. Apparently, I couldn't be clear enough for that stupid bitch. I'd thought that after she had seen me with Melanie, she'd accept that she had no chance with me and she would be deterred. I had even become hopeful when she hadn't called for most of November. Somewhere around Thanksgiving, she'd decided to give it another go. It seemed that the closer she got to her due date, the more needy she became. With just five weeks left, I was sure it was only going to get worse.

I choked on a sip of coffee, realizing just how close that actually was. In five weeks, I would be a father.

Damn it.

I was late. I didn't anticipate having to stop by the office this morning, but I couldn't leave without everything being in place for the new partners who started after the first of the year. Dad had already picked up so much slack for me, allowing me what little time I had with Melanie during the day, so there was no way I could leave him hanging two days before Christmas.

I whipped into the first spot I could find in long-term parking, grabbed my suitcase from the trunk, and practically ran across the lot to catch the shuttle. My knee bounced in anticipation as the bus made slow progress along its course. As soon as it stopped, I rushed off. The double doors slid open as I raced toward them. My eyes swept the terminal, hoping I'd made it there before she had.

Melanie was to leave her car in a long-term parking lot, go to the decoy terminal, and then she would ride the tram around to meet me at the check in counter.

It was impossible to miss the most beautiful girl who ever lived. Her mass of curly brown hair bounced around the collar of her black, knee-length coat, the belt tied firmly around her waist. She stepped carefully from the transit in her black boots, pulling a huge suitcase behind her, looking a little flustered and lost—until she felt me.

I could see the moment she did. Her eyes darted up to meet mine and a wide smile spread over her face. I rushed to her, grabbing her as soon as she was within arm's reach.

It had been far too long.

I breathed her in, savoring. "Mmm."

She giggled at my mumbling against her neck. "Did you miss me?" she teased, kissing me lightly on the lips while she looked up at me, her eyes gleaming. I could feel excitement flowing from her.

"You have no idea." I drew her back for a deep, lingering kiss, showing her just how much I had.

"So, where are we going?" She scanned the flights, searching for some hint of our destination.

I pulled the tickets from my pocket and handed her one. She looked up, biting her lip as she bounced on her toes. "Tahoe?"

I nodded, and she threw herself at me, kissing me as she mumbled, "Thank you," against my mouth.

"That okay with you?" I don't know why I felt the need to ask; I'd already seen her honest reaction.

"Oh, my gosh! It sounds like the best place in the world to spend Christmas with you."

I smiled down at her and kissed her forehead. "You'll love it there. It's so beautiful this time of year."

I knew she'd never been to Tahoe. She hadn't left Illinois once in nine years.

We made our way through the line, checking our luggage and breezing through security. Once they called us to board, we found our seats and Melanie and I got settled. Her posture stiffened as we began to taxi down the runway. She pressed her back into the seat and held my hand a little firmer than normal.

"You okay?" I squeezed back.

"Yeah. I just haven't flown in so long. I kind of forgot what it feels like."

She held her breath as the plane ascended, wincing when the plane dipped slightly just as it pulled from the ground. Her body slowly relaxed into mine the higher we climbed. She watched out the window as Chicago disappeared from view. She looked deep in thought.

"What are you thinking about?"

She snapped her head up in surprise.

"Oh." She glanced back out the window as the last of the city fell away. She sank into me when I wrapped an arm around her shoulders and drew her near. "I was just thinking about when I first came to Illinois...how it felt like a death sentence. Now," she said, playing with my fingers, "leaving for the first time," she turned enough so she could look at me, "it feels like I'm leaving it all behind."

She *was* leaving it all behind. I just wasn't ready to tell her yet.

Instead, I wrapped her up in me. I kissed her softly, reverently, making a silent oath to her and myself that that was exactly what we were doing. We were leaving it all behind.

ꟹ

Carefully, I maneuvered the rented SUV over the snowy roads, relying on the GPS to guide me through Tahoe City. We traveled slowly as we made our way out to the small cabin I'd rented in North Shore. The forest was dense and thick, the night sky covered in heavy clouds as snow flurried around us. The headlights reflected against the white, creating a blinding brilliance that had me gripping the steering wheel while I contended with near-zero visibility. I turned onto a dirt road, wet and muddied, and followed the narrow path to a small clearing that housed a gray stone and wood cabin.

Lights glowed from within, the porch illuminated by the lamp hanging beside the door. The snow on the deck had been shoveled. The rental agent made arrangements for everything to be ready for our arrival, the lights and furnace on, a fire waiting, and the kitchen stocked with everything we'd need for our stay.

Melanie squealed, clapping her hands together when she took in her surroundings for the first time. She unbuckled and leaned forward to get a closer look as the SUV slid to a complete stop. "Daniel...this is amazing."

I couldn't help but smile. She was carefree, without a worry, joyous—exactly the way I wanted her to be every day of her life. This kind of freedom was something I was determined to give her. She stuffed her head into her snowcap and wrapped her scarf around her neck. Her hair billowed out beneath the cap, the brown locks wild and frizzy from the long day of travel and the humidity in the air. She looked absolutely adorable. I didn't realize I was staring until she looked at me, grinning. "What?"

I shook myself out of it and beamed at her. "I'm just so happy right now."

She reached out and touched my cheek. "Me too."

I nodded against her palm, before I grabbed her wrist and brought her hand to my mouth, placing a small kiss on the soft, pink skin.

"Are you ready?"

She nodded vigorously, opened the door, and cautiously stepped out into mounds of soft, white powder.

We were both laughing by the time we made it to the porch, grabbing each other for support as we more so slid across the ground than walked.

I slipped the key into the lock, turned the knob, and pulled Melanie into the warmth.

"Oh, Daniel," she whispered with a sharp intake of air, rewarding me with the biggest smile.

"Do you like it?"

"It's perfect." Her eyes scanned the room, roaming over the darkened planks of the wooden floor. She glanced at the small kitchen and round dining table to the right, but was drawn to the spacious living room. A fire roared in the massive fireplace; the entire face of the wall surrounding it had different variations of gray stone. They meshed perfectly with the walls of rustic, gray wood that completed the rest of the room. The wall of windows that faced the lake was now black and reflecting the flames. She dropped my hand and walked toward the fireplace, running her hand over the back of the large maroon leather couch placed comfortably in the middle of the room. It sat opposite the fire, the gulf between blanketed by a plush black rug.

She glanced at the banister made of thick wood and wrought iron, protectively guarding the stairs that led to the one bedroom over the kitchen.

She turned and took two steps back to wrap her arms around my waist and laid her head on my chest. "Thank you." She looked up, her eyes glowing and open, drawing me into their depths. I captured her lips in a slow kiss, unrushed for the first time in a month. She twisted her arms around my neck. My intense reaction was immediate, my hands at her waist, pulling her against me, instant heat. Forcing myself to slow down, I stepped back and unwound the scarf from her neck and tugged the cap from her head. Her hair was a mess but still so soft when I sank my fingers into it and drew her back to me.

She shivered when my cold hands ran down her throat, exposing her chest. I kissed the soft, pale skin there while my hands loosened the belt of her jacket, pushing it from her shoulders and onto the floor.

"Daniel," she said softly, her breath sweet as it spread over my face. My mouth became forceful. She instinctively stepped back, moving across the floor. Her hands dove into my hair as I leaned forward to fumble out of my jacket. I kicked off my shoes as I stepped with her, her body guiding me, leading me. We somehow stumbled up the stairs.

Flames flickered from the bedroom fireplace, casting orange light across windows set in darkness.

I struggled to hold her close and drag the blanket down the bed at the same time. I raked my arm along the swell of pillows at the head of the bed and swept them to the ground, laying Melanie in their place.

I made love to her, soft and slow. The room echoed with whispered words of love and promises of forever. This—loving her—felt so perfect, so right. And tonight marked a new beginning. I was never again going to fall asleep without her in my arms.

❧

I awoke to the smell of bacon. My stomach growled. I pried my eyes open to see the clock that read eight-twenty. I couldn't believe I'd slept so long. Rolling from bed, I dragged on my pants and ran my hands through my hair, trying to tame the disaster that it was.

I crept downstairs, taking a moment to watch Melanie in the kitchen. She was dressed in red flannel pajamas and black fuzzy slippers, her movements lithe as she made her away around the room. It made my soul soar to see her so at ease and doing something she loved so much. I could see the change from that night those few short months ago when she was so broken—so drained. Now there was life in her eyes when she glanced at me over her shoulder when I wrapped my arms around her waist.

"Good morning." I kissed her cheek.

"Mmm." She brushed her cheek against mine, keeping her attention on the stove as she flipped the omelets in the skillet. "Good morning. Are you hungry?"

"Famished." I grabbed a piece of bacon and popped it in my mouth.

"Me too. Could you grab a couple of plates?" She nodded toward a cupboard. I pulled two down and held them out while she filled our plates with ham and cheese omelets, bacon, and toast. I didn't think I'd ever been hungrier. We settled in next to each other at the little round table.

"This is unbelievable." She gazed out through the huge windows. They were partially fogged over from the warmth inside meeting with the freezing temperatures outside, though not enough to obstruct the view of the crystal blue water that seemed to go on forever. Only the mountains in the distance gave any indication of its end. The branches of the tall pines lining the yard hung low, heavy-laden with snow that layered everything but the frigid fluid lake.

"I thought you'd love it here."

We ate in contented silence, just enjoying the peace of the company we shared.

I wiped my mouth when I finished my last bite. "So, what do you want to do today?"

She glanced back out the windows. "I'd be happy just hanging out here all day, if that's okay with you?"

If it was okay with me? I would be satisfied if we never left once in the next eleven days. Nothing sounded better than being holed up in this cabin with Melanie.

She inclined her head toward the small kitchen. "There's a ham in the fridge, and I thought I'd make that for Christmas dinner tomorrow, and maybe I could make that Italian casserole for dinner tonight? I think I remember you like it..." she said, her voice trailing off as her mouth lifted in a mischievous smirk. Obviously, she'd noticed.

I grinned at being caught. I'd made sure to order everything needed for it when I made the list for the shopper. Melanie had made the same dish on every special occasion she'd ever cooked for us: the two birthdays she'd spent with me, my high school graduation, and twice for Christmas Eve. I couldn't think of anything more appropriate.

She shook her head and laughed. "I would have been disappointed if you hadn't remembered."

After breakfast, we refilled our coffee cups and settled onto the sofa. I wrapped us in a warm blanket and in silence we watched the snow flurries melt as the flakes landed in the water.

We lay like that for what seemed like hours, lost in thought. I ignored my phone ringing on the kitchen table, unwilling to get up and interrupt my time with Melanie. It became increasingly more difficult when it continued to ring every fifteen minutes or so.

When the phone began to ring again, I groaned and threw my head back into the pillow. I tried to keep my frustration in check, knowing there was only one person who could be so obnoxious.

"Just get it, Daniel." Melanie sat up abruptly, her frustration as apparent as my own.

"I don't want to talk to her." Maybe I was acting like a child as I considered smashing the phone that allowed my mistakes to follow me across the country, but didn't I deserve a break from her hounding? She had no right to call me, especially here—especially on Christmas Eve.

"What if there's something wrong?" Melanie was always the voice of reason, though she clearly had no idea of just how unreasonable Vanessa actually was.

"There's nothing wrong, Melanie. She does this constantly. I just ignore it. It'll only encourage her if I answer it."

"Well, you can't ignore her forever. She's your...your son's mother." With as much effort as she put into being strong, pain still laced each word. She couldn't even look at me when she said it, her attention trained on her lap while she did what she believed to be the right thing.

When the incessant ringing began again, I forced myself to stand, my tone a sharp hiss when I answered, "What do you want?"

I stood with my back to Melanie, facing the wall, hoping to spare her the conversation. I winced when I heard the whiney voice. "I...I was just calling to say Merry Christmas."

Was she kidding me? Eight calls to wish me a Merry Christmas? I sucked in a deep breath, trying to control my anger.

"Vanessa, nothing has changed. I told you not to call me unless it's about the baby."

There was silence before she spoke, quiet and pleading, "Please, Daniel. It's Christmas and...and I'm alone."

I exhaled heavily. I had no idea how to deal with this woman. She was completely obsessed and *driving* me insane. A soft, warm hand came to rest on the bare skin of my lower back—Melanie literally standing by my side while I dealt with Vanessa. I pulled Melanie to me, leaning on her for support. I swallowed hard, desperately trying to be civil to the woman who was trying to ruin my life—the life that had just been given back to me.

I spoke to her, keeping my tone even and void of the complete hatred I felt for her, "Vanessa, I'm sorry you're alone on Christmas, but you have to understand...that has nothing to do with me." I couldn't believe I'd gotten that out and still maintained my composure. I focused on the electricity that circulated through my body as Melanie comforted me.

"You need to leave me alone, Vanessa. You're just making this harder on yourself."

I could feel her objection through the phone before she even voiced it. "I'm not giving up on us, Daniel."

"Then you're wasting your time," I said, actually feeling sorry for her for being so incredibly pathetic.

"Daniel—"

"Just leave me alone, Vanessa...please." Melanie squeezed me, shouldering some of the burden in this hopeless situation.

I waited, praying Vanessa would agree and just move on with her life. Really, I should have known better than to hope for something like that.

"I can't do that."

I shook my head at her futile determination, realizing it was no use. There was nothing I could say that would convince her to stop this foolish game.

"Goodbye, Vanessa." I ended the call before she had a chance to respond. I shut off the phone, not willing to give her another chance to disturb our holiday.

I looked down at Melanie, her eyes brimming with concern for me and the pain I'd caused her with my choices. I hated myself for putting her through this. "I'm so sorry, baby."

She shook her head sharply. "I'm here, no matter what, remember?"

"Yeah," I said as I kissed the top of her head.

I knew she would be. There was no question of her devotion, but how could I not feel terrible for putting her through it?

We were going to have to deal with Vanessa for the next eighteen years.

I held the knife steady as I cut into the tomato, slicing through it before turning it to the side so I could dice it, taking the one job Melanie had trusted me with very seriously.

Even though we were alone, it was still the first Christmas we'd spent together in years, so we'd decided to dress up for dinner just like we would have done had we been spending it at my family's house. Right now, I was really enjoying that decision. Melanie moved around the kitchen, looking absolutely amazing in a red dress, her breasts just peeking out from the V-neck. The skirt swished around her knees as she made her way back and forth between the counter and oven.

I found it difficult to pay attention to the task in front of me. My body was painfully aware of every move she made, even though I was trying to give my regard to the very sharp blade coming dangerously close to the tips of my fingers.

She glanced over my shoulder. "I'm ready for those whenever you're finished."

"Just a sec." I finished up quickly.

She pecked my lips. "Thanks."

I sat back and watched as she spread them over the top of the mixture and slid the dish into the oven.

"Would you like a glass of wine?" I inspected the bottles nestled in the small rack and picked out a red that would go well with our dinner.

"Mmm, yeah. That'd be nice." She moved on to prepare the salad.

I popped the cork and filled two wine glasses halfway.

"Here you go, beautiful." I set the glass next to her on the counter, reaching up to massage her shoulders, regretting that I was so incompetent in the kitchen. I figured I could at least make her feel good while she made my favorite dinner.

Luckily, Melanie agreed, groaning at my touch. "That...feels...so...good."

I kissed the back of her head, my nose immersed in her rich brown curls. Swimming in the perfume that was only Melanie, I allowed her aura to ground me. My nerves had spiked, just a bit, knowing where this evening was going. I just had no idea what her reaction would be.

All I knew was I wanted her. I needed to share my life with her—completely—not this messed up situation where I was awarded only a small allowance of her. I was already wholly hers, and I could not bear another day where she was not wholly mine. But above all of that, I needed her safe.

While we waited for our dinner to cook, we moved to the couch, sipped our wine, and immersed ourselves in conversation until the buzzer called us to dinner.

The casserole was every bit as delicious as I remembered, maybe even better. I was sure that impression had a lot to do with the fact that Melanie and I were spending our first Christmas together in nearly a decade. I was now a firm believer in the old adage that you could never truly appreciate something until you'd been without it.

We ate by candlelight. Melanie's face glowed, not just from the flicker of the flame, but with her joy. The smile on her face never faded. Her cheeks were the perfect shade of rose, emitting waves of heat, drawing me in. I found myself constantly reaching out to touch the soft flesh, running the back of my hand over her precious face. We laughed and loved as we ate and drank. We celebrated us. This was a meal I would never forget.

"Merry Christmas, Daniel." She looked at me, her expression soft—adoring. She took my hand under the table and ran her thumb over the back of my hand, her touch so calming yet always fire, never a contradiction.

I intertwined my fingers with hers and stood. Like a magnet, she echoed my movements and rose as well. "Merry Christmas, Melanie." I kissed her tenderly, gently, savoring that constant sweetness that was Melanie. I lingered, manifesting my every affection.

I led her to the fire. The embers glowed red, the flames jumping, crackling, tinged in blue, providing the only light in the room. I helped her to the floor, staring unabashedly as she curled her long legs under her and settled down in front of me.

I didn't know I was so nervous until I realized my hands were shaking.

Fumbling in my pocket, I pulled out the small box and tentatively placed it on the floor in front of her.

Melanie gasped, her eyes flitting between the box and me. "Daniel...I...I don't have anything for you."

As if I could ever want anything other than her.

"Shh, baby, you've already given me everything. And...it's old."

I'd held on to it for a very long time.

She began to reach for it and I stopped her. "I need to say something first."

She looked at me, confused as she withdrew her hand. In quiet expectation she waited while I wrestled with how to best get this out.

"Melanie, sweetheart...you know how much I respect you, right?"

She nodded without hesitation.

"Good. Because I need you to believe I'd never try to control you. But I can't let you go back there. It's not safe."

She immediately refused, just as I knew she would. "No, it's not safe for me to leave yet. He'll know why. We have to give it more time."

"We don't have more time." I lowered my voice, running my fingers through the lock of hair that had fallen in her face, pushing it back in place. "We can't hide this forever, and you can't be in that house when he finds out."

Almost imperceptibly she shook her head. I could see how badly she wanted to agree, but her judgment was clouded. Fear dominated, filling her with doubt.

"Do you really think anything is ever going to change, Melanie? The only thing these last two months have accomplished is making him tighten his hold on you. Another two months aren't going to make a difference, either."

She was silent, her eyes closed.

"Do you understand what I'm trying to say?"

Tears broke free and streamed down her face. She whispered, "I'm scared."

"I know, baby. He wants you to be. Don't you see that? He knows exactly what he's doing, knows exactly how to control you. You are so strong, sweetheart, but you have to use it the right way."

She surprised me by cutting me off. "Okay." She opened her eyes, nodding but still crying.

I grasped her face and kissed her, closed mouthed and hard. My relief was intense, overpowering. I pulled away and glanced down at the space between us, drawing her attention to the little velvet box. "Open it."

She flashed me a soggy, full-toothed grin, and she dried her eyes with her sleeve. She picked up the box and ran her fingers over the velvet top. "Thank you, Daniel. You didn't have to."

Gingerly, she lifted the lid, smiling as she inspected the obviously antique ring, a relic from long ago. She freed it from its confines. "Oh, it's so beautiful," she whispered as she brought it closer, holding it up to examine the detail. She ran a finger over the thick band of white gold encrusted with diamonds that shimmered in the firelight. As she rolled it over, a cry escaped her mouth.

"Oh, my God, Daniel, is this?"

Chapter Twenty-Five

I couldn't breathe, couldn't control the tremors that hit me, rolling through every muscle of my body with the onslaught of emotion.

It was the same inscription as my necklace, the intertwined D & M, except for the date running along the inside.

April 28, 2000. I searched his face, his eyes so hopeful, full of his promise of forever. His voice cracked when he spoke, "Will you wear it?"

I was crying, probably too hard, but I couldn't stop. I found myself only able to whisper his name, praying he could feel what this meant to me even if I couldn't voice it.

He wanted me to wear my wedding ring.

"I'd had it engraved before...before the accident," he said, rushing over the words before taking a deep breath. "I could never part with it because, in my heart, you were my wife. And I want you to know I intend to make that a reality...and soon. But for now, will you wear what was meant for you so long ago?"

My face felt flushed and my heart beat impossibly fast, pounding as it thrummed against my chest. Daniel's love overpowered me as he asked me to acknowledge that day. Our day. A day we had physically missed, but a day our spirits had been present for, a day our souls had always honored. It was a day I confirmed as I nodded, raising a shaky hand to Daniel, my palm extended in offering. He didn't hesitate to take the ring from my hand. He kissed my palm before he turned my hand over and slid the ring to its rightful place.

My entire being hummed.

I gaped at my hand resting in his, the ring a priceless reminder of this love that refused to die.

"I love you, Daniel. Forever." I stared at him through the firelight, witnessed the love alight in his eyes. The energy grew thick, nearly visible at the fringes, a faint shimmer in the air as it enveloped us.

"You are everything, Melanie." He never broke his gaze as he brought me to him, lying us down, side-by-side, face-to-face. His lips were unhurried and worshipful. He took time to revere all of me, leaving nothing in disregard, his love lasting deep into the night.

The rest of our vacation went by quickly, most of it spent in the cabin, content to be alone and without interruption. We'd only ventured out a few times, braving the snow and freezing temperatures. We'd walked down to the boardwalk, always hand in hand, browsing through the quaint stores.

We ate dinner out one night when Daniel insisted I deserved a break from cooking. We dined in a beautiful restaurant nestled on a hill that overlooked the lake. The view was breathtaking, almost as much so as the view from our balcony at the cabin.

We rang in the New Year by sitting snuggled up on the couch with a bottle of wine, the fire raging before us, sharing precious memories of our past and making promises for our forever.

I had never experienced anything so satisfying. My heart was filled to capacity, the joy within me almost overwhelming as it was reflected back in Daniel's face every time he looked my way.

But as I strapped into my seat on the plane preparing to return to Illinois, I knew *this* was what I was looking forward to. As wonderful as the trip had been, I was going home.

Daniel borrowed my phone to call Patrick and Julia since he'd forgotten his charger, and his phone was dead. He let them know we were on our way home. *Our home.*

I made one last call to Mom before turning off the phone for the flight. She'd heard nothing from Nicholas the entire time and said all was well.

We were going to handle this as simply as we could. It was Monday and Nicholas would be at the office. We would get what little I needed from the house, and I'd leave my car there. I wanted nothing that belonged to him. I would take only what I had to have and forget the rest.

I would leave a note asking Nicholas to call so I could arrange to meet him at a restaurant or some other public place, in a place where he could cause no scene and do me no harm. Just to be safe, Daniel would be nearby in case I needed him.

I was going to tell Nicholas the truth. As much as I despised him, he deserved that. After all, I had been a willing partner in all of this.

The seat belt lights flickered on, and Daniel wove his fingers through mine. The plane began to move, readying to make its departure into the early morning light. As the plane took flight, we raced east to meet the sunrise. Faster than I could imagine, the captain came on and announced our decent into Chicago. Daniel smiled at me and squeezed my fingers, murmuring in my ear, "Ready?"

I exhaled nervously in anticipation.

Yes.

Finally—I was ready.

ক্ক

We departed the plane, both of us quiet, contemplative.

"It's going to be okay." Daniel pulled me from my meditation with his soft words and a gentle hand on my cheek. "Tonight is going to be hard, but you can do this, sweetheart. You pick the place and time. Don't give him the option. You need to be the one in control of this."

I nodded. Daniel's suggestion made sense. "Um...there's a little diner Katie and I go to. It's always busy, and I think if you were in the back, he'd never see you."

"Okay." He tried to hide it, but I could tell that he was just as nervous about this meeting as I was.

"We'll just leave a note when we get your stuff."

The tram doors slid open. "I'll see you at *his* house." A small smirk tugged at the corner of his mouth, obviously thrilled to voice that I no longer lived there. "I'm going to pop by the office to sign some papers for Dad. I'll be about fifteen minutes behind you."

"Okay...love you." I kissed him once more before stepping onto the waiting tram. I raised my hand to return the small wave he gave me, grinning as I watched him turn to catch a shuttle to his own car.

I winced at the frigid wind stinging my face when I stepped outside. Chicago was every bit as cold as Tahoe had been. The sky was dark with heavy gray clouds, sagging in their promise of snow. I reached my car, struggling to get my suitcase into the trunk. I paid my parking fee and set out on my last trip to Nicholas's house, unable to pacify the opposing emotions fighting to claim dominance. How could I be so eager to get away from there and so terrified to do it all at the same time?

It was just after three when I pulled up to the house. I opened the garage and parked the car in its spot.

I was officially car-less.

Shrugging, I pulled the keys from the ignition. Those little details mattered none.

I tugged the heavy suitcase from the trunk, figuring its contents would be the only clothes I'd take. I grabbed an empty cardboard box large enough to fit the few things I needed from the office.

I stepped into the house, silent and dim with the advancing storm. I went directly to the office and downloaded a few files from the computer while I rifled through paperwork. I made sure to take the large manila envelope that contained my birth certificate and medical records. There were a few pictures of Katie and me in frames on the desk, and I tossed those into the box as well before looking around to make sure I had everything I needed. It was amazing that everything that was important to me in the last nine years fit into one small box. The only other things I needed were the few pieces of jewelry that had belonged to my grandmother in the jewelry box upstairs and the treasured pictures hidden at the bottom of it.

I heaved the box into my arms and toed the door open, swinging it wide and stepping out into the living room.

"Did you have a nice trip, Melanie?" The cold, steady voice reached me from across the room. I gasped as the box slipped from my hands, the items spilling across the floor, glass shattering as the frames crashed against the tile.

Blood throbbed against my eardrums and ran cold through my veins. My heart didn't know whether to seize or pound its way completely from my chest.

No. Please. No.

But I couldn't deny the dark figure, a shadow sitting leisurely in the large chair in front of the window. The faint amount of light coming in from outside obscured everything but his silhouette. I gulped, trying to hold down the scream rattling in my throat.

"Nicholas...you...you...scared me," I managed to force out, my mind racing. I clamored to find a way to get myself out of this situation. My eyes darted to the door. His eyes trailed mine, keen on my intent.

Even as preoccupied as I had been with packing my things, I still would have heard him enter, and I knew then that he hadn't wanted me to know he was there.

Because he knew.

He had to have been waiting, watching. My stomach clenched. Had he followed me here from the airport?

"Going somewhere?" His tone was laced with a sarcastic bite as he tilted his head to the side. His face slowly came into focus, his relaxed posture a paradox, his expression severe. The fury burning in his eyes was visible even across the darkened room.

His face shifted down, and I noticed the pile of papers resting on his knee. He slowly and deliberately reached down to pick them up, smacking them lightly against his knee.

I knew immediately what they were.

How could I have been so stupid—so careless?

"These are really very interesting." He held them up, pursing his lips, his eyebrows drawn, waiting for my reaction to the pages and pages of cell phone bill. The lines of unknown number were numerous, both texts and calls running in repetition down the columns. The few sparse calls to Katie and my mother sorely stuck out among the hundreds of others. It was clear from the look on Nicholas's face that he knew exactly who my "unknown" was.

So this was it.

I could try to lie, but there would be no denying what Nicholas held in his hand, and I was through keeping my love for Daniel a secret.

"Just let me go, Nicholas. I don't love you, and you don't love me, so—"

His barking laugh caught me by surprise as he jumped to his feet. Not even a small amount of humor accompanied the harsh sound coming from his mouth.

"You think this is about love?"

I cowered back, the broken glass crunching beneath my feet as I backed away from him as he stalked across the room.

"This is about somebody trying to take something that belongs to me. You...are...mine," he growled as he came closer, "and I think it's about time I reminded you of that."

I took the last step I could before I backed into the wall, trapped. His breath was hot and fevered with anger as he stood fuming in front of me. His nose ran down my jaw and to my neck. My body rolled with nausea when his hands came to rest on either side of my head, his mouth against my ear. "You really are a whore, aren't you? Do you know what you smell like?"

I shrank away as he continued to move, his hands roaming over my body. He breathed over me, pushing into me, trying to reclaim me.

I became desperate, frantic, my defenses finally kicking in. I pushed him back and struggled to get away, crying out, begging him to stop. But it only made it worse when he saw what I wore on my left ring finger.

"What...the...fuck...is...that?" he spit through clenched teeth, enraged as his hand came up and twisted in my hair, yanking hard. I shrieked when the other came to the collar of my shirt, the cloth ripping from top to bottom as he tore through it. His hand flew to the button of my pants and he struggled to break it free.

Tears flowed as I slumped against the wall, powerless, my soul crying out as I begged for Daniel. *Please save me.*

It was as if the energy broke through the hopelessness, a quiet voice somewhere in the recesses of my mind.

Fight!

But I heard it.

I gathered all the courage I could find and fought with everything I had, kicking and hitting and clawing and screaming. The sudden attack was not enough to hurt Nicholas, but enough of a surprise to allow me to break free of his grip. I dodged under his arms, escaping down the only open path and into the kitchen.

He was right behind me and knocked me to the floor when he struck me from behind. The sound of my hands and knees smacking against the floor echoed through the room. My face made its own protest as it met the marble tiles. Blood saturated my mouth.

Nicholas wrapped his hand around my calf, the blood pouring from my mouth and smearing across the floor as he pulled me back.

He flipped me over, hitting me hard across the face. "You stupid bitch!"

He held me down, his hand splayed out across my chest, the pressure of his weight suffocating as he struggled with his pants. Still, I fought, trying to kick and break free. He grabbed a handful of hair, lifted my head, and smashed it against the floor. The pain was splitting, staggering, and nearly sucked me into darkness.

Still the voice was there, ringing through the pain, deafening.

Fight!

And I wanted to—so badly. I struggled, flailed, sunk my teeth into the flesh of Nicholas's arm. I barely felt the fist that landed on my cheek. Darkness gathered at the edges of my consciousness. I tried to hang on, but the shadows took hold, spread.

Chapter Twenty-Six

I rushed to the office, signed a few documents, and was back in my car in less than ten minutes. Traffic was light and I was on the highway in no time, racing toward Nicholas's house, on my way to finally bring my girl home.

My heart tightened, overjoyed with that thought. She was actually coming home. Tonight we'd sleep together in *our* bed. To think that after all this time, after so much pain, our lives would be completely joined together.

Melanie's spirit wound itself around me—squeezed and constricted. I smiled at the sensation, yet somehow felt compelled to rub my chest to ease some of the pressure that had settled there.

It was heavy and—wrong.

I shook my head and tried to shake it off.

Raking a hand through my hair, I glanced at the clock, urging the distance away.

I pressed down the accelerator a little further. Agitation raced through my veins, spurring me on, driving me faster.

Fight!

I didn't know where the word came from, but suddenly it was there, and I was voicing it aloud in the car.

Oh my God. Something was very, very wrong. I swerved around a car, cutting back in front of it to take the exit, slamming on the brakes when I came up behind the line of cars waiting at the intersection.

"Go!" I shouted as the cars slowly began to accelerate when the light turned green. I rammed my foot down on the gas and sped around them.

Fight!

It was there again.

I wanted to scream. Instead, I whispered, "I'm coming, Melanie," more desperate and more terrified than I'd ever been.

I took the last turn into her neighborhood, skidding around the corner, the energy frenzied. Fear pulsed through me as the house came into view in the distance, the pull now so great I was nauseous.

I grabbed my phone, praying it had had enough time to charge, and ran across her yard to the front door.

Even with everything silent, I could feel her despair. I cracked open the front door, trying to remain as quiet as possible. I had no idea what I would find.

Cautiously, I stepped inside, searching for anything I could use as a weapon. For the first time in my life, I wished I carried a gun. I crept forward, swallowing down my panic when I saw the evidence of a struggle strewn across the floor, a toppled box with its contents scattered among shards of glass.

The urge to scream for her was overwhelming, though I stopped myself, sure I'd only put her in more danger. I progressed slowly across the room, keeping my footsteps light, cringing when my shoe crunched against broken glass. From somewhere deeper in the house came a rustle, then a low, guttural groan.

My heart stuttered.

Drawn, I moved toward the kitchen. For a moment, I lost the ability to function when I saw them, Nicholas above her, tearing at her clothes, tearing at his—the blood—my girl.

My vision clouded as I was assaulted with the darkest rage, a lust for death I'd never known.

Nicholas, so intent on this most depraved violation, didn't even notice I was there until I'd launched myself across the room. He finally noticed my presence and jerked his head up to look up in my direction just in time for me to ram my fist into his face.

Something crunched and gave way beneath my hand.

The bloodlust surged.

I was on top of him, one hand holding him down while I drew the other back to deliver a slow, deliberate blow to the side of his face.

His head snapped to the side, his eyes fluttering as his consciousness ebbed. Shaking himself off, he sputtered, "Fuck you," through his bloodied mouth. The blackest eyes stared up at me, filled with hate, lost to any compassion.

I itched to wrap my hands around his throat, to feel his pulse die out against my palms as I squeezed the last of his breath from him, to make him pay for what he'd done. To make him pay for ever laying a hand on Melanie.

It felt so good when I gave in, when I watched his eyes bulge in fear.

I pressed my eyes closed when I almost felt the hand on my shoulder, heard Melanie's voice.

No.

I gasped, shocked from the dangerous place my mind had gone.

I cocked my arm back again and hit him hard enough to keep him down.

He slumped to the floor, this time unable to hold onto consciousness.

I sucked at the air I couldn't seem to find, struggled to control the fury that still fought for release, and instead focused on the only reason I was here.

The only thing that mattered.

Sure that Nicholas was no longer a threat, I turned to my broken girl.

Fumbling with my phone, I managed to dial 911 and feel for her pulse at the same time. It beat weakly beneath my trembling fingers, but it was there, thank God.

The operator came on, and I yelled the address, asking for an ambulance and the police, begging them to hurry. The woman tried to ask questions, but I could hear nothing but the ringing in my ears, fear and rage pounding and pushing against every vein in my body.

"Melanie, no...baby, no," I whimpered, tentatively reaching out to stroke her hair, my fingers wetted by the warmth seeping from the back of her head.

"You fucking bastard!" Her face was torn to shreds. A deep wound hung open over her eye, the skin sliced open through her eyebrow, blood still steadily flowing from it. Cuts and scrapes littered her face and another deep cut gaped just under her chin. Her nails were ripped and bloodied, filled with skin and hair from fighting off Nicholas. Her clothes were in tatters, the front of her shirt ripped open, her exposed skin saturated in the blood pouring from her mouth.

Her body had been his aim, it now broken and bruised at his hands.

Groaning, Nicholas rolled, coughing and spitting blood from his mouth onto the floor.

The corner of my mouth trembled, and I clenched my jaw as the urge to end his life flared.

Lifting his head, his hate-filled eyes met mine. I stared at him, my posture protective as I guarded Melanie.

"If you ever touch her again, I will *kill* you," I snarled, my face twisting with hatred.

"She's *my* wife," he spat out.

"No," I shook my head. "She's mine. She's always been mine."

He snorted through his nose and wiped his bloody face with the back of his hand, his cocky demeanor back in full force. "She's not fucking worth it." But the expression on his face told me that he knew she was.

Sirens wailed in the distance, drew near.

He slumped back down to the floor when four police officers entered, their guns drawn in preparation for an unknown situation.

Meeting no resistance, they waved in the paramedics.

"Sir, we need you to get back."

I slid back on the floor and sagged against the cabinet while two paramedics began treatment on Melanie and two others knelt beside Nicholas to assess his injuries. They moved quickly and efficiently over my girl, placing a brace around her neck and compresses against her wounds. I watched helplessly as they transferred her unconscious form onto a stretcher.

The pull I felt for her now was indescribable, the need to be by her, to touch her. I could feel her soul calling for mine, scared and unsure. Even in her unaware state, her lips rolled with my name.

When I could resist her no longer, I squeezed in beside her and took her hand in mine. I whispered in her ear that I was near, that she would be fine. I told her that she was free, that we could now be together. I praised her for being so brave and swore that Nicholas would never harm her again.

"Sir, we need to take her now."

I nodded and placed a soft kiss against her forehead. Her face, even broken and dried with blood, was still the most beautiful thing I'd ever seen. "I love you, Melanie. I'll be right behind you, sweetheart."

Reluctantly, I stepped away and dropped her hand. I trailed behind as they pushed her out the door and slid her into the back of the waiting ambulance.

Jumping into my car, I pulled out onto the road right behind the ambulance.

Grabbing my phone, I meant to dial my dad to let him know what'd happened, but froze when I saw the text message that popped up on my screen, the one I'd been too upset to even register when I'd dialed 911.

Where are you? The baby is coming!

Shit.

I just prayed this was another sad attempt by Vanessa to garner more attention. My hand shook as I pressed the button for voicemail. The generic voice came on and informed me I had twenty-seven new voice messages.

I sped through each one that wasn't Vanessa, for the first time in my life wanting to hear her voice. Nine messages in, she was there.

"My water broke. I'm going to the hospital."

"Fuck!" I screamed into the phone, replaying it so I could hear when she'd called. The message had been left Saturday morning. Two days ago.

My stomach twisted in knots. The first wave of concern I'd ever felt for the child flooded me. Images of Eva's tiny body flashed through my mind—the wires and needles and suffering she'd only known for the two short days of her life.

I skipped forward through more messages, riddled with guilt when Vanessa's voice came on again. "Daniel, the baby's coming. Where are you? Please...call me...I'm scared."

On the last message, no words were said. There were only the soft sounds of a woman crying, familiar enough that I knew it was Vanessa. It had come in late Saturday night.

"Vanessa!" I screamed as if she could hear me yelling at her through the message.

I frantically dialed my father.

"Dad." My voice shook with emotion. There had been too much pressure, first Melanie and now this.

"Daniel?" he asked. "Calm down. Tell me what happened."

"It's Melanie's. She's hurt."

"What?" His voice rose. "What the hell happened?"

"Nicholas." It was all I could get out, but all he needed to understand.

"Damn it," he swore under his breath. "Is she okay? Where are you?"

"Uh...I'm," I took a deep breath, forcing myself to calm down. "I'm following the ambulance. I think she'll be okay...but she's beat up pretty badly."

I could hear him shuffling around, his keys jingling as they scraped across his desk. "I'm leaving right now. I'll meet you there. Which hospital?"

"Mercy. Dad...I...there was a message from Vanessa. I think she had the baby. Dad—" The pall of high anxiety I had experienced spread out, falling over me in a blanket of quiet dread. "He's early."

I felt Dad's pause, his breath absent for a brief moment. When he returned, his voice was soft. "Son, it's not the same. He's just a little more than three weeks early. He should be fine."

"Can you check on them for me? I...I just can't handle all of it right now. I have to take care of Melanie first." Melanie would always be my first priority. And beyond that, I just wasn't ready to face that reality yet.

"Sure, son. I'll take care of it."

The rest of the trip was a haze. The fifteen minutes seemed like a lifetime, my mind trapped in a sea of memories. So much love, so much loss, that familiar pain so prominent, that pain always present when I saw Eva's face.

And, Melanie. I was a fool to have let her go back there alone.

The ambulance pulled into the circular drive in front of the ER, and I found the closest spot I could. I ran across the parking lot and got there just as they were pulling her out.

She was awake.

Relief crashed over me, nearly knocking me to my knees.

Her eyes were glassy, but her soul was alive in them, locking with mine even in their muddled state.

She was going to be okay.

Dad came rushing out the sliding doors of the ER. He was agitated, his graying hair sticking up from where he'd run his hands over his head. The agitation lining his face eased when he saw us. We followed the paramedics inside, and they took her straight to a curtained room and transferred her to the bed.

Dad tugged on my arm, pulling me back into the hallway while they worked around her. He whispered cautiously, "Daniel, the baby...he was born Saturday night. They're here…in this hospital."

My hands went immediately to the sides of my head, trying to force the alarm from my mind.

"He's fine. He's upstairs, in the regular nursery." He lowered his voice even further, unsure of how much information I could handle. "He was five pounds, two ounces, perfect health, no complications." His hand was on my arm, firm, offering reassurance.

I exhaled the breath I'd been holding, looking at the ceiling as I released the fear, the baby's health my solace.

I might not be able to love him, but I couldn't tolerate the thought of something bad happening to him.

"And Vanessa?" I was more than shocked that I cared anything about her condition, but I did.

"She's fine. She had a C-section so they kept her for three days. They should both be released tomorrow."

"Thank you."

"Are you going to go up there?" He cocked his head upward.

I shook my head, glancing at Melanie's room and back to him, ashamed. "I'm not ready yet."

He nodded in understanding but couldn't hide his disappointment. "Okay. Go take care of Melanie. I'm going to call your mother and sister. Neither of them have any idea what's going on. I'll be back in a bit."

"Okay. And Dad...could you call Peggy and let her know what happened? I don't want to leave her in the dark again."

"Sure." He smiled in reassurance, before turning and walking away.

I pulled back the drape to Melanie's room, standing awkwardly in the corner, trying to stay out of the way as the EMTs finished their job and the nurse took over. I wanted to be the one by Melanie's side, the one to fix her, to make up for being too late. I felt useless as they worked over her. The only thing I could do was comfort her from afar. I felt the intense pull as her heart called for mine, her eyes wide with her love but shadowed with the fear that still controlled her nerves. The EMTs left, and the nurse hooked her to a monitor, taking her vitals, scribbling things down in her chart, finally allowing me the room to get to her side.

"Oh, baby. It's okay, sweetheart," I murmured, running my thumb over her cheek.

Her voice was hoarse and low, the narcotics coursing through her veins, ebbing the pain but also her coherency. "What happened to Nicholas?"

"He'll survive." Unfortunately. I looked at the floor before turning my gaze back to her, making a promise I was sure of, though I didn't really know why. "He'll never hurt you again, Melanie. It's over."

"Thank you," she whispered. Even though she was slowly sinking into oblivion, her eyes were intense and without disillusion. "I heard you."

She heard me.

I called out my own appreciation to whatever power it was that led us and brought us together the first time and then again. The one that bound us, the energy that fought for us no matter what obstacles we had to overcome.

I smiled down at Melanie and squeezed her hand, knowing I would never be able to grasp the depth to which I was bound to this woman. "I heard you, too."

Her eyes fluttered closed, though her grip remained firm in mine.

The curtain rustled and a doctor emerged, introducing himself as Dr. Anderson. He was tall and thin, his dark brown hair meticulously combed to the side, his eyes framed by metal-rimmed glasses. Melanie never stirred during his examination. I watched over his shoulder, clearly making him nervous, but I was certain he would be more thorough if he knew I was paying attention to everything he did.

"I'm going to have a plastic surgeon come down and suture these two lacerations," he said, pointing to the one on her eyelid and the one under her chin, "and I'll suture the one in her mouth. The rest are just superficial. We'll also get a CT scan to make sure she's not having any swelling from the trauma to the back of her head and an x-ray of her chest and upper extremities, but from my exam, I'm guessing they'll be negative. Other than that, she looks okay."

The whole time they worked on her, I stayed by her side, her small hand held in mine. My spirit sang with hers, calming her, promising her she was safe, assuring her she would be fine.

I was certain Melanie's body would heal easily but feared her worst scars would be from the emotional damage Nicholas had inflicted on her over the last nine years.

When they wheeled Melanie's sleeping form out of the ER and down the hall to get her CT and x-rays, I sank heavily down in the chair, resting my head against the wall with my eyes shut. I was absolutely exhausted. I began to doze when a light tapping on my shoulder startled me. The same nurse who had tended to Melanie looked down at me apologetically. "Sir, there are police outside who need to speak with you."

I raked my hands over my face, trying to wake myself. Two officers stood just outside Melanie's room, talking quietly as I approached them. "I'm Daniel Montgomery. You needed to speak with me?"

"We need to ask you a couple of questions."

I answered each of their questions as honestly and as straightforwardly as I could, feeling only slightly uncomfortable when they asked about my relationship with Melanie. I could only imagine what they were thinking when I told them of our affair and the events that had led up to this afternoon. They had no idea about our past. They knew only that Melanie had been unfaithful to her husband. No matter what the circumstances, though, Nicholas had no right to hurt her, so I just answered the detectives and hid nothing.

Thankfully, they saw it the same way, another cut-and-dry case of domestic violence. It was obvious who the aggressor had been in the situation, and they promised me Nicholas would be charged as such.

I wandered back to the chair, finding a few moments more rest before they brought Melanie back. She was alert, one side of her face drawn in a small smile when she saw me, though she held herself rigid, guarding herself from moving in a way that would elicit a reaction to her wounds.

"Hi." She reached for me and I wrapped her up in my arms, careful not to cause her more pain, though she seemed to need my touch more than the caution I was trying to impart by not getting too close to her.

"Hey, beautiful. How are you feeling?" I leaned in to kiss her, so lightly my lips barely brushed against hers.

"Sore," she swallowed, clearing her throat. "But I'm okay."

We both jumped when Dr. Anderson rushed in. "So, all your imaging was clear. Nothing's broken and there's just a small amount of swelling around your brain, nothing to be too concerned about, but we are going to go ahead and admit you so we can keep an eye on you overnight."

I trailed behind them as they moved her upstairs to the third floor. The sign indicating *Newborn Nursery 5th Floor* jumped out at me among the fourteen others.

I still couldn't believe this had happened. I thought Melanie and I would have time by ourselves at home, time to talk and decide how we were going to handle this, time to plan. Now I'd run out of time and I was a father.

As much as I needed to tell Melanie, I didn't have the heart to do it. I could almost see the sadness that would cloud her eyes even though her words would be filled with soft encouragement and hope for my future.

She was falling asleep by the time they had her situated in her room. The words were garbled and slurred together as she muttered, "Love...you...Daniel," her tongue numbed by the meds, her mind lulled into a false tranquility.

"I love you forever." I kissed her forehead and drew her covers up under her arms and tucked them tightly around her body, hoping they would provide her some comfort while I was away. With heavy feet and a wary heart, I trudged from her room, knowing I could no longer put off the inevitable. My hand shook uncontrollably when I reached out and pressed my index finger to the five, and I held my breath as the elevator lifted me the two short floors.

Chapter Twenty-Seven

It felt as if I were in the middle of a whirlwind when I stepped out onto the floor. Everything was calm and serene except for the funnel cloud that swirled around me as the energy snarled and crackled. It was as if I were walking through a field of land mines, not knowing which step would trigger the end but knowing it would come. Feelings of regret and fear and grief circled in an endless cycle. What made it worse was that every painful memory of my life came back to originate in a place so similar to this.

My legs became weak when the glass window came into view. Infants' beds were pushed up against it with each baby's name proudly displayed above its tiny head. I tried to focus on the names, but my vision was blurry, my mind rejecting that one of these children belonged to me.

"Sir, may I help you?" A woman in her late thirties looked at me, concerned. "Do you need to sit down?"

"I, uh...I..." I looked at her with a blank expression, having no clue what my own son's name was. "I'm here to see Baby Montgomery...or Levy?"

Fuck.

I didn't even know his last name.

"And your relation to him?"

I choked as I forced it from my mouth. "Father."

She punched a couple of things into her computer.

"He's in his mother's room. I need to see some identification so I can sign you in."

I handed her my license and watched as she printed out the bracelet and secured it to my wrist. I thanked her quietly and turned away, fingering the label that titled me the father of "Baby Boy Montgomery."

I plodded down the hallway, each step forced. I felt ill as I stood in front of Vanessa's room. Using my hand to brace myself against the wall, I tried to come to terms with meeting a son I did not want. It was time to be the man my mother always praised me to be—the man my father had taught me to be—no matter how much I wanted to neglect this responsibility. I took a deep breath and pushed the door open.

I stood in the doorway unable to move as the shrill cries of a newborn infant hit me full force. The child was on his back in the small plastic hospital crib, screaming uncontrollably. Vanessa was in bed, a pillow over her head, trying to drown out his incessant call.

"What the hell is wrong with you?" I spat out, almost unaware I had taken the four steps needed to bring me face-to-face with my son for the very first time.

I barely registered Vanessa's voice as she whined, "He won't stop crying," this tiny person demanding all of my attention. He was dressed in a little white shirt that wrapped around him and snapped in the front, the long sleeves covering his arms. In his hysterics, one hand had broken free of the folded end meant to cover it. His face was pinched and beet red—and absolutely beautiful. The reality of who he was knocked the air from my lungs.

My son.

I shook my head, trying to make sense of what I felt when I looked at this precious child.

I swallowed hard and tentatively reached an unsteady hand out to take hold of his little fist, prying his fingers open to keep him from scratching his face. He instantly reacted and wrapped those same little fingers around my index finger, jerking his mouth toward my hand. The poor little thing was starving.

I gathered all my courage and scooped him up. His cries quieted when he found safety in my arms. I made sure he was secure in one arm, holding him close to my chest as I fumbled around with the other hand to grab the bottle in his bed. I lowered us into the chair. Carefully, I protected his head as I shifted him so I could feed him. I found myself making little cooing noises, shushing him, whispering, "It's okay, little man," against the thin material of the cap that covered his head.

He made grunting noises as he adjusted himself to the feel of the bottle in his mouth, and he began to suck. He fell into a rhythm, taking a few gulps and then stopping to catch his breath.

I wanted to look away and ignore the way he tugged at my heart, but his call was irresistible.

With the bottle balanced between my chin and chest, I pulled the little cap from his head, exposing his thin, blond curls. I ran my hand through the soft fine strands, twisting them in my fingers, quivering with the warmth that sped through my veins.

He released a satisfied heavy breath from his nose and snuggled into my side, still suckling, but at a less fevered rate. I ran the tip of my finger around the shell of his ear and over his cheek. His newborn skin felt like velvet from the soft, protective fuzz that covered every inch of him. His legs were long and thin but, at the same time, plump and healthy. I removed one of his socks so I could see his toes, grinning at how big his foot seemed compared to the rest of him. Cupping the whole thing in my hand, I gently squeezed. He pushed back into my palm, the little muscles in his legs flexing their strength.

He was perfect.

With the bottle nearly gone, his mouth had fallen lax, and I pulled it away and set it aside. I turned him to rest against my shoulder. He stretched, his little bottom sticking out and his legs curling up underneath him, his red lips forming a tiny "O" as he expelled a small yawn.

I couldn't help but nuzzle my nose in the crook of his neck, smelling his soft, clean scent as I patted him on the back and coaxed the bubble from deep within his belly.

His breathing evened out and he fell asleep quietly panting. When his hand came up to rest on my cheek, I nearly fell apart. I brought it to my mouth and placed a gentle kiss against his palm, murmuring, "I love you," into the delicate skin, shocking myself with my own revelation.

Once I had admitted it, I was unable to keep back the torrent of love that came gushing forth from some unknown reservoir. I never thought I could feel this away again. I had always believed that if I allowed myself to love another child the way I loved Eva, it would somehow diminish the devotion I had for her. But my love for her still burned bright, and I would never forget her, the child who had touched me so deeply. She could never be replaced. I would love her forever, just as I would love her brother forever.

I kissed his head as he slept against me, rocking him slowly. We sat like that for what seemed hours. With each passing minute, I fell further and deeper in love with him. Our spirits learned the other, our hearts melding together. I was bound to him for eternity. He was mine, and I would never let him go.

I didn't try to engage Vanessa and allowed her to sleep, something she so obviously needed.

Two faint, timid knocks sounded at the door. Dad peeked his head in, an apologetic grimace on his face. "I hope we're not interrupting. We hadn't heard from you in a long time, and we were getting worried."

I smiled at him in reassurance, gesturing with my head for him to enter. The door opened wide. It was not surprising that his hand was firmly intertwined with Mom's, both of them nervous as they entered the small room. They stopped abruptly when they found me with my sleeping son cradled in my arms. My eyes were red and swollen from the tears I'd shed, this new love un-contained and dancing on my face. Mom and Dad had had no idea what to expect when they found me in this room, but from the relief that poured from them, it was clear that this was what they'd hoped for.

Mom confirmed it when she began crying as she walked toward me and kissed me on the side of my head.

"I knew this would happen." She beamed down at me, then extended the same love-filled gaze to my son as she caressed the small of his back. "He's absolutely beautiful, Daniel. Oh, my goodness, he looks just like you."

I nodded in agreement. He looked exactly like my newborn pictures that Mom so proudly displayed in the den, so much so that I was certain nobody would be able to tell us apart.

"May I?" she asked, whisking him away with very adept hands. Her tone was sweet and melodic as she spoke, swaying her new grandson in her arms. "Hello, sweetheart. You are just precious, aren't you?" Dad sidled to them, joining in the slow dance and running the back of his hand tenderly over the swell of the baby's plump cheek.

She looked at down on me, curious. "Does he have a name yet?"

Vanessa may very well have named him, but I had no clue. For some reason though, I thought not. Everything I'd seen so far had only given him the title of "Baby Boy Montgomery."

I shrugged, inclining my head in Vanessa's direction. "We haven't talked about it yet." I figured that was honest enough. If she had named him without me, that was my own fault. I hadn't been here for his birth, and I figured I'd pretty much given up that right. I would be okay with whatever she chose.

They both turned at once toward her as if they hadn't even noticed she was there. Mom had never even met her, and I could see curiosity burn in her as she stared down at her grandson's mother. Vanessa lay with her back to us, completely still—too still. It was obvious to all of us that she was no longer asleep.

I really couldn't hold it against her. I couldn't begin to imagine how uncomfortable she must feel, witnessing such an intimate exchange by a group of people she didn't know, our only link to her found in the blood that ran through the child.

Reticent, Mom handed my son back to me, mindful of the glaring unease Vanessa was experiencing with their presence. "I love you, Daniel. And you, too, little man. I'll see you both in the morning." Her eyes were damp, filled with joy.

Dad kissed my baby's forehead before clapping me lightly on the back. "Call me if you need me." His simple words always meant so much more.

"I will...and thank you."

They smiled warmly and left the room. The door swung closed behind them and left me alone with my son and his mother. Intense pressure weighed down the air in the room. Vanessa's voice broke through the tension, coarse and muffled by the pillow pressed into her face. "You weren't here."

I sighed, readjusting my son and mustering the strength I was going to need to have this very difficult conversation. It was high time we had it, though, because our son deserved that we come to terms, and I knew part of those terms would include me conceding a bit.

I opened my mouth and accepted some of the responsibility, speaking softly to the woman who I still held a great amount of animosity for, but with whom I also shared this amazing child. "I'm sorry. I should have been."

She sniffled and turned her head in my direction, her cheek flat against the pillow. I focused on her. Even in the subdued light of the dim room, the whites of her blue eyes were a shocking crimson from what appeared to be days of crying. There were dark bags under her eyes, her face looked puffy and bloated, her lips cracked. A huge lump formed in my throat, and I nearly choked on my guilt. She looked awful and incredibly tired.

She barely wheezed out, "I needed you," before succumbing to another bout of emotion that racked her body as she wept into her pillow.

I felt terrible.

"Vanessa," I tried to comfort her from afar, but had no idea how to do that. I really didn't even know her and had no idea what she needed to hear. "I really am sorry I wasn't here. Who was with you?"

Her head snapped up, and she glared at me, yelling, "No one, Daniel! I was *alone*! I don't have anybody. I told you that already."

Cringing at her harshness, I shielded my baby's exposed ear with the palm of my hand. I bit my tongue to refrain from shouting back at her, trying not to make matters worse. We needed a resolution, and I couldn't allow this exchange to end the way all the others had.

I focused on my son's rapid breaths, a reminder of why I was having this conversation.

"I'm sorry, Vanessa. You shouldn't have had to go through this alone."

It didn't seem to placate her, her eyes angry and hurt. "Where were you?"

In the face of such a distraught woman, it occurred to me that lying would probably be a lot easier on her, but I had told her repeatedly that Melanie was my life. She was just going to have to accept it.

"Melanie and I were out of town for the holidays."

She yelped as if she were in physical pain, her fists wound tightly in the sheets. The pained expression on her face was such that she could have been my wife and I'd just told her I was having an affair. It would have made me angry had it not been so pitiful. I scratched my head, sighing as I pushed forward.

"Listen, Vanessa, what you did was wrong, but I can't regret that now." I glanced down at my son. The love I felt when I looked at his face sent my head spinning. I might regret her, but I could never regret him, and I'd accepted that I wouldn't have him without her.

I thought about how terrible it would have been had I grown up with my parents despising each other. I couldn't allow my son to grow up that way. I took a deep breath and made a concession—for my son. "Do you remember when you came to my office that day? When you asked us to be friends? Can we try that?"

She froze, gasping, before turning on her side and raising herself up on her elbow. "You want to be friends?" she asked, dubious, but clearly excited by the idea.

I nodded, forcing a very meek, halfhearted smile.

"And see where it goes?"

I groaned and threw my head back exasperation.

"No, Vanessa." I once again was amazed at how irrational and immature she was.

"Look, I need you to understand something." I didn't know why I felt compelled to tell her, but maybe if I did, if I gave her the whole story, she would finally comprehend there was no possibility of anything ever developing between us. "I know you know very little about my past, much like I know nothing of yours." I paused to search her sullen and dejected face, praying what I was saying would have some sort of impact on her.

"I fell in love with Melanie when I was sixteen." Her sharp intake of air told me she was listening. I hugged my son to me, kissing him softly on the head, giving her a moment to recover. I could only assume she'd believed that dinner was the first time I'd ever met Melanie, and we were sharing nothing more than a torrid fling.

"We were so happy." I laughed wistfully, remembering how incredible those first years had been. "We were so excited when we found out we were going to have a baby. Scared, but happy. We were going to get married as soon as Melanie turned eighteen." I drew in a ragged breath. I felt so exposed sharing this with Vanessa, but for some reason, I wanted her to know. "We were in a car accident...our baby...Eva...she lived for two days." I gave myself over to the pain that surged through me, allowing myself to relive it for that short time.

Through bleary eyes, I looked at Vanessa who had sat up, wringing her hands.

"Her parents separated us. We were both young and naïve. We let our fears drive us apart. For nine years, we believed a lie, but we never stopped loving each other. My heart has belonged to her since the day I met her."

I hesitated before pressing forward. "That dinner you came to?" Vanessa nodded. "That was the first time I'd seen her in nine years. You can probably put the pieces together from there."

She sucked in her quivering bottom lip and turned away as she battled another round of tears, wiping them with the back of her hand. Feeling I'd finally gotten through to her, I felt satisfied we could push forward and unite or at least cooperate and put this child before all of our past grievances.

I laid him against my legs and he stirred, yawning and drawing his legs up to his belly. "He's beautiful, isn't he?"

Vanessa drew in a deep breath, whimpering as she grabbed a tissue from the box. She squeezed her eyes shut and pressed the tissue to her mouth.

"Did you name him?"

"No." She gulped, looking down and tugging at the gown that was twisted at her waist. She took me by surprise when she suddenly rushed the words, "You name him."

"Vanessa—"

She looked up to meet me in the eye. "No...just name him."

She shuffled around, climbed under the covers, and pulled them to her chin. "I'm really tired. Can you take him back to the nursery?"

I nodded, guarding my son protectively in my arms when I stood, kissing him and humming an indecipherable love song as I set him in the small bassinet. Things I had thought would be so foreign to me now came so naturally, changing his diaper and dressing him in a fresh shirt, even wrapping him in the blue and pink striped blanket in the same fashion I'd seen others do time and time again.

As quietly as I could, I wheeled the small bed from the room and flipped off the one muted light. Blackness fell over the room. I reluctantly pushed my son down the hallway to leave him for the night. The movement jarred him awake, his deep, dark eyes fully opening to me for the very first time. I gazed down at him, overcome with a sense of belonging, positive he could feel it, too. By the time we got to the nursery, he was fussing and trying to stuff his fist in his mouth, attesting to his hunger again. I gladly accepted the nurse's offer to feed him in a rocker sitting in the nursery.

I rocked him and kissed his forehead while he drank. I relished the feel of his tiny, warm body in my arms, cherishing this child who had brought this part of my soul back to life.

I remembered those long forgotten dreams of a family, how important they had been, and now this baby boy had made them a reality.

My only worry was for Melanie. She would always have my heart, but now she had to share it. It in no way diminished my love for her; I loved him in a whole new capacity that I didn't even realize existed. All the same, he had become just as important to me as Melanie was. I knew it would be difficult for her, and it broke my heart that something so precious to me was going to cause her pain. I just prayed that in time Melanie would heal enough to forge a relationship with him. There were so many women who adored their stepchildren, and I prayed Melanie would be one of them. I knew she'd want to care for him and would try. I wasn't blind enough, though, to believe there weren't going to be huge obstacles in her path.

I looked down at my son, so pure and innocent, and was unable to imagine a world in which Melanie would not fall completely in love with him. It might take time, but I would be patient.

I kissed my child and whispered, "Goodnight, Andrew Daniel," against his head, proud to give my son my grandfather's name.

Chapter Twenty-Eight

"Daniel?"

I sat up, provoking a stabbing pain from the depths of my head. The splitting headache forced me to squint against the glaring bright lights of the hospital room.

It made me almost regret forgoing the shot of morphine for the ibuprofen the nurse had administered at about five this morning. Daniel was here then, trying to sleep in the chair beside my bed when the nurse had come in.

I had been so tired of feeling drugged and suffocated by the cloud around my mind that I was willing to take the pain over the haze that blurred every thought.

Through scrunched eyes, I scanned the empty room, already aware that I was alone.

Still, I felt safe.

It was over. Yesterday had been a nightmare. Being in that house with Nicholas had been terrifying. I should have left that night three months ago when he'd first struck me. Instead of walking downstairs and into the guest room, I should have walked straight out the front door. It was amazing what I'd deluded myself into believing because I was scared. It was a fear that had nearly cost me my life.

Even here, alone in my room, I could feel Daniel. His presence was near. I took comfort in it, though I really wanted him beside me. With my mind clear, I wanted to look at him and celebrate that we'd made it, that we were free. His presence grew stronger, and I sat up in anticipation, propping myself up on one arm to wait for him.

I was met with the most glorious smile I'd ever seen upon Daniel's face. Total joy seemed to spring forth and flow before him into the room.

He halted mid-stride when he entered, seeing I had already awakened. Hazel eyes devoured me from across the room, washing me in complete adoration, pulling me to their depths. I felt drawn further into them than I'd ever been before, as if the recesses had expanded and his spirit had been amplified.

"Hey," he called in the softest voice, "You're awake. How are you feeling?" He crossed the room to my side, drawing the chair up to sit next to me.

"My head hurts." The pain flared as attention was drawn to it. "But other than that, I think I feel fine."

I turned on my side to face him, and he gathered my hands in both of his, brushing his lips across each knuckle. He leaned in closer, pressing a sweet, lingering kiss against my mouth. He was careful, acutely aware of each of my injuries, managing still to cover every exposed inch of my skin with his praise.

His mouth was at my ear. My body trembled when he whispered near the sensitive skin, "I love you." He sat back to take in my face. His expression was intense, full of devotion and love, but shrouded in compassion and a tinge of apprehension. "Baby, I need to talk to you." My first instinct was to be concerned, but the light in his eyes held a promise, so instead, I watched him with curiosity.

He ran the pad of his thumb over my cheek and moved his hand to rest on my neck. His expression was somber, but his eyes conveyed no real sadness.

I narrowed my eyes at him, unable to make sense of the conflicting signals he was sending. "Daniel—" He shook his head, cutting me off.

"Melanie." His eyes flitted over my face. He chose his words carefully, each one impassioned as it passed through his lips. "My son was born on Saturday."

His announcement echoed through the room and crashed against my ears. His mouth claimed, "My son," while his spirit cried, "I adore him."

I desperately tried to hide it, to conceal the all-consuming ache his news brought me. I wanted to shield from this man the hurt that invaded every fiber of my body. I wanted to protect him from the envy that flowed through me, infecting my heart, my mind, and my soul. I struggled to pretend I did not covet what I could not have, but I couldn't stop the tears from falling. I turned away to spare him my reaction, one I had tried in vain to contain, ashamed of the jealousy ravaging me.

How did I become such a terrible person? Daniel had been given a gift, this child, and he felt a deep love for him that was unmistakable, a love he never believed would be possible for him to feel. I should have rejoiced, but I couldn't.

It just hurt too much.

It felt as if a barrier had been erected, cutting me off from a part of him that I could not share. The void in my life had never been more pronounced.

Tears fell harder when he encircled me in his arms from behind while I buried my head in the pillow. "Baby, it's okay to cry." He wrapped his arm around my chest, pulling me closer to him. "I know it hurts...just...let it out."

His tender encouragement touched me and I gave into it, weeping loudly into the pillow, deep, ragged sobs born of years of insecurity and loss and want and need. And with this agonizing jealousy, it all released simultaneously in a torrent of raw emotions.

Daniel's soft words were there as he let me mourn. He rocked me and whispered comfort, "I will always love you. I'll never let you go. You will always mean everything to me. There is nothing that could change the way I feel about you." His heart was in sync with my fears, mollifying each one as I expelled it from my body.

When he felt me calm, he leaned in closer. He rested his cheek against mine as he almost painfully gripped me to him. "I promise, we will make this work."

Shuddering, I took in a deep breath, resolving that I *would* do whatever it took, knowing that promise depended more on me than anything else. I would take this burden and the sorrow it would bring. I nodded as I wiped my nose and the last of my self-pity into the sleeve of my hospital gown, turning to face the one man I would do anything for. Mesmerizing pools of understanding waited, filled with undying devotion. "I love you, Melanie."

I swallowed, wetting my dry mouth and lips, reaching out to stroke the day-old stubble on his face. "I love you, too." Gathering all my strength, I pushed forward and took the next step. My voice shook. "Tell me about him."

Daniel's expression turned reverent, full of wonder and awe, as if he could not quite comprehend the way he felt. "He's...amazing, Melanie." He scooted his chair closer, taking each of my hands back in his. "His name is Andrew...Andrew Daniel."

Daniel's pride in his son was so obvious as he said his baby's name—his grandfather's name. I wanted so badly to share in this joy with him, but I couldn't find it within me and was more than grateful when movement from the door distracted us. Patrick cleared his throat and a sympathetic smile graced his features as he looked at me. I smiled back, silently welcoming him. He opened the door wide, allowing Julia to step in before him, grasping her hand as they crossed the room together.

"How are you today?" His eyes appraised me as he took a seat on the edge of the bed opposite Daniel.

"Better, thank you."

Julia squeezed in beside Daniel, her bottom lip trembling as she tried not to cry. She embraced me the way only a mother would her own child. "Sweetheart, I was so scared. Are you okay?"

I nodded into her shoulder, my chest tightening as her affection washed over me. There were days when I still couldn't believe I had found this family again. Julia pulled back and cupped my cheek, her expression kind and understanding, seeing the sadness in my eyes for what it really was.

She glanced warily at Daniel and wrapped me in her arms, murmuring against my ear as she ran her fingers through my mass of tangled hair. "You are strong, Melanie, and you will make it through this. I have faith in you, just like I did in Daniel."

I acknowledged her by tightening my hold, praying with everything in me that she was right.

Julia and Patrick stayed only a few minutes, as Daniel's attorney had shown up and was waiting outside my door to begin the paperwork needed to put an end to my marriage.

"Are you up for this?" Daniel looked at me, concerned.

I nodded too rapidly, causing me to wince against the throb in my head. "The sooner we get this over with the better." His smile was warm when he stood, kissing me in agreement. He stepped out and returned only seconds later with his lawyer in tow.

He was much younger than I would have expected, probably not much older than Daniel. He had stark black hair and striking green eyes, and his manner was brash, no-nonsense, and all business. He extended his hand formally, introducing himself as

William Bailey before grabbing a chair against the wall and getting straight to work.

Where his personality lacked, he made up for in knowledge and clear competence. He took me through the forms and answered every question I had without the slightest hesitation.

He explained that Nicholas had been arrested the night before when he was discharged from the ER, only to be released on bail early this morning. He informed me I had no need to worry as I had already been granted the restraining order requested through his office. He left with a promise that he foresaw no problems and expected this to be resolved quickly, especially in light of the domestic violence charges and that I was asking for none of Nicholas's assets.

Daniel rose and shook William's hand, thanking him while William told him he would be in touch by the beginning of the week with an update. He rushed from the room without looking back.

Daniel shrugged as he explained away his attorney's abruptness. "He's the best." We both laughed, releasing some of the pent up stress from the whirlwind meeting and the emotions of the past two days, both of us relieved in knowing that my legal bond to Nicholas would soon be broken.

During breakfast, Daniel stayed at my side. I could tell by his restlessness that he was antsy, torn between being here with me and upstairs with Andrew.

It was there again, the barrier, the wall that created a division between us, the wall that was there because his heart was now hopelessly divided. I knew the right thing to do would be tell him to go, but I found myself too selfish to speak the words.

There was a light tapping on the door. Erin peeked in, wielding an overnight bag filled with clothes and everything I would need to take a shower. "Brought you something." She was a lifesaver. Nothing would feel better than washing this grime away. While the nurses had done the best they could with a sponge bath, it had done nothing to erase how dirty I felt from my ordeal of the day before. Erin stepped in, looking relieved when she took in my appearance. "Oh, you look so much better today!"

I looked at her, confused, having no recollection of her visiting.

She laughed and walked across the room, waving her hand as if to tell me not to worry about it. "I stopped by last night, but you were completely out."

She swept in to give Daniel a quick hug before going to the other side of the bed. She sat by my side, curling one leg under her and facing me. She brushed a lock of hair from my face so she could study me, before she took my hand and rested it in her lap. "How are you really feeling?" she asked seriously, forever straightforward.

Even after all these years, I'd never dream of lying to Erin. Even though so much time had passed, she could still see straight through me. Our bond was still there, and she knew me just as well as she had nine years ago. I still knew her, too, and it was clear she wasn't asking about my physical condition. I grimaced and shrugged.

She patted my hand and stood. "Come on. Let's get you into the shower."

She rushed into the small bathroom ahead of me, pulling toiletries from the bag and placing them in the shower. She turned on the water to allow it to heat up while Daniel assisted me in standing for the first time since I had been brought to the hospital. I cringed with my first step, but as I continued to stretch out my cramped muscles, it felt wonderful.

Erin extended her hand and led me inside, shutting the door behind us. The warm and inviting steam filled the small space. My tired body wanted nothing more than to immerse itself under the therapeutic spray.

"Here." Erin took my arm, turned me away from her, and tugged at the knots on the back of my gown. I could feel the hesitation in her movements and when she spoke.

"He's beautiful, Melanie."

I froze. The air heaving in and out of my lungs and the spilling of water onto the hard shower tiles were the only sounds in the room.

Erin started to say more, but stopped, grabbed a towel from the rack, and placed it near the shower. She averted her eyes as I stepped into the shower and pulled the curtain between us. I submersed my head in the water, breathing deeply as I relaxed into the hot spray that fell on my head and ran down my back.

"You know that he loves you?"

I stalled, pulling my head from the water and looking at her shadowed form.

"Yes."

"Then don't be afraid."

She pressed her hand against the curtain and I pressed mine against hers, wishing I could take her words and live them. I just didn't know how.

She whispered, "Love you," before she left me alone with my whirlwind of emotions.

I stepped back into the spray and pushed thoughts of Daniel's son away to give my heart and mind a moment's reprieve from the pain. For this short time, I would relish in the fact that I would soon be going home, that I was now free, that Daniel loved me no matter what happened.

Truly, a shower had never felt better. The hot water seemed to melt away the tension, and as I washed away the dirt and dried blood from my body, it was almost as if I washed away yesterday's events. I watched as the tinted water swirled and pooled on the tiles, spinning and circling through the drain. The water finally ran clear, and with it, my soul was freed of Nicholas's chains forever.

I knew he had scarred me so much deeper than I'd ever admitted. Of course, I was aware I had been treated badly, but I'd never allowed myself to see just how abusive he was. I didn't know if my broken heart had blinded me to that fact or if I had felt that I deserved nothing better. Either way, none of those things made what Nicholas had done okay. He was an abuser who needed to be held accountable for what he'd done, and I'd stand up in court to be sure that happened. Beyond that, though, I promised myself I would never dwell on the last nine years. I was determined to step from this shower and never look back, only taking with me the valuable lessons I had learned.

I toweled myself dry and slipped into the dark jeans and red sweater Erin had so thoughtfully brought for me. I brushed my teeth and pulled the hairbrush repeatedly through my wet hair. I glanced at my reflection in the foggy mirror and saw my injuries for the first time, thankful that they had not been worse.

When I stepped out, Daniel was speaking with my attending doctor. They turned their attention to me. I sat back on the bed and Dr. Lemmons checked me over once more, assuring me that everything looked great. He signed my release papers and wrote me a prescription for pain medication, telling me to have my stitches removed in ten days.

I was free to go.

When the doctor left, Daniel pulled me from the bed and into his arms. I wrapped my arms around his neck, holding him close, our bodies swaying as we rejoiced. For the first time in our lives, we were free to go home together, where we'd always belonged.

Daniel brushed his lips over mine, the electricity shocking with the light contact. We kissed and danced and held each other for the longest time, unhurried and no longer afraid of being watched, finally free to love.

As our kiss faded and slowed, he hugged me to him again, still rocking us, though his hold felt contemplative. I tensed, anticipating what he would say.

"Will you go upstairs with me before we go home?" His voice was timid, unsure, and so very hopeful as he asked me to meet his son.

I held my breath and pressed my nose to his chest, digging my fingers in his shoulders as I fought against the pain. The energy flowing from his body gave me the strength I needed to nod my head.

I had to—for him.

He pulled back and held my face in his hands, leaving feather kisses on my cheeks and mouth. "Thank you." He looked down at me knowingly, tenderly, sensing each of my fears. "Melanie, I promise, we will make this work," he reiterated, trying to bring me comfort, but the closer I came to meeting his son, the more terrified I became.

Grabbing the bag Erin had brought, he shoved the discharge information into the pocket and slung it over his shoulder.

He kissed me chastely again before taking my hand. I had no idea I was shaking uncontrollably until Daniel's steady grip wrapped securely around my hand. "Ready?"

I wasn't, but I'd never be, and this was a request that I would not deny him.

"Yes," I choked out.

He hesitated, looking at me. "Baby, you don't have to do this right now."

I shook my head, unwilling to take the easy route. "No, Daniel. I need to do this...now."

I had never felt so torn between my need to please Daniel, to sacrifice for him, and the selfish part of me who wanted nothing to do with this child, the part of me that wished he didn't exist. The guilt that thought roused made me sick and my mind chastised my heart for being so cruel. But I couldn't stop it, and it was still there when I took a deep breath and followed Daniel from the room. He led me, never releasing my hand, pulling me forward. Still, I trailed a step behind, my face trained on the ground, concentrating on putting one foot in front of the other.

The elevator ride was short. My head spun and tears stung my eyes when we stepped out onto the floor. How was I going to get through this? We hadn't even reached the nursery and I was already falling apart.

I clutched Daniel's hand, the only comfort I could find. I felt his pulse racing just as fast as mine, but where his raced with anticipation and the desire to be united with his son, mine raced with dread as I walked to meet the manifestation of my every insecurity.

I couldn't even bring myself to look up as Daniel showed the volunteer working the desk his wristband and had a pass made for me.

The buzzer sounded and the door opened. The warmth of the room washed over my face, sending shivers down my spine. Infant cries pierced my ears, coming at me from what seemed like every direction, making me cower against Daniel's side. Wrapping his arm protectively around my shoulders, he drew me in, the energy between us acting as a shield from the pain. My spirit immediately eased. I breathed in and drew from that power, sucking it deep into the pit of my stomach, emboldened as we made our way across the floor.

Daniel stopped just feet away from his child, giving me time to adjust. But I pressed forward, preparing for the surge of jealousy I knew would come. I felt hurried and frantic and knew I should wait and clear my head, but I couldn't stop the steps my feet took. It became suddenly clear the energy I felt was not coming from Daniel at all. His baby boy was crying, a gurgling, rattling cry, so sad it would bring any mother to her knees.

I gasped as I took in his small child, the picture of his father, a perfect replica of the man I adored. My chest rolled with tremors as I felt his call, taking the last step forward to be at his side. I didn't hesitate to touch him, splaying my hand over his tiny chest. Soothed, the child stilled at my touch, his spirit calmed as it met with mine. I closed my eyes, feeling his heart pound, beating strong with Daniel's blood that flowed through his veins. His pull was indescribable, so much like the force that bound me to Daniel, yet so different. It was a perfect accompaniment, an extension of the connection Daniel and I shared.

Daniel moved to my side and wrapped his arm around my waist, tugging me closer while taking his son's hand, smiling wistfully. "He's hard not to love, isn't he?"

I wheezed out through my constricted throat, "Impossible." Daniel and I stayed unmoving for an immeasurable amount of time, our arms wrapped around each other, satisfied to watch baby Andrew sleep in his small crib, his hand firmly gripping Daniel's finger and his heart beating soundly against the palm of my hand. The three of us were enveloped in the cocoon of energy that hovered in contentment, for the first time complete.

I glanced over my shoulder and found Erin and Julia standing at the window hugging each other, their eyes bleary and red as they had watched my first encounter with Andrew.

I smiled pensively and tried to keep myself from shedding any more tears. I'd cried enough for a lifetime, and today was a day to rejoice. Daniel and I had found our heart, and it rested in this small child sleeping safely under our watch.

Erin wiped her face with tissues Julia produced from her purse before coming into the nursery.

Daniel stepped away and pulled his sister into a fierce hug. Both of them murmured their love for one another and satisfaction for the day, their whispers proclaiming, "Thank God," and "I knew she would."

Erin turned and wrapped me in her arms. I hugged her back, whispering, "I'm not afraid anymore."

She nodded and pulled away, dabbing her fingers under her eyes. "I know." She smiled. "So, can I do anything to help?"

Daniel roughed his hands through his hair. "Do you think you and Mom could go and help Vanessa get ready to take Andrew home? I just..." He grimaced, clearly aware he should be the one doing it but just not quite there yet. She shook her head, keeping him from having to explain what she already understood. "No problem."

She patted us both on the back and left Daniel and me to resume our protective stance over his child. We just stood there and watched. We would never be able to get enough of Andrew, so we savored every second we had.

Ten minutes later, Erin rushed into the nursery and tugged hard at Daniel's arm. Her voice was low and alarmed. "Daniel, I need to talk to you."

"What is it?"

"Just come on." Urgently, she tugged again, and he pulled me behind him.

The instant we were out the door, Erin burst. "She's gone!"

"What are you talking about, Erin?"

Erin shook a folded paper in Daniel's face. "This is what I'm talking about!"

Daniel ripped it from her hands and tore at it to expose what was written inside. "That bitch. I knew it."

I stood looking between the two of them, waiting for one of them to fill me in on what happened. Neither of them looked my way, so consumed with what they'd found on that paper. He reached into his pocket and fumbled for his phone, still muttering profanities that Erin continually seconded.

Frustrated, I reached out and plucked the paper from Daniel's shaking hand. I smoothed the crumpled paper against my chest so I could read it. It wasn't addressed or signed, but simply stated, "I can't do this." I had to read it three times before it sank in.

Vanessa had abandoned her son. I was suddenly every bit as angry as Daniel.

My thoughts went to that precious child in the next room. I found myself unable to grasp how anyone could see his face and not fall in love with him, especially his own mother. I turned and walked toward the glass. His small crib was across the room, and I could see nothing of him from where I stood, but I could feel him—the pull—the need within him matching my own.

I barely registered the flurry of activity happening around me as the day progressed. Morning turned to afternoon, and the numerous calls made to Vanessa still went unreturned. There were whispered conversations between Daniel and Patrick, the quick reappearance of Daniel's attorney, people coming and going, the faces of all those I loved strained and concerned as William Bailey made what seemed to be an unending number of phone calls. It increasingly wore at Daniel as he tugged on his hair and paced up and down the corridor. His expression was pained when he paused to peer into the quiet nursery where I rocked his son. I spent those hours meeting all of Andrew's needs while he met mine, comforting the child at the center of the tumult happening just outside.

I kissed Andrew's forehead, wrapped the sleeping infant in his blanket, and placed him back in his crib, still unable to pull myself fully away. I held the side of his bed and gazed down upon the child I would forever adore.

I felt Daniel enter and he came up behind me and wrapped me tightly against his body. He looked over my shoulder to peer down at his son and then leaned in and whispered heaven against my ear.

"Melanie, let's take our son home."

Chapter Twenty-Nine

He was so beautiful.

The sun shone down over us as I sat barefoot, squishing my toes down into the damp grass, my legs drawn to my chest. I watched as my son ran, untroubled and free, across our backyard. His blond curls played around his face as the faint breeze gave way to sudden gusts of wind.

"Mommy, watch," he called. As if I ever stopped.

He climbed the steps to his small slide, his three-year-old legs quick and adept in his favorite activity. His hazel eyes flashed with excitement when he reached the top. He swung himself up and onto his butt, digging his heels into the slide to propel himself forward. His face shown euphoric for the few brief seconds it took for him to reach the bottom.

As soon as his feet hit the ground, giggles bubbled up from within him, his chubby, round face succumbing to a fit of laughter as he raced across the lawn and threw himself into my lap. I exaggerated the impact by shielding his body in my arms as I allowed us to fall back into the cool grass. Laughing, I hugged him to me and breathed against his head.

"You are getting too big, Andrew. You knocked your momma right over!"

He wiggled and sat up, grinning at me and showing all of his small white teeth. "Daddy said I'm a big boy now."

"Yes," I confirmed, my own smile filled with the intense love I had for him. "You are a very big boy!"

He was back on his feet, darting away. He sang the first line of his ABCs over and over while he settled down in the dirt to play with his trucks, leaving me to gaze at the little boy I still could not believe was mine.

Even though it had never been her intention, Vanessa giving up this child had been the most unselfish act she'd ever committed. She had given me a son, a child not borne of my body but created specifically for me, just as his father had been. I'd known it the moment I had felt his pull, just as I'd known that very thing when I felt Daniel so many years before.

Without Vanessa, though, Andrew wouldn't be here. As much as I couldn't stand the person she was, it didn't stop me from waking each morning and silently thanking her for being the vessel that had brought my son into this world.

As he played in the sand, the sun warming his pale, smooth skin against the cool breeze, I saw traces of her.

No doubt, Andrew was his father's twin, his golden curls a near perfect match to Daniel's at the same age, small ringlets framing his precious little face and bouncing with each bounding step he took. Patrick had informed me on more than one occasion that most strangers thought Andrew was a girl, but I still couldn't bear to see the curls cut away. Julia would only laugh and run her fingers lovingly through her grandson's hair, reminding Patrick that he had said the very same thing when Daniel was young.

Andrew already had Daniel's smile, the same one that rendered me helpless. I found myself constantly grateful that Andrew was such a good child because I had no idea how I would ever discipline him. And those eyes, they were as if God had seen his perfect work in Daniel and simply replicated the same magic in Andrew.

Still, Vanessa was there, seen in the faint freckles that ran over the bridge of his button nose and sprinkled out under his eyes, in the hint of red in his hair that could only be seen when the sun hit it just right. It was an odd feeling to be so indebted to someone I hated so much.

That day in the hospital had been a harrowing experience for Daniel. Vanessa had left without signing anything, and the hospital staff questioned whether Daniel was even Andrew's father. Though *we* didn't need medical confirmation that Daniel's blood flowed through Andrew's body, the state did. Daniel had willingly yielded to a paternity test that confirmed him as Andrew's biological father. As stressful as that all had been, it had become the single most important day in my life—the day I went home with Daniel and my son. Nothing could compare to arriving in front of our house and walking through the front door with my family. It was the first time in my life I had ever truly been home.

That April, on what would have been Daniel's and my anniversary, I was given the wedding I'd always wanted, a simple one in which Daniel and I stood hand-in-hand in Patrick and Julia's backyard and professed that we would love each other forever.

The very next day, I signed a petition to adopt Andrew, seeking that he not only be my son in spirit but legally as well. It didn't take William Bailey long to track down Vanessa, and while I could never understand her reasoning behind it, she relinquished her rights to Andrew that day. Two months later, I officially became the mother of Andrew Daniel Montgomery. No longer did I have to live in fear that someday he would be taken away from me. He was mine.

"Andrew, sweetheart, Daddy's going to be home from work soon." I stood, dusted the traces of wet dirt and grass from my pants, and extended my hand to him. "We should head in and start dinner."

His sweet face brightened at the mention of his father, and he barreled over to me, throwing his arms in the air for me to pick him up. I swept him off the ground and into my arms.

"Here, let's get your hands washed." I walked to the kitchen sink and leaned over it, running his hands under the warm water and washing the residue from his afternoon of play down the drain.

I kissed his forehead and set him on his feet. Andrew went straight for his little table standing in the corner of the kitchen. He settled into the small chair, picking a dark blue crayon, his favorite color. He set to work, drawing a picture for his dad, something he did most every day while I cooked dinner.

I looked around the kitchen I loved, warmed by its comfort.

I glanced down at my son, so intent on the picture he was drawing, his small hand flying across the page as he scribbled his wonderful, indecipherable thoughts for his father.

I started on dinner, and seconds later, my phone vibrated in my pocket. I reached for a towel, patting down my hands before digging the phone out to see the name on the screen. I grinned. "Hey, Katie. How are you?"

Katie and I were still very close, though we didn't get to spend as much time together as we would have liked. The last few years had been rough on her and Shane.

Nicholas had been sentenced to only three months in jail for the assault and ordered to undergo anger management classes. To me, the penalty had seemed much too lenient, but in the end, it had cost him his company. During the months he was away, their clients steadily dropped off and no new contracts came in. People seemed unwilling to do business with a company that had Nicholas's name attached to it. Nicholas had always been about image, and he was forced to leave Chicago where people knew him for who he truly was. He'd sold his portion of the company to Shane and left town without a trace.

Shane had changed the company name and Katie went to work for him. Unfortunately, their first year was incredibly trying as they tried to salvage what was left of Shane's years of hard work. He'd used all his profits from Daniel's building to buy Nicholas out, and Katie and he had struggled to stay afloat. Not surprisingly, though, considering Shane's work ethic and skill, it all paid off. By the time Katie gave birth to their son Jordan a little more than a year ago, the business was flourishing, and she was able to turn her duties over to a new office manager so she could stay home to raise their son.

"I'm great, babe, how are—" She was cut off by the shrill cry of Jordan, obviously coming through a baby monitor. Her voice was somewhat muffled but still loud as she pulled the phone away from her mouth, yelling, "Shane, I'm on the phone. Get Jordan." I was unable to restrain my giggle. Their house was screaming chaos every time I spoke with her, but it was a happy, loving chaos in which they all seemed to thrive.

"Sorry," she laughed under her breath. "Every time I pick up the phone, one of my boys suddenly needs me for something."

"No problem. Everything is good here, just making dinner."

"Good. So, Shane and I are taking Jordan to the zoo on Saturday and wanted to see if you guys might want to meet us?"

"I'm sure Andrew would love that. What time?"

"Noonish? Thought we could just get lunch there. Why don't you see if Erin wants to tag along?" Erin had settled in a house just ten minutes from us, and we saw her at least a couple of times a week. She'd always show up unannounced, saying she needed to practice with my son for the children she hoped to have in the near future.

"Sure. I'll give her a—"

The sound of something crashing in the background interrupted us. Shane yelled for help and Katie snapped, her voice no longer directed at me, "Seriously, Shane?" She grunted her mild annoyance into the phone. "I've gotta go, Melanie, Shane just made a huge mess. See you on Saturday?"

"Yep, we'll be there."

"Okay, bye."

"So guess what, Andrew," I said, drawing his attention from the paper in front of him that was now nearly black from all of the different colors he'd mixed together.

He looked up, excited by the tone in my voice. "What?"

"That was Katie, and she asked if you wanted to go to the zoo with Jordan on Saturday. Does that sound like fun?"

He nodded his head, emphasizing the movement. "Yes, I love the zoo, Momma."

I ruffled my hand through his curls and placed a kiss against his head. "Good, because I love the zoo, too."

With the sound of the garage door opening, Andrew jumped to his feet, squealing, "Daddy!" He grabbed the picture he'd colored and raced down the hall to meet his father at the door.

My heart did its own little flip-flop, ever anxious for the reunion with its match. The door opened and Daniel's voice echoed as it carried down the hall. "There's my little man!" Shrill laughter and commotion followed as the daily round of tickling and loud, exaggerated kisses commenced. Loud steps hurried down the hall and Daniel shouted, his question obviously meant for me, "Where's Mommy?"

I hollered back, "Kitchen."

They rounded the corner and came into view. Andrew laughed hysterically as Daniel carried him upside down over the shoulder. Daniel's face was alight with love, glowing with complete joy. "There she is." His voice softened when he spoke, his words holding more meaning than any other could ever know. He stood before me, the energy thick, drawing me to the man I could never live without. He flipped Andrew and set him upright on the floor before he reached out to wrap his arms around my waist. He drew me into a closed-mouth, albeit fierce kiss.

I grinned, my lips still pressed to his, and murmured, "I missed you too."

He nodded, smirking against my mouth, lingering for a second longer. He stepped away and took Andrew back into his arms. "So, what did you and Mommy do today?"

Andrew proceeded to give Daniel a play-by-play of our entire day, his jumbled, sweet words clear to Daniel and me. He ended his speech by telling Daniel of our planned trip to the zoo this weekend.

"The zoo! I can't wait," Daniel said, throwing Andrew into the air, an act I had long since given up telling him to be careful about.

"Okay guys, dinner's ready." I took two of the plates I had already filled, and Daniel grabbed the special one for Andrew. We all settled around the table in the breakfast nook. Daniel's hand found my knee, his thumb caressing over the fabric of my pants, distance for us never an option.

"How was your day, baby?" He watched for my reaction as he speared a piece of chicken and placed it into his mouth.

I really never had a bad day. Some were more stressful than others, but I had been given back my life, and I never let the small things skew that truth.

"Perfect."

He grinned and shook his head, knowing exactly what I meant. He lived his life the very same way.

"Oh," I sputtered through my full mouth, chewing and swallowing my food. "I talked to my mom today, and everyone's coming out for the Fourth of July." Mom came out to visit often, but Mark and my sister had only been here a few times. I couldn't wait to have the house filled with all of my family. In the past three years, we had all become very close. That piece of me had been lacking for so long, and I now found I couldn't go long without seeing them.

The only missing person had been my father. My chest tightened a little as I thought of him. Even though he had caused me so much pain, he was still my father, and I had been willing to forgive him. I had reached out on more than a few occasions, sending him an invitation to our wedding and cards with pictures of my family on every holiday. I had also left him numerous phone messages, trying to get in contact with him. He'd never replied.

When he'd died last year of a sudden heart attack, I'd had to accept I would never reconcile our relationship. As angry as I was at him for being so prideful and unwilling to allow us to come to terms with our past mistakes, I would never deny that his death had been a huge blow.

Daniel smiled and tightened his grip on my knee. "I can't wait to see them too."

It had taken Daniel a while to forgive Mom, but after they'd had several heart-to-hearts and hashed out their past differences, they'd accepted that they had both been guilty of harming the other. Once they had resolved them, though, they'd become impossibly close.

Andrew kept us entertained through the rest of dinner, making us laugh at every turn. His innocent insight into the world was something that left us feeling pure and hopeful for the future. Finished with dinner, Daniel rose to clear the dishes from the table and took them to the sink. "Why don't you give Andrew his bath, and I'll take care of these."

I nodded, released the straps of Andrew's chair, and drew Andrew into my arms. "You ready for your bath, pumpkin?"

Bathing him was hardly a chore. His little body was covered to his chest in bubbles and his face was my very light as he laughed and played in the warm water.

Every moment with him was a treasure.

My son.

Never would I forget Eva, my precious girl I knew only in my heart, but she was there, ever present and forever a part of me. My love for her would never diminish and Andrew would never take her place, but he'd completely filled the gaping hole in my heart that had been reserved only for him. I'd longed for him my entire life; I just hadn't known it until he made his undeniable claim on my heart.

I massaged shampoo against his scalp and through his hair, carefully rinsing the suds away. I wrapped him in a towel, hugging him to me as I walked him to his room and dressed him for his night of sleep. I drew the covers down, and he crawled into his small bed.

Daniel appeared in the doorway, smiling at us. He snuggled in beside me, and we took turns reading our son his favorite poems. Andrew's eyes drooped more and more with each rhyme we sang. When his lids began to flutter, I closed the book and leaned in, kissing him reverently on his forehead. "Goodnight, sweetheart."

He yawned and rubbed his eyes with tiny fists. "Night, Mommy. Love you."

"Love you too."

Daniel scooted in, nuzzling Andrew's neck before kissing him on the cheek. "Goodnight, little man."

Nearing sleep, Andrew muttered, "Goodnight, Daddy," through very tired lips.

We both stood and Daniel tucked him in, making sure he would be warm for the night. I switched off his lamp and flicked on his night-light.

Daniel and I lingered in his doorway, holding each other while we watched our son drift into a deep, restful sleep. His little body rose and fell with each breath he took. I spoke quietly against Daniel's chest, "He's so beautiful."

Daniel drew me in, wrapping an arm around my waist. "Perfect." He leaned in closer and whispered against my ear, "Just like you."

His words brought a rush of heat, the fire ignited as his lips traveled from my ear to my mouth. Immediately, my body reacted to his touch. Every touch, every day, always the same. The need never dimmed.

He stepped back, pulling me into the hallway and pressing me against the wall. He held my face in his hands as he gazed down at me. His eyes filled with adoration and longing, his desire palpable in the energy traveling from his fingertips as they cupped the curve of my jaw.

His voice became rough as his need grew. "Melanie." He crashed into me, mouth and hands and body and soul. He tugged and pulled at the collar of my shirt seeking more. I hummed against his mouth as I rushed through the buttons on his shirt, just as anxious to feel him as he was to feel me. No barriers.

He groaned, grasping my hand and dragging me across the hall to our room, quick to shut the door behind us. He rushed back to me, his kiss forceful. We shed our clothes as we danced our way across this sanctuary that was ours alone.

He wrapped me in his arms and spun us, sinking back onto the bed. His hands gripped my hips as he looked up to me, his gaze filled with intense love that would never lessen. Our connection was not one that could be severed or used up. Our souls were one as our hands and bodies became twisted and entwined, our own existence—a single creation.

He called through hushed breaths, "Melanie," his rapture so much more than physical. "My love." And I spoke his name, "Daniel." A statement, a definition. My life.

I watched my husband, this beautiful man, his eyes drawing me deep into the currents that flowed where our souls met, to the place where we were healed, to the place where we were free. No longer was there the pain, the loss, the suffocating hurt. Now there was life and peace and contentment, all found in this flawless love. What we'd endured had cost us so much, so much I'd never thought I'd survive.

When I look back now, though, I would never change it. There had always been a reason, and I would never regret where the path had led.

Here, loved by this man, his body burning into mine, our spirits consumed by a fire that could never be quelled.

Here, where our son slept peacefully in the room across the hall.

Here, where we were home.

Here, where we'd been Pulled.

Made in the USA
Lexington, KY
30 May 2015